CEO DADDY

A CRESCENT COVE STANDALONE

TARYN QUINN

CEO Daddy
© 2019 Taryn Quinn
Rainbow Rage Publishing

Cover by LateNite Designs
Photograph by Sara Eirew
Model Mike Chabot

ISBN: 978-1-940346-59-5

First print edition: October 2019

ACKNOWLEDGMENTS

Sometimes we make up fictional places that end up having the same names as actual places. These are our fictional interpretations only. Please grant us leeway if our creative vision isn't true to reality.

For those who step up even when you think it's impossible to find your way out of the sadness.

ONE

Hannah

I might be single and alone on New Year's Eve. But I'm not woe as me. No, ma'am. I'm looking at this moment as an opportunity to cherish my solitude.

With a sigh, I set down my pen and picked up my water glass. I should be drinking alcohol at least. Maybe I still would. I wasn't much of a wine fan, but I could use tonight to broaden my horizons. A cocktail sounded nice. Very adult.

A drink I could enjoy happily on my own.

Okay, cut the crap. In my diary, I should be honest. The diary I was writing in while I ate my dinner of consommé—fancy soup essentially—and garlic breadsticks, because who was I going to kiss at midnight? No one.

Joyfully solo, that was me.

In reality, I was fresh off another broken Tinder date. Broken by *me*, no less. I could never quite close the deal. Probably because a date with me held more weight than the usual hookup.

I'd been adult about that too. Virginity was a burden, so I'd just rid myself of it quickly and quietly. No fuss. Until the time came to actually meet Joe Blow in the flesh—yes, that was his name on the site

—and I'd balked. I'd made up an excuse about getting together with an ex and that had been that.

As if I had any exes. Just a few high school boyfriends who hadn't amounted to much.

Since then, I'd stuck close to home, the dutiful older sister who raised her younger siblings after our parents had died in a plane crash. Now that the twins, Emma and Rachel, had turned nineteen and gone off to college, that left me at loose ends.

Alone for real.

"Can I get you anything else? Maybe you'd like a look-see at the dessert menu? The lemon bars are my favorite. They're my mama's recipe."

I blinked up at the grinning blond waitress. At least I thought she was a waitress, though she had a more commanding air about her despite her small town friendliness. "Your mama works here too?"

"Not anymore. She used to own the joint. Then she retired and sold it out from under me with no warning, but I got it back because of my lovable pain-in-the-ass baby daddy. Well, husband too. So, lemon bars?"

I rubbed my temple. Whoa, information overload. "You have a husband? You look…youthful."

Luckily, I'd managed not to say she looked twelve, which was a misstatement in any case. She looked at least sixteen. But not old enough to be married, at least in New York.

She laughed and sat down opposite me at the table. "Sure do."

"And a baby."

"Yeah, she's not even a year old yet. Star's the light of my life. Want to see?" She was already tugging a folding wallet of pictures—many, many pictures—out of her apron pocket.

"Um, sure?"

She showed me an array of photos of a chubby baby with bright green eyes and a drooly smile.

"She's beautiful. Her hair is so dark."

"Like Oliver's. Unless it changes. I hope it doesn't. It's my ace in the hole I wasn't impregnated by the milkman."

Unsure if she was serious, I smiled faintly. "I think I'll try those lemon bars, please."

She nodded enthusiastically and bustled off to the kitchen. She seemed sweet.

Everyone in Crescent Cove was sweet. It was a picturesque village, nestled against the long curve of Crescent Lake. At the holidays, the place really shone.

The big formal banquet room I was seated in was jammed with guests. Most were families, along with a good amount of couples and solo businessmen passing through the area due to the proximity to Syracuse. I lived in between Crescent Cove and Syracuse, in a town so tiny you could miss it if you shut your eyes.

Which you shouldn't do while driving, especially in the fall and winter. We were in deer and wild turkey country.

Spending New Year's Eve in Crescent Cove was a luxury. I didn't have the funds to spare on such things, but I'd asked for money for Christmas from my sisters and my bestie just so I could splurge.

Now I was wondering if it was a huge mistake.

I'd thought I would feel less on my own in a crowd.

Wrong.

I'd had to wait a half hour for this table. There was holiday music playing, and cheerful lights twinkling, and every surface seemed to be decked out with candles and poinsettias and big satin red ribbons. People were laughing and enjoying time with their loved ones.

And I was scribbling lies in my diary about how I didn't mind that my sisters had chosen to return to campus early rather than hang out with their big sister. That I wasn't at all jealous my bestie had a date for New Year's with a guy she worked with.

Worst of all? The prospect of homemade lemon bars excited me more than the gorgeous fireplace suite I'd reserved to spend the evening—you guessed it—alone.

"Here you go. I gave you an extra one. On holidays, calories don't count." The blond proprietress smiled and set the plate in front of me. "Can I get you anything else?"

"Yes, actually, you can. I'd like some champagne, please."

3

"Oh, sure." She nodded as if it wasn't weird at all I was ordering champagne with lemon bars after drinking water since I'd sat down. "Flute or bottle for the table?"

Did she know something I didn't? Was it usual for women dining alone to drink a whole bottle of bubbly? Maybe on New Year's Eve, anything went.

"Bottle for the table, please." The deep voice barely registered. In fact, I didn't even look to see the owner. He couldn't be speaking for my table. I definitely didn't know anyone who sounded like *that*.

Hello, man, not a boy.

The blond shifted away from me and I dazedly followed her gaze to where one of the businessman I'd noticed earlier stood beside the chair opposite me. I hadn't seen his face, just the tidy queue of dark hair on his neck as he was seated. A solo diner, just like me.

Unlike me, he hadn't been writing in a journal with flowers on the tattered cover. No, he'd been flipping through a thick sheaf of paperwork, and he'd barely looked up long enough to order.

I hadn't seen his face, but he'd seen mine. Or else he was in the habit of joining strangers once the alcohol was served. Judging by his well-cut pinstriped dark suit and fancy Italian leather briefcase, he wasn't hurting for money. I preferred looking at those things rather than his features. If his looks matched up with his voice—

Well, let's just say I wasn't in any shape to handle that level of disappointment once he rethought his decision. Because, seriously? Why did he want to sit with *me*?

"Oh." The blond smiled. "Are you joining her?" She glanced at me. "Dinner date?"

Normally, the blond's presumptuousness might have irritated me, but it felt as if she was on my side. Like she was making sure I wanted this guy to sit at my table. I must be giving off vibes that I did *not* know this dude. No matter how handsome he was and how important he seemed, a woman had to be careful.

"Two people eating alone on New Year's Eve should eat together." His deep voice caused a tingle low in my belly. "Sage, you know I'm harmless." His smile was anything but.

The blond—Sage—raised an eyebrow. "So said Ted Bundy." She smiled sweetly and shifted to glance at me. "Your call."

He switched his briefcase to the other hand, allowing me to see the bundle of winter tulips he also held, wrapped with a burlap bow and with pine greenery overflowing the colorful tissue paper. Tulips were a weakness of mine, and I'd never seen a winter bouquet of them before.

As if he'd noticed me staring at them, he held them out as additional incentive. "For you."

I borrowed a page from Sage's book and lifted an eyebrow, saying nothing. But I accepted the flowers. I was no dummy, and the tulips were gorgeous. I could already imagine them in the center of my table at home, cheering me up as I experimented in the kitchen. The pale reds, pinks, and yellows were perfect.

"He can sit."

Sage nodded. "Would you like anything else besides the bottle of champagne?"

"A cup of coffee for me, please." His smile was easy and self-assured, and he never looked away from me as he took the seat opposite me at the table.

Sage left us alone with a waggle of her brows.

"Friend of yours?" I set the bouquet of tulips in my lap and drew a nail through the powdered sugar beneath the lemon bars on my plate. I rued not redoing my nail polish for tonight. The silver was chipped at the edges. Surely, a man like him would notice.

"Oh, Sage? No, not exactly, although we've met a few times. I make it a point to eat here when I'm in town. Something I'll be doing a lot more soon."

He paused as Sage brought over the bottle of champagne and two glasses. She popped the cork and poured for us both, then left us alone again. A moment later, she brought his coffee, which he largely ignored.

I picked up my glass, clinked with my new dinner guest, and sipped. The bubbly went straight to my head as it always did, so I set the glass down.

He was still watching me, his lips curved ever so slightly. He hadn't taken a drink yet.

"I'm Asher," he said as the silence extended uncomfortably. Somehow our personal silence was much more noticeable because of all the excited chatter around us.

"Hannah."

"Nice to meet you. What brings you here tonight of all nights?"

"I didn't want to sit alone at home." *Nice one, Hannah. Can you sound any more pathetic?* "It's a night for parties and fun." I saluted him with my champagne and drank.

Heat flowed out from my belly through my limbs. I couldn't decide if I liked the sensation or not. Or maybe the heat was from Asher's gaze. His eyes weren't as dark as I'd originally believed. With the candle flickering between us, I'd guess now they were a warm hazel, perhaps varying depending on his clothing.

Apparently, his black pinstriped suit didn't offer any appreciable change to them. But whoa nelly, that suit was working wonders on me.

Maybe three-piece suits really were the equivalent to lingerie for a woman. His was definitely revving my motor.

Revving everything.

"So, do you have plans after this? A party perhaps, or some other kind of fun?" He ran his fingertip along the rim of his glass.

"How old are you?" I blurted.

His dark brows drew together. "Thirty-two in March."

"Hmm."

"Is that a good *hmm* or a bad *hmm*?"

"I'm twenty-three. I've never..." I took a deep breath. *Try not to embarrass yourself again.* "Well, this is just sharing some lemon bars and champagne, right?"

"That's up to you. Why don't we start with some conversation and go from there?" His slow smile only served to stir me up even more.

Relax in this gorgeous, commanding man's presence? Not likely.

"Sure. Let's begin with why you came over to my table." I picked up my dessert fork and cut off the corner of one of my lemon bars, belatedly remembering he didn't have one. Sage hadn't brought over another plate.

By accident or design? Even without knowing her well, I could easily see her as the matchmaking type.

"Sorry, it's rude of me to eat when you don't have anything. Here." I set down the fork and lifted the plate toward him, swallowing deeply as he pushed aside the vase and the flickering candle to make room for the plate between us.

"We can share." His fingers brushed mine as he broke off a corner and lifted it to his mouth.

His perfect mouth. His lips were neither too full or too sparse. Just right.

As everything he possessed seemed to be. And I hadn't even gotten a look at him beneath the waist.

Probably good. I didn't need to be any more intimidated, especially by pinstriped thirty-two-year-old cocks. I was already freaked out enough.

Hello, out of my league.

"No fork?" I asked a little breathlessly. He seemed the fork-and-knife-at-all-times type to me.

"Nah. Fingers are better. See?" He broke off another piece and lifted it across the table to me, not dropping so much as a crumb. "Lean forward."

I obliged him and his fingertips brushed my lips as he fed me the treat. His voice was entrancing. I was afraid to imagine all the things he could make me do with just one of those husky commands.

His eyes held me in his thrall so completely that I barely noticed the burst of lemon as I swallowed. The bars were a delicious mix of sweet and tart, but I probably wouldn't have noticed if the dessert had been undercooked and bland.

"Good?"

I nodded and he repeated the move several more times. He wasn't even eating himself, just feeding me. He had long, elegant fingers with a surprising bit of ink swirling down his hands. The bold Roman numerals and heavy, old typeface of a latin phrase were mixed with a bit of artistry.

So incongruous to the buttoned-up businessman. It somehow made him even hotter.

Once, out of the corner of my eye, I noticed Sage start to approach with the bill in hand. She took in what was occurring at our shadowy table, widened her eyes, and sped off in the opposite direction.

I would've laughed had I not been so turned on that I could barely think.

What was happening here? We weren't even talking. Was this what occurred when under the influence of a lonely holiday meant for couples and some expensive champagne? I'd had a couple more sips in between rounds of Asher feeding me. Big, bolstering sips. The kind that made a normally shy, awkward woman feel bold.

"No ring," I said casually—or so I hoped. I'd had plenty of time to see his hand as it came closer to my mouth. "You're single?"

"Very. The kind of single that means I'm alone on New Year's Eve, just as you are." He lifted his thumb to his lips and licked off a stray crumb from the piece he'd just fed me. The movement was far more sensual than it had any right to be. "You are alone tonight, aren't you, Hannah?"

Something about the question and his use of my name made my throat tighten to the point that if I hadn't gulped more champagne, I might've choked. This time, I didn't mind the floaty feeling that overtook my body, or the resulting wave of warmth.

"I'm alone far too much these days. But right now? No. Neither of us is alone."

He nodded, lowering his head for an instant while his jaw locked. He finally took a few sips of coffee before he met my gaze once again. "I have a room upstairs. Just for tonight."

Questions flitted through my mind.

Who are you, Asher?

Why did you pick me to talk to?

Was it just that I looked lonely, so I must be an easy target for sexual advances?

In the end, I didn't really care. We were both alone, and no one was waiting for me at home. What did it matter if I chose this handsome man to spend the evening with? No one would be hurt. And I would finally be able to cross one thing off my bucket list.

Sex with a gorgeous man, check.

Sex, period.

But that didn't mean I'd make it easy on him.

"Who were the flowers for?" I stroked the downy soft petals of the pink tulip on top of the bouquet in my lap.

"My grandmother." He smiled wryly. "She thinks I need to get out more, so she'll approve that I gave them to the most beautiful woman I've seen since..." He trailed off, looking uncharacteristically unsure. Even with only knowing him a very short while, I was quite certain Asher rarely faltered. "Ever."

"I believe you don't get out much after that statement." I rested my cheek on my fist. "My hair isn't really blond, by the way. I put in a rinse today. Truth in advertising and all that."

"It doesn't look blond. Not exactly. More like the color of honey." His voice deepened. "Rich and luxurious."

"Glorious Tones hair color thanks you." I toyed with the stem of my now nearly empty champagne glass. "When is the last time you approached a woman with that line about your room upstairs?"

"Never. I've never had a room upstairs here before." His lips twitched. "And to be honest, I don't have one now. I wasn't planning on staying until I saw you. Writing so furiously in that." He nodded to my abandoned journal. "What were you writing?"

"Where were you going after this?" I countered.

"To my grandmother's. She was going to be who I counted down to midnight with." He finally reached for his champagne and took a single sip. Easing back in his chair, he licked his lips, slowly and surely. "I'd much rather kiss you once the ball drops."

"Which balls are we referring to?"

I didn't know if he'd find me funny or crude. It was usually half and half, depending on my company. But his laughter was quick and appreciative. "You're different than I expected."

"Oh, really? What did you expect? A meek little mouse who'd trot after you and hop right into bed?" Okay, this had to be the champagne talking, because this was next level, even for me.

"No. I wasn't even thinking about bed when I came over here. I just wanted to hear your voice. To see if you ever smiled. You still haven't, you know. Not at me."

"Smiles are earned. Keep trying. You might get there."

"Luckily, I don't give up easily. Why are you alone tonight? No family?"

"No." The lie came easily, and sometimes seemed far too true when my sisters were busy with school and out of touch. My family was a fraction of what it had once been. "Let's just say I live an isolated existence."

It wasn't that far from reality. I was alone too often.

I couldn't stand another moment of it.

"No lover." The word dripped off his tongue, laced with a sensuality that was far beyond my realm of experience.

"No." I tilted my head. "So, what's your story?"

His lips lifted on one side. "I'm a man who works far too much and spends New Year's Eve with his grandmother. What more do you need to know?"

Indeed.

I nodded at the bottle of champagne. "Think we can get that to go?"

TWO

Asher

Coming over to Hannah's table hadn't been in my plans.

I was supposed to eat dinner, read through the dry paperwork I'd brought to keep me company, and go spend the evening with my grandmother. That was all true.

What I hadn't mentioned was the other reason I was headed to Gran's. She was babysitting my daughter, Lily, who was just celebrating her six-month birthday and didn't have a clue that her father was a workaholic. Thank God.

Her *new* father. I wasn't her biological father. Technically, I was her godfather, the one who'd taken on an honorary role in her life thanks to my best friend. I was never supposed to be called into service.

And Billy wasn't supposed to die two months ago with no other relatives, leaving me the sole support for his little girl.

Hannah also didn't know that I was a single parent. Why hadn't I told her? Maybe she wasn't the only one who wanted to be someone else tonight. I didn't doubt for a second she was lying about the no family thing. But sometimes even good people needed a respite from their lives.

I cared a lot about Lily. But tonight, I wanted to be someone other than Asher Wainwright, publisher and CEO of the struggling

Wainwright Publishing Inc. Another man other than the equally struggling single father of the cutest baby girl ever.

Even if I didn't quite know what to do with her.

At least where work was concerned, I'd once felt competent. Now I was drowning on both the professional and personal fronts, and I wanted a win.

Needed one.

For tonight, I would be the man Hannah perceived me to be while her big blue eyes ate me up as if she was equally unnerved and fascinated.

She wasn't the only one.

Something about her utter solitude as she ate her soup and scribbled in her worn book had called to me in a way I didn't quite understand. I hadn't dated in a long time. Not all that long ago in the scheme of things, but a lifetime when considering how many nights I'd gone to sleep with only paperwork for company.

I was married to my job. Trying to save the company my grandfather had built from nothing took almost all of my time. What was left I gave to Lily and my grandmother.

Not enough was left, to be honest, and it was probably irresponsible of me to even consider taking this night for myself.

For myself and for Hannah, who seemed just as desperate for a night away from reality as I was.

Gran would understand. She always encouraged me to try those dating apps or hell, even to just go to a bar and see what happened. Her mindset was much more freewheeling than my own. The idea of meeting a stranger at a bar was beyond my scope.

What do you think this is? You think meeting her in the restaurant of a bed and breakfast makes it much different?

Not hardly.

Hannah was still staring at me, not moving, waiting for me to reply to her statement about getting the champagne to go.

Fuck, did I even have any condoms in my wallet? I wasn't prepared for this.

For *her.*

"We can get a bottle sent to our room." I cleared my throat. "They have gorgeous ones here—"

"They may be booked. It's a holiday, and this isn't exactly a by-the-hour motel." She spoke directly, without the hint of a blush tingeing her features.

I liked that about her. She didn't beat around the bush. So to speak.

Jesus, I was so out of my depth here.

Shrewd, clever, driven Asher Wainwright never made a misstep. If he fucked up, he damn well never admitted defeat. But that was just one side of me. My public persona. The guy underneath, who was still flailing at becoming a parent without going through the steps to get there, who had to figure out a whole new life as well as be responsible for one—that Asher was a few drinks away from getting so blitzed he didn't get up for a day. Or a week.

A month.

So, I couldn't let myself take that tumble. The only one I was allowed was this brief slice of time with beautiful, straightforward Hannah.

"I'll speak to Sage." I was already removing my wallet. I gripped the platinum American Express card as Hannah reached out to still my hand.

"She'll know. This isn't a booty call sort of place."

I had to smile. The term was ridiculous when it came to me and my lifestyle. "We don't have to do anything but talk." Even as I said it, I watched the furrow of her brows and the way her lips tightened in lieu of a smile.

I was still working on earning one. I hadn't gotten there yet.

She released my hand and sat back, crossing her arms over the soft swell of her belly. She was curvy in all the right places, and her deep green dress had a V-neck that drew my eyes right to her breasts. I'd tried repeatedly to keep my gaze above her neck, but she was seriously stacked. Her little cardigan covered her arms and not much else, only serving to draw more attention to her cleavage.

Talk? She nearly rendered me fucking speechless.

"Do you live nearby?" She shifted to unhook her bag from the back of her chair. "Perhaps that is more—"

"No." My voice came out sharper than I'd intended. "Visiting my grandmother, remember? I live in Syracuse."

It was sterling truth. My grandmother wouldn't mind if I brought Hannah over. In fact, she'd probably be pleased as could be if we got naked right there on the living room floor. She worried far too much about my lack of a social life.

But Lily was also there, and I didn't want to explain. Especially not to someone who was just passing through. It wasn't as if Hannah and I would be anything to each other after tonight. I had no time for a woman. My days were filled with work, and my nights were full of Lily.

And figuring out how to bathe a baby without blinding her with harsh soaps or scarring her with water that wasn't the proper mix of warm and cool. And choosing a formula that didn't upset her delicate stomach. And on and on.

Father failure for five hundred, Alex.

Hannah nodded. "Let's see about the room here then." Surprising the hell out of me, she motioned for Sage, who beamed so brightly at us that she was in competition with the candle.

"All set with dessert? Do you need a refill? Or perhaps—"

"We need the check, please."

Sage nodded and clasped her hands against her chest. "Was your meal satisfactory?"

"It was delicious. Your lemon bars are almost as good as mine, and that's saying something. But now we need to go."

I cleared my throat. "About that—"

"We're all set," she said to Sage, covering my hand with her own to shut me up.

Sage put down the folder that contained the bill and left discreetly. As discreetly as one could while still waggling her brows and watching us over her shoulder.

I leaned forward. "What happened to asking about the room?"

"I didn't say I'd ask. I said let's see about the room here." I was so busy staring at her that she had time to sign for the check with a flourish and put down her own credit card. "Which I don't have to ask for, since I already have one and am presently checked in." She closed the bill book and handed it to Sage, who managed to sweep by our table at the exact right instant.

"So you were dicking around with me?"

"No, I was just making sure you didn't get a guilty conscience and confess about your wife. That usually slows someone's roll right down. But no ring," she said again, looking at my hand. "No tan line either. And you didn't so much as blink when saying you didn't live close by. Not that Syracuse is that far."

I slid my credit card back into my wallet and said nothing. I couldn't decide if I admired the way she was taking charge or if it pissed me off.

"I'm sorry, did your sweet, unassuming lay just change into something more challenging? Having second thoughts?"

"Hell, no. But you're not the only one who isn't sweet all the time." I didn't have to fake the growl in my voice.

Clearly, she had more levels than were readily apparent just below the surface. She wasn't the only one.

"Glad to hear it. Because Tinder dates really aren't doing it for me."

The growl was back again, although this time it never left my chest. The sound rumbled there as if I was a disgruntled bear. "You use those apps?"

She gave a dainty shrug. "Hard to meet suitable men nowadays. I never felt comfortable enough to just sit down at someone's table." She tilted her head.

For a second, I was sure she was going to smile. And denied.

"If you want something, you need to go out and get it. That's my life motto."

Or it was, before my business started to crumble thanks to new technologies and changing times. Also before a beautiful brown-eyed baby with red curls fell into my lap.

Literally.

"Time goes by too fast to deal with regrets." I was thinking of Billy now, and how quickly—and unexpectedly—he'd lost his life. He'd had so much ahead of him. So many years to spend with his little girl.

Now I was tasked with standing in for him, and somehow making him proud. That mantle weighed heavy on my shoulders, even heavier than keeping the business afloat. At least with the business I had some idea what I was doing, even amidst the changes in the industry.

With Lily? Clue-fucking-less.

"And I'm something you wanted?" Hannah asked quietly.

"Isn't that obvious?"

"I didn't even see you looking my way."

"You were to wrapped up in that book." I tapped the cover with my thumb. "Diary, is it?"

Smoothly, she tucked it into her bag. "More like an agenda. Some journal aspects too, you could say."

"So, your life is busy enough you need to keep a running to do list."

Her pale brown eyebrows lifted. "You, sir, are asking far too many questions for a random hookup."

"Keep calling me *sir* and maybe you'll distract me into forgetting them."

Her lips parted a fraction, and I swore I could hear her rush of breath despite the conversation all around us.

"Here's your credit card, Hannah." Sage set down the bill folder. "Hope you two have a nice night. Don't be a stranger, Asher." She wiggled her fingers in a wave and moved on to the next table.

Hannah took back her credit card, slipping it into her wallet. "The nice thing about Sage knowing you is it gives me some comfort you may not be a serial killer."

"She only knows me to say hello and goodbye when I have dinner. We aren't buddies. And remember, even she mentioned Ted Bundy earlier."

"Thank you for allaying my fears."

"You take far more chances on those apps."

"I cancelled my last date with Joe Blow. Let's go."

Arching a brow, I rose and moved around the table to help her out of her chair. She did not wait for my assistance and was soon halfway across the room.

I followed her out, my gaze firmly on her swaying hips in her clingy dress.

Goddamn, she was gorgeous.

I came up behind her in the foyer when she stopped at the base of the sweeping staircase that led to the second floor. She turned toward me and shocked the hell out of me by placing the room key in my hand. Then she leaned up on her tiptoes and spoke near my ear—which was pretty damn close, since she seemed on the high side of average height and her heels gave her just enough of a boost. Her breath smelled sweet and fruity, a cross between the lemon tarts we'd shared and the champagne.

"You probably prefer to be in charge. So, let's pretend the room is yours."

I caught her wrist before she eased back. "Let's get one reality straight."

Blue eyes huge, she nodded.

"For tonight, you're mine."

She wetted her lips. "Same goes, Asher."

Just her saying my name had me going harder than the beams that held up the damn ceiling.

"*All* night."

Again, she nodded.

Christ, it burned me to acknowledge that all too soon, she would no longer be in my sphere. And that was crazy. "I won't go further than you want me to, but now's your chance to say no."

She'd have a million other chances to say no, but of course I hoped she wouldn't want to. I wasn't trying to scare her, just figure out what her limits were.

Even what mine were when it came to her. Right now? It didn't feel like I had many left. She'd tested my boundaries in ways I'd never expected, simply by being herself.

Unless even her personality was a game, just like her mysterious persona. If that was true, I didn't want to know.

17

I wanted the fantasy every bit as much as she did.

"Yes is the only word I plan on saying tonight." She jogged up the stairs, weaving around a couple who was coming down.

Swallowing hard, I followed her to the room. She waited while I unlocked the door, then stood aside to allow me to enter first.

She went right to a small vase by the door and shifted the fresh flowers over to make room for the tulips I'd given her, fussing with them for a moment before stepping back.

The lights were off, but the fireplace was burning. Whether Hannah had left it that way, or it was one of the features provided by the staff, the flickering firelight added a warm glow to the rich furnishings in the room. Even in the low light, opulent touches seemed to be mixed in with the rustic decor. A four-poster bed in knotty pine was paired with what appeared to be a handmade quilt. An Aubusson rug in jewel tones drew the eye to the large fireplace with its wide mantel still decorated for the holidays.

Across from the door, huge windows framed the space. Outside lights glimmered on the lake. The bed and breakfast had the perfect view of the water, but tonight that view was obscured by snowflakes. The few meandering flurries that had been falling when I'd come inside for dinner had turned into a deluge.

"The storm is here," Hannah murmured, dropping her bag by the bed to rush to the windows.

I was tempted to turn on the lamp so I could see every bit of her, but I didn't know if she'd shy away at such intimacy. The dancing flames offered just enough light, streaking her long fall of light brown hair with hints of gold.

When I came up behind her, she barely seemed to notice. She laid her hand upon the glass as if she could touch the snow even through the window.

"Were we supposed to get a storm?"

"Oh, yes, it's been forecast for days—" She broke off when my arms encircled her waist.

She felt so good. Solid, warm. Strong. The scent of lilacs wafted over me from either her perfume or her shampoo. Fuck, I'd never smell them again without thinking of her and this moment.

Of us alone in the firelit dark while a storm raged outside.

Then she stumbled backward, stomping on my foot. And I laughed.

"Sorry. Sorry. I shouldn't have moved. I just didn't expect you to be so—"

"Close?" Her unexpected bout of nerves after her bravado downstairs was refreshing. Maybe the mask was slipping a bit?

"No. Hard. All over." She cleared her throat and shifted toward me, lifting her head. "I was distracted by the snow."

I gripped her chin, rubbing my thumb over the shallow dent in it. "Must not be that impressive if snow is more interesting than the prospect of being alone with me."

"First big snowfall is late this year."

"That it is." I brushed her hair back from her face. "If I don't have any condoms on me—and the chances are probably 60/40, odds not in our favor—I want to lay you in front of the fireplace and devour you all night long."

When she only watched me with heavy eyes, I moved in that much closer until our bodies were flush. Wedged together. Carefully, I drew her full lower lip between mine, tugging softly with a scrape of my teeth until she let out a low moan.

The sound tore something open inside me. Later, I'd wonder if I had really lunged at her, cupping her face in both hands as I kissed her. My lips molded to hers and my tongue delved inside, sweeping over hers before I explored every nuance of her mouth. Then our tongues were twisting together, sliding against each other while she pushed up my suit coat and spanned her hands over my lower back through the thin cotton of my shirt.

Not enough. I needed to feel every inch of her pressed against me. Naked.

No clothes again, ever.

Fuck, I was out of control. Already. Still. She made me do things I normally never would. Hell if I understood it. Even approaching her had been far outside my comfort zone.

My life wasn't for me anymore. It was for the business. For Lily. Even for my grandmother.

But this…*this* was all for me. And for Hannah. Especially for her.

"Asher." Her harsh whisper as she moved back made me open my eyes. Everything was fuzzy and indistinct except for the fiery blue of her irises.

What had we unleashed here?

"I'm so—"

She stopped me with a flick of her thumb over my lips. Lipstick probably. Already I wore her on my skin.

I wanted more of her on me. Surrounding me.

"I have a condom in my purse. Two, actually. Though I have to say that whole devouring thing?" she said breathlessly. "Suits me just fine."

THREE

Was I really doing this?

Yes.

A thousand times yes. First and foremost, I wanted to be rid of my pesky virginity, but this man... There was no way I was supposed to be this lucky. To have a man like Asher want me. To actually be shaking a little in his need for me.

It was beyond my scope in about a thousand different ways. But here we were. In the ultimate romantic getaway spot.

I mean, for God's sake, there was actually snowstorm raging outside. I'd read this in a romance novel or seven. Heck, I'd watched it on the deluge of Hallmark holiday movies I'd binged this season.

Though the Hallmark movies weren't nearly as carnal as I was about to get.

I cleared my throat. "Let me just go clean—"

"No. Don't overthink this. If you go into that bathroom, you'll come out with a million reasons why this is insane."

"Oh, no. We're doing this." I was resolute. I had high hopes based on his kissing skills. Because whoa, boy, did he have skills.

I was getting this done. I was going to treat myself in every way that counted this New Year's, dammit. The room, the ambiance, the man.

God, did I ever hit the jackpot on the man.

He grinned down at me, then loosened his tie and jerked it out of the knot. "Oh, we're definitely doing this." He looped the unfurled tie around my waist and dragged me in close.

Shocked, I laughed up at him and braced my hands on his chest.

"Finally, I got a smile." He leaned down and flicked his tongue along my cheek before burying his face in my hair. "Dimples even."

I lifted my shoulder against the ticklish spot. "I hate them."

"There's something about a woman with dimples."

"Yeah, we look like a perpetual fourteen-year-old." I pushed him back when he dug deeper to scrape my neck with his five o'clock shadow.

"No fourteen-year-old ever kissed me like you do."

My breath shorted out in my chest. That was a good sign. Maybe I wouldn't be totally inept at this sex thing. "I should hope not. Unless you were fourteen at the time."

His dark eyes lit with the devil. I was sure of it. And I wanted to let the devil in. "Maybe when I was twelve. I've always been an overachiever."

"I just bet." I shivered when his hand slid up my back to find my zipper.

"Right now, I need to get my hands on your skin. To watch the firelight kiss every inch just before I do."

"You're sure you haven't done this before?"

"Seduced a woman?" He peeled the dress away from my shoulder so it pooled between us. "I'm no innocent, Hannah."

Oh, but I am.

Part of me screamed to tell him, but I didn't want this to stop if he got weirded out about it. To chance that this could end without me getting what I needed.

I pulled my arms out of the dress and let out a slow breath as the material slid down to swish around my ankles, his tie floating to the floor as well.

"Sweet Christ."

"I hope that's good."

"So good." His eyes seemed even more intense in the dim light. As if there were shadows living in them. Some that made me wonder beyond my own selfish needs.

But others—like the heat growing between us—pushed away the pesky thoughts of reality.

His fingertips trailed up my middle. That was an area where things weren't as tight as I wished some days. I baked and liked to eat my own cooking. But wonder filled his expression, not exasperation or disdain.

He lightly traced the lace of my forest green bra. I'd worn the one set of underwear I owned that wasn't made of cotton and designed to be purely functional. I'd specifically bought it to match this dress and this night. For the wild, sexy Hannah I wished I could be, not the careful woman who spent too many hours dreaming up recipes and food combinations.

I wanted to be an adventurous woman who took exactly what she needed.

My head tipped back as he made lazy circles around my tightening nipple before plucking one lightly, then the other. Just that brief touch left me breathless.

It wasn't me fumbling in the dark when the nights got too lonely.

This was a real man touching me. Wanting me.

Suddenly, warmth blossomed over the lace followed by a strong, sure pull from his lips. His tongue pressed against the lace, wetting it and making it malleable enough for me to feel every movement he made.

My fingers slid into his hair. The short hairs tickled as I grasped enough to hold him in place. I didn't need to worry—he wasn't stopping. No, he was more than happy to keep going with his light touches chased by little nips of his straight white teeth gleaming in the darkness.

I couldn't look away as his laser focus became my lifeline. A rhythm only he seemed to understand and I ached to figure out.

Each pull from his teeth and mouth arrowed down between my thighs. When I swayed, he caught me, when I tried to back away from the intensity, he pushed for more.

I threw back my shoulders as he opened the clasp on my bra. I should've been worried that they weren't as perky without all the support, but his jaw tightened as he cupped them together and met my gaze.

"Fucking beautiful. You were made for firelight. Made for me." He swung me up in his arms and strode over to the fireplace. On the way there, he looked around.

"Bed?" It was pretty big. Not sure how he could've missed it.

Especially since I was the one who'd had the bubbly.

Speaking of, had Sage forgotten to send up our requested bottle? Or was it waiting for us in the hall?

Not that I intended to stop long enough to find out.

"No. I need you spread out just as I said. In front of that fire where I can worship this lush, perfect body."

I swallowed. "Oh, boy."

One corner of his mouth tipped up. "Are you amenable to that plan?"

"Is there a contract to go with it? Where do you need me to sign?"

He laughed. "Maybe just that condom in your stash."

"Bag." I pointed to the mint paisley bag on the floor by the bed.

He rerouted to that side of the room and lowered me enough to grab it without putting me down. I dug into the little side compartment and dropped the bag again. Two condoms would need to be enough.

Please God.

As he passed the bed, I snatched the throw blanket at the bottom. He laid me gently on the floor, then grabbed the pillows off the bed and scattered them behind me. He knelt over me, his dress pants hugging him from thigh to knee and more importantly, just along his zipper.

And mercy, did the fabric hug it tight.

I could see the curve of him and everything clenched inside of me.

There might have also been a little bit of panic since this was my first time.

Then again, Asher didn't seem to be average in any capacity, so why would that particular appendage be any different?

He untucked his shirt the rest of the way and slowly unbuttoned the crisp pearl-colored shirt. A tight white T-shirt stretched across his chest. So many freaking layers.

If I'd been a little braver, I would have risen up to push the shirt up and out of the way, but let's be real.

Every part of me was shaking at the idea of exactly what was under those gloriously tailored slacks.

Even his undershirt was something more than off the rack. Ripples of muscle showed under the superfine cotton. And the hint of something else.

Another tattoo?

"The way you look at me. God, I hope I don't disappoint you. I'd hate to lose that gorgeous expression."

"I think the worry is the other way around."

"You couldn't disappoint me. You don't look like the kind of woman who lays there like a dead fish."

A quick laugh rolled out of me. "That's a thing?"

"You'd be surprised."

"I'm sorry you've had to deal with that."

"Let's not talk about anything other than us."

"I like the sound of that. Just like the first time."

His smile softened. "I'm as nervous as the first time."

"Yeah?" I swallowed hard. "Me too."

He reached behind his neck and tugged the shirt over his head. His neat hair was tousled a bit and I liked it even more. Not so perfect. Especially when I was anything but.

He tossed his undershirt aside and crawled over me. "Now I can finally get you skin to skin."

The arrow of hair fanned down his pecs and trailed down his muscular stomach. I trailed my fingers through the fine hairs there and shivered at the warmth of his smooth skin. "So beautiful."

"You're the beautiful one, not me."

I followed the winding beads of his rosary tattoo. So much ink on someone I'd thought was so buttoned-up upon first glance. "I beg to differ."

He closed his eyes as I followed the intricate lines and shading to his neck before he lowered himself to rub against my breasts. His groan matched my own as he covered me and my mouth.

My legs opened for him and the soft wool of his pants cushioned the decadently hard line of his shaft as he moved lightly against the lace of my panties.

Such small barriers, and yet they felt like too much.

I wanted his skin on me—all of it.

I curled my arms around his shoulders and moaned as he settled on top of me.

"Am I too heavy?"

"No. You're perfect." I curled my leg around his hip. I'd never had a man between my legs like this. The few boyfriends I'd had were more interested in getting a hand between my thighs than in actually fitting themselves against me. Forget taking the time to touch and kiss with meaning.

Asher's mouth slid down to my neck and back to my breasts. He stared up at me in the firelight, his dark eyes dancing with flames and intent while he sucked my nipple with just a little too much force. Enough that I arched up off the soft rug.

Again, the pleasure arced through me and pooled under the lace of my panties. I was probably going to leave wet marks on his beautiful suit. Before I could mention that fact, he curled his arm under me so my shoulders bowed back, giving him more access.

As if there was a single place left on me from my neck to my breasts he hadn't touched.

I ached for more. So much more.

"God, I want to taste you."

"Aren't you?"

"More." He slipped down to the underside of my breast and to the soft line of my rib cage. "Everything."

"I..." I didn't have an answer for that. I craved every bit of experience, but I wasn't sure how much honesty he could handle.

He scraped his teeth around my belly button, just above the dip of my panties. "May I?"

"Anything."

"Oh, don't give me that opening. I'll take it all. I'm a greedy bastard."

I swallowed down the rush of fear under the excitement. If this was the one and only time I'd have this chance, I wanted it all. Even the extra frosting of that amazing tongue where nothing but my fingers had been. "Show me."

He inched lower and tucked the tips of his fingers under the stretchy lace and dragged them down my legs. Rather than looking down at the most hidden part of me, he stared into my eyes as he lowered his mouth to me. Our gaze was locked for what felt like forever.

"Breathe, Hannah."

I let out a soft laugh and it faded into a groan as his tongue slipped through my wetness. "Oh, God."

The rumble from his chest buzzed along my thighs before it reverberated through my skin to where his very clever tongue was tucked. I resisted the urge to push him away. It was intimate and overwhelming, but then there was nothing but a wash of intense pleasure as he flicked his tongue around my clit with a skill I didn't want to think about.

Instead, I concentrated on the way it made me feel.

As if I was floating and drowning at the same time. The sounds of my wetness made me want to push his head away, but it seemed to intensify his need for more. The greed he mentioned seemed to diffuse into me and made me stretch up with little tendrils of need.

Instead of pushing him away, my fingers slipped into the longer hairs at the top of his head and held him closer. He groaned against me and slipped a finger underneath where his tongue had been. Sliding it into me while I gasped.

I arched off the rug and reached up with my other hand for the pillow above my head. Anything to hold on and not fly apart as one finger became two and he stretched me.

"You're so fucking tight. As if you were made only for my mouth, my tongue, my fucking fingers."

I panted out a sob. "Yes. No one else's." That was the truth. No lies there. "Never anyone else's."

He slowed and looked up at me. "Never?" He stopped driving his fingers deeper into me. "Hannah?"

I swallowed. I didn't want to lie, but if he stopped—dear God, I'd kill him and cry for a month, maybe even a year.

He turned his hand until his thumb was tucked under my clit. My brain shut off and I lifted my hips for more. Madness clawed at my brain like a fever.

"No one?" His voice was reverent, not accusatory.

I turned my head away. "No."

His fingers slipped out of me.

"Asher, please."

"God, Hannah. I could have lost control. I was a second from ripping my zipper open and driving into you."

Yes. Yes, I wanted that. So very much. To just have him let go and I'd finally be whole. To finally know what I was missing.

A tear slid down my temple. "Please don't stop."

"I couldn't." He quickly moved up to me, turning my face to his. "I wouldn't. I just don't want to take you like an animal. You're twisting under my mouth and you taste so good." He covered my mouth and I gasped at my taste on his tongue—now on *my* tongue. He tugged on my lower lip. "Taste that?"

I let out a shuddering breath. "Yes."

"Times a thousand for me. You taste like honeyed peaches and perfection."

I'd never look at peach pie the same way.

He cupped my cheek, brushing away the tears that had leaked out. "I don't deserve this gift, but when I said I was a greedy bastard, I meant it."

I covered his hand. "And I meant it when I said I wanted everything. Show me."

He inched back off of me. "God, you're going to kill me, but that's what you're going to get. But your first time isn't going to be on the floor." He lifted me again and I yelped. "Round two maybe."

"Round two could have been on the bed."

He grinned and set me down on the huge mattress. "I want to make this amazing for you. I'm an overachiever."

Oh, Lord. I wouldn't make it through this if he made it any better.

My gaze fastened to his hands as he lowered his zipper and peeled back the pinstriped charcoal wool to the jet black boxers underneath.

I swallowed thickly. That was a lot of man in there. A whole lot.

He stepped out of his pants and tossed them on the chair near the bed. Socks went with it before he climbed back up between my legs again. "We'll figure this out together. The first time for both of us."

I reached up to stroke back the little lock of hair that fell forward to mar his perfect face. "As long as both of us aren't acting like virgins."

He laughed. "Definitely not." He covered my mouth with his and lightly stroked his way down my torso to between my thighs. His sweet kiss turned heated, then grew wilder as he groaned. "So wet for me," he said against my mouth.

"So ready."

"I'll let you know when you're ready."

Up close, I could see the little flecks of gold in his hazel eyes. Almost predatory. I shivered, but not with fear. I'd been holding onto my virginity for so long, it had seemed as if I'd never know what it felt like to be with someone, let alone a man like Asher.

I didn't even know his last name.

Maybe that was better. There was nothing outside this little snow globe we'd created. No baggage, no family, no burdens.

A space of time that was only about us.

My hips lifted as he slowly stroked one then two fingers inside of me. He took his time to learn my body. Even when I tried to urge him on, to go faster, he stayed the course.

He had his own plan for how this was going to go.

I was so impatient to reach the finish line. To just get him inside of me to feel part of something—*someone*. But Asher had his own agenda.

And that included death by endless orgasm.

Each time I got close, he backed off and slowed his tender movements. Added a kiss to my shoulder, my neck, even my collarbone. But he only touched me between my legs.

I arched up to get that deliciously soft hair of his chest against my skin, but he shifted so it was only about me and his fingers.

"Relax, Hannah. Just let me inside."

"That's the freaking object of this and yet..."

The rumble in his chest ended in a low chuckle. "We have all night and only two condoms."

He was right, but I was so restless and lost. I didn't have any choice but to follow him.

I turned my face to meet his mouth and wrapped my arms around his neck. He gasped into the kiss and the long, strong hardness of his shaft dragged along my inner thigh. "Yes," I said against his mouth. "Closer."

He tore his lips away from mine and inched down to my hips. "Is that the way you want to play it?"

I sat up on my elbows. "I don't want to play anything but you inside me. Fill me up, Asher. Please."

His eyes were wild, but his determination was overriding everything.

I fell back on the pillows. I didn't know this man, but I knew one thing. I was on his timetable.

He yanked me down then hooked my knee over his shoulder and all his teasing double-timed until I was writhing on the bed.

Fingers, tongue, even his breath was focused on the very center of me. I tried to grab onto his shoulder, but I swear my brains were leaking out my ears. I pushed pillows out of the way and grasped the headboard as he feasted on me.

There was truly no other word for it.

My thighs shook as he slipped two fingers inside me and lapped at me. I arched up as the crackling fire, the dim light, even the howling wind outside fell away and there was simply nothing but my own harsh breathing and my heartbeat throbbing under his tongue and reverberating in my head.

"Fuck, Hannah." He bit down on my inner thigh as he thrust inside me again and again with his fingers.

I couldn't take it. The pleasure mowed me down and left absolute destruction in its wake.

Then he was gone and I couldn't articulate what I needed. *Something.* Even while I basked in the ruins of what he'd done with me, there was something missing.

In an instant, he was back. The was no space between us this time. Just him ranging over me before he parted my sticky thighs and slid forward.

Finally.

"I'm sorry," he whispered in my ear, but I was already too far gone.

Too far past the point of no return.

I accepted him inside me as if I was made for him. A twinge of discomfort, then a fullness I'd never dreamed possible.

He curled his arms under my back and enveloped me from chest to waist as we joined in every single way. He cradled the back of my head, his fingers tangling in my hair as he held me still. And watched me as he broke down every defense I'd ever thought I had.

I could deny him nothing.

Even if I'd wanted to, he wouldn't allow it.

He stretched me out, wrung me out, and demanded more. Sweat poured between us thanks to the roaring fire beside the bed, but I didn't care.

I wrapped my arms and legs around him. Maybe even my heart.

The friction of our bodies, and the seeds of my orgasm, grew until his name was a chant against his mouth, his neck, even his shoulder as I tried not to scream the roof down.

My name was a plea, then an oath as he finally released his rigid control and drove into me. I chased him, the fire, the edges of insanity, and a moment before he did, I broke.

Fully and inexorably.

He filled me in more ways than should have been possible. This stranger shouldn't have been able to touch me so deeply, so completely.

Yet somehow he'd left only the ashes of Hannah Jacobs in this big, beautiful bed.

What I'd become next, I just didn't know.

The rage of our own personal snowstorm eventually abated. The sweat cooled and our wild breathing slowed. Still, his heart beat a steady tattoo against mine while I traced a never-ending circular pattern on his back.

There were no words between us. None that could really convey just what *that* had been.

Finally, he slid away and sat on the side of the bed to dispose of the condom he'd luckily remembered to put on. My brain had been in a very dangerous place where I wouldn't have questioned it.

That in itself was damn scary.

I sat up and gathered the sheets over me.

"Don't think you're going anywhere. We have all night."

I gave a nervous laugh. "Even if I wanted to, the snow says no anyway."

He turned toward me. "Do you want to?"

I lifted a shoulder. "No. But this can only be for tonight."

Everyone knew fairy tales ended, and I wanted to take control of mine. I knew better than most that nothing good lasted forever.

He narrowed his eyes and his gaze flitted to my hand.

"Hello, remember that pesky virginity thing?"

"Right." He stood and the firelight bronzed his perfect skin. And mercy, all the rest of him too.

I rubbed my legs together. I could still feel him there, like a permanent imprint.

Emotions and desire had coalesced into something hazy and feverish. Something I'd drag out on the lonely nights to remember when I'd done something just for myself.

I snuggled down into the blankets as he walked around the bed and into the small bathroom before returning.

"Enjoying the show?"

I grinned and pulled a pillow in front of me to hug it tight. Maybe then I wouldn't lunge for him and embarrass myself. "Maybe."

He lifted the edge of the blankets and crawled back into bed with me before taking the pillow away and tucking it behind his head. "If you're looking, I get to as well."

I burrowed deeper into the covers.

"Now you're going to play shy?"

I shrugged. "Orgasmic haze has left the room."

"I should fix that then." He pulled the covers over both our heads and dragged me closer.

The kisses were filled with laughter. I didn't realize I had that in me after all the intensity of before. And to be honest, I didn't know Asher had that side of him. There was a touch of charm in his reactions to me at dinner, but for the most part, there had been an aching loneliness that I'd recognized and been drawn to.

This part of him made things warm and expand in my chest. Things that I had no business feeling for a man who was a one-night stand.

By choice. I'd rather this be one perfect, happy memory than for it to turn into something tinged with regret.

That wasn't for tonight.

Instead, we found ticklish spots on one another and new screams filled the room. There was only laughter and the rich rumble of his teasing voice as he covered my entire body with stubble burn.

It was so worth it. And when we came together a second time, it was soft and dreamy, the exact opposite of the wild storm we'd made between us the first time.

If I'd been a more fanciful woman, I would have called it something more.

Wished it could be.

When he turned me so he could curl around my back, the firelight shimmered with more than just the gasps of my pleasure.

I felt more cherished by a stranger than anyone in my life since I'd lost my parents. When he slipped inside of me, stretching me so perfectly, I laced my fingers with his across my middle. We moved together in a rhythm of heartbeats and the snap of fire while the wind howled outside.

I reached back with my other hand to grasp the back of his neck as he buried his face in my neck. His low, throaty groan was the loveliest end to our evening.

We slept in a tangle of legs and arms. No fighting for pillows or deciding which side of the bed we'd sleep on. There was no side. Just us in the center with no space in between.

I woke with the dawn as was my habit, no matter how many hours of sleep I'd gotten—or not gotten.

There definitely hadn't been many with Asher.

I laid there for a few moments, appreciating the weight of a man behind me for the first time in my life.

It had all been so brief.

My chest ached as I slipped out of his arms and tucked a pillow beside him when he reached for me.

I moved to the window and saw the streets were already plowed. A snowstorm was no match for the cleanup crews in central New York. I dressed in silence then crouched beside the bed for a moment to watch him sleep. His hair was mussed and the harsher lines around his eyes had eased in slumber.

So beautiful. And he'd made me feel exactly the same. Beautiful and whole and strong.

I just had to be strong enough not to make it more than it was.

My bestie Gabriela had a phrase for this.

Fuck and run. Split before reality intervened.

Because really, what could we have in common outside of bed? He'd been all about work before he stopped by my table, and I wasn't ridiculous enough to think I could compete with his likely high-powered job.

Nor did I want to try.

Suddenly, his eyes snapped open. He went from sound asleep to wakefulness in a blink. Sadness filled his gaze before his expression became steady and blank.

"Were you going to say goodbye?"

I brushed the back of my hand along his bearded cheek before he jerked away from my touch. Sighing, I stood. "You knew what this was. *We* knew what this was. Would it be better to do this after breakfast?"

His jaw tightened. "Guess we won't find out." He rolled to the opposite side of the bed before he swung his feet to the floor. I got one more flash of his spectacular butt before he firmly shut the bathroom door.

Part of me wanted to go to the door and knock. To talk to him and tell him just how amazing last night had been. Maybe even find out more about him. A last name and a number.

But that wasn't how this ended.

I might be a virgin—scratch that, not anymore—but even I knew that the morning afters were never easy. What were we supposed to do? Shake hands or kiss? Go for one more condomless round? Yeah, that was smart.

I heard the shower turn on and closed my eyes for a moment.

No.

A quick and clean break was best.

I shook my hair back and straightened my shoulders. *Big girl panties, Hannah.* I swung my weekender and my purse over my shoulder before my gaze settled on the small vase on the table by the door.

My secondhand tulips.

I plucked them out of the vase and tucked them carefully in my purse. They were mine now. Just as last night was forever mine, no matter how it had ended.

As soon as I stepped into the hall, I saw the champagne in a bucket beside the door. It was only then I glimpsed the *do not disturb* sign Asher must've hung when I wasn't paying attention.

I picked up the bottle of champagne and tucked that away too.

Another reminder. I'd drink it and recall every detail of this perfect, unforgettable night.

Then I looked back one last time.

"Goodbye, Asher," I said quietly to the room and closed the door behind me.

FOUR

Asher

Two months later

A MEETING AT ELEVEN. ANOTHER MEETING AT NOON. THEN LUNCH, followed by another meeting.

Already my day was a shitstorm.

My sales manager had quit with no warning, leaving me to meet with several of our biggest customers. I had little time to get up to speed on their accounts and even less time to consider if my long-term, trusted employee had taken off with all his sales contacts in tow. If so, whatever company he landed at next would benefit from all the relationships he'd built while being paid by Wainwright Publishing Industries.

But I didn't have time to dwell on the possible misuse of company resources. Not when my grandmother was on the phone, upending my life in her sweet, chaotic way.

"When is this trip again?" I sorted through the piles of paper on my desk, desperately searching for my Day-Timer.

Lately, that brown ring-bound book was my life raft. If I put the task in a little box with a time and date, then I could check it off when it was completed. All those checkmarks were in my win column.

Examples of things I'd managed to address and handle in a timely fashion.

Yes, my world might be spiraling out of control, but this was how I held everything together. I put it on the calendar and I dealt with each item at a time.

"March eleventh through the seventeenth. It's already in your Day-Timer. I put it there last month."

I stopped searching and smiled, amused as always at exactly how well she knew me. Then the dates finally sunk into my head.

"Mid-March? I have the Free Papers Expo that week. Who is going to watch Lily if I'm out of town? Most of it is local, with only one overnight but—"

"I'd suggest friends, but you'd have to stop working long enough to make some. I know it's not the same for you since Billy died, but you have to stop hiding in work sometime, Snug."

The old nickname smoothed away the tickle of irritation. "You know, most people see me as a formidable man. Yet you call me that."

"You'll always be my Snuggle Bunny even if you tower over me. Now stop stalling and tell me when you're going to do something about this nanny situation."

I sighed. "I interviewed two of them. What more do you want?"

"Did you hire either of them?"

"Of course not. They weren't right. I can't leave Lily with just anyone." I straightened my tie. "I'll muddle through. Maybe Vincent can cover for me at the expo."

"Right, and then you'll just take a week's vacation because I'm traveling with my group of fuddy-duddies. We're going south in August, so you better make time then too."

"August is a long time from now." And I wasn't sure if I'd make it through this week, never mind five months away. "Let me handle the March vacation first, okay?"

"That's how you deal with everything. Mark it down as something to handle. Tell me this, do you ever enjoy anything anymore? Ever take a day or a night for yourself? Not since New Year's Eve—"

"Gran." Her name was an admonition. I was not going there. I'd been doing my damn best to pretend that night had never existed.

Not because it hadn't been good. Far from it. Somehow that night with Hannah had been the best one of my life. And it couldn't—wouldn't—be repeated, so there was no point in dwelling on it.

"I'm just saying. A healthy adult male needs certain activities to keep his equilibrium."

"Seriously?" I was not blushing. Absolutely not. I ran my finger along the inside of my collar. It was just warm in here.

"Don't play coy with me. I know you're not making time for the important things in life. I was so happy you went out on New Year's and came home with lipstick on your collar to boot. I was hoping we'd see more of that young lady around here, but I should've known you'd go right back to work as if nothing ever happened."

"You know the situation with the paper. If I let up for even a minute, we could lose everything."

"You're not going to lose everything, but maybe you should."

Stunned, hurt, I sat back in my desk chair and stared sightlessly at the rows of projections in Excel on my computer screen. One of the many reasons I loved my grandmother was because she didn't have a whit of interest in the family business. She didn't care about money, unlike my mother who considered financial worth before she spoke to a person.

Okay, she wasn't quite that bad, but bad enough.

But for my grandmother to openly say she hoped I failed? I'd always counted on her support, even if she didn't quite get why maintaining what I saw as the family legacy was so crucial.

"Snug," she said a moment later, breaking the silence. "Don't misunderstand me. I know how important the paper is to you. It does my heart good knowing how much you care about making your grandfather proud. He's gone, but you'll never forget him, will you?"

"No," I murmured.

Sharing penny candies while sitting in my miniature rocker at his side when I was a boy. Laughing as we sat in a fishing boat in the early morning fog and waited for tugs on the line. Perching on his lap and pretending to drive his big old Oldsmobile in the driveway when I wasn't more than five.

No, I would not forget.

"But there's ways you can honor his memory other than working yourself to the bone. Times are changing, honey, and you can't reverse the clock. Much as you might want to. Much as I might want to, matter of fact." She laughed, but I could hear the sadness just beneath it. "He would want you to be happy most of all. In your early days of running the business, you were. Now? Not so much."

"I'm happy spending time with you and Lily. She makes me laugh every single day." That was sterling truth. "Even more now that she's starting to crawl. Heaven help me."

I still didn't have the faintest idea how to be a parent of a baby. A little girl, no less. But Lily was not listening to my pleas to stay small and safe in her crib. She was determined to walk, whether or not I was ready.

In the meantime, I was setting out quilts for her to crawl on and covering up every outlet I could find with safety covers.

Or at least I had managed that in the bachelor pad I currently lived in. But I'd decided shortly after the new year that Lily could not grow up in an apartment in the city. Well, she could, but I had plenty of money, so what was I saving it for if not to spoil my loved ones? She was my daughter now, and I didn't want her to lack for anything. She deserved a big backyard in the suburbs with a giant swing set and room to run.

Hell, perhaps someday I'd even get her a pony. Wasn't that every little girl's dream? I'd need acreage for that.

Someday. Maybe.

In the meantime, I'd recently closed on my dream home for now in Crescent Cove. It boasted five bedrooms—although I didn't quite know why I needed so many—along with a fireplace in several rooms, including the master bedroom. It also had four bathrooms, a huge backyard, and a Jacuzzi tub among other amenities.

It was a lot of house for one man and one baby. Unless I managed to convince my gran to move in, which was doubtful because she claimed to need privacy for her and her "boyfriend."

Yes, my sixty-seven year old grandmother was getting way more action than I was.

"All the more reason you need some help. I don't know why you see hiring a nanny as admitting failure. You simply can't be everywhere at once, Snug."

"I'm well aware of that fact. As I'm about to be late for a meeting with the advertising director of athletics at the university."

In truth, I wasn't late yet. I added in extra time before and after every appointment, just in case. I was the kind of guy who preferred my dates—back when I'd had some—to be on a form of birth control while I used a condom, because ample protection was best.

And birth control related to the current line of conversation, how? Jesus. My brain was everywhere at once lately.

I rubbed the knot in my forehead. I blamed Hannah for this. She was the reason I had sex in mind so often nowadays when I'd once relegated it to the shelf where it belonged.

Even thinking of her name made me shift in my chair.

Over the past two months, I'd worked fucking hard at erasing that word from my thoughts. Every time memories of that night we'd shared plagued me, I threw myself into work or into tending Lily. Eventually, the flashbacks disappeared, even if now and then, I had to use a scotch chaser to rid myself of them.

She'd had no use for more of me, and I didn't have time for a relationship, even a casual one. Not that anything between Hannah and myself would ever be casual.

It simply wasn't possible.

"Why don't you let me handle the next few nanny interviews? I know you met with a couple of women and they weren't quite right, but let's be real. I know more about what you need in a nanny than you do. Besides, I can help screen for any of those DILF hunters."

"Say what?" I let out a baffled laugh. "What is a DILF hunter?"

"A DILF is a dad I'd like to fuck."

"Gran!" There was no questioning my face being hot now. I was tempted to stick my head in the vase of fresh flowers my secretary had placed on the corner of my desk just to get some cool water on my flushed skin.

"Don't 'Gran' me. As I'm your grandmother, that means obviously I've had sex at least enough to produce your father. And I kept going after that, trying to get it right. Some was just for practice's sake."

Her bawdy laughter made me grin despite my embarrassment. "I don't get the dad thing. Aren't most of the men you meet dads?"

"Not me, silly. At my age, children are a liability, not an attractive feature. I'm not looking to score with any Tony Randall types. Have your kids at an appropriate age, for pity's sake."

I couldn't argue there.

"But yes, it's an actual thing in the dating world. Women are out there hunting down non-suspecting single dads like bucks on the first day of target season. Their camouflage clothing is miniskirts and push-up bras."

"What? Why would any woman get excited about a man with a child? Doesn't that mean less time for them?"

"In theory, but women are primed to find good protectors. It's in our DNA, much as we may hate it. Plus, some find single fathers working hard on behalf of their children as sexy. You're a double DILF."

"Come again?"

"You're working hard for a baby you didn't even have yourself. So, during DILF open season, bagging you would be like getting a huge-racked buck. And they won't use a tree stand to take you down. More like a burp cloth and some Ravish Me Red lipstick."

"You aren't making sense, but yes, fine. You can meet with the next nanny interviewee. Assuming there are any. No one has answered my ad recently." No one suitable anyway.

"Maybe it's time to look beyond ads. I'll see what I can come up with."

"No weirdos," I admonished. My grandmother was a sweetheart, but she had a tendency to pick up stray humans just as she did with stray animals. "Keep in mind, this nanny will be influencing Lily, and it's important that she—"

"Yeah, yeah, I'll make sure to keep the felony convictions to a minimum. Have fun at your meeting. Ciao, Snug." She hung up before I could do more than stare in exasperation at the phone.

I was truly afraid to find out who she would come up with.

But I couldn't worry about that now. I was really almost late, thanks to our extended phone call.

I grabbed my jacket off the back of my chair and shrugged into it, cursing the latest snow warning to flash across the corner of my computer screen. The end of February meant they were pretty much constant nowadays.

And snow made me think of Hannah. How she'd touched the window as if she wanted to feel the cold flakes on her skin.

Shut it down.

I grabbed my Day-Timer on my way out the door. I had my meeting to concentrate on.

I'd also probably have to meet with a new nanny candidate sooner than later. Then there was everything I had to deal with when it came to moving Lily and I into our new house.

The one thing I didn't have time to think about?

Hannah.

I wasn't ever going to see her again. Just the way she wanted it.

Just the way *I* wanted it.

FIVE

MARCH WAS COMING IN LIKE A LAMB. IT WAS DECEPTIVE, BECAUSE storms were forecasted for later in the week and into next. But for now, me and my cardigan were taking it.

I looked down and smiled at the tug on my charge's bright purple leash. Latte, a Yorkie with some other mixture in his bloodline, was the newest client in my recently hatched dog-walking business.

So, he was my *only* client. It still counted. I had a client. I had a business other than my fledgling food delivery operation. That was a bit more off the ground, but not by much.

Along with those two income streams, I also had a weekend job at Crescent Cove's coffee shop. That was new too. I could've had more hours if I wanted them, but I wasn't the best at working for someone else. Hence, my own tiny businesses.

In time, I hoped to be able to support myself entirely through my own efforts. I was good at budgeting, so I could make do on little. Until then, a couple of weekend shifts as a pastry maker helped fill in the gaps.

And walking little Latte while his people parents were at work—one of them at the same coffee shop where I worked—gave me a chance to get some exercise. Good thing too, since I'd noticed this morning my jeans were a little snug. I'd had to suck in a breath or two while I was tugging up the zipper.

Too much sampling my own goodies probably. Hey, being a cook-slash-baker had to have some perks, right?

Latte led me over to a patch of grass near the pizza shop. My mouth watered at the thought of a slice. I was about to dig in my pocket to see if I'd remembered to tuck a few dollars in there when Latte dragged me on to the next patch of lawn to sniff, this one in front of the real estate office.

I glanced up at the stately columns that framed the wide porch, smothering a sigh. It must be so fun to find a house that had everything you'd ever wanted. To figure out every detail and make sure every bit was to your liking.

Not quite the same as living in the too big cookie-cutter house that had belonged to my parents. It wasn't really that big, but it was a lot of house for just one woman living on her own. My sisters hardly ever spent time at home anymore, if they could help it. Even on breaks, they tended to be out with their friends or picking up a shift or two at the pizza shop for some extra spending money.

Finding new accommodations—a fresh start—as soon as my businesses started turning a profit was at the top of the list.

Latte walked over to the nearest bush and cocked his tiny leg. Whew. No need for the plastic bags tied to his leash yet. Then he made a liar out of me by walking over a few feet and squatting dangerously close to the sidewalk.

"No, no, Latte, not in this town. There'll be none of that." Discreetly, I tried to nudge his brown rump toward the center of the lawn. He would not budge.

Let the poop commence.

I sighed again and closed my eyes for a second, focusing on the warmth of the sun on my back instead of the pile of steaming poo awaiting me. I turned my head and shielded my eyes to look across the lake, taking in the rays shimmering off the still icy water. Chunks had broken free near the shore, but out in the middle, Crescent Lake was still frozen solid, unexpected warmth or not.

A sudden yank on the leash had me reeling forward. I did a fancy two-step to avoid the present Latte had left me and nearly tipped over into the baby stroller wheeling up the block in our direction.

It wasn't operating under its own steam, thank God, but it took me a minute to realize that. All I could see was the cherubic little girl in the seat, clapping her chubby hands and reaching for the dog now straining to get into her buggy.

"Oh my God, I'm so sorry. He's friendly, as you can see. Latte, no."

I scooped him up and cradled him to my chest, hoping like hell the older woman manning the stroller wasn't the litigious sort. Latte hadn't bitten the little girl, but some people were far too eager to start trouble. Especially in prissy small towns. Crescent Cove seemed to contain a lot of kind, friendly people, but one could never be too sure.

"Oh, don't worry about it. Lily was enjoying him. As you can see." The woman laughed and slipped off her funky purple and pink sunglasses, then reached around the canopied top of the stroller to ruffle the baby's russet curls. She was still straining toward Latte, her little mouth screwed up in a pucker.

Latte was straining just as much in my arms. He'd definitely made a new friend. But I wasn't going to push it.

"Go ahead and set him down again." The other woman tucked a file folder under her arm bearing the words Hamilton Realty. Must've just come out of the real estate office, which was why she'd seemed to appear out of nowhere. "Go on now," she urged when I hesitated. "They're about the same size. They won't do each other any harm."

"If you're sure."

I set down Latte and he scrambled toward the baby, popping up on his hind legs for the little girl to awkwardly pat his head. The dog's tongue never stopped flicking out over her arm, which only made her laugh.

"This is the perfect day for a nice walk, isn't it?" The woman shielded her eyes and glanced across the street to the lake. "Now that we have this business done, we're headed over there. Maybe you too, with your handsome little gent?"

"Oh, he's not mine. I'm a dog-sitter." I bent to remind him I was close by, just in case he decided to get too frisky. "His name is Latte. And your little girl, she's Lily? She's a beauty."

She let out a rich laugh. *"Mine?* Hardly. This shop's been closed for years. This is my great-granddaughter, Lily Louise. Prettiest little girl you've ever seen, isn't she?"

"Great-granddaughter? You can't be serious."

Upon closer inspection, the other woman did appear a bit older than I'd guessed from my first fast glance. Grandmother, all right, I suppose I could see it. But great-grandma? Wow. I needed to invest in her skin care regime. She looked fabulous.

"Oh, I'm very serious. Turning sixty-eight this year." She tilted her head. "And you, you're just a youngster."

"Not that young." I threw back my shoulders and drew myself up to my full height. Average all around, that was me. "I'm twenty-three."

"Yes, definitely a youngster then." But something in her smile grew sly.

I didn't know why, so I leaned down and smiled as Lily stuck out her gummy hand to me. She'd just had it in her mouth, then Latte's, but who was I to stand on ceremony? I pretended to shake and she giggled, her deep brown eyes dancing. "Hello there, Lily Louise. Pleased to meet you. I'm Hannah. You've already met Latte—and Latte's tongue."

Latte turned his head to give my wrist a lick in a show of solidarity.

"He's quite the spiffy little guy. With surprisingly large gifts to leave behind."

"Oh, God, I forgot. Sorry." I stumbled up and turned around, wrinkling my nose.

"Here, let me help." Before I could say a word, the chic older woman hustled around the stroller to take the leash from me. "Look at that, we match." She held the leash up against her purple sweater and motioned down to her purple suede boots.

"Oh, those are killer." I stared down at them wistfully and hoped she didn't check out my ratty tennis shoes. My budget didn't extend to such hot boots. "Thanks—"

"Bess," she filled in when I paused, holding out her hand for a quick shake. "Sorry I didn't introduce myself sooner. Usually, the kid gets all the attention. As she should. Look at those cheeks." She reached down to pinch the baby's ruddy cheek and Lily giggled, clapping her hands.

"She's gorgeous. And um, sorry, but I have to...just one second." I shifted to scoop up Latte's little present and tied off the bag. Then I glanced around for a place to dump it off. Discreetly.

Bess cleared her throat and nodded to a small green receptacle for just such items to the side of the pizza shop, right above a bowl of water on the ground for their "canine customers."

"Thank you," I mouthed, jogging over to dispose of the baggie. I'd have to remember that was here, especially if I expanded my dog-sitting business as I hoped to.

Multiple ways of making a living. That was the ticket. And a sure way to stave off boredom too.

As well as thinking too much about sexy men I'd slept with a mere block away from the spot where I was now standing.

Nope, I was definitely not thinking about *that*.

After spritzing my pocket bacterial spray on my hands, I hurried back to Bess, Lily, and Latte, the latter of whom was now leaning against Bess's leg and gazing up at her adoringly.

Miniature con artist.

"Looks like you've found a new admirer." I smiled and accepted his leash, although the furry beast was in no hurry to leave Bess's side.

"I have. And so has she." Bess chuckled as Latte pitched himself at Lily's lap yet again. The baby giggled and slapped her hands, reaching for the dog over the stroller barrier that separated them. "She so would love a pet. Snug would too, if he'd let himself."

"Snug?"

Bess grinned. "Oops. He would kill me if he knew I was using his nickname in front of strangers. Not that you're a stranger. You're a friend now. So, friend, feel like a stroll?"

Maybe I should've felt a little bowled over by her take charge attitude, but I didn't. Friends were few and far between in my life, and ones who could spend some time walking with me and my canine companion in the middle of a weekday were even scarcer.

Besides, one of the things I loved most about Crescent Cove was the small town atmosphere. Everyone was so welcoming here. So, why not?

I smiled as she tucked her arm through mine and we started walking up the street in the direction I'd just come from. With her other hand, she pushed the stroller while I held onto Latte, who seemed equally excited to have added on to our walking party.

We crossed at the crosswalk to the lake, making small talk about the surprisingly nice March weather, our strides keeping pace despite the difference in our ages. Clearly, Bess was used to a walking regime and I so was not.

That needed to change. My slightly too tight jeans agreed.

We wandered up the sidewalk along the wide swath of still ice-encrusted grass. Stubborn pools of snow remained, seemingly impervious to the warm sun. But the sound of melting icicles grew near every building and everyone we passed on the walkway wore a smile.

Spring had sprung. Or at least that was what we were all pretending today, before the next storm arrived.

"So, if I may be so bold, along with walking little fellas like this guy," Bess smiled down at Latte, who was trotting along beside me, "what else do you do to keep yourself busy?"

"Do you mean like hobbies?"

"Sure. Work, hobbies, the whole shebang."

"Well, actually, my main hobby is my work. I bake and cook. I work on weekends at the coffee shop up the street. Have you been there?"

"Brewed Awakening? Absolutely. I stop in for a cuppa every time I take out my Lily here. That Macy who runs the place, she's a pip."

"She sure is."

"Surely a young lady like yourself does more than just walk sweet little dogs and serve coffee a couple of days a week. Oh!" She paused and slapped a hand to her chest as if she was surprised. "You must have a boyfriend, pretty girl like you. Or maybe a husband? Though really, if you haven't taken the plunge yet, take it from someone who knows—you have a lifetime for marriage, so make sure you have your fun first."

It felt as if she was fishing for something, but I couldn't tell what. Maybe I was just so out of practice at making new friends that I didn't know what counted as normal getting-to-know-you conversation anymore.

"Nope, no husband. No boyfriend either. I keep busy with my jobs. I also have a food delivery service for a few families in my neighborhood. You know, I prepare meals for busy working moms and dads and they pay me."

"Well?"

"Excuse me?"

"Do they pay you well? Because I know of a job where you could make good money. No, make that *great* money. Assuming your references check out."

I frowned. *Ah-ha.* No wonder my spidey senses had been activated. "I'm sorry, but I'm not interested in any of those MLM-type businesses. Aren't they basically just fancy pyramid—"

Bess barked out a laugh. "No pyramid schemes here. Not even close. This job is on the up and up, I swear. As if Snug would let me break even one law. He's a fuddy-duddy."

"Snug is your grandson?" I tugged on Latte's leash to get him to move past a questionable food wrapper on the snowy grass. There wasn't much litter in a pristine town like Crescent Cove, but every now and then, something snuck through.

"Sure is."

"Is he a lawyer or something?"

"God, no, bite your tongue. I wouldn't allow one of my relatives to enter that vile profession."

Okay, then.

"Why, it's almost as bad as being a car salesman. No, he runs the newspaper in Syracuse, among other things."

"Oh."

"But see, he's on his own with this sweetheart here," she gave the stroller a light rattle, "and he practically refuses to ask for help. He claims every person he interviews isn't right for the job. So, I figured I'd look around for someone myself."

"Wait, you need a babysitter for Lily?" I could do that. I supposed. I'd had enough experience helping to take care of my sisters when they were little.

I wasn't terribly excited about being thrust into a caretaker role again, I had to admit. Dog-sitting was one thing. Tiny humans—no matter how snuggly and cute—were quite another. I didn't want a traditional office or desk job, but I also didn't want to have to be responsible for anyone else right now.

Taking care of my sisters after my parents' deaths had been a lot to handle. I loved them and wanted the best for them, so I'd done it despite my many misgivings. I hadn't been ready to be a parent at that age. Or hell, this age. I'd barely lived myself. And yes, being a nanny was different, since I could return Lily at the end of the day, but I'd still be in the role of nursemaid.

However, Bess had mentioned great compensation, and she certainly didn't seem to have money issues from her attire. Assuming her grandson was the same, and if he ran the newspaper, he probably wasn't struggling financially, right? This job could push me along the path to financial independence that much faster.

Lily let out a gurgling laugh as Latte veered close to the stroller and stuck his furry face inside, tongue flicking everywhere.

Then there was adorable Lily herself, with her sweet giggles and her eager expression. God, she was so tiny. Would I be able to manage taking care of her?

"Not a babysitter per se. My grandson works a lot of hours. He needs a lot more help than just the occasional shift here or there." Bess pushed her sunglasses on top of her head and rolled her dark, perfectly made-up eyes. "Even if he doesn't know it yet."

This was sounding more complicated by the minute.

"I've never taken care of a newborn."

"Why, she's not a newborn. She's eight whole months now, aren't you, dandelion?" Bess reached down to tug on Lily's wiggling purple-socked feet. More purple. "She's not a fussy one either. Snug got damn lucky. She's basically an angel. Other than her diaper situation." She winked at me and I let out a weak laugh, lurching forward as Latte decided to chase a butterfly.

And I really thought I was capable of taking care of a baby? This dog was a handful.

"Are you an only child?" Bess asked before I had a chance to say anything.

If I even *had* a reply.

I was starting to feel like a mute, my few words retreating into the lockbox in my head. Bess was the kind of forceful person who made me reel back and evaluate. I knew how to stand my ground, but at first, I seemed like a pushover.

Wrong.

"No," I said after a moment. "I have two younger sisters. Twins."

Bess's eyes gleamed. "How much younger?"

"They're nineteen and away at college. Bess, I'm really not certain I—"

"Do you have a criminal past?"

"Huh? Of course not."

"Are you apt to ignore a crawling baby? Because this one is starting to scoot around pretty good."

Latte stopped dead on the sidewalk a few feet ahead of me and I came to a halt right behind him.

"Nope, you're paying attention. So, I have no fear you'd let my great-granddaughter get into mischief."

"Um, thanks. But I still don't know if I want the job. I didn't even interview for it."

"What do you think this is?" she demanded, making me blink.

"You aren't the one responsible for hiring for the position, are you?"

"Not officially, but if Snug can't get things done, then someone else has to. He'll drag his feet on this until Lily's in college if I let him."

"Isn't she his baby? That's up for him to decide, I'd say."

Bess stopped pushing the stroller and cocked her hip, her gaze penetrating mine. For a second, I was sure I'd finally driven her back with the pointy tip of my verbal sword.

"You've got fire. I like you. A lot. What are your salary requirements? We'll meet them."

So much for driving her back. Looked like I'd need a cavalry for that.

"I don't have salary requirements. I'm just walking this dog. Latte," I called out in exasperation as he headed for a small family coming toward us on the walkway, their young son in front. Then he leaped in the air just high enough to snag the string of the kid's balloon.

The kid was not amused. He started to bawl.

"Hang on just a second. I'll get your balloon back for you. Latte, come here." I wrangled the dog into submission, gently prying his mouth open until I could fish out the balloon's string.

While I performed this operation, Lily banged her hands on the stroller behind us. Bess murmured soothing words, yet Lily would not be deterred. Soon, she started to cry too, just like the kid.

Yay.

She quieted the moment I freed the balloon from between Latte's teeth. Then she stuck out her hand and made a distressed sound that any woman could recognize—although we usually made that noise at the sight of hot shoes, not balloons, but same difference.

"Oh, dear," Bess murmured while Lily wailed as I handed off the balloon to the kid. Who pushed it back at me with disgust, ignoring his parents' admonishments, due to the "dog slobber" all over the string.

What a lovely child. No wonder I didn't want to be anyone's nanny.

Spotting a temporary food vendor a few feet away near the gazebo, I offered the kid my brightest smile. "How about I buy you a hot dog to make up for what happened?"

The kid grinned, his tears drying in a flash. Dad wasn't as impressed as he gripped his son's shoulder. "Stafford doesn't eat processed meats."

"How about a comic at the store?" Bess leaned in and gave Stafford a conspiratorial smile. "I'll trade you the balloon for a comic, how's that?"

Warily, the kid nodded, side-eyeing his father.

"He's just fine. I'll get you another balloon." The father was about to pitch it in the nearest garbage can when I plucked it out of his hand and passed it to Lily.

Who beamed brighter than the sun.

Once Stafford and his stern-faced parents continued on, Bess flashed me a huge smile and nudged the stroller forward. Lily was quiet and content, bobbing the balloon. Any minute now, she'd shove the string in her mouth. "You've got a way about you, Hannah. What's your last name, by the way?"

I was worn out enough by the last few minutes that I couldn't do anything other than smile weakly. I needed to get a bottle of water or something. The relentless sunshine was actually making me feel dizzy. "Jacobs."

"Are you all right, sweetheart?" She gripped my arm and towed me up the street. "Let's get us some fro-yo. You look like you need some sugar."

Maybe I did. I wasn't sure what I needed right now.

"Just say you'll think about the job," she added as the silence stretched between us. "Sleep on it tonight, then we'll talk tomorrow. How's that?"

Saying anything other than *no* to her felt like a dangerous proposition, but I was weakening because of the revolving yogurt sign in the window of the shop just ahead of us. Right now, I'd say anything to put a pause on this conversation for a little while. "Yes, tomorrow."

SIX

Asher

"You did what now?"

"I pre-screened a nanny for you. There is no reason for you to even interview her. My instincts say she's right on the money, and she has tons of work references."

I pressed a fingertip to the muscle jumping in my temple. One of these days, I'd just name it after my grandmother and be done with it. "Tons of nanny references?"

My grandmother suddenly got busy straightening the magazines fanned out on her coffee table. "Tons of work references," she repeated.

To give myself a moment, I walked down the hall to my grandmother's homey blue-and-yellow kitchen to pour myself a glass of orange juice. That I didn't add a shot of vodka was a miracle.

I'd taken a rare Saturday off to hopefully relax and spend time with Lily and my grandmother. I needed desperately to unwind after the endless meetings I'd endured all week.

All month.

All year, it seemed like.

Trying to fill in for the salesman who had split with our client list was a full-time job in itself, never mind doing my own job and dealing with dwindling circulation numbers and all the rest of the fires that needed handling on a daily basis.

To say I was fried was an understatement.

Now my grandmother was pulling the rug out from under me and hitting me in the head with it.

When I was reasonably certain I wouldn't snap at her, I returned to the living room. She was now dusting the mantel. The mantel she hadn't dusted in my presence in years.

Who was this woman she'd invited to her home?

"Look, I know you mean well," I began, sitting in the navy blue armchair that had once been my grandfather's.

"That trip is happening soon, Snug. I'm not leaving you on your own with an infant. If that's the case, I'll just cancel my trip."

Oh, she was pulling out the big guns now. She knew I would never allow that to stand.

"You can't."

"I surely can. You're overworked as it is. Do you think I can't see the lines under your eyes? How long has it been since you've slept well? Never mind had an active dating life."

"What does one have to do with the other?" I knew damn well where she was going with this, and if I'd been smart, I would've bitten my tongue.

"Have you ever heard of stress relief? A man has needs. God knows women do too, and you notice how much sunnier my personality is than yours? You're blocked up."

Yep. There we go. Back on that track again.

I drank my juice and said nothing. That she wasn't wrong was irrelevant.

Discussing my sex life—or lack thereof—with my grandmother was a non-starter. I had bigger problems. To be honest, it wasn't as if my libido was even making itself known lately. I'd been working so much that I was usually exhausted when I finally got home to tend to Lily.

Most of the time, I barely remembered I still had a dick. It just wasn't a factor in my life.

"Or friends. What about them? You used to have Billy to go out and blow off steam with. Do you even have any other male friends?"

I raked a hand through my hair. "Jesus, he's been gone four months. Sorry if I didn't immediately go out and find a new best friend."

"Forget a new best friend. *Any* friends. It's just like dating. You don't need to put a ring on a woman's finger to have some fun. Isn't there anyone you can call up to go shoot some pool?" She pointed at me with her neon purple duster on a stick. "You need a few laughs. Maybe even to get good and soused."

"Right. And who's going to take care of—" She started to smile, widely, and it was my turn to point. "Do not go there. I have not met this woman yet."

"Are you saying I'm not capable of hiring a competent nanny? There's no one on this planet who loves that baby girl more than me and you know it."

Regret tightened my chest. She was right. I was ashamed it was the truth, but there was no denying that it was.

Of course I cared about Lily. I'd been fond of her even before she had been put into my care. I had started off as her godfather after all, and Billy and I had been close since our college days at Syracuse University.

But that was different than being her father. I would give my life to protect her—and would certainly use all my resources to make sure she had everything she ever needed—but I hadn't grown to feel the way a father should.

It bothered me a fucking lot too. She deserved that love.

Unfortunately, I just didn't have it in me quite yet, although I kept hoping one day it would just appear, like flowers in the yard after a hard, cold winter. It would've been growing underneath all the time, seemingly dormant. And then one day, it would be just...be there.

I hoped.

"No, I'm just saying it's my job. I need to make sure I find the right person. Don't you see the horror stories in the news? If I pick the wrong person and something goes wrong—"

"You'd never forgive yourself. But you're only one person. No matter how thin you spread yourself."

The doorbell rang and I gripped my now empty glass, amazed it didn't shatter from the pressure. My displeasure must have registered on my face because my grandmother let out a sigh. "Just give her a chance, all right? That's all I'm asking. If it makes any difference, she didn't want this job. I had to talk her into it."

"Excuse me? You just hired someone off the street?"

"I went with gut instinct. You should try it sometime. Hannah's the one, I'm sure of it." Her confidence might've bolstered me if the name Hannah hadn't streaked through me like lightning.

It couldn't be.

Hannah was a common name, wasn't it? Especially for those in her age group.

Her probably too-young-for-me age group. I wasn't going to turn into one of those guys who tried to reclaim their lost youth by chasing younger women.

But I hadn't cared about her age that night. She'd pulled me to her in a way I hadn't been pulled since…well, ever. I had never reacted to another woman as strongly as I had to Hannah.

It was just wishful thinking hoping she'd shown up here. Seriously, what were the odds?

Besides, it wasn't as if I wanted to see her again. We'd made an agreement. I didn't have time in my life for anything or anyone else, regrettably not even her.

Not that she'd given me any indication she was looking for more than one night either. We had both understood the score.

Then afterward, she'd tried to duck out on me as if we'd shared absolutely nothing. If I hadn't awakened when I had, she would've been gone without a word.

For the best, I reminded myself as my grandmother finally stopped staring at me and went to open the door.

I could only imagine what she'd read on my face. Normally, I was good at keeping my expression blank. That was a valuable asset in business.

But not when it came to my grandmother. And evidently, not when it came to Hannah.

Any Hannah. If this woman wasn't my Hannah, she definitely wasn't getting the job. There was no way I could say that name every fucking day and not remember how Hannah's long, gorgeous hair had spilled out around her in front of the fire, and the sound of her moans as she neared orgasm. The way we'd laughed together under the covers before our hands had started wandering all over again.

I remembered far too much.

The low hum of voices in the foyer cut off abruptly. "Bess, I can't do this."

Fucking hell. I sat up straighter in my chair and stared at my glass unseeingly. Within the span of four words, I knew.

It was *her.*

"Just come in and meet my grandson."

I locked my jaw and moved my glass to the side table.

Oh, she already has. Don't worry about that.

"I don't think that's the best idea. Really, I shouldn't have even come."

I walked into the front hall to join them. "You're right about that, because you don't want this job, and I don't want to hire you."

My grandmother gasped.

Hannah did nothing.

She didn't so much as blink at my arrival. Of course not. Because I might've entertained the fact that there could be more than one Hannah in town, but more than one Asher was much more unlikely. That meant she'd known exactly what she was walking into.

And she hadn't wanted to come.

That lack of goodbye on her part the morning after had conveyed her feelings quite succinctly. This was just adding a period to them.

My grandmother frowned. "This is Hannah Jacobs. Hannah, this is my currently impolite grandson. Do you two know each other?"

I cocked a brow and looked to Hannah for that one.

After a moment, she tucked her hair behind her ear and glanced at my grandmother with a weak smile. "I don't suppose you could leave us alone for a few minutes?"

"I certainly could, but why?"

Hannah cleared her throat. "I'm good at diffusing tricky situations. I just want to convey to Asher that perhaps he has the wrong opinion of me."

"But how could he if he doesn't know you?" My grandmother pursed her lips. "And how did you know his name was Asher?"

Hannah's forehead wrinkled in confusion, as I'm sure my own did. Actually, forget the wrinkles. I probably had furrows deep enough to swim in now to match the troughs under my eyes.

"That's his name, isn't it?"

"It is, but I never called him that to you."

"Oh, that's right. You called him Snug."

"Oh, for fuck's sake. Seriously?" I rubbed the side of my head and debated walking out on this whole conversation. If Lily hadn't been asleep upstairs, I would've just left them to deal with the fallout.

Seeing Hannah again had been like being doused. Not with water, but with flames. And my previously disinterested cock agreed. Somehow being annoyed at her for not wanting to see me again— even if that had been our agreement—only made the fire burn hotter.

Except now I couldn't even be irrationally pissed at her, because she hadn't known I was the man my grandmother had called Snug.

Could I be any more emasculated?

Oh, yes, I could, by Hannah not wanting to see me again. She hadn't even been uncomfortable about the possibility, since she'd had no clue I was the man she would be meeting today.

Just an unlucky booby prize.

And on top of that? She didn't even have the dignity to look shocked or dismayed or *something* at the sight of me.

"I slipped, all right?" My grandmother stood up straighter. "Look, I'm not sure why there's so much tension right now, if you two truly don't know each other," her dubious expression indicated what she thought about *that*, "but I think we need to sit down and have some sweet tea and cookies and figure this shit out."

I opened my mouth to argue with her, but she'd already spun around to charge into the kitchen. So, I did what any man would've done in my situation.

I turned around and left Hannah standing alone in the goddamn hallway.

If she'd followed me, I would've at least had a target for my frustration. So, of course, she did not.

Hannah was hopping on all of my buttons with her beat-up tennis shoes.

Halfway back to my grandfather's armchair, I frowned. *Those* were the shoes she'd chosen to wear to a job interview?

Then again, why not? She didn't want the job.

Even in her battered shoes, jeans, and a T-shirt, with no makeup and her long hair in a ponytail, she was gorgeous. Possibly even more gorgeous than she'd been on New Year's Eve when she was all dressed up. Not that I understood how that could be so, since she'd knocked me out then. And I obviously still hadn't gotten all the way back up.

Leaving out my dick. Suddenly, that part of me was having no trouble remaining engaged.

I sat in the chair I'd just vacated and debated taking Lily to my office. Even dealing with her while trying to get some work done was better than this.

My grandmother hurried into the room with a tray containing a glass pitcher of sweet tea and a platter of her frosted lemon cookies. They weren't bars at least, but even the lemon reminder from the night Hannah and I had spent together was too much.

With all that had gone on the last couple of months—*how* had it been two months already?—I couldn't believe I even remembered. But it seemed as every detail from that night was etched into my memory.

Especially the intimate ones.

Annoyed at my manners, or lack thereof, I got to my feet. "Here, let me help you."

Except I wasn't fast enough. Hannah rushed into the room to assist my grandmother. Then my grandmother mumbled something about getting the glasses and vanished.

Hannah busied herself with fussing with the plate of cookies, tucking one or two that nearly slid off back into the center.

"Wondering if they taste as good as yours? I can assure you, they do not."

I hadn't had her lemon cookies. My grandmother's *were* quite delicious. But I'd said the comment to be rude, although that wasn't my typical nature.

Hannah's lips trembled before she firmed them. She turned away as my grandmother entered the room with three glasses on yet another smaller tray.

"There we are. I have some lemonade if you'd rather—"

"No, no, Bess, thank you. The tea and cookies are perfect. But I'm sorry, I can't stay long."

Naturally not. Since the mere sight of me was obviously off-putting enough that she needed to flee.

Except she hadn't wanted the job before she knew it was me.

Still, the impossibility of our situation was hard to ignore. Had blind luck pushed her my way? Or something else?

I waited until my grandmother and Hannah had taken seats on the sofa before I got right to business.

"So, how did you two meet?"

"Ordinarily, he's a charmer, I swear," Gran muttered.

Hannah simply dabbed her mouth with her napkin. I guess she didn't want to weigh in on that score.

"I have a dog-sitting service. I was walking one of my customers' dogs when Bess went out for a walk. Latte took a liking to Lily. Her great-grandchild," she stressed, narrowing her eyes at me as if somehow I'd forgotten our familial relationship.

Or as if she was none too happy I'd left that detail out of our night together.

Why, I couldn't fathom. Was no-strings sex different with a single father? She hadn't seemed to mind.

It wasn't as if she'd been completely forthcoming either. I didn't know she was a dog-sitter. Did that even count as an actual job? It wasn't my place to say how she made her money, but it was a far cry from my daily lifestyle, that was for sure.

And if I was more than a bit envious at the freedom that seemed synonymous with such work, I must be sleep deprived.

"Does your expertise at walking canines somehow grant you skill with human children?"

Hannah's jaw locked just before my grandmother slammed down her plate. "Asher Heathcliff Wainwright, you have no call to speak to a guest like that in my home. What is the matter with you today?"

Before I could reply, Hannah let out a laugh, but she quickly coughed into her hand to cover it. "Heathcliff? Such a romantic name."

My grandmother shook her head and picked up a cookie. I'd been given a momentary respite from her ire thanks to Hannah's comment. "His mother had her flights of fancy."

"Does it hold true, I wonder?" Hannah sipped her iced tea.

"Does what hold true?"

She still didn't look my way. "Heathcliff was a difficult sort. Sometimes we become our namesakes unintentionally. A sort of kismet."

"He's not real," I snapped.

This was not the first time someone had commented on my middle name, but it seemed particularly annoying coming from her. I was already pissed at her for wanting her so much.

Which was not her problem at all, yet I couldn't help holding her responsible.

That was added to the indignity of her not wanting to take my nanny position, even before she knew it was mine.

I wasn't above being ridiculous, and today proved it.

"No, but he's a staple of literature. He may as well be real. I can't begin to count the ways *Wuthering Heights* has influenced storytelling and movies and even culture—"

"Why don't you want the nanny job?" I demanded.

I expected her to deflect and deny. That was what most polite, uncomfortable people did. I was surely showing no tact whatsoever. But she met my frank question with an equally honest answer.

"Because I don't want to take care of anyone else right now but me."

For a moment, the truthfulness—and pain—in her statement reached down deep inside me to where I felt the same.

I hated myself for feeling that way. For the small moments of resentment that crept in when I became irritated at having to worry about Lily when I should be focusing on the newspaper. I was the only one who could pull it out of the hole we'd fallen into. I was the only one who cared enough.

And yet, I was all Lily had too.

Not entirely, of course. My grandmother adored her. She treated her as a true great-granddaughter, just as she had from the day Lily had been brought into our world on a permanent basis.

I was the one who was struggling to adapt to the new role that had been thrust upon me. Maybe if the newspaper had been thriving, maybe if *I* had been thriving, and not so exhausted and frustrated and worn thin, I would've been able to bounce back quicker.

Maybe I wouldn't have felt as if I was drowning.

Rather than my grandmother arguing with Hannah—God knows I couldn't have since I felt the same, much as I hated admitting it—she simply nodded and set her half-eaten cookie aside. "I understand. I hoped you would change your mind, because I truly feel in my gut you are the right one to help my Snug—"

"Jesus, can we not?"

She ignored me. Probably as she should have, since I was being a dick right now. "But my great-granddaughter is far too precious to foist on anyone." She rose and dusted off the crumbs on her purple pants. "I apologize for wasting your time, Hannah, and I do hope we can still be friends."

"Oh. Well, yes. Of course. My apologies for the trouble." Obviously flustered, Hannah finished off her tea and cookie—palming the other fast enough she probably figured my eagle-eyed grandmother wouldn't see—and stood.

I did too despite the fact I was not ready to let her out of my sight again. But now thanks to my grandmother, I had her last name.

At least I had a route to finding her again. If I so chose.

"Thank you for coming." My voice was stiff, but that couldn't be helped. I couldn't look away from her. Couldn't miss another couple moments in her presence. "I'll walk you out."

Hannah picked up her purse with the hand not hiding the cookie and attempted to smile. "Thanks."

I motioned for her to go ahead of me. She'd made it about three steps when a loud cry sounded from upstairs.

All three of us froze. Then I sprung into action.

I ran for the stairs, shocked at Hannah blocking my path. She was already heading up too.

"You don't know where you're going. Move."

She kept right on heading up, her speed swift enough that I couldn't fault her for slowing me down. As if she'd been here a million times before, she followed the baby's cries into the nursery, and I burst into the room behind her with my grandmother on our heels.

Lily was half out of her crib, seemingly hanging, precariously close to falling.

"Lily." My panicked shout spurred Hannah into action. She picked up my baby before I could, cradling her in her arms like a natural, murmuring to her while Lily cried.

Almost immediately, the baby's tears began to slow.

With my heart still in my throat, I glanced at my grandmother. Although she was clearly still upset, her expression said one thing clearly.

I told you so.

SEVEN

I CUDDLED LILY CLOSER TO MY CHEST, SHOCKED AT HOW RIGHT SHE FELT in my arms. I wasn't sure when the last time was that I'd held a baby, but this one might as well have been meant for me.

That wasn't even considering that I might be holding her the wrong way. I was supporting her head, just as I was supposed to, but she was so long. Probably why she'd almost vaulted out of her crib, for heaven's sake.

She was a tiny little baby. Well, age-wise. Wasn't she?

"She's only eight months, right? Isn't that what you told me?" I asked once Lily's sobs had eased into hiccupping gasps. Poor thing.

"Yes." Bess hurried over to stroke Lily's head, murmuring softly to her great-grandchild.

Asher, I noticed, kept his distance. He'd certainly rushed in here fast enough. Was his worry so easily assuaged?

"She's just so long. And is she crawling?"

Asher tucked his hands into the pockets of his suit pants and said nothing.

"Yes, she's getting about pretty good. Not standing yet," Bess added, as if anticipating my next question. "I've been working with her, holding out some of her favorite toys and having her make her way to me if she wants them. She seems advanced to me. Definitely more advanced than my Danielle was at her age." Bess scooped her fingers through Lily's wispy red curls before moving to the crib. "Guess that was what this was all about, huh? A bored, mischievous little girl."

"Could've been the loud voices too." I lifted my chin. "Unless she's used to those."

"What are you implying? That my—Lily is used to hearing arguments in her home?"

"I don't know. You tell me." Somehow I managed to keep my gaze squarely on his. "Do you argue a lot with her mother?"

It probably hadn't been a strictly necessary question. I wasn't taking the nanny job—was I?—and this situation wasn't my business.

Too bad it was harder to convince my heart of that. Or my belly, which had been flip-flopping since the moment I'd laid eyes on Asher again this afternoon.

If I was being truthful, it probably hadn't stopped since we'd met on New Year's Eve. Every time thoughts of him entered my head, I was in trouble. No matter how I tried to keep them out, they were persistent. *He* was persistent.

Right now? He was pissed at me. Again.

I'd always thought I was a rather inoffensive person, but Asher seemed to have no trouble finding things to be irritated at me for.

So different from how he'd been that night. I supposed that made sense. What crazy woman would sleep with a stranger who wasn't even friendly?

Me.

We were still strangers for all intents and purposes, but my skin was tingling and too tight and I couldn't quite stop staring at his lips. And remembering what they'd done.

With relish.

"Her mother died during childbirth. So, no, I do not argue with her, nor would I if she was alive." Asher's flat hazel eyes pinned me in place as my breath stalled in my chest.

The silence that fell was so dense that even Lily stuck her little fist in her mouth, her inquisitive brown eyes now riveted on mine. It was so much easier to look down at her sweet, innocent face than to meet Asher's accusatory gaze.

"I'm sorry. I didn't know."

I hadn't known any of this. I couldn't even blame him for leaving me in the dark on so much, as we'd agreed to just one night. But I also couldn't help being envious of the nameless, faceless woman who had borne him this beautiful baby.

It wasn't my place. Wasn't my life.

Tell your green heart that.

"Gran, would you mind leaving Hannah and I alone for a few moments?" When Bess hesitated, he added, "Please."

She nodded and walked out without a glance back.

I clung to the baby.

His baby, whom I wasn't in any hurry to return. God knows why.

"The mattress is too high," I blurted as soon as Bess shut the door behind her and closed us inside.

Together.

Asher crossed his arms, straining the seams of his wrinkle-free white dress shirt. "Excuse me?"

"Lily's mattress is too high. That's why she was able to climb up. The height of the bed should be lowered. Or there are sleep snugglers, which help keep the baby secure in this little wrap-like thing. It's almost a sleeping bag, but they don't mind it. That way she can't just decide to climb whenever she wants."

Utter silence met my unsolicited advice. I couldn't say I was surprised.

"For someone who doesn't want to take care of anyone else, you're full of suggestions."

"It was an issue with one of my sisters too. That was a lifetime ago, but she was always trying to escape. My mom had to get creative."

"Hmm."

When it became clear he wasn't going to say anything else on the matter, I stepped forward to give him back his daughter. If it physically hurt to surrender her, I chalked it up to some kind of weird hormonal imbalance. Damn PMS.

Even if my period had been a no-show so far this month. It had to arrive eventually. Maybe that was why my symptoms were worse than usual.

But instead of accepting Lily graciously, he laid his hand on my arm. She looked back and forth between us, her tiny rosebud-pink lips pursed.

My heartbeat kicked into gear, and I had the most irrational urge to laugh.

I don't know what's going on either, kid.

"You really didn't know she was my grandmother." Though his voice was so low I had to lean forward to hear it, his expression was fierce.

"No. How could I have? I didn't know you had...*this.*" I indicated the baby in my arms with my chin. "I also didn't know your last name. Wainwright." My brain finally clicked into gear, and my eyes flew wide. "Not *the* Wainwrights. The mogul? Bess said you managed the newspaper—"

I stopped at his laughter and shook off his hand. "Why are you laughing at me?"

Bess *had* said that, hadn't she? Or some variation therein.

"I'm not laughing at you. Exactly. Just an ironic choice of words." He nodded at his daughter, but he made no move to accept her. "You look good holding her. Far better than I do."

I frowned. The vibes I was getting from him regarding Lily weren't exactly making me want to dump her off on him and run. Exactly the opposite.

He seemed uneasy around her. His own child. How could that be? I mean, Bess had made it clear that her "Snug"—a more unlikely nickname I'd never heard before—was in desperate need of a nanny, but she hadn't indicated he was incapable.

But that seemed wrong too. Somehow Asher Wainwright didn't seem like the sort of man who ever faltered.

Yet here he was, faltering.

Unless his behavior was due to something even more sinister. Maybe he wasn't uncomfortable around Lily. Maybe he didn't love her as a father should.

Surely he didn't blame her for the loss of her mother?

Almost unconsciously, I drew her back against my chest to nuzzle the top of her head. She was so small and alone. So utterly helpless. She wasn't responsible for anything, least of all something so tragic.

"See." His voice sounded rough now, almost like sandpaper. "It's as if she belongs in your arms."

"Because I'm a female? That's my job, right? To nurture and care and clean." Even as I said the words, the leading edge of my irritation faded as I looked down into her face. She was smiling up at me, I would've sworn it.

It was probably due to gas or who knows what else. I didn't care. Her smile warmed me with a soft, happy glow.

When Asher didn't respond, I spoke to the baby instead.

"Guess you don't mind me holding you, even if you probably don't remember me from the other day. But we made fast friends then, didn't we? Remember Latte?"

"Latte." Asher's voice didn't sound any less gruff. In fact, it was even more so.

What kind of heartless man could be bothered by someone doting on his baby girl? A baby I was beginning to think desperately needed it. At least she had her great-grandmother.

Thank God for Bess.

"The dog you were walking," Asher said into the silence. "When you coincidentally came across my grandmother."

I didn't know if he was intentionally sounding like a dick, but I wasn't having it. I also wasn't going to upset Lily, not when she finally seemed settled.

"Actually, *your daughter*," I stressed those two words, "fell in love with Latte. Since even a fancy Wainwright like yourself doesn't own the sidewalk, I figured we could walk on it. If you don't approve, feel

5

free to tell someone who cares." I delivered this with a sunny smile, my voice as even as a ruler.

Lily blinked open her big brown eyes and made a face. There was no outwitting a baby. Especially one who was ready to climb before she even walked.

"It just seems so unlikely." He shrugged and tucked his hands back in his pockets. Guess it was better to touch silky fabric than his own child. "Us meeting again."

"Another chance meeting after our first chance meeting? Yeah, so strange. Especially since Crescent Cove is so huge. That under three-thousand population definitely makes it hard to run into someone more than once." I rolled my eyes. "And I didn't even run into you. I ran into Bess. If she hadn't gotten it into her head that I would be perfect to help out with Lily, we wouldn't even be having this conversation."

"No clue where she would've gotten that idea."

I didn't have to look at him to know he was watching me cuddle Lily. "She didn't see me hold her or anything," I said through gritted teeth. Worse, I could feel my cheeks heating.

As if I was embarrassed I liked his little girl. More than he even seemed to.

"She said you needed help," I continued. "I didn't want to do it, but your grandmother is friendly and sweet and well, look at *her*." I gave Lily a little impatient rock in my arms, and her lips rounded into an O. But she didn't cry.

Small favors.

"She is adorable."

"Say that as if you mean it, why don't you?"

"I know why I'm irritated at you, but maybe you'd like to share why you're annoyed at me?"

"You have no reason to be irritated at me. I came here to help you."

"To help Bess," he corrected. "You didn't know you'd be helping *me*. Right?"

I narrowed my eyes. "Sure you aren't a lawyer instead of a businessman? You're suspicious enough for one."

He shrugged.

"Is it that hard for you to believe I wasn't interested in getting another shot at you?"

"Interesting turn of phrase." He tilted his head, assessing me in a way that almost made me forget I was holding a baby. From the heat in his eyes as they swept over me, I might as well have been naked.

I definitely felt that way right now.

"You know what? What you think is not my concern."

"Aren't you even going to ask why I was irritated at you?"

"Irrationally irritated?" I kept my tone sweet despite my decidedly uncharitable thoughts.

This ass had taken my virginity. Could I get a refund? It was unfortunate the only receipt I had was the X-rated tape that kept wanting to play behind my eyes.

"I won't dispute you that it's irrational." I was so shocked he was agreeing with me that I almost didn't notice he'd stepped closer.

Until he cupped my chin and lifted my face to his.

"It's irrational for a man to be mad at a woman who doesn't want to see him, when that was the agreement all along. When he has no time for her in the first place."

I tried to focus on what he was saying and not the insistent pressure of his fingers on my skin. Light and possessive, warm and dominating. How it could be all of those things at once, I didn't know.

Maybe I was just too long deprived.

"I don't have time for you either, so don't trouble yourself."

His lips curved for an instant. "And she only hears the last part." His thumb brushed along the edge of my lower lip, barely skimming it, but a breath rushed out of me just the same. "That is what I've missed the most. So responsive. Is it to me, I wonder, or to any sensation at all?"

"Add it to your list of unanswerable questions. Now if you don't mind—"

"I *do* mind. I mind very much knowing you're on this planet, walking the streets of my town, and I can't have you."

A thrill went through me, causing my arms to involuntarily band more tightly around his child. She let out a soft whimper, and I glanced down to make sure she was still sleeping.

"And that," he murmured, his cinnamon-laced breath wafting over my mouth as physically as a kiss, "is just as arousing. You don't want this responsibility. Yet your first thought is for her."

"Your daughter," I reminded him, since he didn't seem to want to say the words.

Something unreadable passed over his face. Then he was moving even closer, his shiny wingtip shoes crowding my worn-flat sneakers. "My responsibility," he agreed, his Adam's apple bobbing up and down. "Which makes you off-limits, even if you were interested."

"I am not."

"The lady doth protests too much." His mercurial smile flitted away before I could enjoy it. "But in this case, I'll gladly go without if it means Lily won't. So, name your price."

"What?"

"You heard me. Name your price for agreeing to take care of her." The pinch of his fingers on my chin tightened, then he let his hand drop. "Whatever it will take, it's yours."

"A few hours a week? How long?"

Right, that was what I should be asking. Instead of telling him no straight out.

How was I supposed to keep my professional boundaries with Asher when he was so...Asher? Especially when my feelings were already becoming far too unmanageable where he was concerned.

And clearly, he'd just recently lost his partner. His *wife*?

"Full-time."

Okay, I could deal with that. Maybe. Depending on what his idea of full-time actually meant.

"Like thirty-five or forty hours a week? And we'll need a trial period, to see if it works out. Because I really don't think I'm the one for this job—"

"As Lily makes a liar out of you." He touched her cheek for a heartbeat before slipping his hand into his pocket.

And my heart ached for his little girl even more than it currently ached for me.

"Asher, how long?"

"Full-time," he repeated. "You'll be my live-in nanny."

EIGHT

Asher

"Snug, I'm leaving in two days."

Halfway across the parking lot to my car after day one of the Free Papers Expo, I blew out a breath. I'd hoped to swing by the gym for some stress relief before I swung by my grandmother's to pick up Lily, but my grandmother had called before I'd made it two feet past the door.

"I'm well aware."

"Are you also aware that it's customary to train someone before you leave them to handle a new job all on their own?"

"I'm handling it."

"Oh, really. It didn't sound that way when Hannah called to give me her contact info yesterday. She might not have been excited to take on the position—and I'm still not sure how you managed that feat —but even she's starting to wonder who hires someone on the spot then vanishes."

I opened the driver's door to my Mercedes and tossed my briefcase on the passenger seat. "You're speaking to me right now. Doesn't seem like I vanished."

"Have you spoken to her?"

"No."

"When do you plan on it?"

I hadn't.

All right, so that wasn't entirely true. I knew I'd have to deal with her, but I had a lot going on. Besides, just lining up a nanny—even if I wasn't enjoying the benefit of her services quite yet—had lifted a load from my shoulders.

Assuming we were right about her latent nanny capabilities.

It would've helped had I actually seen her references, even of a personal nature. I didn't think she was secretly a serial killer, but as of now, my only testimonials for her were my grandmother's gut feelings and my dick.

And my dick didn't know jack about how to take care of a baby.

"You know what today was. I was meeting with clients and investors and industry people all day."

"How did it go?"

"Fine." I knew she was just trying to help so I exhaled, long and slow. "I was going to spend an hour at the gym, so I'll just spend it stopping by Hannah's instead. What's her address?"

A phone call would've sufficed, but I told myself I was already in my car and Lily had a sitter for a little while longer. Face to face was how I conducted as much of my business as possible.

That was all this was. Business.

Plain and simple.

"Before I give it to you, I have a question. Do you know Hannah?"

I reached up to loosen my tie. All of a sudden, my clothes felt too restrictive, despite the fact that my suits were practically a second skin. I worked in them, relaxed in them, fucked in them—

No. Not that I fucked period lately, but I'd never indulged in an afternoon quickie or dinner date bathroom romp. I wasn't that sort of man. Everything was separate. Defined. I didn't understand being ruled by passion. It just didn't compute.

Or it hadn't used to. Now I wasn't so sure.

"She's now my employee, is she not?"

"You know very well what I mean."

"You mean before you introduced us."

My grandmother waited.

"I don't know Hannah Jacobs," I said firmly, and it didn't feel like a lie.

Not entirely.

The woman I'd met on New Year's Eve had seemed different than the Hannah who had appeared in my grandmother's living room. Halves of the same whole perhaps, or maybe her true nature had been hidden behind the facade she'd worn that night. I'd worn one as well.

So, no, I didn't know her. Not nearly as much as I wanted to, and that was a goddamn problem.

"Sure about that?" But this time she didn't wait for a response, just rattled off Hannah's address.

"Thanks. And do me a favor? Don't call to warn her I'm coming over."

"Pray tell, why not?"

Which meant she'd intended to do just that.

"I don't want her to change her mind about the job before I speak to her."

Or refuse to see me, after deciding she'd rather not be alone with me after all.

"Didn't I just tell you she was inquiring about the position herself? Not that she sounded overly enthusiastic, gotta say, but that she hasn't backed out is a miracle. Especially since you haven't exactly upheld your half of the bargain."

"I will." I started my car. "I'll be home to relieve you in an hour, tops. Thank you."

"You know I love this baby."

"I do. Thank you for that too."

"You don't ever have to thank someone for giving love. It's free." With that perspective adjustment, she ended the call.

It took me longer than I expected to reach Hannah's. Somehow I'd forgotten that she'd made a passing comment about not living in the town proper.

Yeah, not even close. She was halfway to Syracuse, therefore requiring me to turn around and head back in the direction from which I'd just come.

That was my fault, however, since I hadn't reread the address my grandmother had given me until I was nearly back to Crescent Cove.

Lost in your thoughts, hmm? Wonder why.

I finally pulled up in front of Hannah's place, having passed a number of other houses much the same as hers tucked away in this cul-de-sac. More models were being built at the end of the lane. Most of them seemed like dull repetitions of each other. No distinguishing features, no children's bicycles laying haphazardly on the lawn—at least until the next snow came. Definitely no fun and whimsical touches to make each home individual.

My own new house wasn't much different. It was a bit larger and more child-friendly due to the enormous yard. I'd been happy with it until looking at these soulless replicas had made me realize that mine was much the same.

Not like my grandmother's home, one of the oldest on her block. She was forever having to repair this or that, but it had so much character. Her house also had a porch, just as my new place did. I wouldn't have purchased it otherwise. To me, porches meant family and friends.

There wasn't one of those in sight here. That seemed like the biggest insult of all.

I parked beside an older sedan with little pockets of rust over the wheel wells. It didn't match the house, but a quick look inside revealed it was tidy and well-kept.

And I was going to walk up to the front door before the neighbor peeking out between the lacy curtains next door labeled me as a creeper or a potential thief.

I ascended the two steps to the small stoop and rang the bell. No one answered. I pressed it again. And again.

Wasn't that Hannah's car? It certainly seemed as if it might be.

Unless it was a boyfriend's car. Maybe they were occupied upstairs.

Christ, I wasn't going to put those thoughts in my head. My

mistake for not asking if she had someone in her life now. It didn't have a bearing in any case.

Just business, remember? She's Lily's nanny.

I hoped.

With that in mind, I rang the bell again. That was the only reason I was here. Perhaps she was taking a shower or was in a distant part of the house.

Perhaps she knew I was here and was ignoring me.

If that was the case, I was going to turn around and head home. She deserved the courtesy of a call before I showed up on such short notice.

Even if I didn't fully believe she'd stick around to speak to me without the buffer of my grandmother between us.

Then again, she'd agreed—sort of—to taking the full-time nanny position in my home. I hadn't specified she'd be living with me, but surely, she knew how this worked, right? I'd assumed she'd be in a small apartment, not *this*.

Wrong again.

Ringing the bell one last time, I rocked back on my feet. If she didn't answer, I was leaving. Even I respected some boundaries.

Just as I was about to turn away, the inside door swung open.

Hannah appeared in the doorway, her brown hair flying out of its topknot thingy and falling across her face. Under one arm, she held a huge silver mixing bowl and a whisk.

"Oh." Her throat visibly moved. "It's you."

Not the warmest welcome I'd ever received, that was for sure.

"Did I interrupt?" Knowing full well that I had.

She stared at me owlishly, then reached up to pull out one of her tiny earbuds. "Sorry, I couldn't hear you. I try to get into the zone when I cook and these help."

"Are you making dinner? My apologies."

"Well, yes, but not for me, and not for today. I'm prepackaging meals for my clients. Do you want to come—"

"What clients? The ones you dog-sit for? What do you do, package up some doggy stew for them?"

"Hardly. Their owners handle their dietary needs just fine without me. Though, hmm, that's an idea." She moved to a side table, set down her mixing bowl, and tugged out a notepad from the drawer and scribbled on it with a stubby pencil.

A gust of wind from behind me nearly knocked me off my feet. She didn't notice.

"Healthy stews and treats," she mused. "Pre-portioned. That's good. Cheaper price for higher quantities. I wonder if I should add cats too?"

I had not one clue what she meant. Obviously, my day at the expo had worn me out more than I'd realized. That gym visit obviously hadn't been optional. My brain was sluggish.

"Listen, can I come in?" Before the wind blew me off the stoop.

I wasn't certain she'd care.

"Sure, sure." She gestured behind her and kept scribbling and muttering.

I stepped inside the wide, cheerful foyer and marveled at how tidy everything was. She was a capable homemaker. Unless...

"Do you live here alone?"

She turned to me with the pencil now stuck behind her ear and the mixing bowl back in her arms again. The notepad was tucked in the front pocket of her apron. "Yes."

"All alone."

"Yes," she repeated.

I tucked my hands in my pockets and rocked back on my feet. "Hmm. Okay."

"If you're trying to ask if I can afford a place like this, the answer is no, not really. Which is why my schedule is fully booked. So, if you don't mind if we chat while I continue my food prep, that would be awesome."

She'd taken a step away when I reached out to cup her cheek. She halted, her big blue eyes widening so much it was almost comical. Until I saw her lower lip was trembling to match.

Was she afraid of me? Why?

"Flour on your cheek," I said lightly, rubbing it away with my thumb.

"Oh. Thanks. Caught up." She brushed the back of her hand over her cheek and hurried up the hallway, leaving me to follow.

The kitchen was huge and modern with all the latest appliances and plenty of workspace, which was good because she'd covered every surface with pots and pans and more gadgets than I could even identify.

This wasn't some quickie operation. When she said she had clients, she hadn't been lying.

"What exactly is it you do?"

She gestured impatiently at the mess. "I cook and bake for those with time crunches. Isn't it obvious?"

I had no desire to show how little I understood what was happening here, so I just left that alone. "How many clients do you have?"

"Not all of them are consistent. Some take weeks off, and some are on the mini plan. That's only one or two meals a week."

"How many, Hannah?"

She didn't even need a moment to count them up in her head. "Sixteen."

"Sixteen clients you cook and bake for. How many dogs do you dog-sit for?"

"Mostly just walking now, until I expand my services. But I'm up to three. I have a fourth I'm talking to because of my Facebook ad, so I'm hopeful that may pan out."

First, she was meeting men on Tinder, now it was random clients from Facebook. How was that safe?

I slipped my hands back in my pockets. I tended to reveal my thought process when I fisted one and tapped my thigh. A tell I hadn't been able to ever quite shake. "That's it? No other jobs?"

"Just the one at the café. But that's only on weekends." She shrugged it off and went back to mixing.

No problemo.

"Did you neglect to recall the one you're supposed to be doing for me?"

It was only when she took a moment to answer that I realized she still had the other earbud in, and the tinny music had started playing again. I leaned forward and tugged it out, lifting it to my own ear as she scowled.

"What the hell is this?"

"Biggie Smalls."

That name didn't mean much to me. Unless it was something on the classic rock channel I could blast during the rare occasions I had an open road in front of me, I was clueless.

I handed the earbud back to her, and she reluctantly dropped the set into her apron pocket next to her notepad. "No, I didn't forget the nanny job. I was beginning to think you had."

"I've been busy at work."

"Bess started filling me in on some basics. We can continue that way."

Was I mistaken, or was that hope in her voice?

"She can certainly help, and there's plenty of things she's more versed in when it comes to my—Lily than I am. But there are times you'll have to deal with me."

"I'm sure." She tucked away a wayward strand of hair. It was streaked with blond, like a few others flying around her face. "She was reluctant to tell me much since she hadn't been able to connect with you. If you're having second thoughts—"

"Like I said, I was working. It's a particularly intense time right now. As for having second thoughts, no, I'm definitely not. I came over here to ask when you'd be moving in."

It was probably cruel not to feel her out first, to make sure she understood the parameters of the position before I dropped that bomb on her. But really, it was standard for full-time nanny jobs, wasn't it? If she didn't know that, it was hardly my fault.

She didn't speak. I wasn't even sure she was still breathing. The color leeched out of her already pale face until those big blue eyes were all I could see.

Yes, I was a right bastard. There was no denying it.

"If it's easier for you, you can live here for a while first."

"Are you serious? Why would you want to move me into your house? I've never even seen it. Shouldn't I see it first?" She turned away and pushed her hands through her already disordered hair, making my stomach tighten.

I was doing this all wrong.

"We can go see it, sure. It's not fully set up yet, but yes, whenever you'd like."

She made a sound that seemed perilously close to a sob. Inside my pockets, both hands fisted.

Fuck.

"Or not. We can ease into the living-in part of the nanny job, if you'd rather. You seem occupied here." I looked around at the joyful chaos that surrounded us. "There's just one problem."

That sound again, deep in her chest.

Oh, shit.

My shoulders locked as she shifted toward me. She was *laughing*. A little maniacally, but still. It was so rare to even see mirth in her beautiful eyes or for her lips to curve.

Full-tilt laughter was unimaginable.

"Let me get this straight. We slept together, no-strings attached, and now you want to hurry up and move me in your house to be your full-time nanny, although you still haven't seen fit to inform your sweet grandmother that you banged me?" She whisked tears off her cheeks with her thumbs. "Seriously, Asher, if you want to have sex with me again, you don't have to work this hard."

It was my turn to stare. I couldn't even begin to unpack all of what she'd said.

Except that last part. And my traitorous cock had just taken notice of the tight pink T-shirt she wore under her apron, and her bare calves peeking out from under her cropped jeans.

Calves? Really? Since when were they an erogenous zone?

Since right now, apparently. My whole body had become one. Only activated by *her*.

Goddamn Hannah Jacobs.

Despite the fact that my dignity was lying in tatters on the floor—I was not moving her in so I could have easy access to sex, thank you—my baser nature was still intrigued by the last part of her statement.

If I didn't have to work that hard, it meant that....

No.

No, Lily's well-being came first. If I was paying Hannah, I wasn't having sex with her.

I exhaled and pushed a hand through my hair. "I realize you don't know me well."

"Or at all, sexual congress aside."

"I haven't heard that term used in twenty years. Maybe not even then." It was oddly hot, in a puritanical sort of way. "Regardless, Lily comes first. I would never move you in to satisfy my urges. If I even have them." Which I wasn't admitting to.

"Really." She crossed her arms, regarding me with a tilt of her head. "This isn't some kind of Hallmark special move."

"What? God, no. What are they showing on the Hallmark channel now?"

She waved it off. "I'm just saying, this nanny scenario is like the foundation for half the tabloid affairs I read about. No, I don't read about tabloid affairs," she added, correctly guessing my next question. "I just hear stuff."

"I would never take advantage of my position that way." On that point, I wouldn't waver. "Lily deserves someone who is wholly committed to her. Like I—" I stopped and exhaled again.

Like I should be.

I was financially, as well as when it came to keeping her safe. It was the loving her like a parent should part of the deal I hadn't quite managed. It was early days yet. She was still Billy's in my head. Would always be Billy's. He deserved a space I didn't belong in.

So, where did I fit exactly?

Staying away was less complicated. And more cowardly.

"She had a rough start in life," I said into the silence. "I want to make up for it as much as I can."

Hannah frowned. "You know I had misgivings about taking the job. She's a sweetheart, but the main reason I followed through was because I have mortgage payments to make. If I move in with you, what point is there to me keeping this house?"

Before I could reply, she moved to the window and gripped her throat. "I could sell it," she whispered, almost to herself. "I could."

"You don't have to." Her gaze whipped to me. "If you want to, sure. But I understand needing a backup plan if the job doesn't work out."

But it would. It had to. Hannah was literally Lily's only hope.

Right now, she was mine too.

"I don't know if I'll be a good nanny. But I also know I don't want to be trapped behind a desk either. I want to be in a kitchen, or outside in the sunshine."

"Or the wind," I said drily as crumpled winter leaves blew past the window in the breeze.

"Whatever. I want to see the seasons. *Be* in them. Good, bad, or otherwise. I don't want to live inside a box. My mother did that, and it kills me that she never really got to see much of anything before she —" She stopped and swallowed. "Before she passed."

There was no stopping myself from fisting my hands, not when her pain was so physically palpable. "I'm so sorry."

Such inadequate words, when all I wanted to do was to take the hurt away. Whatever it took.

"It's okay." She didn't smile to make the uneasy moment smoother. That wasn't her way. She just let it stand as it was.

I respected the hell out of her for that, along with so much else. She wasn't a pushover. But she had a giving heart. I'd seen it for myself when she interacted with my grandmother and Lily.

And even with me.

"I don't want to force you into this job."

She snorted.

"It might not have seemed that way. How you were with Lily changed everything for me. I didn't want someone off the street to have the position, and I was dead-set on not hiring you—just like I didn't hire the women I interviewed before you. Neither of them felt right. Neither of them rushed to hold Lily when she cried and held her as if she mattered."

Hannah nodded.

"But I'm going to be frank with you. My grandmother is leaving town for a few days with her friends, and I have a big expo for the trade paper association. No one else can handle it for me. My right hand man, Vincent, would try, but he's not me. I'm the face of the company, and I need to be there."

Hannah waited, again not filling the gaps.

Damn, I liked this woman. It made things more complicated, but maybe it didn't have to. I was an adult. I could ignore my needs.

I'd done it for so long now.

"I don't know how I'm going to juggle both this week. Hell, I'm not sure how I'd juggle Lily period if I didn't have my grandmother, but that's a separate issue."

When Hannah still didn't speak, I swallowed hard and went for broke.

To hell with my pride. Lily was worth me losing every shred of it.

"Jesus, don't make me beg. I need you, Hannah."

NINE

"I NEED YOU, HANNAH."

Ironic words to replay in my head as I sat on the ice cold examination table in my doctor's office.

I was swinging my legs like a kid's. I couldn't keep still. A bad habit of mine, especially when I was nervous.

Right now, I was about to hurl. And I wasn't even certain it was solely from nerves.

It couldn't be possible.

It just could *not* be.

I couldn't be a high school health class warning statistic. I'd waited twenty-three years plus to have sex. Far longer than any of my friends or even my younger sisters. It just wouldn't be fair.

Then again, what was? My flying-phobic mother had finally found the bravery to go up in my father's plane only to lose her life on her very first flight.

I'd say that proved fairness was a fairytale.

But I had to be overdue for some good luck. I'd even added a few coins into my karmic bank account by agreeing to meet Asher at his house today once he left work. If I hadn't had this appointment this afternoon, I could've made it easier on myself and spent the time with Bess instead, going over some of the particulars for Lily.

Instead, I'd had a very important test to take, where passing meant I'd have to take care of someone for the next eighteen years.

You don't want to get stuck taking care of anyone else, huh? We'll just see about that.

If Dr. Ellis didn't return soon, I was going to flip the hell out.

She'd had a situation with another patient, but she was adamant about speaking with me. I'd had the same doctor since I was a baby. In a small town, everyone knew everything about everyone else, and your doctor sometimes was more like a friend than a physician. Usually, I appreciated that personal touch.

Not right now.

I wished I'd just peed on a damn stick like everyone else. But I wanted to be sure. No chances. Better to deal with the situation head-on. Positive action. Positive thinking.

Positively about to lose it.

The door opened and Dr. Ellis stepped inside, looking a bit harried despite her gentle smile. Her snowy hair was in a neat updo and she looked perfect from her tidy white coat to her responsible navy pumps.

Me? I was a half-crazed hot—literally—mess who couldn't stop bouncing in place.

"Sorry about that, Hannah. It's a zoo in here today. You know how it is before a snowstorm. Worse in here than the grocery store."

"What snowstorm?" Normally, I was a weather buff, but I hadn't been paying attention to much that didn't involve cooking for my clients or was period-related.

As in where was mine, because it definitely hadn't arrived on time.

"You haven't heard? This weekend, we're expecting two feet." Dr. Ellis laughed and sat on the edge of her desk. Since she was a small-town doctor, her setup wasn't as fancy as I imagined it might be in other larger facilities. "March weather can be fickle, can't it? But that's not why you're here."

For a second, thoughts of being shut in with Asher and his baby had overtaken even the possible occupancy of my uterus. I really did not want to deal with being alone with him right now. If I wasn't pregnant, it would be hard enough, because he was right about a couple of things.

It wasn't proper having a personal relationship while I was taking care of his daughter. Lily's welfare needed to come first, not any pesky entanglements that could affect our working situation.

Definitely not any orgasms. I was certain those would affect far too much of my life, as they had already.

Case in point where I was currently sitting, jiggling my legs like a kid hyped on too much sugar.

Asher needed me. How he was so clueless at taking care of his own offspring, I had no idea. Didn't having a child bring with it some natural wisdom about the role?

You're about to find out.

"No, but thank you for the heads up."

"You won't need to stop at the store. Your kitchen is always well-stocked." She smiled and shuffled paperwork. "Although perhaps you'll have to add some new additions. You're pregnant, Hannah. Congratulations."

I didn't blink. Didn't swallow. The fingers I'd dug into my thighs as I swung my legs went numb, just like the rest of me.

Minus my whirling, chaotic brain.

"Hannah?"

"Yes. I'm sorry. Are you sure?"

"Very. There's no mistaking it."

"But I got my period last month. Maybe the test is wrong."

Dear God, please rethink this and make it wrong.

It was probably far too late for prayers. That one crazy night had changed my life.

Changed *his* life.

How was I going to tell Asher? He barely had time for the daughter he already had.

I officially had a baby daddy now—and he already had another kid.

Fuck me.

"Sometimes that happens shortly after implantation occurs. Some women even bleed every month for part of their pregnancy. The process is as individual for every woman as a fingerprint."

"That's reassuring." I tugged at my ragged thumbnail and hopped to my feet. I had some meals to deliver this afternoon and a new dog to take out for his nightly sabbatical before I met Asher at his house for a tour. "Well, thanks. If we're finished now, I'll just be going."

"Hannah, wait." Dr. Ellis rose and came around her desk to peer down at me through her round Lennon-style glasses. "Typically, I give some counseling at this stage. Just so a woman is aware of her options."

"Options." I rubbed my forehead. Already I knew those options weren't for me. I might not have planned on a baby, but I would be having it. "You mean abortion."

"And adoption," she added gently, reaching for a few pamphlets on her desk. "If you'd like, you can read these over, and we can talk after you've done some thinking."

I waved them off. "No, thank you. I'm keeping the baby."

It was too soon for me to say *my* baby. None of this felt real. I was still wondering if I'd wake up in bed anytime now.

"Okay then. I'll prescribe you some prenatal vitamins."

"Prenatal. Right. Because it's not just about me and my impending panic attack."

She smiled kindly and I nearly bristled when she moved forward to touch my arm. My reaction turned her smile into a frown. "I take it this wasn't news you were hoping for."

Mutely, I shook my head. I felt guilty for admitting it. I had to be a heathen. What kind of woman didn't jump for joy when she found out she was expecting?

So many women tried to have babies and could not, and here I was, easily pregnant—so freaking easily—and not tossing confetti.

I was just...numb. Shocked. Scared witless even through my paralysis.

"I was a virgin until New Year's. It was only one night." I swallowed hard, shoving down all the babbling I could barely contain.

I don't know how to be a mother. I don't even fully know how to take care of myself.

How can I? I don't have my own mother anymore.

I had no one to go to. No one to counsel me. My sisters were more experienced than I was, but not when it came to this situation—and Lord, I hoped that remained true for a good long time.

My bestie Gabriela would definitely have no idea what to do about something like this. She was a good time girl who didn't get slowed down by much. Clearly, she employed better birth control than I'd used.

Or else Asher had super active sperm to go along with his workaholic tendencies. Perhaps that was why he never spoke of Lily's mom. Considering the situation with me, it was probably a little awkward, but even so. He'd made a baby with her, so you'd think he would find it hard not to mention her loss, even in passing.

Unless it was the same situation as it was with us. Maybe he'd driven by and implanted a baby in her without knowing much about her. If so, he really shouldn't be going around with that weapon out of its holster.

Like…ever.

"What method of birth control did you use?"

I didn't flush, but it was a close thing. "Condoms. Multiple."

Because we hadn't stopped at one time. Of course not. Had to make sure he hit the baby-shaped bull's eye.

Dr. Ellis's eyes widened. "Not at one time."

I let out a quick laugh before panic strangled it in my chest. "No. I was a virgin, but I wasn't clueless. Anyway, Asher knew plenty."

She tried to keep her expression emotionless, but she didn't succeed. She knew that name.

If you gotta get knocked up, might as well do it by a super rich dude who is known throughout the town, right?

I covered my face with my hands. "Look, don't tell anyone, okay? Please."

"Hannah, you know whatever we discuss is confidential. You don't have to worry."

"But you know him. That much is obvious. Or you know *of* him."

She slipped her hands into the pockets of her white coat. "I apologize for not tempering my reaction. But yes, I know of Asher. " She sighed. "Such a hard situation."

"Yes." I didn't elaborate. I didn't feel right about discussing Asher's life with someone else. Not that I knew much. Dr. Ellis probably knew more than I did.

The whole town most likely did too.

My doctor's office wasn't in Crescent Cove itself, but it was just beyond the outskirts. Close enough for Dr. Ellis to hear scuttlebutt for sure. She probably knew the players in a way I did not, living in my own minuscule town nearby with my head buried in pots and pans and now cleaning up doggie poop. Even my jobs in Crescent Cove were new enough that I wasn't yet familiar with many of the townspeople, although I was learning.

Just not fast enough.

"He really stepped up for Billy and Lily. So, forgive me for speaking out of turn here, but if one of your concerns is that Asher isn't father material, duty is his middle name." She smiled and reached for the folder—*my* folder—behind her while my brain spun on hyperspeed. "Let me write you that vitamin script, and you can be on your way."

"Dr. Ellis, who's Billy? I know Lily. Know of her, I mean, since I was actually just hired to be her nanny. Ironic, right?" I let out an uneasy little laugh. "I know her mother died in childbirth. But Asher never mentions her, and he's definitely never mentioned Billy. Who is he?"

Dr. Ellis stopped writing in mid-sentence and looked up at me. "It isn't my place to say. I shouldn't have even acknowledged being familiar with Asher's situation in the first place. But I've known you since you were knee-high to a grasshopper, Hannah, and you've dealt with so much recently on your own. But I don't think you'll be on your own in this."

"Please tell me what you know. He hasn't told me anything."

She frowned. "He hired you as his nanny and didn't tell you the particulars?"

"He told me about Lily's mother dying. That's it. And he didn't really hire me in the first place. It was his grandmother who wanted me to be Lily's nanny. We didn't realize at first who the other was." I drove my hands through my hair, ripping apart my braid. "I just want to hide and make all of this go away, and I can't. I have to be an adult and God, I'm not ready. I still feel like a little girl myself, with no mother to hold me and tell me everything is going to be all right." My voice cracked and I was horrified at the hot rush of tears burning behind my eyes.

I wasn't a crier. I *wasn't*.

Dr. Ellis studied me with compassionate eyes. "Billy died in a construction accident last fall. He was a single father to a baby girl. Asher was Lily's godfather." She released a long breath. "I'm friends with Billy's neighbor. The whole neighborhood chipped in to start an education fund for that little girl, which turned out to be unnecessary considering, well, who Asher is. But we wanted to help somehow." Dr. Ellis finished writing on her little pad and set down my folder before coming closer to wrap me in a brief hug.

I clung to her like I was drowning. Between what I'd just learned about Asher and Lily and my own baby—

God, how was I going to figure all of this out?

How were *we*?

TEN

Asher

HANNAH WAS LATE.

First day of work, and she was a no-show. Great sign.

Thanks, Gran.

Technically, this wasn't her first day. My grandmother wasn't leaving until tomorrow, so that would be Hannah's official first day with Lily.

I'd been able to shuffle some of my meetings at the expo, and Vincent was stepping up so I could come home earlier and help out. I wasn't planning on monitoring Hannah, and God knows, I was no expert myself, but maybe between us, we could figure some of this out.

I wished I could bottle whatever innate kid smarts my grandmother possessed, but alas, no. It probably also had helped that she'd raised her own daughter then partially raised me when my own parents had been lackadaisical at best. Not neglectful exactly. They'd just found much more interesting things to do with their lives than being good parents.

My father was on the west coast now with his new wife and his stepchildren, whom he seemed to have a better rapport with than me. I truly wasn't bitter. Sometimes the fit wasn't right, even when the people in question were related. My father and I were opposites in every possible way.

As for my mother, she lived in Rhode Island, and I saw her now and then. We also weren't close. We weren't distant either exactly, just more like acquaintances who shared a last name than mother and son.

Thank God for Gran and my grandfather. Because of them and their influence, I'd once believed I had a chance of doing right by my own kids someday. Assuming I was blessed with any. I'd never thought much about the possibility.

That was for someday, along with considering marriage. Dating was one thing, at least occasionally. But serious relationships were on the distant horizon. Possibly after retirement once I wasn't working day and night.

Then there was Lily. My plans had flown out the highest window, and I was still trying to catch them before they hit the ground.

I couldn't expect my grandmother to give up her life for me and my responsibility. She'd already done so much. Hannah would be a huge help to fill in the gaps.

If she ever arrived.

As Lily started to cry, I crossed the living room to turn her swing on a higher setting. I'd had it on the lowest one, but she seemed to enjoy more motion. A flick of a button and a piped-in kiddie tune filled the room. She only cried harder.

This was going well so far.

I scratched the back of my neck before crouching to rummage through the baby bag my grandmother had packed for me in case we needed to go out. She'd put together several of them, as if I couldn't possibly assemble the needed items in a hurry without help.

She wasn't completely wrong.

After four months plus, I should've been better at all of this. If I hadn't immediately thrown myself even harder into the newspaper, I might have been.

But I understood how to balance profit and loss sheets. I grasped how to make up shortfalls in advertising revenue, even if I hadn't yet deciphered how to plug all the holes. I knew how to innovate when the tried and true no longer got the job done.

I did not know how to cuddle and soothe and sing lullabies.

For one, my singing voice sucked.

I also wasn't a cuddler. I wasn't even much of a hugger, despite what my grandmother insisted on calling me. What I'd done when I was seven didn't have a ton of bearing on my personality at thirty-two.

Christ, thirty-two with an eight-month old and I still didn't have one clue what I was doing. And worst of all? Those knowing brown eyes, so like my best friend's, didn't hesitate to accuse.

Anyone else could do this right. Not you. You're just a glorified pencil pusher.

Fine, she probably wasn't thinking that in those exact words. Billy wouldn't have been either. He just would've grinned and said he'd given me ample opportunities to hold her, but I'd always begged off.

No begging off now.

I glanced up at the ceiling.

Bet you're laughing at me up there, buddy. I can practically hear it.

Lily continued to cry, pumping her chubby bare feet. She wouldn't keep on socks or shoes, no matter how hard we tried. Almost as soon as we put them on her, she was wrestling them off.

Stubborn like her father.

Both of them.

I sighed and dug out a banana-flavored applesauce pouch. "How about this? You like this, don't you? Gran said you always grab for it right away."

Sure enough, her tears dried in a flash. She stuck out her hands, whining a little until I handed over the goods. She frowned at the twist top and tried to stick it in her mouth before I took it back, once again unleashing more tears.

Short-lived this time, thank God. They stopped as soon as I undid the top and pushed the applesauce pouch at her puckered mouth. She grabbed it and started to suck eagerly.

I exhaled. See, I could do this parenting thing.

Good thing, since Hannah was still MIA.

Rising, I pulled out my phone. Almost an hour late. She wasn't making the best impression, that was for damn sure.

I glanced back at Lily, blissfully sucking on her applesauce and swinging back and forth to some inane children's song. Then again, what options did I have? My grandmother was leaving for a few days, and I shouldn't lean on her so much anyway. It wasn't fair.

Today, I might have no choice.

I'd just tapped the speed dial button for my grandmother when the doorbell rung. A quick glance out the front window indicated Hannah had arrived.

Finally.

I tugged open the door. "You're late."

Hannah was facing away from the door, her long dark sweater pulled tight around her in deference to the clear cold day. Later, snow would come, but for now, everything was calm, and the sky was streaked with the faint colors of a growing sunset. Pinks and golds and blues that washed over her face as she shifted toward me and I locked in on her red-rimmed eyes.

My chest seized. "You've been crying? Why? What's wrong?"

She didn't bat a single dark eyelash. "Why didn't you tell me you lived in a mansion?"

"It's hardly a mansion, and even if it was, that isn't why you've been crying."

"You're right." She rubbed her thumb over the corner of her mouth. "Did you hear *Supernatural* is ending?"

"What's *Supernatural?*"

She rolled her eyes and brushed past me to enter my mansion—uh, house.

I'd barely had a chance to shut the door behind her and flip the locks before the excited squeals and giggling began. I stepped into the living room in time to see Lily fling her applesauce pouch like a projectile and thrust her arms out toward Hannah, who was already acting a hell of a lot happier to see the baby than she'd been to see me. Hannah wasn't smiling, not quite, but she was talking in that cooing voice that most seemed to employ when speaking to small humans.

She unstrapped Lily from her swing and scooped her up into her arms before bending to retrieve the applesauce pouch. At least it hadn't spilled. "Some aim you have on you, little girl. You gonna play baseball and put up your dad in a fancy nursing home someday?"

Lily laughed while I frowned. "I'm nowhere near needing a nursing home, thank you."

"Good to know." Hannah's gaze swept over me in a way that didn't match how she was cradling Lily.

What had gotten into her? I couldn't put my finger on it, but she was acting different. Weird. How I could tell that just from our few moments of interaction, I didn't know. It wasn't as if I knew her very well. Or at all, really.

Except biblically. I remembered every minute of that particular night.

"But if that's a crack about our age difference, I'll remind you I have no trouble telling time. You, on the other hand—"

"Why don't you have any furniture?"

I glanced around the room. I barely noticed how little it contained because I didn't spend much time here. I'd just moved in. As it were. I probably should hire some decorators.

Then again, why bother? Who did I have over besides my grandmother? Lily surely didn't mind.

Hannah, however, didn't seem too impressed.

"I just moved in."

"How just?"

"Recently," I said through gritted teeth. "I'm sorry if the place isn't to your liking."

"It isn't that. It's just unexpected. You have this huge place—so much house for a man and his daughter. Then you come in here and it's virtually empty."

She walked around the perimeter of the room, pausing by the enormous fireplace that had been one of the selling points of the house. There were a few of them, but this one and the one in the master bedroom were the largest. Perfect for cozying up on a winter's night.

Alone. As I did much else. But I liked my solitary existence. At least I had, not all that long ago.

"I've been working." The excuse seemed flimsy even to me. "I suppose I should hire someone. Maybe a whole team, get it done faster."

Hannah turned with Lily in her arms, who was looking up at her adoringly, and my heart clenched like a fist. Like *my* fists, currently tucked in my pockets. "You can't do that. A house should reflect you. Your choices, your sweat and hard work. You can't pay for someone else to pretend to be you."

"You can pay others for just about anything."

"Said like a rich, entitled man." Her tone was light, but the jab still struck its intended mark.

She was already on the move, crossing through the dining room, lifting her brows at the long table with enough place settings for a crowd. It had belonged to my grandparents and my grandmother harbored no illusions about holding formal dinners "at that old thing" anymore. It was a priceless antique and a family relic to boot, so I'd kept it in storage until I found my house. There was also the huge ornate china cabinet that went with it, standing mostly empty except for a single set of fancy dishes that my grandmother had passed down to me.

"At least you have things to eat on."

I didn't tell her I never ate on that china, because I was sure she would've deducted points. When it was just me, I ate on paper plates. Why make a mess for just one? I ate out a lot too, usually rushing between meetings or on my way home. Or I ate at my grandmother's, when the silence and shadows grew too deep.

In the old days, I'd caught a lot of my meals with Billy. We'd spent a lot of time together, both before and after he'd had Lily. I hadn't really had time for other friends with work, so I hadn't made them.

Now I didn't know what I'd do with a friend. I wasn't sure I even remembered how to be one.

I followed Hannah and Lily into the spacious, bright kitchen, watching silently as she opened the double oven before doing the same to almost all of the cupboards, above and below. The scarcity of food got a raised eyebrow, as it did when she opened the refrigerator and found it nearly empty minus sandwich makings, formula, and a few premixed snacks for Lily. She was still more interested in her bottle than actual food, but we kept trying.

"I didn't figure you for the usual bachelor with just a head of lettuce and beer in his refrigerator, but you're scarily close." She shut the refrigerator and turned to me, setting the baby on her hip. "You can't live like this with a child."

"Lily has everything she needs." There was no helping the defensive tone in my voice. "You haven't seen her nursery yet."

"I don't mean just what she needs. You hardly have the makings for a balanced diet in there. Where do you eat, if not here?"

"Out."

She sighed. "I'm assuming your grandmother makes sure you're fed now and then at least."

"I'm a grown man. I don't need anyone taking care of me."

"Oh, really? And where's your proof of that?" She gestured behind her and Lily reached out for Hannah's arm, nearly toppling from her perch on Hannah's hip. Lily's little face reddened, a sure sign tears would follow, but Hannah just scooped her up securely again and continued on her house tour.

She clucked under her breath at the nearly empty basement-slash-family room, sniffed at the generic brand of detergent in the laundry area, and let out a long sigh at the pile of mail and magazines stacked in the foyer. But when she entered the den, she let out a soft sound of pure pleasure at the shelves of books. They extended all the way up the walls, high enough that there was a rolling stair ladder like in the bookstores to accommodate the uppermost rows. Plush cushioned seats stretched under the windows that framed the room, showing a view of the driveway and the big side yard.

Snow clung to the glass in fat flakes, the promised storm arriving on gusts of wind that rattled through the trees. Hannah didn't seem to notice. She was scanning titles, one arm securely around Lily while she talked softly to her, sharing her finds.

"Oh, Stephen King. He's scary. Too much for you. Same for Dean Koontz. Kylie Brant. Serial killer? Yeah, no. Where's the shelf for smart little girls?"

Feeling more than a little foolish, I pointed at the bottom shelf. "Those there."

Hannah marched over to me and held out Lily, who looked as panicked as I did.

I could hold her. I could. I did all the time.

Well, sometimes.

Occasionally.

Hannah's face softened. "Just for a second. I want to look at the books."

Swallowing hard, I lifted Lily into my arms. Her forehead wrinkled as she stared fixedly up at me, her gaze saying everything I was thinking.

You suck at this.

I adjusted her in my arms so she was more comfortable, then reached up with my free hand to sort of pat her head. Awkwardly. While Lily stuck her chubby fist in her mouth and started to self-soothe.

I couldn't blame her. I needed to self-soothe too.

"Oh, look at all these Little Golden Books! You have so many. Wow, seriously old." Hannah sat down cross-legged on the antique rug and paged through a couple of them.

"From my childhood."

"Super old," she said over her shoulder, although for a second I thought I saw a glow in her eyes.

So brief that it might've been a flick of a lighter in the darkness.

"Keep that kind of talk up and I'll begin to think you have some kind of older man fetish." I hoped Lily wasn't listening. Not that she cared much for what I had to say when she had her delicious hand to snack on.

Hannah continued flipping through the book. "Who's saying I don't?"

She was acting weird, all right. Not flirty exactly. But she definitely wasn't backing down if things went in that direction.

Maybe she was testing my resolve from the other day. Maybe this was all a game to her.

Maybe I was too fucking horny and it was highly inappropriate while holding a baby in my arms.

"*The Shy Little Kitten? Scuffy the Tugboat?* No way. Oh, these are so sweet. You kept all these?" She glanced at me. "For your own kids?"

She'd already looked away again by the time I managed to speak. The excitement on her face and in her voice was intoxicating, but it vanished far too fast. "I guess so. I'm not sure why we kept them. My grandmother was their steward though. She bought me almost all of them."

"Not your mother?"

"My mother didn't worry overmuch about my reading habits."

I carted Lily over to where Hannah sat and joined her on the rug. I made a cage out of my spread legs and set Lily on the floor, surprised that my arms were aching a bit. Not from being sore, but because they were now empty. Lily had felt right in them.

Hannah looked at where Lily was trying to push herself up using my legs for balance, her lips twitching. Still not a smile, but if anyone had been able to get one from her, it was Lily. "She's ready to run."

"Not yet, dear God. I have to finish babyproofing the house."

"Easy enough to do when it's empty."

"That's a good point. Maybe I'll leave it this way." Thoughtfully, I scratched my chin.

"This room isn't empty." Hannah craned her neck to take in the ornately carved desk that had been a holdover from my apartment. My laptop and my files were stacked on top. "There's even seating that isn't the floor." She nodded to the chaise across from the desk, another piece from my apartment.

"This is where I spend most of my time. For you, it'd be the kitchen." Almost as an afterthought, I reached out to tuck a stray strand of hair that had escaped from her braid behind her ear.

She sucked in a breath as if I'd held a lit match to her skin. Lily whipped her head around, searching for the cause, shifting toward Hannah as if she could help.

Instead of dropping my hand, I leaned forward to slip it under her braid, casually cupping the back of her neck.

Lily watched us with huge eyes, gnawing on her lower lip.

"Such an angel."

"Are you talking about me or your daughter?" For some reason, she lingered on those last two words, and they hung heavily in the air between us.

She didn't know, did she?

I certainly hadn't told her. I didn't think my grandmother would have either. And Hannah definitely hadn't let on before that she knew Lily wasn't biologically mine.

But Crescent Cove wasn't a huge place. People talked. It wasn't a secret that I'd adopted Lily after Billy's death.

I had far too many single women approaching me in the grocery store for that very reason. I might not have ever heard the term DILF —or else I'd blocked it out—but my grandmother wasn't wrong that there was such a phenomenon. Its existence was the main reason I'd turned to grocery delivery services.

If I had to speak to one more woman meaningfully squeezing melons while she eyed me up and down...

"Lily. I'd call you something else."

She wet her lips. Whether she knew that was a provocative move, I didn't know. She'd been a virgin.

Until that night.

Until me.

Until *us.*

Every possessive molecule of my body roared to life at the thought. I was the only man she'd been with. Ever. And perhaps I wasn't the only one remembering how it had been between us.

Focused on her mouth, I leaned in, my gaze lifting to her eyes. The panic trapped in those startlingly blue depths made me pause. "Hannah?"

She reared back and jumped to her feet, sending the pile of children's books tumbling to the rug. "Sorry, I have to pee." She practically shouted it as she fled from the room.

"The bathroom is down the hall, second door beside the—" I trailed off as a door shut somewhere in the distance.

Either she'd already found the bathroom or she'd split. Rightly so.

Christ, I was an asshole. I'd promised not to make any moves on her because of Lily, and I hadn't even made it a full hour since she arrived.

Lily looked at me accusingly, then sank down onto my leg. Once I'd steadied her, I waited for her to drop her tiny head into her hands. She seemed as defeated as I felt.

So much for having my libido under control. It was as off the rails as the rest of my life.

I could only hope Hannah wouldn't file a suit against me for inappropriate workplace behavior. Or do something even worse.

Like leave.

ELEVEN

I GRIPPED THE SIDES OF THE TOILET AND PRAYED TO DIE.

This could not be morning sickness. It was evening. Not to mention, I hadn't had a lick of it until I'd known I was actually pregnant. Unless Asher's child had decided to put on a show to let me know he or she was here.

Got it, kid. You can stop anytime now.

Wiping a hand over my sweaty forehead, I leaned up to hit the flusher, then another two times for good measure. Gross. The bowl had just stopped circling when once again, I felt that telltale feeling in my throat.

Seriously?

I stared up at the ceiling and tried counting backwards. Then times tables. Then a list of all the reasons I hated men and their penises, especially Asher's.

I'd just made it to needing a Tylenol for your achy jaw post BJ— and this reason was one I'd borrowed from Gabriela, because I'd never even given a blowjob—when the threat of puking again became a reality.

Once it was over, I wiped my mouth and rolled to my side on the floor.

Dear God, make it stop.

I laid there, clutching my belly, wondering if maybe this was actually a case of food poisoning. Not from my cooking. Absolutely not. But after my doctor's appointment, I'd stopped off for a sandwich at the café. Vee's chicken salad on a croissant was delicious, and she was as skilled behind a cutting board as I was.

But maybe the chicken was bad. Maybe there was a salmonella outbreak.

Oh, God, yes, please.

Because if I was going to have to deal with this for months on end, I might as well off myself now.

Morning or evening sickness didn't last the whole pregnancy, did it? Unless my child was an alien.

An Asher alien.

A cry sounded from another part of the house and I tried to get up. It took two tries—Asher's bath mat was surprisingly comfy—but I gained my feet just as the door shook from the force of his knock.

"Hannah, you need to come out. Now. I'm sorry. I didn't mean to do that."

Still a little woozy, I held a hand to my head. "You didn't?"

"No." A pause. "Okay, yes, I did. You probably can tell I'm very attracted to you."

The irony made me shake my head as I gazed down at my belly. So much for thinking my cooking had been the culprit for my tight jeans. More like Asher's swimmers.

"Other than the fact we've already..." I cleared my throat. "Not particularly. But thank you."

"Thank you?" he echoed. "Did you miss the part where I just tried to kiss you?"

"Huh. No kidding. Seriously?"

I wasn't a complete moron. I'd been aware of his hair tucking and leaning in routine, but the kiss warning hadn't gone off in my brain. Probably due to the more pressing concern in my stomach. And throat.

I wiped the sweat off the back of my neck. And all over.

"Hannah, you don't sound like yourself. Please, come out here and we'll talk."

Rather than respond, I moved to the sink. I'd rinsed out my mouth half a dozen times, plus washed my hands a time or twenty with his spruce-scented bar soap, when I chanced a look at the mirror. Offhandedly. Just to make sure I didn't look as bad as I felt.

There was no stopping my moan.

Dear God, did he need an eye exam? How could he be attracted to me right now? I looked hideous. Blotchy face. Red-rimmed eyes. My face even seemed puffy. Too much salt?

Too much *baby?*

"Hannah? I'm coming in." He didn't give me a chance to say no before he flung the door open. Because I hadn't locked it. I'd been more focused on getting to know his toilet than worrying about potential interruptions.

Though now that I was thinking about it, I did need to pee. Badly.

Asher stepped inside and halted, his expression conveying everything I'd feared. Hot mess was an apt description for the look I was currently sporting.

"Are you okay? You groaned."

I nodded weakly. "Sorry. Just a little bit ill."

Hi, understatement. Nice to meet you.

"Oh, shit, really? Like a bug or something?" He was already sliding past me to open the medicine cabinet. He emerged with a first aid kit.

I couldn't help laughing. "What are you going to do with that?"

He frowned. "You're laughing?"

"I've been known to now and then, yes." He was the oddest man sometimes.

"Not around me, you don't. Your laugh is beautiful." He reached up to tuck my hair back again, and I let him because he had a way of charming me that I didn't have any defenses against.

He was just so...Asher.

"I haven't had a lot of reasons to laugh for a while now." I cleared my throat and made myself focus on the kit in his other hand rather than the warmth of his fingers still tucked behind my ear. As if he couldn't bear to move back.

He must be seriously sex-starved. How long had it been for him anyway? Surely, it couldn't have been since we…

Hmm. Could it?

"I understand that. I do," he said, although I hadn't argued. He finally let his hand fall away from my face, then tucked it in his pocket. "My best friend died in the fall."

It was hard to keep my face composed. I felt so guilty for not letting on that I knew. But if I did, then we'd probably have to discuss Lily. And I didn't know if I had the mental fortitude for that right now. Just remaining upright was difficult enough.

"I'm so sorry. What happened?"

Ugh. I'd just had to ask that, hadn't I? Might as well compound the guilt over not admitting that I already knew.

"Construction accident. Freak thing. He had a ton of years on the job, but he was up on a roof and—" He broke off as I swallowed hard. "You don't need to hear all that. But losing him was tough. The hardest thing I've ever been through, other than losing my grandfather."

Since I already knew Lily's mother hadn't been his partner, I didn't bother with that line of questioning. Not even for the sake of pretending not to know anything. I'd tell him that I knew soon enough.

Probably as soon as the room stopped spinning.

"I'm so sorry," I said again, brushing my hand over his arm. "A best friend can be as close as family. Sometimes closer."

"Yes." He nodded and shut his eyes. "Like a brother to me." He released a breath and opened his eyes again, looking down at my hand on his arm before he met my gaze. "Let's get you into your room."

"My room? I didn't plan on staying today, Asher. I didn't bring a bag. I thought this was just an exploratory visit."

That was one word for it.

"Yes, well, I'd like you to stay here on a more permanent basis, as we discussed. But nothing is set in stone. Besides, I don't think you'll be leaving anytime soon anyway."

"Why?"

Instead of answering, he opened the first aid box and pried out what looked like two small candies. "These were my grandfather's special elixir." His voice was somber as he placed them in my palm and closed my fingers around them. "They'll help settle your stomach, guaranteed."

"Is it that obvious what kind of ill I meant?" I frowned. "How old are these things? And what's in them?" I couldn't take just anything, now that I was having a baby.

God, would that idea ever become more normal? The word *baby* blazed through me like fire every time I even thought it.

"There's no expiration date on them. Made out of natural stuff. Honey, ginger, mint. A few other ingredients. I'd take one now and save one for an emergency. They'll fix whatever ails you. He used to swear they were magic."

I eyed them dubiously in their wax paper wrapping. "I don't want to take your last few."

"I have a few more in here. Go on, I insist." He smiled down at me and for a second, I got dizzy for a whole new reason. God, he was gorgeous. "I won't poison you, Hannah. I need you too much."

How I longed to hear him say those words in another situation. When we were naked and in bed, wrapped up together. Nothing between us but skin and sweat.

Oh, and that bean-sized baby growing in my belly that would change everything.

More changes.

But if Dr. Ellis had been right, at least I wouldn't be alone to figure them all out. That wasn't even what I was most frightened about. Asher had already begun to prove himself as a stand-up man who handled his responsibilities. Not that I relished being another one of those for him.

I was scared *I* wasn't up to the task of being a parent. That I couldn't give to a child when I still felt so hollowed out and empty inside after the loss of my parents. I had barely lived myself, and now there would be a new life.

And what about Asher? He'd been thrust into a role he'd never anticipated. To saddle him with another child when he clearly didn't know what to do with the first almost seemed cruel.

As if fate was laughing at us.

Two incompetent strangers, thrown together to raise a baby.

Two babies.

Except we didn't feel like strangers anymore. And my feelings in his direction were already overwhelming. I wanted to know more about him. I wanted to spend time with him and Lily. I wanted to make him smile and to watch his serious hazel eyes soften as he looked at me, just as they were right now.

I wanted far too much, and telling him about this baby might kill my chance at all of it. It would change me from the woman he was attracted to into one more responsibility.

One more task on his list.

"Why can't I leave?" I whispered, far too aware of how much I wanted to stay.

In this mostly empty house with its magical library and comfy bath mat and baby laughter.

With *Asher.*

He put the first aid kit back in the medicine cabinet and nudged me out the still open door. Without saying anything, he took my hand and led me down the hall and up the stairs.

I should've shaken him off. We weren't a couple. But I liked his big hand enclosing mine far too much.

At the top of the stairs, he turned and headed down the hall past several doors. He opened one slowly, and I swallowed a sigh as the nursery came into view.

The fully outfitted nursery, where so much of the rest of the house had still been in transition.

Soft butter yellow walls were decorated with zoo animals that matched the brightly colored rug on the hardwood floor. A tall white rocker piled with pillows stood between the windows, and I gasped as I glimpsed all the snow outside.

Holy crap, when had *that* happened? Exactly how long had I been tossing my cookies?

Asher stepped behind me and cupped my shoulders. When he spoke, it was near my ear, fluttering my messy braid. "Told you."

"Guess the forecasters were right."

"Guess so." A shiver went through me as I tucked the candies into my jeans pocket. Was I imagining things or had he pressed his lips against my earlobe, just for a second? "I hope you don't have anywhere you need to be tonight."

TWELVE

YES, I DO. RIGHT HERE.

But in lieu of answering, I moved to the crib. The railings on this one were much higher and the mattress was lower. Either he'd had the setup at this house correct the first time or he'd listened to my advice.

I grinned as I took in Lily's little face pressed against the bars of her crib. "Aww, you're in jail, huh, honey? You're being so quiet. So good."

Somehow the praise sprung Lily into action. She lurched to her feet and banged her fists on the bars, then lifted her arms toward me as I leaned over to free her from her pretty white prison.

"You're definitely her favorite," Asher observed as I picked her up and cuddled her close. I was beginning to get used to the feeling of a baby in my arms.

Good thing.

I nuzzled her soft red curls. She smelled like powder and soap and...eww, dirty diaper.

On cue, Lily let out an inhuman wail.

"That time again, hmm?" With a resigned exhale, Asher came forward to pluck her out of my arms.

Shocked into silence, I watched him lay her efficiently on the little changing table beside the crib. He swapped off her old diaper with a minimum of fuss, pausing for a second to tickle her chubby belly. Baby giggles filled the room.

Such a wonderful sound.

He put the clean diaper on her, then struggled to get her back into her green striped onesie. I hurried forward to help, but he muttered, "I've got it. This is the one part I can do."

I stepped back and let him show off his skills.

When she was dressed again, he passed her back to me like a sweet-smelling, slightly squirmy football. She snuggled into my embrace like she never wanted me to let her go.

My chest ached as I turned with her to the window. "She should go out and play in this kind of weather. It's probably the last storm of the season."

"You're sick."

I remained quiet. I wasn't going to tell him that my sickness had already abated.

Not yet anyway.

Soon enough, I would have no choice but to reveal all. For today, for him, I could pretend our lives hadn't irrevocably changed.

And for me.

"I'm feeling better." It wasn't a lie.

"Yes, but going outside in the cold with a baby might wear you out. Although if you try that candy, you might be protected." He raised his eyebrows at me as I glanced over my shoulder at him.

"You're relentless, Wainwright." I shifted the baby so I could thumb one of the candies out of my pocket. "Humoring you," I added, unwrapping it and popping it into my mouth.

It didn't taste particularly good, but the honey eased the lingering irritation in my throat and the mint was pleasing enough. Within a few minutes, I couldn't deny I felt a little better. My touchy stomach had been given enough time to settle, of course, but I could give Asher this small win.

"You're right. It's magic."

Asher nodded as if he'd expected nothing less. Then he went to the closet and withdrew a pair of bright purple boots and a pair of mittens, along with a navy blue snowsuit.

Lily stirred in my arms, her legs already pumping.

"She's excited?" I guessed.

"No. She hates this thing." He shook the snowsuit, and Lily made a face. "But she loves snow, and she knows what this means."

Yet again, he plucked Lily out of my arms. I waited for him to dress her to go outside as capably as he'd changed her, but he glanced at me expectantly.

"Some help, please. We don't have long before she messes up her diaper again. Or wants to eat. Or both at the same time."

I helped him bundle her into her snowsuit before we got her into her mittens and boots. She immediately started trying to get the boots off, banging her feet and making faces.

With a sigh, Asher tipped back his head as if he was used to this routine.

"Not a fan of footwear, I'm guessing?"

"No. She hates shoes and socks. Sometimes she hates clothes, period."

"Oh, naked baby, huh? Are you a naked baby?" I pulled down Lily's hood to make her laugh. She fought it off and I did it again, playing peekaboo with her while Asher went down the hall to get his own gear.

He returned wearing a leather coat and a long blue scarf that seemed handmade.

"A present from an old girlfriend?"

Why had I said that? Probably to keep from flinging myself at him like a horny chick who had no fear of getting pregnant.

Too late there.

"Hardly. I've never dated a woman who knits." He angled his head. "Do you?"

I snorted. "Do I look like the crafty sort?"

"You look like you could do anything you put your mind to."

"So do you. Hold your daughter." I passed Lily to him. He fumbled her for a few seconds before settling her on his hip as he'd seen me do.

I nearly smiled. Progress.

It wasn't until we stepped outside onto the wide porch with its twin rockers and copper wind chimes, now circling madly in the breeze, that Asher's voice snapped out again. "Where's your coat?"

I was wondering the same. Actually, I knew right where it was—hanging on its peg in my coat closet. I just hadn't expected the weather to turn this cold this fast. "Didn't realize I'd be playing in the snow this afternoon."

"Here. Hold your...Lily." He handed the baby to me and quickly shucked off his jacket. I started to protest, but he wrapped it around my shoulders before taking Lily back into his arms. "Much better."

Since my teeth were a moment away from chattering, I shoved my arms into the sleeves and basked in the warmth. In the glorious smell of leather and Asher's woodsy cologne. "Thank you. But you'll freeze."

"I'm hot-blooded." Jauntily, he flipped his scarf over his shoulder. Lily grabbed for it and shoved the end into her mouth, causing him to laugh.

"I can vouch for that." I'd made it halfway down the stairs when a perfectly packed snowball hit me in the back. I pretended to ignore it, but as soon as my foot hit the snowy walkway, I scooped up snow and flung it over my shoulder at them, giggling as most of it blew back in my face.

"Great job packing the snow." Asher shook his head in mock disappointment and turned to set Lily on a little pile near the steps. She immediately began whipping her arms through the snow on either side of her as she laughed and laughed.

Lily's giggles were the sweetest thing I'd ever heard.

I was so distracted by her antics that I wasn't paying attention as Asher crouched to pack another snowball, which he then winged at me. I screeched as cold streaked down my back.

His response? He laughed so hard he almost fell on his ass.

"Would've served you right," I said while he scrambled to right himself.

I turned to pack some snow of my own, taking my time to shape the ball. It was coming down so hard that I had to keep blinking it out of my eyes. I would probably get a chill soon, thanks to Asher's sneak attack, but I was pretty toasty in his jacket.

I shifted back with my arsenal of three snowballs and nearly swooned at Asher helping Lily smash the snow between her palms. He was leaning over her and she was pounding the snow with delight. Her cheeks were already ruddy from the cold. I hurried over to pull forward the sides of her hood—and realized far too late that Asher had laid a trap.

A snowball came flying right at my face. I ducked and slipped, falling backward onto the sidewalk.

All at once, fear rushed into me.

Genuine fear.

Not, *oh, yeah, I'm pregnant, hope I'm okay,* but actual cold-blooded terror at the thought of something…well, dislodging my baby.

My baby.

Thank God. I wasn't a worthless mother after all. Maybe I really could do this.

"Are you okay?" Asher's voice was thick with worry.

I struggled to sit up and nodded, casting my gaze down at my lap.

You okay in there, bean?

Pea was probably more accurate at this point. I didn't know all the stages, but he or she had to be minuscule right now.

So easy to harm.

"Hey, hey, look at me. Did you get hurt? I'm sorry. I should've been more careful. Let me carry you inside." Asher tipped up my chin, his beautiful hazel eyes narrowed on my face. They were the greenest I'd ever seen them.

Sneakily, I pulled a snowball from my pocket and nailed him dead in the nose.

Mashing it in for good measure while he sputtered and laughed and called me names not befitting a parent.

He grabbed my hand, now red and nearly numb from playing in the snow with no gloves, and kissed every one of my fingertips. When he finished with that hand, he picked up the other and did the same, then tucked them between his palms to rub some warmth back into them. Snow dripped from his face, clung to his eyebrows, and his hands were as red or redder than mine, but he didn't seem to notice. All his attention was centered on me.

Suddenly, I wasn't that cold anymore.

"Deserved it." The rumble of his voice tweaked something low in my belly. "My penance is to carry you inside."

I nudged him back and looked up at the cloudy sky, currently a slate gray tinged with the orangish-pink hues that came with a storm. His house had so many security lights that the lawn was well-lit. Beyond that glow, the world was freezing and dark.

Being here with him and Lily made me feel safe and warm. Even if my ass was parked on an icy sidewalk and snow was falling so very fast.

"I'm too heavy to carry."

"Even a guy like me who doesn't date much knows that the only acceptable reply is you're as light as a feather."

He started to rise but I stopped him with a hand on his cheek. "You don't date much?"

"No."

"Define much."

He took a few seconds to answer. "You're the only woman I've slept with since... I don't know. It's been a damn long time." He took a quick, deep breath. "What about you?"

"I've never slept with a woman. Should I try it?"

I waited for him to suggest a threesome or something else that fit the typical crude male response. Instead, he somberly shook his head. "I don't recommend it. It's terrible."

"Oh, is that so? Is that why you found me arousing even after I'd been draped over your toilet?"

His smile almost made me smile, and that never happened. But I'd laughed so much in the last half hour. Being with him and his baby girl made me happy.

Scarily so.

"I'd find you arousing in any and all states." His gaze dropped to my mouth and lingered. "Problem for me, since now I'm paying your paycheck."

"One of them," I reminded him. "And it's only a problem if we make it one."

"Is that so?" His gaze still hadn't left my lips.

And I liked it. A freaking lot.

Rather than answer, I glanced over my shoulder to where Lily was happily bouncing her legs and throwing snow on herself. "Your daughter seems to enjoy this weather."

"Told you. She'd stay out here all night if we let her."

It was such a small, stupid thing, but that he included me in the decision-making process for Lily made warmth spread inside me. "I'd love to play out here with her some more, but next time, I better bring some gloves."

Asher frowned and grabbed my hands again, bringing them to his mouth to blow lightly on them. The heat from his breath tingled over my skin. "None in your car?" When I shook my head, he frowned again. "You should have a kit in case of breakdowns. Spare gloves, jumper cables, tire iron, donut, an extra coat, a spare—"

"Asher, I can't use those things, minus the coat and gloves. So, why have them?"

"I'll teach you. Do you have AAA?"

I was afraid to tell him and cause him to stroke out. "Hey, Lily," I called, not expecting the baby to look up guiltily. She'd been shoving snow into her mouth. "You're going to spoil your dinner if you keep eating that."

She kept right on gnawing on her snowy hand.

"You already have Mom Eyes." Asher sounded impressed. "Didn't even have to look her way to know what she was doing."

Little did he know.

I got to my feet with his help, and we went to join Lily. Well, I did. Asher went in the house and returned with two pairs of men's size gloves, one set for each of us.

We played in the snow with Lily until my nose was frozen and running and the promised chill had sunk deeply into my bones.

Asher wasn't much better. He'd sneezed about half a dozen times, which shouldn't have been as cute as it was. Even Lily had had enough.

Bright side? As soon as we brought her in and gave her a bottle, she was ready for bed. I'd barely finished the lullaby I was singing to her before she conked out.

I rose from the rocking chair in the nursery and carefully placed her in her crib. Asher checked to make sure the baby monitor was working, then drew me out of the room.

"Hungry?"

"I could eat." I couldn't hold back a shiver.

Preferably while huddling under a dozen thick blankets.

"I'll fix us something."

At my dubious expression, he laughed. "You didn't look in the freezer. I have stuff I can heat up. Made by my grandmother."

"Oh. Okay. Whew. I thought you were going to cook."

"And you assume I can't?"

"It's the usual way with most bachelors. Are you going to prove me wrong?"

Sheepishly, he scratched the side of his neck. "Alas, no."

"Thought so."

"While I'm heating up dinner, you should take a hot bath. Warm up. I'll start a fire."

"In the living room?" He'd indicated in passing earlier that the place had a few of them.

"I could," he said carefully. "But there's also one in the master bedroom. We could eat in there."

"On the floor?"

"Or in bed."

When I didn't answer, he stepped back. Both figuratively and literally.

"There's a room made up for you too. You can just go to bed on your own if you prefer. It's not fancy," he added as if he figured I expected to sleep on 1000-thread count sheets. "I assumed you'd want to have a hand in designing it, so I just made sure it had the basics."

"All I need is a bed." I pushed a hand through my hair, afraid to imagine how it must look after our time outside. Oddly, I didn't much care.

The way Asher gazed at me this evening had never changed. He always looked at me as if I was a goddess. It was addicting.

Intoxicating.

Frightening as hell, especially considering everything I wasn't telling him.

"We have those." Asher smiled and turned away, but I laid a hand on his arm to make him face me.

"I want to sleep with you. I do."

He frowned. "Sounds like there is a *but* coming. Message received. I know the job thing makes it awkward. I can't decide if I'm grateful to Gran for bringing you back into my life or mad at her for making it so I can't be with you." His frown eased into a smile, as his expressions so often did. That his smile made the worry lines around his eyes turn into sexy crinkles was just a bonus. "Nah, that's a lie. I'm grateful. I'd given up hope of ever finding you again."

My heart started beating way too fast. "Did you try?"

"No." His eyes darkened until I couldn't see where his pupils ended and his irises began. "We made an agreement. I'm in no place for a relationship. As you indicated you weren't."

"Did I say that?"

If I had, I was a moron.

I was so used to being alone now that I was too wary to risk caring about someone, only to lose them again. As much as I claimed I wanted freedom, the biggest box I'd ever been trapped in had no sides.

Loneliness was endless and vast, with no date of reprieve.

Asher chuckled. "More or less."

"You said it first."

Maybe. I wasn't even sure. I'd been in hardcore defense mode.

So determined to lose my virginity and learn all the secrets of the world. But I wouldn't fall in love and get my heart broken. I would leave before that happened.

So much for that.

He chuckled again. "I don't remember that part."

"Me either. My memories are centered on other things that happened that night."

"Me too." He was back staring at my mouth again, and the wild heartbeat in my chest was now also beating between my thighs. "That was the other reason I never looked for you. I knew if I found you, I wouldn't be able to let you go this time."

I had to tell him. It wasn't fair to keep such important things secret.

Two important things. My guilty conscience was about to explode.

"I know Lily isn't your daughter," I blurted, shutting my eyes while the words echoed in my head.

That was how I told him? Really?

He didn't move back. Nor did he look away once I dared to open my eyes again. "I wondered if you might know. Or had figured it out."

"Why?"

"It's common enough knowledge. Billy's accident was big news for a while." He dipped his hands in his pockets. "I'm sure you figured something was up when you saw how fucking clueless I am when it comes to taking care of her."

"No. I assumed you were the typical workaholic rich guy who couldn't wait to pass her off on someone."

His jaw locked. "And now?"

"Now I see you're trying the best you can. No one hands out manuals on how to be a parent, even if the kid is biological. Never mind if you fall unexpectedly into the role."

"I've made mistakes. If it hadn't been for my grandmother—"

I reached up to cup his face, waiting until he had no choice but to meet my eyes. "You're doing everything you can for that little girl. If I didn't believe that, I wouldn't be here."

"She deserves more." His voice was raw. "I don't feel how I should feel."

"Love grows, no matter who it's for. Her father chose you because he thought you could handle the job. I may not know you well, but I can tell you don't just deal with things. You do your very best. Always."

"What if my best isn't good enough?"

"Not possible."

"You don't know me, Hannah. You just said it yourself." He focused on me far too intently. "Perhaps you're just seeing what you want to."

"Not possible," I repeated, finally releasing him.

I didn't want to. Which was exactly why I had to.

The silence stretched between us. I couldn't stand it anymore.

Couldn't bear to let him hurt alone when maybe I could help alleviate some of it.

"Just in case you didn't know, there's something about grief no one tells you. Sometimes when you're grieving, you don't have any love left to give anyone. Not even yourself. Even if you want to. Even if you're desperate to." I paused to ensure my voice wouldn't wobble. Taking breath after breath while my chest fought to close in on itself. "Grief shuts everything down. You can't think around it. Can't feel through it. Your emotions are locked away behind it. But they're there, I swear it."

Maybe I was making the same promise to myself. Absolving myself as well for not instantly bonding with the baby inside me.

Although maybe, just maybe, I was. At least I was starting to. I'd only known for a few hours. And Asher didn't have a clue yet.

But at least I'd told him what I knew about Lily. The rest would come soon. I'd find the words to tell him the unexplainable. The absolutely crazy.

God, I hoped.

THIRTEEN

Asher

I WAS ASKING FOR TROUBLE, BUT I COULDN'T MAKE MYSELF BACK AWAY.

Not now.

Hannah understood. She'd gone through the very same things I'd experienced the last few months. Losing her parents had wrecked her and changed her life.

Just as my life had been changed.

Sure, it was different. But Billy had been as close as family to me, and on top of that, I'd been tasked with taking care of his precious little girl.

She was all I had left of him. And every single day he'd been gone, I was sure I was failing him. Dishonoring his memory and invalidating his trust by bungling all of this so badly.

But I wasn't alone. I had my grandmother and now I had Hannah. They were helping me figure all of this out. One minute at a time.

"Billy and Lily," Hannah mused. "Did he do that intentionally?"

"Huh?" I scraped my fork over my plate, getting every last bit of the chicken, cheese, and corn casserole my saint of a grandmother had left in my freezer. She'd even stocked waffles and frozen fruit for her precious Snug for the morning, complete with a sweet note.

131

It would be a long while before I bugged her for calling me that again. My stomach was too grateful.

That wasn't the only part of me feeling gratitude. I was also glad that Hannah and I were sitting with our knees touching on a quilt in front of the fire, eating and talking and laughing.

The laughter mostly came from me, a miracle of its own. But she'd almost smiled a few times now. I was beginning to fully understand why she couldn't. That didn't mean I wouldn't keep trying to make her feel the way she so effortlessly did with me.

Happy.

"Their names rhyme."

I set down my fork and frowned. "Yeah. They do. Weird I never noticed."

She shook her head. "You're so observant in some ways and so clueless male in others."

I shrugged. "He just loved the name Lily. So did Solange, his girlfriend."

"She died in childbirth, right?" Hannah bit her lip. "Why is that still happening? Childbirth should be safe."

"I don't know. Some weird medical thing. They didn't catch it until it was too late." I rubbed my eyes.

Remembering what my best friend went through when his daughter was born just stirred up everything about Billy's death. They were so linked in my mind. Lily had lost so much at such a young age.

I'd spend the rest of my life trying to give back even a fraction of what she'd lost.

"Oh." Hannah set aside her food.

"You didn't eat enough." I nodded at her still half-full plate. "Want me to feed you?"

"What, am I Lily now?" Her lips twitched, but her eyes were far too heavy. The blue was like storm clouds, dark and turbulent.

"They were so in love when they made Lily." I leaned back on my hands and gave up trying to shove the memories away. They were rooted far too deep.

I've got news, man. Big news.

Oh, yeah? Like what? Did Solange finally agree to move in with you?

Better. Well, she did that too. She's moving in. Know why?

Because you told her you'd finally get a better place, one with actual windows?

No, asshole, because we're having a baby.

"Had they been together long?"

I stared at Hannah, dragging myself back. "No, actually. They met and it was instant chemistry." There was no denying the roughness of my voice. I couldn't help it. There were too many parallels between my buddy's relationship and what had happened between Hannah and I. "He told me he fell in love with her that night."

I didn't even know what that felt like. But I wanted to spend more time with her. I loved seeing her eyes sparkle with hidden amusement, even if it was at me. Especially when it was at me.

And every time she picked up Lily, something moved in my chest. Cracks opening up along a predetermined fault line. Then like plates of the Earth, locking into place.

Hannah toyed with a frayed thread on her sweater. Despite my admonishments, she hadn't taken that warm bath yet or changed out of her wet clothes. At least she was seated close to the roaring fire. "Do you think that matters?"

"What?"

"Do you think it makes a difference for a baby, if their parents are in love or not?" She huffed out a breath. "I don't mean later, while the child is growing up. I mean at the moment of conception."

"I don't know."

"Me either." She drew her knees up to her chest and pulled her long sweater around her, almost as if she was hiding.

I didn't know what she was getting at, but maybe this was her way of us getting to know each other.

"My parents probably weren't, but I can't say it made any difference in my life. I gravitated to my grandparents early on anyway. I think kids figure out how to get what they need."

"Yeah, but that doesn't mean the child still doesn't feel unworthy, deep down." She rested her head on her upturned knees and peered at me through the tumble of her golden brown hair. "My parents were madly in love. At least in the beginning. In later years, my father got bored. Turned into a bit of a daredevil."

"And your mother?"

"She turned into a people pleaser. All she wanted to do was make him happy. Sometimes she didn't pay as much attention to us because she was all about him."

"You have sisters, right?"

"Twins. Huge brats, both of them, but I adore them. They're whip-smart and beautiful and so much trouble."

I had to laugh as I moved her hair out of her face. She startled, but she didn't shift away. "Beautiful, huh? I don't believe it." I made my tone light so she knew I was teasing.

Hannah was simply stunning. It didn't surprise me an iota that her sisters were too.

"I grew up taking care of them when my dad was off doing crazy stuff. My mom spent her life chasing after him. They liked to travel and he flew private planes and surfed and went on safari or whatever else caught his fancy. She agreed to anything he suggested. Well, except flying. She wouldn't get into his little prop plane. Not until that last day." Her eyes filled and my gut twisted.

"Hannah." I wrapped my arms around her and she burrowed into my chest, tucking her head under mine. She pressed her cheek to my chest, and I knew she could hear the rapid thundering of my heart.

"I've never had this," she whispered. "Not since my mom died. I never had anyone to hold me."

"Well, you're in luck." I stroked her hair. "Free hugs given here."

She looked up at me, her dark lashes starred with tears, and I would've given her the world if I could have. "Promise?"

I wasn't even sure what I was agreeing to. Free hugs forever? That seemed innocuous enough. I would've promised her so much more.

Right then, perhaps anything.

"I promise."

She shivered and I tipped up her chin. "Your clothes are still damp.

You were already sick today. You need that warm bath. Or warm shower. Dealer's choice."

"I'm feeling okay right now." The little purr she made in her throat went straight to my cock.

Sure enough, she noticed.

She licked her lips and shifted against me, her eyes twinkling in the low light from the fire. "You're feeling pretty good too."

"Can't blame me for reacting to a gorgeous woman." She shivered again and I wrapped the messy end of her braid around my hand. "Who needs a hot bath."

"So bossy. Is this how you are at work?"

"If it gets the job done." I gave her hair a tug. "What would get the job done with you, blue eyes?"

"Did you just give me a nickname?"

"Not the most creative one, but yes, I guess so."

"I like it."

She slid away from me. I was still missing the feel of her in my arms when she pulled off her sweater and let it fall around her. Beneath, she wore a thin V-necked top and well-worn jeans. Without hesitation, she took off her shirt and undid the button and zipper, wiggling the denim over her hips.

Her simple white cotton bra and panty set had little roses between the cups. Sweet, almost chaste. She reached up to undo what was left of her disordered braid, setting all that glorious thick hair free, and my mouth went dry.

"I'd say we both could use a nice warm bath, don't you agree? That Jacuzzi tub in there looks big enough for five."

"Three."

My choked response made her lips curve for barely an instant. Didn't matter. I'd seen her smile just for me.

"Think we are just fine then. Why don't I get the tub ready while you check on Lily?"

"Why don't you," I echoed as she rose.

She tugged off her socks. "You mean you'd rather I go see to Lily?"

"Yes. No. Christ." I rubbed my hands over my face. "Sorry, all blood in my head rerouted south. You're fucking gorgeous."

"Sure you don't need glasses? I've seen my hair tonight."

"Perfect 20/20. And don't say that again." I grabbed her calf when she stepped out of her jeans. "Can't you tell how crazy you make me?"

"I can. I'm just waiting for it to change."

"It's been more than two months. It's not changing."

She tossed her jeans at me and headed into the en suite bathroom, her heart-shaped ass bouncing in the very best ways. "Then get a move on, Wainwright. I've never soaked in a Jacuzzi."

"Shit. I don't have any condoms."

That stopped her dead momentarily. "You still didn't buy any?"

"To use with who? I told you there's been no one else. And it's unethical to do…this."

"That again." I tried not to watch her perfect ass sway, but it was pretty much a lost cause. "Come find me when you forget your supposed rules."

A moment later, she leaned around the doorway, dipping forward enough that her tits nearly spilled out of her low-cut bra. "Don't forget you're far too old for me too."

"Hannah, you're pushing your luck." Just as my dick was pushing against the confines of my pants.

"And you should never deflower an innocent virgin in a one-night stand—"

I threw her sweater toward the bathroom door, and she backed away, laughing. Then the water turned on in the tub.

Fuck. I stood and started gathering our plates. I was not standing on ceremony and missing a second of this.

We could make our own rules.

FOURTEEN

Hannah

THE SOUND I MADE AS I SLIPPED INTO THE JACUZZI BORDERED ON orgasmic.

Could someone climax just from a few well-placed jet sprays and hot water? And I didn't even mean on my clit or anywhere interesting. Right now, my sore legs and aching hips were getting lots of play.

Either I'd jarred myself on the cold sidewalk more than I realized or pregnancy was already kicking my ass.

Along with feeling like heaven, the tub also allowed me to hide my belly. I'd been more nervous about revealing that part of myself to Asher than my breasts or between my legs. He'd seen them already in any case. But my stomach was a big old baby neon sign.

Or so it was in my head. As if he would be able to tell I'd gained five pounds.

Could he?

Probably not until the pre-sex haze cleared anyway. Afterward, maybe. He was fairly observant when he wanted to be.

He was also ridiculously sweet. But that whole lack of condoms thing wasn't keeping me from, as Gabriela called it, a thorough dicking.

Especially since condoms were not a factor in our lives right now.

I was so clean I was squeaky. I was pretty sure Asher was too, judging from his overall level of preparation and nonexistent list of current lovers.

Just me. And wasn't that the most wonderful thing ever?

Wait until he finds out you're knocked up.

A shadow crossed the doorway. I sat up straighter before remembering angles and my stomach situation. I slumped back down and swallowed hard. "Could I trouble you for a loofah?"

"A what?"

"A loofah. It's a mesh spongey thing to wash with." I swallowed as my gaze dropped to Asher's bare chest. The surprising amount of muscles and tattoos he mostly hid under his business suits—other than the wrist and hand ones—were as much of a surprise now as they were the first time I saw him naked. "Never mind."

He bent to open a cabinet beneath the spacious double sink, emerging with a few stubby candles and a washcloth. "Suitable?"

"Yes, thank you. Are you going to light those with the power of your mind?"

He tossed me the washcloth and it splashed in the water. "You have a very smart mouth. I didn't fully realize the night we met."

"About all you realized then was how tasty my lemon bars were."

They hadn't even been mine, but I'd shared them with him. Perhaps someday he'd get to try the ones I made.

Maybe. Everything felt so tenuous right now. I had to try to live in the moment.

Tomorrow? What tomorrow?

"Wrong. I also noticed you were a screamer." He disappeared into the other room.

I caught myself smiling as I lathered up the washcloth with some of the citrusy cedar-scented bodywash in the tub.

Mmm. No wonder Asher smelled so good.

I lathered my neck and shoulders before moving to my belly, deliberately avoiding my breasts. I had a feeling they would be far too sensitive, and I was already skating along a thin edge.

Had I really screamed? Moaned loudly for sure.

The door creaked open again and Asher returned with a small tray that contained the lit candles. A portable baby monitor poked out of his trouser pocket.

My heart gave a hard tug.

He flicked off the overhead lights and set the candles near the tub. The baby monitor crackled as he set it on the countertop and he muttered under his breath, fiddling with dials and buttons.

As sexy as I found the lean muscles shifting in his back, and his perfect peach of an ass snugly displayed in his well-cut pants, the hottest thing about him was his concern for his daughter.

When he shifted toward me and tugged at his zipper, the bulge in his boxers came in a close second.

"May I join you?" The slight hesitation in the question had me leaning forward, completely oblivious to my bare breasts bobbing out of the water.

Until his jaw locked and his eyes glazed.

I rubbed the soapy loofah over my thighs before it slipped away in the water. "It's your tub."

"May I join you?" he repeated.

Every part of me buzzed and hummed with anticipation. Even Asher's impeccable manners excited me. I knew he had a more commanding side and waiting for it to come out was yet another turn-on.

"Please do." I hadn't meant for my voice to sound husky.

He inhaled as he shed his trousers and boxers, his gaze not meeting mine until he was fully nude. The thick curve of him drew my focus. And how.

When he spoke again, all I heard was white noise.

Damn, he was built. No wonder I was pregnant. I was amazed I hadn't gotten inseminated just from seeing him naked.

Maybe I had.

"Hannah." He tried again. "Hannah?"

I just licked my lips. He let out a low groan and slipped into the Jacuzzi across from me. "Never mind."

"Where did you get all the ink?" I asked when I recovered my voice. "It's so not like you."

"A few have special meaning. Others were dares when I was with my—with Billy." He exhaled. "Besides, are you sure you know exactly what I'm like yet?"

His voice was low, barely audible over the bubbling water. Or else I was fixated on studying his body again, partially disguised as it was by the foam.

"No, I'm not sure. But I want to know everything."

The heavy-lidded look he gave me didn't register surprise, but I could feel it in the tension in his body. His legs were braced on either side of mine, not touching. So close I could feel his heat and how rigidly he was holding himself still.

Two strangers, naked in a tub. Who'd made a baby, even if one of them didn't realize that yet. Yet we didn't want to get too much into each other's personal space.

I started to laugh.

He nudged me with his calf and that made me laugh harder.

"Not sure if you're up on hot tub protocol, but when a guy gets in with you, maybe cool it on the chuckles?"

I wiped my streaming eyes. "Just we're a little ridiculous. So careful and polite, and it's so past time for all of that."

"Is it now?"

I sucked in a breath and inched forward, stretching my legs over his thighs. He didn't move. Didn't even seem to breathe as I dragged myself toward him. It took everything I possessed to reach out and touch his face. The sharp lines of his cheekbones, the curve of his temples where sweat beaded on his skin, his granite jaw. I explored him, watching his wary eyes shift in the weak candlelight from hazel to a blazing green. My thumb slid along his lower lip and he nipped it so gently I could only gasp.

The sound seemed to set him off. He pulled me against him, hauling me right into his lap. My bare center met the hard length of his cock and I gasped again, shocked at the arc of pleasure that shot through me.

Then his mouth was on mine, and the pleasure grew like a wildfire.

His hands moved up my back to my shoulders as he angled me right where he wanted me. He kissed me hungrily, desperately, drawing me closer until my breasts mashed to his chest. I cried out from the surprise jolt, and he immediately reared back.

"Too fast? I'm sorry." He panted between the words, but his concerned gaze never left mine.

"No. Sorry." I tried again, pressing myself against him with less force. This time, my breasts didn't hurt. Just twinged in the sweetest way.

As if he knew exactly what I needed, he touched my breast with infinite care. I bit my lip, fairly certain I might shriek if he twisted my nipples right now. Instead, he touched me so tenderly that my eyes grew damp and my breathing stuttered.

"Better?"

"Much. Sorry. Just—"

A little bit pregnant here. Touchy boobs. Who knew?

Only the rest of the world.

"It's okay. I'm obviously overeager. We should've done this in a bed." He blew out a breath. "Or maybe in one of those snowbanks outside. That might've worked to keep me in check." His gaze dropped to my cleavage. "Then again, probably not."

Knowing I made him so crazed was freeing in the very best way. Only one thing was still making me hesitate. Make that two.

One was the pea-sized child growing inside me. The other was the one sleeping down the hall.

They both came first. They had to.

"Are you sure you're all right with this?" He continued to caress me. Never rushing. Offering just enough pressure that the need between my legs climbed and I couldn't help rubbing against his cock.

His nostrils flared. "I'll take that as a yes?"

"Yes," I whispered, wrapping my arms around him. He was so solid and muscled, so strong and hot in my embrace. Capable of withstanding anything.

Unlike me right now. I felt so fragile. So easy to break.

I looked up into his eyes and the worry there nearly shattered me. Fuck my wants. This man deserved to know who he was sleeping with. I wasn't just his one-time hookup. Not anymore.

Now I was the mother of his baby.

But I was also a coward. And when he kissed me again, framing my face in his big hands, I dismissed the reality pressing in around us. He was everything I yearned for. Such certainty and warmth and passion.

Full of life, when I'd spent so much time looking back at what I'd lost.

His mouth slipped down my neck, his teeth leaving little points of pain that tugged at my clit. He moved lower and drew my nipple between his lips, our gazes connecting. I didn't know if it was because I couldn't possibly hurt when we were linked that way, or if I was used to the feeling, but nothing hurt now. That low stirring in my belly grew, and I arched into his erotic kisses, dipping my head back. My hair bobbed along the surface of the bubbling water while he kissed and touched me, his mouth relentless.

I was so primed by the time he slid a hand between my thighs that I nearly came. I was so close. There was no building period, no need for rocking into his strokes to get myself there. I was already on the verge, breathing hard, the tips of my breasts taut and aching and wet from his kisses.

"I want to put my mouth here too," he growled against my throat, his fingers sliding into me so deeply that darkness shimmered at the edges of my vision.

"I must advocate for water safety—oh, God." He drew his fingers back then pushed them in again, so deep that I simply forgot what I was saying.

And his thumb brushed over my clit, just right…

"Asher." I stared at him as my body quaked around his fingers. I gripped his upper arms, holding on for dear life when he didn't stop. Just kept demanding more from me while the steady flame of green in his eyes burned.

I came again. Or still. It didn't seem to have an end. His mouth touched mine and he answered with a groan of his own as I trembled.

"I need another ten of those." His kisses turned rough. "Another twenty."

"You haven't had any yet. Whoa." Still holding on to him, I eased back to breathe. I was still shaking. "I think I'm dehydrated now."

His raw chuckle against my cheek made me smile. "I should've brought in the bottle of wine I have on hand for emergencies."

"No."

"Don't like wine? You liked champagne well enough at the bed and breakfast."

All at once, the warm haze faded, leaving me far too clear-headed.

This wasn't right. Wasn't even slightly fair to him, a man who'd been nothing but decent to me.

He was decent, period. He'd been dealt a shitty hand by life with the loss of his best friend, but he'd manned up like a goddamn champ.

Now you're about to suckerpunch him again.

"It's not that." I slouched down deeper into the froth as if I could disappear. Static crackled on the baby monitor, and I cast it a quick look before it fell silent again. "Those condoms? We don't need them."

"No?" His face was friendly. Curious. Open. Lines of strain fanned out from his eyes, and his jaw was still tight, but I suspected that stemmed from his heavy erection.

Give the guy a damn BJ first. At least let him get off.

I would have. I wanted to, God knows. My nipples tightened just from staring at his cock. But even that felt wrong. My mistake had been pretending for even a few minutes that I could do this.

It was bad enough spending the day with him while hiding how our lives had changed. Being intimate with the guy and keeping this to myself? A hundred times worse.

Yes, he would be shocked. Overwhelmed. As I was shocked and overwhelmed.

Maybe between us we could figure this out. Make some kind of plan. He was good at those. And he had a kid already. The role of father didn't sit easy on his shoulders yet, but perhaps it was kind of like having cats. Having two was barely more work than having one.

God, we were so fucked.

"Hannah? What is it?" He glanced at the baby monitor again. No more crackling, but there were definite whimpers emanating from the speaker. They seemed soft, the humming water nearly drowning them out.

Too bad it couldn't disguise the thud of my heartbeat in my ears. It was like a ticking time bomb.

"We should see to Lily." I was already rising to grab one of the fresh towels on the bar.

"Wait." He touched my thigh, reddened now from the steamy water. "You're sure we're okay? That what happened here was okay?"

The only way I could hold back the tears was by turning my head to the side. "Everything we did here was perfect. I'm just sorry that you—" I forced myself to look at him, blinking so fast he probably thought I had an eyelash stuck in my eye. "That you didn't get to finish."

"Hopefully, we aren't through here?" He glanced at the monitor as Lily's whimpers turned into full-blown tears. He dropped back his head and drew in a long breath. "Get back in the tub. Let me handle this."

I was already wrapping the towel around me. It wasn't even just to escape. I felt pulled to that baby, just as I had from the first time I'd seen her.

"Hannah." He motioned for me to pass him a towel, then climbed out and quickly dried himself off. His erection tented the cotton, but he ignored it as if it didn't exist. "I'll be right back. Relax. Seriously. She probably just had a scary dream and she'll be back to sleep in no time."

From the sounds coming from the monitor, that wasn't the case. But I humored him by nodding and shedding my towel. His jaw locked again before he left the room.

I slipped back into the hot tub. There was no orgasmic sigh as I sank into the water this time. I just buried my head in my hands.

He didn't come back right away. No, he stayed in the other room, singing to Lily

Singing to her, for God's sake. And his voice was terrible, which somehow only made it sweeter and more poignant.

Tears rolled unchecked down my cheeks. There was no stopping them. Hormones be damned.

Everything I'd bottled up for months came rushing out, because a man I barely knew was singing to a baby I'd just met and was already growing to love.

I didn't know how long I sat there. The hot tub bubbled endlessly. Eventually, the singing stopped. I leaned against the back of the Jacuzzi, wondering how I'd missed the little built-in headrest. Leaning against it and closing my eyes was a no-brainer.

I was worn out. Raw in every possible way. Maybe I'd just take a quick catnap.

Footsteps sounded nearby. I tried to raise my head, but it was as heavy as a boulder. Instead, I let myself be lifted, lulled by the strong arms holding me close.

All I'd ever wanted was someone to hold me.

"So tired," I mumbled.

"*Shh.* I know, baby."

His voice rumbled through me, soothing me without effort. I didn't move when he laid me on the bed. I had my arms around his neck, but I didn't want to let go. His laughter felt like forgiveness.

He didn't leave me. His body curled tight to mine, a protector in the night.

I slept.

It was still dark when I opened my eyes and startled in the unfamiliar place. I threw back the covers, momentarily confused by the heavy arm across my midsection. Then it all came back to me and my face flooded with warmth.

I glanced over my shoulder and swallowed deeply at the sight of Asher's face cast in moonlight. He was stupidly beautiful for a man. His features were rugged, yet his eyelashes were long and his mouth was soft in sleep. Vulnerable.

As vulnerable as I felt right now.

Which was why the boldness growing inside me didn't make sense. Nothing had changed. I touched my stomach.

My *bare* stomach.

I'd slept naked with him, which seemed like one more intimacy. He wore a T-shirt and flannel bottoms, his version of keeping me safe from him. Clearly, he hadn't wanted me to wake up and think any expectations existed.

Except my own.

My pulse racing, I curled back into bed. I tugged the covers up again and stared at him in the silvery darkness.

His eyes opened and the words were right there.

I'm pregnant.

He smiled with his eyes still cloudy with sleep and I reached for him, drawing his mouth to mine. One unhurried kiss led to a dozen more. I pushed my hands under his T-shirt, touching his hair-roughened skin, learning him in all the ways I hadn't before. The waistband of his bottoms slipped down and I slid my hand lower, cupping him where he was already so hard.

I wanted to take my time. To bring him to the same pinnacle he'd brought me. But I was impatient, and he didn't hesitate to oblige me. He shoved his pajama pants down and buried his hand in my hair as I dipped my head to kiss my way along his groin. He smelled like that citrus bodywash I'd used in the tub, and I wondered if he'd showered in the glass stall in the corner of the bathroom after he put me to bed.

He'd taken care of me, just as he did with Lily. Even if he was convinced he sucked at it.

God, he was so wrong.

I turned my head and tasted him, just one long lick. I didn't have a clue what I was doing, and I wasn't brave enough to look at him to see if I was on the right path. So, I followed the cues from his body. How his thighs tensed and his shaft subtly swelled when I gripped him to lift him to my mouth. I licked him there too, shifting against the bed and pressing my thighs together as he rubbed my back.

Pleasuring him was giving me something too. My nipples hurt in the most delicious way. And my clit pounded, needing stimulation too.

For right now, the anticipation was plenty.

His hand wound into my hair, drawing my head up so I had no choice but to meet his eyes as I sucked lightly on the crown of him. His thumb traced over my cheek and I drew on him harder, every part of me clenching when he rolled his hips and flexed upward. Pushing him slightly deeper, matching the careful pull of his hand in my hair.

Always so gentle. Loving me without words.

I reached down to stroke his soft sac, unprepared for him to haul my head up off him. I gasped and he crushed his mouth to mine, tasting every bit of himself on my tongue. "Can't. Hold. On." Each word was punctuated with a kiss.

My heart slammed against my ribs as he gripped my hips and yanked me on top of him. I started to say something—what, I didn't know—but he was beyond his limit. He parted my sticky thighs and groaned at how wet he found me.

"Yes. Fuck, yes. Let me have you."

I nodded, although I didn't know if he'd uttered a question or a prayer.

His thumb skated over my clit and I shuddered, closing my eyes. He nudged against my entrance, carefully inching inside. I didn't want that right now. I needed something more. A way to smooth over the jagged parts of myself that only seemed to settle when I was with him.

I braced my hands on his stomach, rolling my hips until he was fully seated. Following instinct, I drew myself upward. Every drag of his flesh against mine set off nerve endings I hadn't even known existed. Then I sank back down, biting my lip around the moan I couldn't contain.

"Christ, you're beautiful." He pushed his hands through the hanging ropes of my hair and framed my face, kissing me wildly as my body took over, lifting and lowering again and again. Chasing that elusive feeling I'd only ever found with him.

Not just an orgasm. I could have those on my own. Less spectacular ones, sure. But he wasn't the keeper of the climax.

He made me feel...safe. Wanted. Appreciated.

Needed for *me,* not what I could offer. Stripped down to nothing, I was enough.

He grasped my hip and shifted me underneath him, his mouth like a fever against my breasts as he drove into me. He tugged my leg up over his shoulder and I arched, reaching behind me for the pillows to anchor myself.

There was no holding back now. No waiting. No hesitation.

I quivered beneath him, around him, bowing my back at the pleasure that sang through me with his every thrust. It didn't stop. His teeth skimmed my nipple and I cried out, caught between pain and ecstasy. He pumped into me, wringing more from me than I'd known I was capable of. I bit down on the pillow, trying to smother my sounds when he timed touching my clit with his endless strokes.

"Come," he whispered, before he kissed me and gave me no other option.

I clutched his shoulders, needing to hold on while he so thoroughly destroyed me. I kept right on holding him when he buried his face in my hair and let out a shout. He plowed into me one more time, prolonging the moment until we were both sweaty and gasping.

No beginning. No end.

Finally, he lifted his head and pushed the tangle of hair out of my face. He kissed me so softly that my heart ached as much as the rest of me. "Okay?"

I smiled weakly. "So much better than okay."

He smiled back before his gaze drifted to the monitor beside the bed. It was blissfully quiet. "I should probably check—" He broke off and frowned, his troubled expression barely visible in the silvery moonlight. "We forgot a condom. I mean, I didn't have any, so—" He blew out a breath. "What was that about you saying earlier we didn't need them? Did you go on the Pill?"

I'd hoped to have a few more minutes to bask in the afterglow. Not long, because my conscience wouldn't let this go on any longer. I'd wanted to tell him earlier, but apparently, I'd needed to check out for a while. And sleep in a cloud-like, huge bed that dwarfed my own at home, with Asher's muscled arm cuddling me close.

But the time had come. No more delays.

"No, I'm not on the Pill. I don't need to be." I faced him squarely. "I'm pregnant."

FIFTEEN

Asher

IN TIMES OF CRISIS, SOME PEOPLE CLAIM TO SEE THEIR LIVES FLASH before their eyes. You know, right before a bullet rips into them, or an attacker swings out with a knife.

In my case, I saw the rest of my life flash before my eyes after Hannah spoke, not the past.

I saw late night feedings.

Changing endless diapers. Picking up one baby, slapping on some Pampers, then passing it to my grandmother as I moved to the next one in the assembly line.

Singing "Baby Shark" until my eardrums exploded.

Balancing one baby per hip while I dealt with colleagues and scheduled meetings and tried to maintain a shred of sanity.

And sex? Sex would not be a factor in my life ever again, obviously. There would be no time for such frivolity. Not to mention it had landed me in this situation.

"Asher?"

I rolled out of bed and went straight into the bathroom. Where I stared at myself in the mirror and wondered if I was too old to run away from home.

Hannah did not follow. I didn't blame her.

You're being an asshole. She's dealing with this too, you know.

I still couldn't believe it. I was sure I'd wake up in bed alone any minute. Hannah wouldn't even be there, because she would've refused to spend the night. We needed to think about what was best for Lily.

For this new baby.

A new baby.

Good Christ. I hadn't even gotten a handle on parenting the last one.

I splashed ice cold water on my face and took care of business, then eyed the bathroom window and debated if I could fit through it. Probably not. Besides, I'd have to face this eventually.

That was what I did. Dealt with things straight on. Without even an ounce of immaturity.

I stepped into the bedroom. Hannah was curled up on the bed, her honeyed hair tumbled over her face. "You should've disclosed your… condition before taking the nanny job."

Once the words were out, I had no idea what on earth had possessed me to say them.

She should have told me right away, but it was hardly a deterrent to her employment.

I mean, how could it be? The kid was mine.

Mine.

I sank to the floor right where I stood and dropped my head into my hands.

If she thought this behavior was odd, she did not say. Instead, she swung her long legs over the side of the mattress and tugged the sheet around her. "I would have disclosed it before accepting the nanny job had I known." Her voice was cool. Practically dripping with ice. "Actually, I don't recall ever saying yes so much as being badgered into it."

"Sure. Right. Blame me. I made you take the nanny job. I suppose I made you sleep with me too. Both times."

"You didn't make me have sex with you either time. I quite enjoyed it."

Although I suspected that frost in her tone was a defense

mechanism, I had a few of my own, and they were all just as detestable. "Enough that you didn't think you should tell me about this new development before you sucked—"

"Asher." My name was a whip that shut me the hell up.

Why was I being such a dick to her? She hadn't caused this. It took two. But she was so goddamn calm, and inside me, it felt as if a hurricane was raging.

"You've never been in my situation. You have no right to question why I do anything."

I scrubbed my face. My eyes were burning as if I hadn't slept at all. Between watching over her and Lily, I hadn't gotten much. "You're right."

There was no point in asking if she was sure. She had to be. She was supremely competent and wouldn't just take one test and assume. Although how often was even one test wrong? Probably not that often.

"Did you see a doctor?"

She rolled right on. "Furthermore, I tried to tell you earlier, before Lily had her bad dream. I didn't want to fall asleep." She rose, yanking on the sheet when the bedding got tangled. "Carrying a whole other life inside you is exhausting. Surprise."

The knot in my throat made me swallow hard. "Hannah, I'm sorry."

But she wasn't listening to me. "Do you think I wanted to tell you this? I knew you'd freak out. I've watched how you struggle with Lily. You're so much better with her than you give yourself credit for, but you don't see it. It'll take time. I know that. I *know* that," she repeated, drawing the sheet around her so tightly I wondered how it didn't cut off her circulation. "But I don't have that time. I'm carrying this child now. And we have to deal with reality, not start blaming each other like children."

She was right. Of course, she was. Except I'd never once acted like a child. At least before tonight. I'd always shouldered my responsibilities stoically. Never asking for assistance from anyone.

Until now.

"You were supposed to be the one to help me," I muttered. "Funny how that worked out, huh?"

She didn't look at me before marching out of the room and slamming the door.

Almost on cue, Lily started to wail down the hall.

I buried my head in my hands again. She wasn't wrong to be pissed at me. I'd said some doozies in the span of just a few minutes. But she claimed to understand my position. She didn't have a clue, as evidenced by that slamming door. Doing that with a kid around was basically a recipe for making the rest of your night hell.

But naturally, she didn't get that, because she'd never been a mother before. Not until now.

Now that she was having my baby.

Jesus Christ.

I pushed myself to my feet. Without any conscious intention, I went to the dresser and started pulling out fresh clothes. Jeans, boxers, sweater. I pulled them on, then opened the door and went down the hall to find my boots, jacket, and wallet.

The baby was still crying. Every whimper she made tore a hole inside me, but I wasn't thinking straight. Wasn't thinking at all.

I had to get away from here.

I grabbed my keys. It was okay, because Hannah was with Lily. Even as pissed as I was—at myself, most of all—I knew she'd take care of my little girl.

It wasn't fair of me to put her in that position. And it wasn't because she would be collecting a paycheck either. She already cared so much about Lily.

Cared about—

I shut it down as I yanked on my jacket. Lily would be fine. Hannah would be fine. I was just taking a time-out.

Oh, yeah? Then tell her you're leaving. Don't be the bastard who finds out she's carrying your child and leaves her to handle it alone.

The problem was I had never once been a bastard. Ever. I must've been overdue, because I couldn't seem to stop myself.

This time, I was the one who slammed the door behind me.

Some sick asshole part of me wanted Hannah to worry. To fret that I'd done something so out of character and split. She thought she had me pegged.

Everyone thought they knew me. Even my grandmother. I was about as predictable as a sandwich.

Until tonight.

I stopped dead on the porch at the sight of all the snow. My car was blocked in. The plow service hadn't come by yet. It wasn't much past midnight. We'd barely slept for an hour or two before she'd awakened and blown my mind.

In more ways than one.

I didn't even know where I intended to go. Normally, I'd head into the office and pour my frustrations into paperwork and whatever else I needed to deal with to get ahead for the rest of the week. But that was what dutiful Asher did. I didn't want to fucking work. I wanted to get blistering drunk and act like an idiot.

I wanted to not be me for a while.

The only reason you can be a jackass is because you know she's here. Just dump and run, why don't you?

I yanked on the gloves I found in my pocket and rushed down the steps. Fuck it. I'd walk it off.

Last call was two a.m., wasn't it? Just enough time for me to pour some libations into me and make all of this disappear for a while.

Just as well that I wasn't taking my car. I couldn't drink if I had. This way, I could take an Uber back. Or stumble home.

Or faceplant in a snowbank and see if anyone ever comes looking for me.

Why would she? She already had this situation under control. Oh, she'd said I didn't understand where she was coming from, but she certainly hadn't seemed eager for *my* input. She'd basically said she knew I would freak out.

And look at that, here I was, freaking out.

Sandwiches were probably actually more unpredictable than I was.

I made my way down the sidewalk. Nothing was shoveled, because I hadn't done it yet and neither had either of my neighbors, spread out as they were. So, I walked in the equally unplowed streets, hunching my shoulders against the cold. It hadn't seemed so frigid when I was out here before. Playing with Hannah and Lily had taken my attention, I supposed.

Hannah always had, from the very first moment I'd laid eyes on her.

The night we'd made a baby.

Snow fell and blinded me as I walked. I fumbled for my phone, then realized I'd forgotten it.

For the first time, panic surged through me and stalled my breath. I was completely out of touch. What if something happened?

I nearly turned back. But the little devil on my shoulder pushed me forward, and I stumbled on the snowy street as if I'd already had too much.

I didn't even know where I was going. This neighborhood was essentially new to me. Crescent Cove wasn't very big, but there were so many small pockets of neighborhoods and side streets.

On one of them I came upon a small bar that looked as if it had been forgotten by time. It wasn't that far from Main Street, at least geographically. Otherwise, it might as well have been on the moon.

The place looked practically deserted. Not shocking on a night this stormy, but I suspected it might be a regular situation. Most smart people stayed home on nights like these.

Whoever had called me smart?

A car and a Jeep sat in the lot. Only one of them appeared to have been running in this century.

A blinking neon sign above the weathered door read Sharkey's. Did he own the beater car? Or was he the owner of the Jeep? I couldn't imagine anyone picking that name for a watering hole if it wasn't their own.

Tentatively, I turned the door handle.

Devil, don't desert me now.

I stepped inside the murky darkness of a rather ordinary drinking establishment. Tinny oldies music piped from unseen speakers, and the lone TV high on the wall was tuned to the sports highlights.

Only one patron sat at the bar. He wore a ball cap and a heavy down vest with a flannel shirt beneath. He didn't look away from the TV as I grabbed a stool.

"Hey."

He finally turned my way. "Hey. You lost too?"

The guy seemed around my age, give or take half a decade. I'd expected him to be some wizened old fisherman, judging from the way he was hunched over his frosty beer mug.

His mostly empty beer mug.

"You could say that. Is there a bartender in this joint?"

"Quit yer bitching." A bubblegum-chomping redhead strolled out of the back on high enough platform heels that I hoped she never encountered spills. "Whatcha want?"

This was definitely not my usual sort of place.

"An old-fashioned, please."

She looked back at the wall of bottles behind her, selected one, and plunked it down in front of me. "Here you go." Then she disappeared in the back.

"She's not the usual bartender," the guy beside me offered. "She's just filling in. Doesn't give a shit about this job."

I pried off my gloves. "You could've fooled me."

The bottle wasn't even opened. It definitely wasn't a high-end whiskey either. But who was I to judge? I just wanted to get fucking drunk.

When I struggled to get the bottle open with the opener on my keychain, the guy beside me grabbed it and did the honors. "Not much of a drinker?"

"What makes you say that?"

His gaze dropped to my legs. "Your jeans look starched. Not part of the usual uniform."

The guy's jeans seemed pretty tidy themselves, but I couldn't argue. "I don't think I've gotten properly drunk since college."

"Twenty years ago?"

Affronted, I tossed back the whiskey. And nearly choked until my eyes bled. "Try ten."

He cocked his head, drank a little more, and nodded. "Yeah, I can see it. Sorry. The snow made your hair look grayer."

"Gray*er?*" I leaned forward and tried to see my reflection in the mirror backing the bottles on the wall behind the bar. "I don't have any gray. At least I didn't before today. Now? Very possible."

"What happened today?"

"I knocked up my New Year's Eve date." I sank back on the stool and braced my palms on the sticky bar top. Sightlessly, I stared straight ahead. "I can't believe I just told you that."

I also couldn't believe I'd referred to Hannah that way. Although it had been technically accurate until a few hours ago when we crossed that line again, it wasn't the truth. Hannah had never just been a hookup to me.

She couldn't be. Even if we had never met up again after New Year's, I would've always seen her as the one who got away.

The one I let leave.

I tossed back more of the whiskey and savored the fiery aftertaste as it worked its way down. Tonight, I'd been the one to walk away.

The regret inside me burned almost as much as the cheap alcohol.

"And you can't even blame getting toasted yet." The guy beside me set down his empty mug. He looked around as if he wanted another beer, but good luck there. "One and done situation?"

"No. I mean, we thought so, but she's my daughter's nanny now, and we just slept together again tonight, and Christ, I need to drink faster." I took another few swallows and wiped the back of my hand over my chin. "What is happening to my mouth?"

"Can't answer that, as I don't know you from Adam." He stuck out a hand to me. "I'm Austin Lancaster, by the way. I'm new to the area."

"Me too. Well, kind of. I'm from Syracuse. Recent Crescent Cove transplant." I shook his extended hand. "Nice to meet you."

"Name?"

"Huh?" Then I laughed. It was probably good I rarely drank. Clearly, I was not a natural. "Asher Wainwright."

Austin's dark brows climbed toward his equally dark hair. "The newspaper Wainwright people? Fancy building with your name splashed over it?"

I considered lying, although I'd never denied my legacy to anyone. On the contrary, I'd let fighting to maintain it define me for so long that I wasn't sure who I was outside the realm of business.

"Yes. That's me. Well, I didn't start the paper, but I inherited the publishing company."

Austin whistled. "Wow. You gotta have much more top shelf stuff at home." He nodded at the whiskey I hadn't stopped steadily sipping.

I'd probably singe off the lining of my throat before the night was through, but the buzz in my blood was nice. Even my chaotic thoughts were settling. I hadn't had that kind of reprieve since...

Hannah. Hannah gave me that same sort of break from the weight of my responsibilities.

Yet somehow in our escape, we'd created another one.

Together.

Not just me, not just her. It was a joint project, and I'd left her to handle her end alone.

I rubbed my fist over my suddenly aching forehead. Christ, I was a right bastard.

"You have any idea how a guy who hasn't had sex in years impregnates someone on their first try?"

Austin coughed and wrapped both his hands around his mug. His chunky gold insignia ring caught the dim light. "I don't know. Luck?"

I frowned. "You think it's lucky? I already have one. And I didn't even make that one myself."

Austin's mouth quirked. I couldn't say I blamed him. I knew I sounded like some kind of crazy right now, but I couldn't seem to shut my trap. "Depends on how you look at it, I guess." He scratched his scruffy chin. "As to your question, if not luck, maybe you...stored up?"

It took me a moment to follow. When I got there, I started to laugh. "Probably true. My grandmother says it isn't healthy. Jesus, my grandmother. I didn't even think about what she'd say." I shut my eyes and shook my head. "See what happens when she goes away? Everything goes all to hell."

"What she would say about what? The knocking up part? From my experience with grandmas, they're usually overjoyed at the prospect of babies."

I opened my eyes. "You're supposed to be on my side."

"Am I? So, you want me to agree you getting some hookup pregnant who is the nanny to the baby you didn't make—yet you call your daughter—is a calamity. Do I have that right?"

"Yes. No. I don't know."

"You don't know if I have the facts right?"

"No. The calamity part. I mean, it should be. Am I father material?" I jerked my thumb at my chest and jabbed myself hard enough to bruise.

"You look like it."

"Hmm." Was that a good thing? Why had Hannah wanted to nail someone who looked like a daddy?

Different kind of daddy. The other kind I doubted had any trouble getting action.

"That's not an insult. Just saying you look stable. Mature. God knows you have the financials covered." He nudged my shoulder with a grin. "Don't suppose I can hit you up for a loan sometime?"

"Wait until I save my company first, okay?"

Austin's eyes narrowed.

I cleared my throat. "Good job on keeping up with my fucked-up life, by the way. I have trouble following it myself, and you grasped it all like a pro." I lifted the whiskey to my mouth and wondered why the distance seemed to have grown. Of course, the bottle was a third empty now. I was probably reaching my limit.

Did I have a limit?

I knocked back some more. Maybe not.

"Thanks. My boss always praises my linear thinking." Austin's dimples flashed.

"That ring? Police? I couldn't quite make out the insignia."

He shuddered. "Bite your numb tongue."

I tapped it against the roof of my mouth. He wasn't far off. "Fire Department?"

He saluted me with his empty mug before banging it three times on the bar. Miss Sunshine shot out of the back, gave him a refill, and split with a scowl for me.

I probably wasn't drinking the whiskey fast enough. Then again, consuming this whole bottle might literally kill me.

"Yes. New York's Bravest, except some miles away from the city."

"It's an honor to meet you," I said solemnly. "I'm also glad you can't arrest me if I end up forgetting to pay and stiffing the bartender for this bottle."

"I heard that," she called from the back.

"It's an honor to meet you too. I've never met someone actually made of cash money. Although you mentioned something about saving—"

I waved it off. "Hello, I'm working on being drunk. Don't listen to me. You live near here?"

"Yeah, Morningstar Lane. Renting a place, with an option to buy. Assuming I come up with the money. I'm in line for a promotion, but it means longer hours and it's hard with Joey."

"Wife?" I rethought the name. "Husband?"

Austin shook his head. "Kid sister, but I'm basically her dad now. Our parents passed on last year."

"Oh, I'm so sorry."

"Thanks. Me too. It's a rough situation." Austin took a long drink.

"I don't suppose she's under two? Lily could use a playmate." Then again, Hannah and I would be providing her with one soon enough.

My head swam and I started to push back my stool. I might actually need to put my head between my knees so I didn't pass out.

Austin clapped my back. "You okay, man? You don't look good."

"Yeah. Sorry. Just gonna lie on this floor for a day or two. Don't mind me."

"Seriously, not *this* floor. My boots stuck to it the whole way in." He pulled me more upright on the stool and kind of shoved me against the bar so I would have some support. The guy was way more athletically built than I'd realized upon first glance. Made sense though, since he was a firefighter.

All I pushed around all day was pencils and Pampers.

Luckily, I was still reasonably physically fit due to all the hours I spent in the gym to compensate for all the sex I wasn't having.

Probably a good thing, or who knows how large a family I'd have now. Evidently, it wasn't safe for me to recreationally knock boots.

What had Hannah worn that first night anyway? Pumps?

Welcome to the Brady Bunch part deux.

When I didn't reply, Austin smiled. I had a feeling he could tell my thoughts were spinning like a Tilt-a-Whirl. "Oh, and sorry, Joey's almost eleven. She's at her first sleepover tonight, and I was going stir-crazy at home, so here I am. She has trouble making friends, and if this one doesn't work out..." He rubbed his hand over his scruff and exhaled heavily. "Anyway, think you're out of luck with the playmate situation. But, hey, with your new baby on the way, at least your kids will always have a friend, right?"

Right. Bright side.

Dots encroached on my field of vision. Many, many dots. "I don't suppose you have a spare oxygen tank in your vehicle?"

"Dude, you are bad off. You probably shouldn't be drinking. How about I get you home?"

"I should go home. You're right. I'm not this guy. I'm decent. Honorable." I shoved away the whiskey bottle. I'd drank far more of it than I should have. "I wore a condom the first night. Responsibly. Not tonight though. But she was already pregnant. So, doesn't count." I grabbed his shirtfront as I stumbled to my feet. "Right?"

"Sure thing, pal, whatever you say." He patted my back and turned me toward the bar again. "Hate to ruin this *Oprah* moment, but you have the money for that whiskey, right? My card's maxed beyond my tab."

"Oh, sure. Right. Of course." I took out my wallet and thumbed out a credit card. I was about to call for the bartender when she swept out and grabbed it off the bar. "His too," I called.

Austin shook his head. "Nah, man, thanks, but I'm not that bad off.

Just a little squeezed from trying to buy a house for us and getting situated in a new town. For fuck's sake, she's gonna be a teenager soon. Her clothes are never right, and kids are so damn mean." He cracked his knuckles. "Anyway, thanks."

Somehow I smiled. "You're welcome. You remind me of—" My smile fell away.

He wasn't Billy. Billy was dead. Just because I'd spent a few minutes drinking with this guy didn't make us buddies. And he definitely didn't replace my dead best friend.

Nothing could bring Billy back. Eventually, I'd come to terms with that.

Lily was mine now. No one would come and spirit her away to her real family. Just as Hannah was pregnant. That baby was a reality too.

Wasn't it? She intended to have the child, right?

She had to. I mean, she had all the choices in the world, but we'd made that child and so what if I wasn't ready? Life didn't follow a schedule.

Too bad I only grasped that when my blood was humming and I wasn't quite stable on my feet.

"Remind you of who?" Austin asked.

I shook my head and it nearly rolled off my shoulders and across the bar. "Just someone I lost. A friend. The best friend I ever had."

"Ah, Christ, I'm so sorry. I shouldn't have asked."

"It's okay. It's been five months give or take." As if that made it all right.

It didn't. Nothing ever would be again.

"Hey, I've got an idea," Austin said as I signed the slip the bartender presented to me. She snatched it and returned my card and was gone again in a flash.

She had an unusual style of bartending, I had to give her that.

"Going home and sleeping it off?"

"Yeah, that too in a few minutes. But how do you feel about some foosball first?"

I followed the direction of his gaze toward the row of tables in the back. There was a pool table, a couple of dart boards, some video game machines, and the aforementioned foosball table.

"Closing time is in twenty," Miss Personality called.

I pushed away from the bar. I debated slipping the whiskey bottle in my jacket pocket but decided against it. My quota of bad decisions had already been reached. "Sure. Maybe I can win one out of two."

"I wouldn't count on it. I was foosball champion two years running at Syracuse."

"You went to SU too?"

Austin nodded and removed his ball cap, revealing a disordered mop of short brown hair. "Dropped out two years in. I wanted to party, and it was expensive to get a degree in that particular occupation." He laughed and moved to one side of the foosball table. "Might go back though, if it'll help me move up. Or maybe just for personal enrichment."

I took my side and gripped the edge of the table. My buzz had faltered briefly, but it was back now. I was going to hang on to that fleeting feeling of bliss for as long as I could. "Party for as long as you can. Adulthood lasts the rest of your damn life."

"Ain't that the truth, brother." Austin flipped a few rows of his foosball dudes and flashed me a wolfish smile. "Let's play."

SIXTEEN

"Shh, shh, that's a good girl."

I rocked Lily as she whimpered softly and wondered how I'd gone from being painfully solitary to a mother of two in a matter of months.

Two-word answer: Asher Wainwright.

I wasn't Lily's mother, just the nanny. Her mother was gone, and now she had a father who was afraid to love her and a great-grandmother who loved her enough for half a dozen people.

Maybe I wouldn't be Lily's nanny anymore. It wasn't as if I'd gotten used to the job yet. But before I'd told Asher I was pregnant, I had never really considered the possibility he might not take part in the kid's life.

Might not want *me* to be part of Lily's life either, once he knew.

I smoothed a kiss over Lily's sweaty brow and smiled as she clutched my shirt in her chubby fist. I hadn't wanted to put on any of Asher's clothes, and I didn't have any of my own there except what I'd worn that day.

A quiet rage simmered inside me, layered under the hurt and fear. I'd worked so hard to build a sense of stability for myself, both financially and emotionally. That had meant pulling away a bit from the world, as I grieved and tried to figure out what I wanted to do for the rest of my life.

Now everything was in flux.

The only thing I knew for certain was I wanted my child. Wrong timing or not, we'd make a way for ourselves.

If that was without Asher, then it just was. I wasn't going to beg. I also wasn't going to tolerate being an emotional punching bag while he processed his own shit.

I swallowed deeply as I gazed down at a now sleeping Lily in the light from the moon. I didn't want to lose her from my life. It was nuts I could've become this attached this soon, but somehow we'd bonded.

As I'd thought I had bonded with her asshole of a father. The man who was currently running the streets doing God knows what.

I wasn't looking at the clock. Wasn't fretting at all.

Liar.

I didn't know where he was. If he was okay. I did know this behavior was not like the Asher I'd come to know. Whether this fit of pique would last or just be a passing moment, I wasn't sure.

Either way, I'd have to shore up my defenses. He had a way of sneaking under them.

Down the hall, a door closed. Softly this time, not with all the bluster of a couple of hours ago. I sat up straighter in the chair, drawing Lily close. She didn't stir beyond nuzzling her drooly little chin underneath my neck.

I stared at the open doorway, waiting. Barely breathing. Even so, I wasn't prepared when Asher appeared in it, looking so big and rumpled and...male.

So very male.

Something inside me twinged, and it definitely wasn't annoyance. There was some lust in there too, but not only that. When he leaned against the doorjamb, his hair all messy and dark and wet from the snow, his clothes wrinkled, his eyes heavy with a combination of fatigue and things I didn't want to think too much about...

I wanted to hold him. And yes, get naked and climb in his lap, but also be the one to comfort him and rub those lines away from his eyes.

Even if coming clean about our situation had inadvertently helped put them there.

My first inclination was to rise and go to him, despite what had happened. I'd been the first one to slam out of that room, and that had been wrong too. But the instant I moved, I smelled the alcohol on him. It wafted out of his pores, or off his jacket.

Ugh, I didn't even know.

I cupped the baby's head in my hand and pressed my back against the chair. I could only imagine my expression.

But I didn't have to imagine his. He was staring at us in a way that tangled up everything inside me in complicated knots. His gaze was hot, but tender too. He never looked away.

"I'm sorry." His voice was rough, as abrasive as uneven concrete. "I'm still pretty drunk."

"I could smell you."

"Really?" He lifted his sleeve and sniffed. "Think you smell the bar on me. I didn't have that much."

"No? Then why is your voice slurred?" I didn't add that it was also sexy, which was ridiculous. But it was as if normally hyper speed, ultra-focused Asher had dialed himself back a few notches. Leaving him a little slower, a little softer, a little more unguarded.

One hundred and twenty percent dangerous as he walked toward us with long, unhurried steps. The nursery wasn't that big, but it felt as if our eyes locked forever while he crossed the room.

"I had some whiskey. Got drunk. It helps me not to think so hard. Not in a rush to have it end." He licked his lips. "Are you going to kill my buzz, Hannah?"

Asher saying my name should be a criminal offense. "I'm just sitting here, minding my business."

"You're sitting there, rocking my baby." He leaned over and braced his hands on the arms of the rocking chair, and my heart went into overdrive. I would've sworn I heard it knocking against my ribs. "Both my babies. Isn't that right?"

I didn't say anything. What could I say? He'd admitted he was drunk. I could smell the alcohol on his breath. It wasn't repulsive. If anything, that hint of the forbidden pulled at me. As if I could ride his high with him.

A high I couldn't have on my own any longer. Not for quite some time.

"Your lips are trembling." He touched my lower lip with his thumb and it was a damn miracle I didn't crush Lily in reaction. Every part of me braced.

He sensed it, because he backed off and tucked his hands in his pockets. "I'm sorry," he said again after a moment.

"For what? For coming home drunk?" Only after the word was out did I realize how foolish I was being. This wasn't my home. Even if he'd invited me to stay there, it was just for Lily.

I was getting all tangled up in something that wasn't meant for me. "Yeah."

"What about for leaving in the first place? For getting mad at me because we made a baby *together*?"

He fisted his hands in his pockets, making them bulge. "I'm not mad at you," he said quietly. "I never was. I regret causing you to think that. It was a fucking dream you walked back into my life."

Before I could reply, he touched the top of Lily's head, just a brush of his fingers, and strode out of the room.

He's drunk.

He doesn't know what he's saying.

It may not even be true.

A fucking dream? Really?

Then again, our day together had been pretty unreal before I'd spilled the baby crackers. Dream was actually a pretty apt description.

Except he'd claimed to have a buzz—and his voice had definitely indicated that—but he seemed entirely too lucid for someone who'd spent a couple of hours drinking.

Unless Asher even got drunk differently than other people.

I rolled my achy shoulders. He did *everything* differently than other men. Was that why I couldn't keep my distance?

But I didn't run after him. No, I took my sweet ass time. Once I was sure Lily was still asleep, I tucked her in her crib and turned on the little music mobile that seemed to bring her comfort. She didn't move. Hopefully, she'd get some rest now that she had a full belly again, thanks to the bottle of formula I'd given her earlier.

After a quick stop in the bathroom to freshen up—and give myself about fifteen pep talks—I went down the hall to the master bedroom. Clothes and shoes were all over the floor, as if Asher had let them fly.

On the bed, Asher was sprawled out, completely nude.

Completely hard.

It was insanely stupid that I didn't turn around. Clearly, he wasn't in a talking mood. From the state of his erection, there was a good chance he'd, uh, primed the pump since he'd left the nursery.

But I didn't want to talk either. I definitely didn't want to fight. He'd apologized, and God, I wanted to believe he meant it.

In the middle of the night, nothing seemed wrong.

What felt wrong was standing on the opposite side of this doorway another minute, watching him watch me.

I took off my shirt and let it drop onto the floor with Asher's clothes. He leaned up on his elbows, staring at me intently. Memorizing every detail as I undid my braid and snapped the band around my wrist. I didn't take off my panties. I didn't know why. Maybe so I'd have one last barrier if my common sense returned.

Or maybe I just wanted to watch him fuck me while I still wore my chaste white cotton.

I crawled across the bed to him on my hands and knees. I was still self-conscious about my body, more so as I knew it was already starting to change, but it was hard to feel anything less than beautiful when Asher's gaze was drinking me down. He held out a hand and drew me toward his chest, groaning as my breasts pressed against his skin.

"I like coming home to you," he whispered before our mouths met with just as much hunger as earlier. And just as much as that very first night, when we'd chosen to get naked by firelight rather than talk.

This was a much easier language for us to share.

I slipped my hands into his hair and nibbled on his lips, bearing down harder as he cupped my ass. He squeezed hard before delving between my thighs to toy with my panties. Rubbing me through them, and then under them, his fingers finding the heart of me unerringly and slipping inside.

"Wet for me."

I bit his lower lip. "That's the state you left me in."

His groan blazed through me, a sound I echoed at the deep press of his fingers. He pushed all the way into me before drawing out in a slow, slippery slide. He did it another time, harder. My clit throbbed and I ground against him, fumbling for his cock. The damp tip slid over my nipple, and I wasn't sure which of us moaned louder.

He rolled me beneath him and spent his share of time sucking on my nipples. Both of them, including the one that had to taste like him. His pupils blew wide in the moonlight as he carefully tended to me, his teeth sharp, his tongue so erotic. But he was gentle with my breasts. He knew I was pregnant now, and he must've remembered my reaction in the hot tub earlier, even through the alcohol. His gaze remained on my face, minutely gauging my reaction to every movement he made.

All the while, his heavy cock slid up and down my cleft, making me squirm and bite my lip.

He inched down my body, dropping kisses as he went, hovering over my belly. I didn't know how he'd react, but he stared at it for the longest time until I had to touch him. I brushed my hand through his hair, and then he rested his cheek on my palm.

There weren't words, so I didn't try to fill the silence with them.

The momentary sweetness made me warm all over, but in no time, he was slipping downward again. He kissed my navel and continued on, nudging aside my panties to lick me where I was already so soaked. My clit pulsed under his attention, and I strained toward his mouth, spreading my legs wider while he lapped at me. He didn't rip my panties or remove them, just enjoyed me despite them.

God, he enjoyed me.

As I enjoyed him. I relished every push of his fingers inside me, every swipe of his tongue, every heated glance meant to ensure I was with him each step of the way.

The orgasm rolled through me, swift and merciless. I smothered my cries in the pillow beside me, digging my nails into the back of his neck when he turned into an overachiever and decided to give me another. He didn't even pause long enough to let me catch my breath.

My only option was to come. And come again.

I still hadn't fully stopped quivering when he rose onto his knees and gripped his cock. He moved my panties out of the way and circled his shaft over my still overstimulated clit before he leaned down to kiss me, so sweetly the backs of my eyes burned. I tasted the alcohol mixed with me on his tongue, the combination hotter than it had any right to be.

"Hold on to me."

I wrapped my arms around his neck as he adjusted my legs around his hips and drove inside me. I wasn't even sure if my panties were still intact.

I so didn't care.

He swallowed my moans, extending our kiss while he withdrew and buried himself inside me once more. He did it again and again, his movements deep and decisive, his arm like steel where he braced it beside me on the pillows.

So much for drinking too much affecting a man's ability to fuck. It certainly wasn't affecting Asher.

But it was time to make him just as crazy as he'd made me.

Scraping my nails down his back, I flexed around his cock inside me and licked my lips, nice and slow. Then I slid my hand into my still semi-intact panties to strum my clit, testing both of us. I had never done this before in front of a man. Had never touched myself just to feel good, not for the express purpose of a climax.

He ate me up with his eyes, his thrusts coming even faster. Deeper. Harder. Bumping that delicious spot inside me that made my legs shake and my breaths turn to pants.

I rubbed myself just that much more quickly, loving the pressure from his fullness inside me. He grabbed my wrist and brought it to his mouth, sucking on my fingers as he shoved my underwear over even more and redoubled his strokes.

Every time he bottomed out inside me, I gasped. And clutched him that much tighter.

He finally let out a low groan and went off inside me, those warm pulsations going on for so long that my body had no defense. I came again with a whimper against his shoulder, clinging to him through the waves of pleasure and the aftermath that always arrived too fast.

"I love giving you your firsts." He rolled onto his back and took me with him.

We'd made a bit of a mess, but obviously, neither of us was inclined to tidy up right now. Instead, we stretched out like starfish and hoped we could breathe again without wheezing sometime soon.

"Which first now? Drunk sex?"

"You're not drunk." The concern in his tone had me lifting my head. I didn't particularly appreciate him going paternalistic on me, but at least it proved he cared about the baby.

"No. I haven't drank since New Year's." I tapped his sulky mouth. "I meant you."

"Oh. Could you tell I was drunk?" He glanced down at his body as if he was ascertaining certain parts of him were still attached.

"You told me you were, remember?"

"Hmm. I'm not sure I am anymore. I think the last of it drained out of me when I saw you rocking Lily."

"I fed her again too. She was unsettled tonight. Wonder why." I propped my chin on my stacked arms. "Which first?"

He brushed my hair out of my face. "Earlier tonight, that was the first time you sucked a man's cock."

I winced. And tried not to shift my thighs together from the thrill those words gave me. "That obvious?"

"No. You were incredible. I could just tell."

"Mmm-hmm. Speaking of firsts, I doubt you get drunk that often."

"It wasn't my first time, but it's been a very long time. Billy and I used to go out most Friday nights. That changed, of course, when he met Solange and they had Lily. The Fridays were few and farther between."

"And you got wasted every time you went out?"

His chuckle was like smooth, expensive silk against my skin. "Hardly. But I tested my limits sometimes. I met someone tonight who reminded me of those days."

Involuntarily, I stiffened. "Oh, yeah? Was she pretty?"

"Try a he." His smirk was entirely too smug. "I guess he was kind of pretty though, in a manly way. I'm sure he has no trouble meeting women."

I snorted. "Unlike you. Too bad you're so ugly."

"I didn't have time for women."

My pulse quickened. *Didn't.* Definitely in the past. Did that mean that he did now? He certainly didn't seem to have cleared his schedule.

"Does he?"

"I don't know, but he's a single dad too, to his kid sister. He's had a rough go of it too." Asher pinched the bridge of his nose. "Christ, he made me laugh. It was like it was with Billy, except it wasn't. It couldn't be."

His pain was a palpable thing. I wanted to pull him close, to hold him while he poured out his feelings.

But he wouldn't, and I'd just regret trying to encourage him to. So, I tried a different tact.

"Where did you go? And don't just tell me the bar."

"I did go to the bar."

"Elaborate."

He folded one arm beneath his head and stared up at the ceiling. His other hand still rested possessively on my ass. "There's a place called Sharkey's not far from here. I ended up there. Basically, it's a dive. The bartender gave me an entire bottle of whiskey."

Horrified, I narrowed my eyes. "You did not drink a whole bottle of whiskey. There's no way in hell you could've gotten it up if you had. Not with your lack of tolerance."

"Gee, who's the expert here?"

I didn't want to say it. I almost didn't. "Try the girl who watched her dad get pissed-face drunk more than once and knows well enough the effects. He couldn't even stand up when he drank a whole bottle of hard liquor, never mind aim with your precision."

He was silent for too long. Enough time that I knew he was pitying me. "Hannah, I'm sorry."

I eased away from him and drew my knees up to my chest. All of a sudden, I was so cold. "You can stop saying that anytime now."

"But it's true. I hurt you, and I didn't mean to. The reasons I left tonight didn't have to do with you nearly as much as me."

"They had to do with you feeling responsible for a kid you never intended to make."

"You're right. I didn't intend to make a child. Maybe ever. I didn't know if it would happen. I also didn't intend for Billy to fall off that fucking roof, or for his little girl to end up with my last name. I didn't intend to have to rock her to sleep from nightmares. I wonder if she knows, if she senses her real daddy is gone and is never coming back. If she even remembers him. If she compares me." He sat up beside me and raked his hands through his hair. "I didn't intend for life to be so fucking complicated."

On that point, we could agree.

After a moment, he reached out to rub my back. "I like having you here. I know it's new. You took this job with Lily, and maybe you figured you'd tell me once the dust settled."

"I found out yesterday. Remember when you asked me why I was late?" I tightened my grip around my knees. "That would be why."

"Yesterday," he echoed dully.

"Yeah. So, I'm no more 'settled' with this idea than you are. My doctor ran through the options with me and—"

"What options?"

"The usual ones. Anyway, she told—"

"You're not having an abortion."

"No, I'm not, but not because you insisted on it. Your opinion didn't really factor into my choice."

His mouth curled into a sneer. "Nice to know where I rank."

"Don't give me that. You're not my husband. We aren't a couple."

Some part of me was screaming out for him to deny that. To say something like, *hey, we screwed around a few times, maybe that makes us in some kind of relationship.* It wasn't much, but I'd take any bone I could get right now.

But softening the blow wasn't Asher's style.

"No, but until we decide otherwise, I'm your employer. And I'm that child's father, whether or not you like it."

"Nice to see which title you put first. I'm going to take a shower and go to bed." I didn't want to repeat what had happened earlier, but I also didn't want to share his air at that particular moment.

I was too hurt, and I wasn't even sure I had any right to be. But I wasn't sure what rights he had either.

We were both too gun-shy and too new at all of this to be able to have a rational conversation. At least right now. Maybe after we got some sleep—or perhaps within the span of the next six and a half months—we could get through a discussion about this topic.

Asher looked pointedly at the mattress we were sitting on. "This qualifies as a bed."

"It does." One I'd been eager to sleep with him in, until he'd made sure I remembered I was the hired help. "I also have one you made up for me down the hall."

He exhaled. "Whichever you prefer."

I'd prefer to stay in your arms.

But I didn't dare do that, in case I was setting myself up for a very large fall. One that would affect more than me. More than Lily.

And I'd be wise to remember that the next time I wanted to let my hormones take over.

I made myself get out of his bed and walk to the door, gathering my shirt as I went. My panties were far too damp and stretched all to hell, thanks to his strong hands yanking them out of the way.

Another fantasy checked off the list at least. I'd have to be happy with that.

"Goodnight, Asher."

This time, when I closed the door behind me, I didn't slam it.

Sometimes softness was far more powerful.

SEVENTEEN

Asher

I SLEPT FOR FOUR HOURS AND GOT UP FOR WORK.

That was all I knew how to do. Force myself to keep going, one foot in front of the other. But today, I'd had to down three Tylenol and a strong cup of coffee before my feet would work.

Damn hangover. I hadn't even been drunk all that long.

That was life. You played, you paid. I was lucky if I even got to play first.

I grabbed the first suit that came to hand in my row of practically identical ones and dressed in the muted morning light. It was still early, and I didn't expect Hannah to be up yet. We'd gone to bed late, and she'd been sick yesterday—

I shut my eyes.

Sick from a baby, you asshole. Not food poisoning or the flu. And you gave her ginger candies. No wonder she wouldn't consult you for any-damn-thing.

I hadn't known. Hadn't even guessed. Because we'd used condoms, and it had only been one night.

It had only taken one fall to kill Billy. He'd been young, capable, strong. The two situations weren't at all related, except that *just once* was plenty.

Before I left, I wrote down a list of numbers where I could be reached in case of emergency, plus a few extra notes regarding Lily's preferences. Hannah and I hadn't discussed anything such as hours, or if she'd be staying here at least for this week while my grandmother was away, or hell, even salary requirements.

That would need to be taken care of this week, as awkward as it was considering the situation. But she'd agreed to take on a job and I'd agree to compensate her, so we needed to get it handled. And this way she would be protected if our personal relationship soured—any more than it had already—and she would be on the books as Lily's official caretaker.

Assuming she still wanted to be.

That she hadn't split showed how much she already cared about my little girl. I wouldn't take advantage of her financially on top of everything else.

We just needed to actually *talk* to each other.

We'd made a baby, and we'd fucked, and we'd fought. Then we'd fucked and fought again. There hadn't been much time for any sort of conversation that didn't involve our loins, or the fruits of them.

I rubbed my forehead and tacked on a quick note at the bottom of the paper.

I'm assuming you're still working for me. If I'm wrong, you know where to find me.

Great, defensive with touch of dickishness. The exact tone I needed to convey after last night's colossal mess.

I hope we can figure this out.

. . .

I took a deep breath and studied my hurried scrawl. *One more step. You can do it.*

Hannah, I'm sorry.

A text came in from Vincent. He was already on the way to the trade show. Did I want to take the afternoon shift?

No. I wanted to be anywhere but here right now, as horrible of a person as that probably made me.

I set down the stubby pencil. The words I'd written seemed so inadequate. She deserved a face to face apology, but I didn't know what to say. How to explain. I couldn't puzzle out my own thought process right now.

Work was what I knew. What I was good at. Or I'd been good at it once. I just had to see my way through this period. Emerging on the other side would be Wainwright Industries' greatest triumph.

And mine, other than mastering the art of the perfect diaper.

I tucked a bottle of water in my soft-sided briefcase and stepped outside into a frosty morning. The barren trees glistened with snow and ice and the lawn was covered with a pristine layer of fluffy snow. The driveway had been plowed, as had the road itself. I would have no trouble getting out.

Halfway down the steps, I stopped and puffed out a breath. I hadn't said goodbye to Lily, as was my habit. Already I was conceding that space to Hannah. Far too eagerly, if I was being honest. She seemed to have the whole baby thing under much better control than I did.

Not even just because she was carrying one.

Mine.

At the sharp twist in my chest, I gripped my briefcase and turned back. I wasn't going to run out of my own home. Not again. If I happened to see Hannah while I was saying goodbye to Lily, so be it.

I headed upstairs and stopped in the doorway to Lily's room. Her mobile was spinning merrily, playing some sweet tune. Lily was staring up at it with her fist in her mouth.

"Hi there, sweetheart," I murmured as I set down my briefcase.

Her gaze swung to me and she let out a giggly gurgle before sticking out her arms. I looked over my shoulder, sure Hannah was probably behind me.

Nope. Lily wanted me to pick her up.

Carefully, I lifted her into my arms. She grabbed a fistful of my hair and tried to drag it into her mouth, her big brown eyes fastened to mine with a plea I wasn't strong enough to resist.

So what if she sucked on my hair? It would dry.

We moved to the window and I spoke in a soft voice to her as I narrated what I saw. The smoke pluming out of chimneys, the snow-covered cars rumbling down the street, the kids charging down the mostly shoveled sidewalks with their brightly colored backpacks. Lily gnawed on my hair and listened for a good moment or two before she screwed up her pretty face and started to cry.

Not five seconds later, I also screwed up mine.

"That time again, huh?" I took her to the changing table and after shedding my jacket, made quick work of her very dirty diaper. "One good thing, at least you can't spray my suit," I told her.

She looked up at me unblinkingly.

She couldn't, but maybe the new baby would.

Swallowing hard, I tugged out a new snuggly outfit for her in soft green. On the front it said *my grandma loves me mostest,* which I knew to be true.

I smiled. Hopefully, Gran was having fun on her trip. With her boyfriend.

Oddly, the thought of her actively dating didn't cause an immediate pulse-pounding headache. Probably because I was in no place to judge. She always had a good time and picked her dates well. She also didn't have to worry about pregnancy or sticking her giant foot in her mouth so many times it got stuck there.

"She's the smart one, right, Lily Patch?" I tugged the outfit into place and set her on her feet, laughing a little as she tried to step forward.

Then she did it again.

"Holy sh—crap, Lily, are you walking?"

Unsurprisingly, she didn't answer, just jammed her hand in her mouth.

She'd tried a few times, but she'd never gotten very far. A blessing for sure. A walking baby was a lot more work than a crawling and climbing one.

Before I could try to get her to walk to me again, she fell back on her butt and chewed on her fingers, her cheeks reddening. She let out a sob and I rubbed the back of my neck.

Now what did she need? Could it be time for another bottle? Hadn't Hannah mentioned feeding her before bed? That hadn't been all that long ago in the scheme of things, as evidenced by my dry, gritty eyes.

"Hang on, kiddo." I set her back in her crib and went to the kitchen to warm up a bottle of formula. Hannah's door was still closed.

Maybe she'd left. I couldn't quite blame her if she had. But no, I knew she wouldn't do that. To me? Maybe. Just never to Lily.

Hell, she probably figured Lily needed her influence. She wasn't wrong.

I brought the bottle back to the nursery. Lily was still crying, knuckling her streaming eyes with one hand while she sucked on the other.

"Come here, sweetheart." I tried to pick her up and she kicked out at me, sending the bottle rolling away. I sighed and retrieved it before picking up Lily and propping her on my hip.

My gaze landed on the rocking chair where Hannah had sat with her the evening before.

I didn't think I'd ever forget that moment. Knowing she not only cradled Lily but that she had my child inside her…

Even if I had not one clue what to do with said child, I couldn't deny the feelings he or she aroused in me. More and more with each passing hour.

I lowered myself into the rocker and attempted to give Lily the bottle, but she kicked out again. Only my nimble reflexes saved it from going flying again.

"Not hungry, hmm? Diaper is clean. What's left? Do you miss Hannah?" My voice dipped on her name as if I could conjure her that easily.

Worst of all, I was pretty sure I missed her too, although it had been mere hours since I'd seen her last.

But she needed her rest. They both did.

Christ.

Lily kicked out again and shoved her other hand in her mouth to join the first. Her face was getting redder and redder despite her cries lowering to rather pathetic whimpers.

If she kept that up, we'd wake Hannah whether or not we meant to.

I set Lily higher up on my lap and fumbled out my phone from my trouser pocket. I did a quick one-handed search for possible explanations for crying babies, which ranged from diaper rash—her bum had seemed fine to me—to allergies—I had no idea to what—to teething.

Since Lily was currently rubbing her mouth against her hand and drooling all over the place, I decided that was a good guess.

"You growing some teeth in there? Let's see." I reached toward her face and she turned it away, her tears ratcheting up again.

So, that wasn't happening.

My next step was to do a search to find out how to help. Popsicles, Orajel, and a visit to the pediatrician were some of the top suggestions.

My phone buzzed in my hand. Another text from Vincent, this time saying he'd had something come up and he would appreciate me handling the morning sessions after all. We were also still a go for the overnight Friday night. Saturday would bring a full slate of meetings and social gatherings at the conference space in the Catskills, our free paper organization's official wrap-up to the week's activities.

I stared down at Lily. Fuck, how had I let that slip my mind?

Oh, that's right. Spending the day with Hannah and Lily. Sleeping with Hannah. Finding out she was pregnant. Getting drunk. Sleeping with her again.

All of that was enough to make anyone forget, I'd say.

And Lily was still crying.

"I'll pick up some Orajel for you tonight, honey. Or Hannah will."

Lily's tears slowed and she blinked at me.

"Hannah?" I tried again, just to see her reaction.

She burped.

Close enough to a smile.

I smiled at her, about to rise to transfer her back to her crib, when she burped again and spit up on my shirt.

Glancing down, I sighed. It wasn't as much spit up as usual, which made sense since she hadn't eaten recently. Maybe this was related to teething?

Who the hell knows?

Why wasn't there a comprehensive handbook for being a father? I didn't mean one of those that glossed over the basics. I wanted one that dealt with every possibility in detail and with pictures.

Unless the pictures would scar me for life.

I picked her up and set her back in her bed, speaking soothingly to her all the while. Then I took off my suit coat and undid the buttons on my shirt before removing it and stepping into the hall. I was just tugging my undershirt up from behind my head—she'd soaked me clear through both—when Hannah's door opened down the hall. She stepped out just as I yanked it off the rest of the way.

I gripped my shirts in my fist, taking in the sight of her in the top from yesterday that barely skimmed her thighs. Her hair was wild around her shoulders and her eyes were sleepy and soft, rousing me in unspeakable ways. Especially when her gaze dropped to my bare chest and lingered there before she looked up again and licked her lips.

"Must you do that?" I said under my breath.

Without giving her time to answer, I turned to head into the master suite with its connecting bathroom.

She followed.

"Do what exactly? Breathe your air? Exist on your planet? Complicate your tidy little world?"

"That's a good one." I tossed the soiled shirts in the hamper and grabbed a handful of tissue to wipe my chest with soapy water.

"Why are you naked?"

"I'm not naked. I have trousers on." Ones that were becoming more uncomfortable by the second.

Did her voice always sound that seductively low in the morning?

"Lily?" she guessed.

"Yes. I think she's teething. Can you get her some Orajel today? If you're able to," I added in an attempt to be conciliatory.

It was the least I could do since I wasn't so much as glancing her way. A smart man knew when he was outmatched.

"Sure. I can do that if you tell me what you meant in the hall." While she spoke, she pulled down a hand towel and passed it to me. Apparently, she wasn't impressed with my tissue clean-up job.

Considering the tissue was hanging off my fingers in sopping clumps, I couldn't fault her logic.

I dumped it in the trash and dried off my chest with the towel instead. "Pardon?"

"Don't 'pardon' me, Asher Wainwright. Tell me what you were referring to."

I opened the drawer under the counter and withdrew the spare pair of glasses I kept in there for mornings such as this one. I slipped them on and turned toward her, frowning at her sound of distress. "What?"

"Nothing." She fled, calling out a response over her shoulder. "I'll get the Orajel."

"Hannah—"

She shut the bedroom door just as I reached it. This woman was going to be the death of me.

Even so, I couldn't deny how knowing she was taking care of Lily helped to ease the relentless knot in my chest. The new one in my groin, however, wasn't as easily placated.

A few minutes later, I was dressed in a new shirt and undershirt and on my way out the door with my jacket and briefcase. More calls came in as I drove to the trade show location, but I ignored them.

My head was full of Hannah.

Always Hannah.

Was she taking a shower now? No, she'd mentioned taking one before bed. That explained why her hair had seemed a little damp in that stolen glance I'd taken of her before her casual move had nearly killed me.

As soon as I arrived at the trade show venue, I pulled into a space and grabbed my phone. But not to return the work calls that had come in.

Nope, I had more pressing business.

You wanted to know what I was referring to? Your mouth. How it drives me crazy when you lick your lips. Yet you do it all. The. Damn. Time.

I didn't know if she'd reply. It was probably better if she didn't due to the long day of work I had ahead of me. But I sat there waiting like a chump just the same.

When her text came through a moment later, I swallowed deeply before reading it.

Yeah, well, I'd feel bad except glasses. GLASSES.

I frowned as I flipped down the car mirror to look at myself. They were standard specs. What did she mean?

Do you have a glasses fetish or something?

Her response was a row of flesh-toned middle finger emojis.

I was grinning when I headed inside. Maybe this day wouldn't be so tiresome to get through after all.

When I emerged late that afternoon after a full slate of meetings and panels and a long, tedious business lunch, I was exhausted. Add in a couple of hours manning the newspaper's "information booth" and dealing with questions from prospective advertisers, and fried was my middle name. It wasn't that long ago I'd become energized at talking with colleagues and strategizing. Now I just felt like none of the tired old ways of handling increased competition from social media could possibly make up for our losses.

The whispers were growing that the newspaper business was a dying breed, especially in print. Forget whispers. They were growing closer to a roar.

And here we were, still arranging deck chairs on the Titanic. Offering sales on advertising and slashing revenue when the whole medium itself was on a downward spiral.

I'd just reached my car when my phone went off again. It seemed as if people had been contacting me all day. I stuck it in the holder and accepted call.

"Wainwright."

"Asher, it's Daly. I just wanted to say I think it's a brilliant idea. I never thought you'd do it, man, but if now's the time, then just go for it. What are you tackling next?"

I blinked. Daly was a sort of friend, the kind you made through work and treated congenially when you saw them then never thought of them otherwise. I knew I was tired, but I couldn't make sense of what he was saying.

"Next?"

"Don't be coy with me. The word was all over the place today. Vincent's certainly stepping up, isn't he? I have to say, it's a bold move to drop the weekly and turn your focus to a monthly newsmagazine with more in depth pieces on local business and agriculture. Pairing it with an online version is—"

"What the hell are you talking about?"

Silence fell across the line. "Oh." He coughed. "You really don't know what I'm talking about?"

The vise around my vocal cords was barely allowing me to speak. At the same time, my shoulders felt suspiciously light. I was defensive, of course. This was my company. My baby—until I'd begun to understand the difference between a child made of figures and facts and a very live breathing one with a heartbeat and gummy smiles.

"No, I don't. But obviously, I'm missing some vital details about my company. Thanks for the heads up."

"Wainwright, wait."

I didn't wait. I ended that call and immediately FaceTimed

Vincent, who answered from the conference room he was still in at the trade show venue. "Asher? What's up?"

In the old days—just a few months ago—he'd called me "Boss". I'd waved it off, since I had always considered us to be friends. We'd been working together for years. Maybe that was my problem. I hadn't exerted enough of an iron rule in the office. How often did I even see Jason? Not often, and he was Wainwright's CFO. Oh, he showed up to weekly meetings, but otherwise, good luck catching him at his desk.

I hadn't pressured him. Nor did I ride Vincent's ass for coming and going pretty much as he pleased as well, including weeklong trips to Saint Tropez on a damn near whim. They did their jobs and the company had been doing well—better than well—so I'd had no complaints.

Now I was scrambling to keep a foothold in a social media world that no longer had much room for a weekly print paper, and Vincent was using his free time to figure out how to steal my grandfather's legacy out from underneath me.

"Hello? You FaceTimed me—weird, by the way, but I'm rolling with it—and now you're not saying anything?"

"I wanted to see your eyes when I ask you if you're trying to take over my company."

Vincent didn't blink. "No. But maybe I should be."

"Excuse me?"

"Let's be real, Asher. Your mind hasn't been fully involved in the business since—well, you know quite well since when."

"Oh, is that so?"

"You know it's so, man. I'm not trying to make it harder on you, but in this climate, there's no room for distractions. Your life has been one giant one for the better part of six months. It certainly doesn't seem like that will be changing either."

Vincent could say that again. He didn't even know about the latest thing that had rocked my world. No one did, except Hannah and I.

Unless she'd told someone, and if so, they were probably judging me right now too.

"What would you have me do? Ignore my responsibilities at home so I can work here twenty-four seven? You haven't seen me jetting off to Saint Tropez recently."

"No, but perhaps you should. The reason I needed that vacation is because I've been busting my ass securing funding despite our shortfalls and trying to convince our advertisers and business partners that we still have something to offer them. Why don't you ask Jason what he's been doing night after night when you've had to run home to deal with feedings? He's been crunching numbers, trying to balance books that can't be balanced." He eased a hip on the conference table he was standing next to. Files and papers were scattered over it in all directions. "Our business model doesn't work any longer, Asher. It just does not."

"The commercial printing side is still quite liquid." Even I could hear the defensiveness in my tone.

"Yes, it is, but the weekly paper is dragging it down. We need to cut that ball and chain loose before it sinks the entire operation."

"That's not your call to make."

"No, you're right. Your name is the one on the building, right?" His mouth twisted into the remnant of a smile. "I'm just the street kid who worked his way up and won't stop until your company makes it through to the other side. So, no, I'm not trying to stage a hostile takeover. More like I have some ideas of what could be. I still have the passion you used to have, Boss."

I wanted to argue with him. How dare he question my passion when he was spreading rumors or whatever the hell he was doing about my company?

Except what if he was right? I hadn't enjoyed work for a while. I couldn't say exactly how long. It had become something to handle. To conquer. I wanted to be able to look back and say I'd brought the business through its roughest period. I'd righted the damn ship, against all odds.

Then I could be certain my grandfather would be proud of me.

Right now? He would not. I wasn't doing a good enough job for the business, and I certainly wasn't nailing my personal life. I had two children now—for all intents and purposes—and their mother didn't think much of me at the moment. Not that I entirely faulted her there.

Wait, she was our baby's mother. Not *theirs*. I was paying her for a service. We weren't some happy little family. How could we be, when all it seemed we knew how to do was hurt each other?

"I didn't spread rumors all over town," Vincent continued, as if he didn't realize the barrage of thoughts he'd caused. "I just talked to Daly. My mistake. I thought he was trustworthy."

"No one is trustworthy," I said before clicking off. Then I just stared at the phone in my hand.

Vincent and I were supposed to do the overnight trip together in a couple of days. That gave me enough time to ready a response—either to take his suggestions under advisement, truly hear them out and give them a chance, or to cut my losses.

And let my right hand man go.

EIGHTEEN

I found a double-padded play mat for our little Houdini. I left it just outside my office. Maybe we can put it together when I get back. Lily is determined to give me gray hair, I'm sure of it. I swear, I checked on the video app nine times last night.

I left money for groceries and whatever else you need since it's shopping day. You have my numbers if you need anything while I'm out of town.

Maybe a cooking lesson when I get back tomorrow. You can show me how you make vegetables actually taste delicious.

ASHER

I PROPPED MY CHIN ON MY HAND AND READ OUR LITTLE COMMUNITY notebook again. He'd been so damn distracted the last few days. Gruff and almost curt, but here, on paper, we worked so well. I got to see some of the real Asher I remembered from our first night together.

Sometimes they were bullet points about some parenting article he read, sometimes it was a funny thing Lily did during the night.

I flipped back a few pages and smoothed my hand down his neat, slashy handwriting that was a mix of block letters and cursive. Here, there was the softness I remembered.

Dangerous thoughts, girl.

I wasn't even sure which Asher was the real one. We just didn't know each other enough. Obviously, we had done well enough that we'd made a human, but other than that, not so much.

Not to mention the fan of actual hundred-dollar bills he'd left me.

Plural.

Like he'd leave for his mistress.

Okay, not mistress. There would need to be sex still going on for that to be a factor, but still. It seemed a little excessive for the three of us for food for a week. It wasn't as if I cooked with truffle oil, for God's sake. And didn't he know me? I was the original budget girl. I could make a dollar stretch.

Well, ten dollars. Hello inflation.

Then again, my salary was enough to buy groceries and rent a house. Weekly.

I hadn't even wanted to discuss money with him because of the pregnancy, but I had to be able to take Lily to any doctor's appointments that came up.

I barely read the agreement we'd finally signed, salary included. Everything was just so damn overwhelming. Cooking was easier to deal with.

I pulled over my iPad and flicked through the series of recipes I'd been putting together. So far, I'd come up with twenty-seven recipes for the winter season for my new company. In fact, I had four slow cookers simmering as well as two brand new Instant Pots I'd bought with my first paycheck.

I'd put extra money on each of my sisters' food accounts at college and I still had a tidy stack of money sitting in my bank. More money than I'd seen in a damn long time. I should feel a little guilty for how much, but seeing how much he flashed around for groceries...

Well, the guilt thing was definitely not a factor anymore.

I was in the middle of updating my website for *Hannah's Helping Hand Boxes* when a text popped up on my screen.

"Finally, an adult conversation," I muttered aloud.

I was doing that a lot lately.

I quickly replied to my best friend's text and rushed to the front of the house to meet her. Lily was down for her mid-morning nap and I was in hardcore work mode during the two hours she slept. Especially since Asher's note was very accurate. Lily was definitely a Houdini these days.

Speaking of Houdini, I checked my phone app for the crib monitor just before I got to the front door. The little girl was still in angel form —aka sleeping. Though that wouldn't last for very much longer. I did a quick check through the peephole on the front door—couldn't be too careful—and swung it open.

"Hi." I rushed toward my bestie and gathered her into a fierce hug.

"Hey. Did someone die?" She patted my back weakly.

A quick prick of tears hit me sideways at the familiar vanilla and orange blossom scent of my best friend in all the world. "No. It's just been a damn long couple of weeks." I got a hold of myself and stepped back. "Wow, you look great." I tipped my head. "Did you cut your hair?"

Gabby—Gabriela Ramos, to be exact—pushed her way into the house and unfurled her miles long scarf from her neck. I was pretty sure she'd made it. If it was an Instagram fad, my bestie usually tried it. Knitting had been all the craze last year and I had two scarves to show for it in my closet.

"I did. Thank you for noticing." She spun around in the foyer before dumping her overnight bag and coat on the little bench. "This is quite the gig, girl."

"I know. Asher is insanely rich, obviously." I hung up her coat and gave her the wiggle fingers to pass over her scarf.

"Asher, huh?"

Hmm. I suppose most nannies would go with Mr. Wainwright. *Oops.*

Gabby peeked down the hallway that ended in the huge formal dining room we never used. Her huge brown eyes were a little shell-shocked. I knew how she felt. The house was very luxe, but somehow not cold. "Well, those Wainwrights sure knew how to embed themselves into Central New York. I'm pretty sure they singlehandedly covered the cost of the rebuild on the gazebo in the park in Syracuse after that big storm took out the roof."

"How do you know these things?"

She shrugged. "I don't know. Stupid trivia sticks in my head. You know, like recipes stick in yours."

"How's John?" I hung up her coat and scarf in the main closet.

"Who?"

"The guy you were seeing around New Year's?"

"Oh, I got rid of him already. Okay, so technically he ghosted me first, but I totally was going to do the same. He was boring with a capital and italicized B."

I shook my head. Gabby went through men like she went through her Instagram fads. But she was sweet, so men flocked to her like lemonade on a hot day. She could charge a damn ten spot for a glass of her lemonade and they'd keep coming back for more. There was something about her that made men want to take care of her.

Unfortunately, she loved to let them. And the ones she chose didn't have a long-term plan about anything, including her.

I'd lost count of how many times she'd gotten her heart broken, but somehow she always got up and tried again. She was convinced Prince Charming was out there.

"I started seeing another guy, Frank, but then he kissed me, and the spark died a tragic death bathed in halitosis."

I scrunched my nose. "Yeah, that won't work."

"No way. I like kissing and the duck and cover should only be used for fires or hiding from Mami during the holidays when she asks me why I'm not married already."

"She does realize we're in our mid-twenties, right?"

Gabby shot a look over her shoulder as she sailed through the living room to the large archway that led to the kitchen. The open floor plan of this house meant there were many different ways to explore it. "As far as Mami's concerned, I should be spitting out a second kid by now. If it was good enough for her, it's good enough for all her girls."

I instinctively put my hand over my still flat belly. Well, mostly flat, since I'd enjoyed my cooking a little too much since my sisters had gone away to school.

Eating my feelings? I chose to look at it like I was making sure my recipes worked.

Even if things with Asher didn't work out, I had the Ramos family to lean on. Bonnie always treated me like one of her daughters. She had four of them by blood, so what was one more? At least that was what she always told me.

Maybe I'd have to believe her someday.

Especially since Asher and I couldn't be in the same room without tense silence or child-rearing conversations wedging between us. And none of them were about the baby I was carrying. We both kept avoiding that one.

It was all about Lily right now.

Safe in all ways. It was as if she was an actual mutual wall we spoke over every day like neighbors. Until the nighttime. Then we went to our separate corners. After we cleaned up from dinner and put Lily to bed, Asher would close himself into his home office and do… whatever it was moguls of large companies did. I wasn't sure because he never shared anything with me.

Except the hot, heavy looks across the hallway in the middle of the night when we fought over who would take care of Lily when she awakened with one of a half-dozen needs. The last few nights had been teething in the extreme. Everything was fair game for her mouth lately.

I was pretty sure her drool was going to be part of my DNA soon.

"Girl, I'm never going to keep those five pounds off my ass if you keep cooking things with biscuits."

I caught up to Gabby and met her at the huge kitchen island. "Keep those paws off my dough. It's not done resting yet."

"Speaking of, how many deliveries do I have to make today?"

"Seven."

"Hey, that's pretty good."

I shrugged. "It's growing slowly. Better than the three it was last week."

"Word of mouth. My mom talks you up all the time. Of course, she calls your website the Facebook, but small steps." She put air quotes around the word Facebook.

I laughed. "Are you sure I'm not keeping you from anything tonight?"

She pulled the top off one of the slow cookers and moaned. "Bathing suit season? What's in there?"

"Beef stew."

Before she could reach into the bubbling food and burn herself, I smacked her hand. "Sit, I'll make you a bowl."

She made a face at me but followed direction. "What time does the kiddo go to bed?"

"It's only ten-thirty in the morning."

She rolled her eyes. "I know, but I'm thinking about tonight already. I even brought a bottle of wine." She glanced at her watch. "And it's eleven, thank you."

That wine was going to be a party for one. God, I had to tell her everything and I so didn't know how. "I haven't even made the gravy for this yet." But I ladled out a bit of vegetables and meat because I knew she'd eat it regardless of the biscuits and gravy. "I can make you a sandwich."

"Nope. I'm ready for whatever that is."

I shook my head and added a little broth. "Thanks for coming over to help."

"Sure. It's easier for me to do the deliveries around the transcription work I do than for you to put Lily in a carseat. Not that a cute kid doesn't help sell stuff. They'd probably think you were a single mom and double their order."

I swallowed. That would be a true statement in a few months. "Yes, well, if things get a little bigger, we'll both be making deliveries. At least that's the hope." I pushed aside the panic of telling my best friend all my news. "Anyway, that handy bilingual thing keeps you busy all the time, so it's still a big ask."

She waved me off and gave me heart eyes as I set down the food in front of her. "All good. It gets me away from the screen. Ugh. I love my mother's food, but you do the best comfort food in the damn state."

"Even if it doesn't have Spanish spices?"

She hovered her nose over the bowl. "Rosemary is just as good."

I floured the marble countertop and used my steel cutter to make little piles. "I added another half-dozen recipes to the site. Hopefully, that will make people want to try me out."

"How many do you have cooking today?" She waved her spoon.

"Six and three different kinds of cookies prepped in the fridge."

"You're crazy. That's six different full meals for one client each."

"It's a good way to try out the recipes. And whatever is left I freeze in man-sized portions for Asher. His hours are crazy."

"So, how is that going? That's a lot of man flesh to have to work around. Not sure I could do it without trying to pounce on him. Especially since I looked up Mr. Asher Wainwright on the internet just to get a look see of how gorgeous this new daddy was—and girl, that's some wrong."

I dumped the biscuit dough out of the bowl. "Fine. Not a big deal."

Just got very pregnant and then decided to have sex with him a couple more times like an idiot. No big deal.

Was I supposed to just blurt it out?

Oh, God. How was I going to tell my sisters?

Everything was such a cluster. Except cooking. That I could do. And focus on so that I didn't lose my mind completely.

"Somehow I do not believe you. He's hot with like five fire emojis."

More like ten. Even more so when he was naked. In my limited scope, it was a rare man who looked just as good in a suit as out of one.

"He's attractive, but that's not a big deal."

Except that he follows me into dreams almost every night.

I kept reliving the night of the New Year's Eve snowstorm. How he touched me and never stopped. How he was wild for me and made me just as wild for him.

"Tell that to your flushed cheeks, chica." Gabby leaned forward, her spoon dripping on the counter.

I picked up my spray bottle and towel to clean up after her.

She only rolled her eyes and lifted the bowl, scooping up another piece of carrot before putting it back down. "I don't blame you. It's like a Hallmark movie come to life. Sweet single dad who needs you desperately. Talk about fantasy. I mean, I don't know if he's sweet, but I'm assuming he's not a monster. Though I've watched the ones with the grumpy guy who's inept, and those are equally hot."

When I didn't say anything, she put the spoon down with a snap. "What?"

She squinted at me.

"What?"

"How could you?"

"How could I what?"

"Are you flirty with this dude?"

"Can we stop talking about Asher?"

"I don't know, can we? Seems like he's an interesting topic."

"Not really. We barely speak."

We just like to use our tongues and other body parts.

God, so many other ways to use our mouths.

"Okay, so what's the problem? You can have the hots for your boss. We're heading for 2020. It's not that big of a deal."

"I'm pregnant."

"Whoa. What? When did that happen? Weren't you a virgin like a second ago?"

I studied my floured fingers, picking the sticky dough off with painstaking slowness. "Not exactly. More like three months ago."

"And you didn't tell me? Wait—you actually finally got a dicking and you didn't tell me? First of all, that's not cool. But baby? Who? How?"

"I don't know!"

I was pretty sure her jaw was heading for the floor. "You don't know the dude's name? Who are you?"

"No, I know his name. I mean, I don't know how it happened. We used a condom, dammit. I finally got up the courage to go for it with a man who made me feel something and I got pregnant right away."

"*Madre di dios.* My worst nightmare. Then again, I was more like seventeen when I let Paul Carson pop my cherry. But we're *not* talking about that."

"Or the fact that you let Paul do the popping. What were you thinking?"

"There were extenuating circumstances and an unfortunate amount of Fireball in my system. He was a really good kisser, but don't distract me. This is not about my virginity."

It was remarkably easy to distract her, but of course, this had to be one of those rare times she didn't go off on a tangent.

"So, you had a one-night stand that ended up with…" She looked down at my middle. "How far along?"

"New Year's."

"And you didn't tell me?"

"I just found out. I'm one of those weird women who almost has her period even after she's pregnant, which seems excessively cruel since that should be a perk. At least it's not an ongoing thing. Just tricked me into believing I was in the clear."

"That is weird, but why didn't you tell me? Was it that bad? Was he a vagrant or something?"

"No. He was amazing. It was amazing," I sniffed as the tears sprang out of nowhere.

After that incredible night, now I had this little bean growing inside me. And I couldn't be mad about it, even if I didn't know how to work things out with Asher right now.

She rushed around the kitchen island to me. "Oh, no. Don't you cry, then I'll start crying." She threw her arms around me. "It's okay. We'll do this together just like we do everything. I just wish you'd told me. You know you don't have to do everything alone, right?"

"I know." I rested my cheek on her shoulder, her soft sweater soothing me just as much as her familiar scent. I didn't stay there long though, or I'd be a bawling mess. It was my default just to deal with things and move on.

"So, flirting with the hot rich dude is definitely a bit weird. I get it."

"Yeah, about that."

"Oh my God. You already slept with Asher too? When you get going, you really get going."

I had to laugh, because what else could I do? "Not exactly. I mean, yes, I slept with Asher, but—"

"But what? Wow, by the state of your cheeks, I'm going to say you have the keys to orgasm city, but again, you didn't tell me." She shook my shoulders.

"I couldn't. I didn't want to even own up to it myself, especially since we ruin things as soon as we get naked. It's like he puts his size-twelve foot in his damn mouth directly after."

She tilted her head. "Size twelve? Wow, so he's rich and hung? That seems unfair."

"Why? Because he has big feet?"

She gave me bland look.

"How am I supposed to know?"

"Well, you've been with two guys."

"Uh, no. It's Asher's baby."

"Wait." Gabby pushed her hair back from her face, exasperation lighting her eyes. "You've only worked for him for a week."

"Yeah, it's complicated."

"I need more food to understand this whole thing. Like a lot more food. And you need to explain. Pronto."

I looked back down at my unevenly cut biscuit dough with a sigh. Even talking about Asher made chaos take over my life. How many times had I divided up biscuit dough this week? Oh, only every day.

She went to the large crockpot and fixed herself another bowl. Then spotted the cheese biscuits I'd put aside for my clients.

"Hey."

She took one with a shrug. "Your penance for not telling me about all the good-goods, woman. Now spill."

And I did. I told her about the snowstorm and how wonderful it had been for a first time. At least I only had my experience to go by. Of course, then there was the fact that I split the morning after as if it had been a dirty little secret. Then about Bess and how I ended up working for him and just how insane my life had become.

Gabby's huge brown eyes were saucers by the time I was finished. And another bowl of stew was gone.

"Wow."

"Yeah. So, you can see it's been a tense few weeks."

"Yes, but it didn't have to be. You could have come to me."

"I didn't know how." I dumped my overworked biscuit dough into the trash. Crap. That would set me back, and Lily could wake up any minute. "I was trying to put it behind me and to get my business going. Hello, I just sent my sisters off to college. I really wasn't interested in doing this all over again." I pointed to the baby bottles in the drying rack.

"Your sisters weren't babies when you took over."

"No, but I helped raise them. I'm well-versed in this whole thing. But Lily is so sweet, and Bess is a force. And God, the money seemed like it would be good. Then I walk into this crazy mansion and find Asher."

"Hello, one hot night dude."

"I figured I would do this until *Hannah's Helping Hand Boxes* got off the ground. I didn't even know I was pregnant when I took the job. Well, he sort of strong-armed me into it, although I already adored Lily. Then…" I sighed.

"Then you have a baby daddy and a boss. You really are a Hallmark movie. A dirty one, but whoa."

"Shut up."

She waggled her eyebrows. "Seriously. You got way lucky with the good nookie thing. That doesn't usually happen the first time."

"Orgasms are the least of my problems. I have a half-going business, yes, but…"

"But what? You have a rent-free situation here and an adorable baby to babysit while you get things going. Hell, you can finally sell your folks' house. You never loved being back there anyway."

"Except I might need that house, after all."

"The girls are super happy at college. They don't even come home for vacations anymore."

"Yeah, well, I might need it for *my* baby."

"You told Asher, right?"

"Of course, I did. It's so damn awkward we don't even talk about it. I can't count on him sticking around."

"Fuck that."

"Gabriela Maria!"

She flushed. "Don't use that mom voice on me. It's a good one though. You're a natural."

I lowered my forehead to the cool marble countertop. I needed a time out. "I hate you."

She continued to eat. Loudly. At least from her slurps I could tell my food was good. "Nah, you love me. Now that I've completely killed my diet, let's start packing these badboys up, huh?"

I straightened up. "That's a good plan."

As if she was waiting for me to get ready to work, Lily's cries came crackling out of the baby monitor. "Hold that thought."

"Want me to start?"

My hands itched to do it. I had a particular way I wanted things packed up. But honestly, something had to give. I needed help if my business was going to continue to grow. "Thanks. That would be great. The boxes are in the cupboard right by you."

She bent down and started rummaging around. "These are so cute."

I grabbed my phone. "I'll be back in a few minutes."

She waved me off. "I've got this. No worries."

Maybe things were looking up a little. I climbed the stairs to the nursery and wished to God I'd checked the video sooner. "Oh, Lily."

Evidently, Houdini now knew how to get herself out of her diaper as well. And it definitely wasn't a happy diaper.

It was time to try one of those sleep sacks I'd talked about with Asher. They would limit her mobility just enough so she couldn't scale any cribs. Or fling any poo.

I scooped her up and headed right for the bathroom. It was going to be a long day.

Welcome to your new life, Hannah.

NINETEEN

"Lily, no." I sighed and dumped the two pans I'd planned to wash into the sink.

My favorite little redhead was nearly unrecognizable. She had Spaghetti-Os plastered across her cheeks up to her hairline. Little triangles of hot dogs I'd cut up for her littered the floor around her high chair. She was just starting to get the hang of human food on a hit-or-miss basis.

The rest of the hotdogs had been my lunch, now cold.

I usually made something far more nutritious for her, but I was seriously dragging after my girls' night with Gabby. Even minus the wine, we'd talked well into the night. And because she was a devil, she'd gotten way too many details out of me about Asher.

Add in the five hours of sleep I'd managed to get—thank you, Baby Orajel—and I was ready for a nap with the kiddo. Lily, however, had no such plans for sleep. Plus, she needed another bath thanks to her abject failure with finger food.

Emma had loved Spaghetti-Os. I remember her being just as covered in them when I helped my mom with lunch time.

I blinked back the quick prick of tears. It was times like this that made me miss my mom the most.

The fact that I was sure I had a picture of Emma in a similar state as Lily made me grab my phone off the counter and catch it for posterity. Maybe Asher would enjoy seeing it. I stuffed my phone into my back pocket and reached for the baby wipes I had at the ready. "You, my little princess, are a hot mess." I started with her hand and picked noodles out of her fist with the first wipe. "My goodness. What would your dad say?"

"He'd say, what the hell happened to my kitchen?"

I spun around, the smashed pasta smearing across my apron. "Asher, hi." My heart picked up speed as I quickly turned back to Lily. "Oh, this is nothing. You should see what she did with peas yesterday." I moved to the side. "Say hi, Lily Patch."

Her delighted squeal filled me with joy. She was truly the cutest baby.

When I glanced back at Asher, instead of the soft smile I usually found on his face, he was frowning. Exhaustion dug brackets along both sides of his distractible mouth. He was still wearing his aviator sunglasses and his scarlet tie was askew.

"How was your trip?"

"Fine."

My spine tingled. His voice was tight. "You caught us right in the middle of crazy lunchtime. She's discovering the glory of—"

"Processed food? Is that what you're feeding her? What you'll be feeding our baby?"

"Excuse me?" I dropped the baby wipe I was using. Lily immediately picked it up off the tray and stuck it in her mouth. Her sweet laughter turned to instant tears at the taste of the light soap in the material. "Dammit," I muttered as I unlocked the tray to unbuckle her.

"What happened to my kitchen?"

"I was working on my meals for my business. I was just about to clean up when your daughter decided to fling her food. So, yeah, I was a little backed up on the dishes."

"Your sole job should be taking care of Lily. That's what I pay you for."

I hugged Lily tighter to me. I knew he wasn't *this* guy deep down. He was too good with Lily—and with me when he let himself relax—but right now, he was the rigid Asher who made me want to pack my stuff and run.

"This agreement only works as long as we both are happy with it. What am I supposed to do when that is no longer the case?"

His jaw locked. "You're truly that unhappy?"

There. The flash of fear made me want to hug both of them to me and never let go. But I was still me. I'd pushed aside everything I needed before to be the rock for someone. Two someones—and it was happening all over again.

Guilt swamped me, even as my spine stiffened. I couldn't let him railroad me. Lily was the most important person in all of this.

And our child.

"I'm not just a mom, Asher. I'm not even totally a mom yet and I know that. I want more. I'm always going to want more. It's okay for you to have a career and not me?"

"I never said that." He raked his fingers through his hair. "You're the most capable woman I know."

Lily tucked her face into my neck, her cries subsiding as I swayed with her. "Then don't come in here with that attitude and take out your crappy day on me."

His face closed off. "Don't claim to know what's going on with my day."

"Why would I? You just come in here with a scowl instead of coming to see her. She missed you last night."

He tipped back his head.

I knew it was a direct hit. I also knew it was a shitty thing to say when he was exhausted, but I just didn't care. I was tired of his crap.

I was pretty much tired of everything.

"I have to get her cleaned up." Lily reached out a hand for him as we walked by. I couldn't hold her away from him. It wasn't fair. To his credit, he didn't shrink away from her sticky fingers. He leaned down and kissed her chubby little hand, and his scent made me want to lean into him to let him hug me. To make me feel a little bit better. And that was far too dangerous.

I couldn't count on anyone but me. Watching everyone walk away from me reminded me of that every damn day.

"I'm sorry, Hannah. I would never belittle your work. I just don't want you to think you *have* to work. You, Lily, and our baby are all that's important to me."

"You have a funny way of showing it." My voice was raspy with emotion. I knew he meant it, but he sucked at showing it unless I cornered him.

Before he could say anything else, I escaped the kitchen and headed upstairs. Lily's lower lip trembled, but she didn't make a sound. She only clutched me tighter. "I'm sorry, little one. He just makes me crazy."

By the end of her bath, she was laughing once more. I took a little extra time to play with her with the tub soap I'd picked up. The foam was colored and stuck to the tiles until I rinsed it away. Keeping her in the tub seat was growing more difficult. Independence was her middle name. I used the low flow setting and rinsed her off as well as the walls.

We were both giggling by the time I bundled her up in her turtle hoodie towel, then we played on the new mat that Asher had bought for her. I couldn't wait to put it down until he got back. Not with her level of acrobatics and urge to climb.

I was forever worried I'd come in too late and she'd break an arm or her freaking neck.

But this time with her? The afternoons where we sat and read half a dozen books? This was our favorite time. Her fluffy reddish-brown hair was getting curlier by the day, and her eyes were so often wide with fascination.

She'd burrowed inside my heart so quickly. The place she'd made would be hers forever, I was sure.

She curled in close, her thumb in her mouth. She wasn't a thumbsucker by nature, but when she was tired, it seemed to be the first thing she looked for. I read *Winnie the Pooh* to her for the third time and didn't make it through the story before both of us were asleep.

I woke to Asher slipping the baby out of my hold. I was so exhausted I'd fallen asleep sitting up. His soft singsong voice almost immediately soothed Lily back to sleep.

If I was smart, I would've told him to wake her. When she napped too much in the afternoon, it was impossible to get her to go to bed, but they were so sweet together that I couldn't pull the trigger on sense.

He set her down and leaned over the crib rail, his large hand stroking her back with such gentleness that my chest tightened. When he backed away and turned to me, it was almost as if he was embarrassed to be caught tending to her. But then he reached his hand out to me and helped me to my feet.

Instead of letting me go, he drew me closer, touching his forehead to mine. He always seemed to smell of leather and ink, a soothing combination of old and new.

As his large hand smoothed over my back, there was a distinctly different flavor to the emotions rolling through me.

Sweet Asher was something I didn't quite know how to deal with. That he did such a quick and distinct turn into the physical man I still dreamed about left me breathless. He didn't ask for anything more than closeness. The air was charged between us and I didn't think I would have said no if he'd leaned down and kissed me.

The indecision swirled in his hazel eyes, but then he brushed a soft kiss over my temple and slipped away from me.

I was about to chase after him to ask what the hell I was supposed to do with these feelings when Lily stirred. Asher paused in the doorway, but I waved him off and scooped her up. We'd slept most of the afternoon away.

And my schedule was now a hot mess.

I got her dressed and we went into the hall. I shook my head at the closed door to Asher's office. "Come on, little girl. Time to pack up dinners for Gabby to pick up."

After we went downstairs to the kitchen, instead of finding a mess,

I discovered Asher had done all the dishes. He'd even put them away. Frankly, I was shocked he knew where they went. Then again, I'd find out just how little he knew when I went looking for pots and pans.

But it was the thought that counted. And he'd saved me about thirty minutes of cleanup.

I dragged in the pack and play from the living room and set Lily up with her favorite toys as was our routine. She was an avid fan of Harry Styles and Taylor Swift, which was the brunt of my current favorite playlist. Sometimes a woman just needed some angst and happily ever afters mixed together.

The rest of the day was a blur. Gabby didn't have enough time for a visit, so it was just the two of us for the duration of the day. Asher didn't even come down for dinner. Then again, I didn't go up and invite him down.

But we had a schedule and he knew it. At least that was what I kept telling myself when I was cleaning strained carrots off of Lily's face.

Maybe it was just as well he'd stayed locked away. It was probably for the best we stayed to our own spaces for a bit.

I left a wrapped plate on the counter for Asher and went upstairs to do our nighttime routine. For once, Lily went down without any issue.

At a loss with what to do with myself, I tried to curl into the chair in my bedroom with my journal. It had become more of a work and recipes catch-all these days, but it wasn't holding my interest as it usually did. I was restless in the extreme. Part of me wanted to march down to Asher's office and ask him what the hell was going on between us, but the other half of me didn't really want to know.

Answers meant I'd have to face all this…stuff. Raising a baby with a man I barely knew but ached for. A traitorous body that was growing a human but didn't really feel that different.

In all of the baby books I was reading, they talked about changes and hormones and so many different aspects of pregnancy. Me? I just wanted to strip down to nothing at night. Spring fever or pregnancy? Who was to say?

I hadn't had nausea since the first day. For all I knew, that could've been nerves.

Sore boobs and increased sex drive were the only signs I could really identify with. I didn't even know if that was because of being pregnant or having good sex that I hadn't realized I'd been missing.

I couldn't settle all evening. In the end, the only thing that sounded good to me was ice cream.

I peered down the hallway. Both Asher's bedroom and office doors were shut. Well, his upstairs office. He also had a library downstairs, a room I tended to love to hide out in. I didn't want to analyze if he was working more upstairs to leave me to the library.

Some things were better left alone.

I slipped out, my robe swishing around me as I sneaked down the stairs. The lights were off, so I knew Asher had finally gone down for something to eat sometime between Lily's bedtime and mine.

I went right for the freezer. "Where are you?" I whispered as I dug deeper into the bottom freezer drawer of the fridge. I knew I'd stashed a half gallon of peanut butter fudge.

"Looking for this, perhaps?"

I screeched and whirled around. My heart skipped as I shoved the drawer closed. "Are you trying to give me a heart attack?"

The quick flash of white in the moonlight told me he was more amused than contrite.

"Why are you eating ice cream in the dark?"

"Could ask you the same."

"Well, do you have another spoon?"

"No, but you can share mine."

I crossed my arms to disguise my very braless state. I could get my own spoon, of course, but something told me to go sit with him at the little bench seating in the corner of the kitchen. The slats from the shutters left him in shadow, but there was enough light to tell me he was sitting there without a shirt.

Go back upstairs, Hannah.

Ignoring that voice was always bad for my panties. Hell, it was the reason I was in this whole situation. Yet I found myself crossing the room to sit across from him at the little table where we occasionally shared a meal. Only this felt far more intimate.

Still, I didn't turn on the light. I liked the dark. Liked the softness between us.

Maybe we needed the cover of night to actually be civil toward one another.

"I see you were feeling a little heated tonight too?"

He glanced down at his chest. "I've been stuck in a suit for days. I didn't even want to wear a damn T-shirt tonight."

"Can't say I mind." I glanced down at my chipped nails. The last vestiges of my girls' night were already fading since I did so much with my hands during the day.

God, my palms were itching to reach across the table to see if his chest was as warm as I remembered.

"Good to know you like at least part of me."

"Feeling sorry for yourself again?"

He scraped a spoonful out ice cream out of the carton. "Never let me get away with anything, do you?"

"Well, you know you're attractive. All hot men know they are."

He looked up from the carton. "Excuse me?"

"Oh, so you don't know you're rocking a six-pack or eight-pack or whatever is going on over there?"

"Would you like a better look?"

"No. I remember."

He didn't say anything, but that smile was back.

"Are you going to share?"

His lips twitched, but then he held out the spoon. I'm not sure what possessed me to lean in and accept it, but he watched me very carefully slide the creamy perfection off the spoon. I may have licked my lips a little more than necessary. Maybe.

The groan that left him made me smile back. It felt good to regain a more even footing with him.

At least we were both equally crazy.

"What are you doing down here in the dark?" I asked.

His smile faded. Dammit, I couldn't just let it be us sitting here enjoying a treat. Nope.

"Couldn't sleep." He scraped off another spoonful for me.

"Me neither." I took it and the cool sweetness melted on my tongue.

"Why?"

I shrugged. "Restless. Hot. Bored. Take your pick."

"D, all of the above?"

Another spoonful and an ice cream headache would be heading my way. When I shook my head, he ate the next one.

"What about you?"

"I have some decisions to make that I'm not all that happy about."

"Is that why you've been so grumpy?"

He gave me a mercurial half-smile. "Some of it."

"And the rest?"

His dark eyes shined in the semi-darkness. Sometimes the hazel edged toward the deepest brown shade. "Takes a lot of work to stop myself from crossing the hall every night and slipping into your bed."

"Oh." My heart hammered as I twisted my fingers under the table.

"I know I don't deserve that privilege."

I didn't know how to react to that confessional. Not when I had a similar problem following me around. "We never had a problem with the bedroom, Asher."

"No, we sure didn't."

I wasn't exactly sure how to avoid that landmine. If we talked about naked time, there would be ice cream pooling on the table. Probably under my butt when he put me up on the table. You know, for instance.

Lord, I didn't need to be thinking about that. I was already hot and bothered with his oh-so-male scent in the air between us. Especially mixed with my favorite ice cream of late.

"What decisions do you need to make?" I asked instead of going that road.

"Just going to ignore the hallway thing?"

"Right now? Yes."

211

His stupidly long lashes swept over his cheeks, and the shadows of the moonlight carved his angular face into even more fascinating lines. All of it mixed together to draw me closer to him—and not just for his sweet treats. His salty ones were just as alluring.

And that line of thinking was definitely going to melt the ice cream.

Instinct pushed me to take a chance. I stood and nudged him over on his side of the table. I pushed the ice cream away and took his hand. "What's weighing on you so much?"

He swallowed but didn't say anything.

I cupped his cheek. "Saying things in the dark makes it easier. That's how my sisters would tell me the scariest problems they ever faced. Then again, theirs were more about how to break up with a boy."

"Well, this is sort of a breakup."

I braced. Was that what this was all about? He didn't know how to let me down easy? To walk away?

"I'm thinking about stepping down from my company. At least the day to day operations."

"What?"

That was not the angle I was expecting.

"I won't bore you with the specifics of the publishing business, but needless to say, things are changing in a big way. I've been holding on to try to maintain the legacy my grandfather built. The newspaper that he loved with everything inside him. It was the most important thing to the Wainwrights and…"

"And it's not to you?"

He bowed his head. "No." His voice was little more than a sandpapery whisper. "I used to live for the paper, and now the only thing I love about the paper is—"

"Memories," I finished for him.

His shoulders sagged as if my understanding helped to unburden him. "Yes."

"Are you thinking about selling it?"

"No. No, I'd never do that. There's far too much history there."

"But…"

"But this is the thing I used to share with my grandfather. The paper was everything to him. It used to be the same for me."

"What changed?"

"I don't know. Maybe it's the enormity of running everything. All the endless administration. I don't know how he did it all."

"Well, I'm sure he had a team. A good business is about more than who is on the masthead. I'm sure he taught you that."

"He did, but he also never let me forget about the importance of leaving the Wainwright name behind when I'm gone."

"But if you're leaving it behind to no one, how does that work?"

"That's the problem. I'm drowning in the business part without any of the love. All I remember is how my grandfather would beam when he talked about the newspaper. When he brought me to the printing room to show me how it all work. Ink forever stained his fingers, even when he wasn't actually a newspaper man any longer. He loved being part of the stories."

I tipped my head against his shoulder. "When's the last time you read the newspaper?"

"Every issue."

"I mean, really read it."

He raked a hand through his hair.

I pulled down his hand and laced our fingers under the table. "A long time?"

"I honestly can't remember when I've read more than the headlines I approved. I'm not the editor. We have one of those, and even he's been going to Vincent more than to me."

"If you love it and want to get into the creation side again, that's not a bad thing."

His hand tightened around mine. "I don't."

"You know Bess only wants you to be happy. She's not exactly the most traditional person, Asher."

"I know, but I feel like I'm letting everyone down. The more time I'm at work, the less time I'm here with Lily. The less time I'm here with you." His voice was rough and low. "But then I'm here and I know I'm dropping the ball at work. Vincent has been taking on more duties and has so many ideas. Good ones that I've been ignoring."

I let him keep talking. It all came out in a rush. The plans Vincent had for expanding the brand into a monthly magazine instead of a weekly newspaper. Possibly moving from only paper media into podcasts and maybe even a news show, although that was farther in the future.

I could hear the thrum of excitement under the guilt.

I couldn't disagree with Vincent's ideas because that was the way I got world and entertainment updates. Various podcasts were the only reason I was remotely informed. It was the easiest way to consume information while I was cooking.

Finally, Asher ran out of gas. "I can't disappoint Gran. She's done so much for me."

It wasn't my place to tell him what to do. But knowing how much was on his shoulders made everything make so much more sense.

"It guts me to think about telling her that I hate it. And I hate that I hate it. How can so much change in a few years?"

I pulled his hand over to my middle. "Things can change in just a few months."

He gripped the still mostly flat expanse of my stomach, and I cupped both of mine over his. "It's not selfish to want more than work. To want a legacy that includes a flesh and blood family. Talk to Bess. Talk to Vincent."

I turned into him and he curled his arms around my shoulders as if it was the most natural thing in the world. He held me so very tight. Almost too tightly, but I didn't pull back.

I needed some of his strength too. And while our little baby was coming freaking fast, I felt like I wasn't alone for the first time.

As if maybe we were building a legacy too.

TWENTY

Asher

AFTER A LONG MONDAY, I WASN'T ANY CLOSER TO A DECISION ABOUT Vincent.

We hadn't discussed anything other than the usual work things last week. Our overnight away at the trade show wrap-up had been more of the same. Somehow we'd come to an unspoken agreement not to speak about anything but that day's agenda.

Coming home to Hannah on Saturday had been both a blessing and a curse. I'd stopped at the gym on the way back because I'd been too full of anger and frustration. I didn't want to bring any of that home to her and the baby. They didn't deserve that.

Yet I'd still snapped at her about stupid canned pasta.

Over the past week, I'd probably let on more than I wanted to. She was an intuitive woman. And I wasn't nearly as good at hiding my thoughts as I'd once believed.

My poker face must have vanished right along with my supposed passion.

I knew one thing. I had no problem feeling passionate toward Hannah, as our ice cream middle of the night date had proven quite well.

Resisting that woman was proving to be hell on my libido. And my heart.

Other niggles of interest were starting to take hold too. I didn't know if opening up to her—or trying to, despite the freaking walls upon walls we both had around us—had unlocked some of the other juggernauts inside me, but I was becoming curious about things that had never fascinated me before.

Like podcasts.

Daly had mentioned that word in passing the other day, and it had been stuck in my head ever since. I'd done some research over the weekend when I'd been closed into my study at home, communicating with Hannah with notes and iPad videos because it was easier. Less sticky.

Less likely to end up with us naked. We were both understandably wary about that.

Perhaps Vincent was righter than I'd given him credit for. I'd felt more flickers of excitement from looking into what equipment doing a news podcast would require than I did about selling advertising and plotting media campaigns. By far.

I hit replay on the video on my computer screen one more time. Before the picture came into focus, baby laughter filled my office. Despite the headache brewing behind my eyes, I couldn't help smiling. Hannah clapped her hands and the laughter grew louder as Lily pumped her legs and smashed her hands gleefully in the bowl of applesauce Hannah had placed before her. A dollop landed on Hannah's forehead and she sighed, still smiling. Her adoration for the baby was evident in every line of her face.

As soon as it ended, I played it again. With every viewing, the tension in my shoulders and behind my eyes bled away.

She'd started doing the videos by accident, I think. She'd tried to take a photo and had accidentally recorded a clip instead. Once she sent it to me, I'd asked for more. I liked seeing the record of their days together. There was no pressure for me, since I wasn't there to mess things up.

No, I was at work, messing things up here instead.

My phone rang and I grabbed it without looking. "Wainwright."

"Snug, your favorite person is home."

I grinned. "All in one piece?"

"Yes. How's my Lily girl?"

"She's good. Teething we think, and on the verge of walking." Another of Hannah's video clips had shown Lily attempting another step. That one I'd received while running as if a serial killer was chasing me on the treadmill Sunday morning.

My life might be fucked up, but I was in excellent cardiovascular shape.

"And I have a surprise for you."

"Funny that." I glanced back at the screen where I'd paused the video on a still of Hannah leaning over Lily's high chair. Her sweater draped just right so that I could imagine what she would look like with a swollen belly.

Soon enough, I'd know for real.

I cleared my throat. "I have a surprise for you too, Gran."

"Oh, do you now? Is your surprise that you're finally getting along with that sweet girl? She doesn't know you only strike out like a bear when you have a burr in your paw."

With effort, I dragged my gaze away from Hannah. Her honey-colored hair had tumbled into her face and she was caught in a laugh, her dancing blue eyes alight. I loved seeing her happy. Moments like that had been far too rare between us. Other than the snowy afternoon we'd spent with Lily, I'd barely even seen her smile. I needed to change that.

Just as soon as I broke the news to my grandmother that she was going to be that title twice over in a matter of months.

"My paws are just fine. How was your trip?"

"Don't try to change the subject. I hope you're doing better with Hannah. She's a lovely woman, and she stepped up when we needed her most despite your bad attitude."

"Yeah, about that—"

"Hang on a second. Chris, can you grab that bag for me? Thank you, sweetness."

I frowned. "Chris? What happened to…Harry? Was that his name?"

I hadn't paid all that much attention once I'd ascertained that her last boyfriend seemed to be a decent guy. She never dated anyone questionable, so I dealt with most of her relationships the same way I did with the ones I wasn't having—I buried myself in work.

And now work wasn't a refuge any longer. At least not for me.

"Oh, Harry met someone in Virginia actually. Nice woman. Killer poker player. Do you know he won over a grand on our last hand the final night of the trip? I still think he cheated." She laughed, her voice lacking rancor.

"Wait a second. Harry left you for another woman and then took one thousand from you in cards? And you're laughing? Also, since when do you bet that kind of money?"

"We were on vacation," she said as if that explained everything.

"And that's where you met Chris?"

"Yes. He lost his wife last year and this was his first trip. He nearly aged out of the group, but they let him in, thank goodness."

I frowned. "Aged out? How can you be too old for a seniors' group?"

How old was this guy, anyway? Did he even still have teeth?

"Not too old, too young. Let me talk to you later, Snug." She turned the phone into her shoulder and had a hushed conversation with her younger man, ending it with a laugh before returning to the phone. "We'll talk tonight, all right?"

Gran hung up and I decided I'd dealt with enough insanity for one day. I didn't have any more meetings, thank fuck, and I had gone to the gym this morning before heading in. The only thing left to do was for me to go home and help Hannah with Lily. She was probably overworking herself as usual, juggling far too much.

As if cooking a vast menu for humans wasn't enough, I'd seen scribblings in the margins of the Lily-related notebook we passed back and forth with recipes for dogs and cats.

So much for her dropping that idea.

So, if she wouldn't ease off voluntarily, I would help her. It was a distraction from my own tangled business at the very least. And if I had ideas for her to scale up while economizing her efforts, well, she could take it as free advice. I tugged on my suit jacket and reached for my overcoat with a grin. Or set the kitchen on fire, which was just as likely when it came to Hannah Jacobs.

On my way out the door, my phone buzzed with Vincent's ringtone. I didn't pick it up.

Bitter? Nah. I was an expert at compartmentalism. I didn't know how I wanted to deal with him yet, so I wasn't.

What I wasn't doing was letting him go. The more I turned the situation around in my mind, pulling at corners and shoving them back into the puzzle, the more I wondered if the one who needed to go was me.

I just didn't know what that meant yet. What that would look like. And if I'd still be the man I thought I was on the other side.

Blasting music on the drive home evened me out even more. I roared into my driveway with "Lola" by the Kinks screaming out the windows. I was singing along—badly—but I was enjoying it just the same.

"Fuck." I stopped the car, remembering that Lily was inside, possibly sleeping. I couldn't remember the last time I'd played music that loudly, so it normally wasn't a factor.

I'd just stepped out of the car when Hannah burst out on the porch, her hair in a messy pile on her head. "What's going on?"

I looked around. I'd parked the car in my usual spot, and nothing appeared amiss in the glow from the motion sensor lights over the garage. At a loss, I checked my watch. It was past six-thirty, which wasn't bad for me lately. I usually stayed at work far later than that.

"I don't know?"

"You were playing music?" She rushed down the steps. "I heard it all the way up the block. Your windows were down in this weather?"

Again, I glanced around. It was a clear, cool night with a scattering of stars just beginning to pop. The days were getting longer, but the nights still begun early around here. "It's nice out."

"Nice? It can't be more than forty."

I shrugged. I'd shed my overcoat in the car and was just in my suit jacket. "Feels nice to me. What are you doing?" She was crossing the driveway to me, her forehead pinched with worry.

She didn't reply, just leaned in close to sniff at my clothes. Then she pressed a cool hand to my suddenly warm forehead. It wasn't only my face that was hot. All of me was on fire, just from her touch.

Her eyes narrowed. "Are you feverish?"

She didn't follow it up with another question, but I heard it just the same. "Am I drunk?"

She didn't deny it, merely stepped back and crossed her arms over her chest. "Fine, if you want to put it out there. Are you?"

"No. I haven't had a drop. I'm not your father, Hannah."

The shutters came down over her eyes and I instantly regretted what I'd said. But what did she expect? I'd been drunk once in our acquaintance. So, just because I was singing and happy for one moment, she assumed the worst?

She's obviously dealt with plenty of worst in her life.

She started to turn away until my fingers gently closed around her forearm. I drew her back against me, sliding my hand down to bracelet her wrist so I could feel the wild thud of her pulse. I brushed my mouth over her hair as I spoke, wanting the words to reach her where she'd already retreated. "I shouldn't have said that. But you shouldn't assume I was drinking because I did it once. One time, Hannah. I hadn't had any alcohol in the better part of a year. Not even when Billy—"

She shifted to gaze up at me, her eyes heavy and troubled in the thin shaft of light from the garage. "You were singing. Blaring music. What was I supposed to think?"

"That maybe, just maybe, I was happy."

Her expression of puzzlement tore a laugh from my chest. I understood that look in my soul. "I don't fully understand it either. A hell of a lot is messed up or in flux right now. But I left work today and I was in a good goddamn mood, even so." I touched my thumb to the corner of her mouth. "I have to think that's because of you."

Panic flared in her eyes before she glanced over her shoulder. "I have something on the stove. And Lily is—"

I cupped her cheek and turned her face back to mine. "This will just take a second."

Slowly, so slowly, I drew her up on her tiptoes as my mouth touched hers. As gently as the wind ruffling the still bare branches of the trees, as carefully as I might've coaxed out a skittish deer. Pouring everything into the easy slide of my mouth over hers.

Waiting forever to see if she'd respond in kind or shove me away.

She made a frustrated noise in her throat and fisted her hand around my tie, choking me when she dragged me closer. I laughed and wrapped my arms around her, lifting her against me while the kiss went on and on.

Dimly, I heard the sound of tires rolling over the pavement. Didn't care. I nibbled Hannah's lower lip and debated just carrying her inside to finish this on that sturdy bench in the front hall. Or I could just back into the car—

"Asher." Hannah pulled her mouth from mine with a ragged hiss of breath that made me swear. "Open your eyes."

I didn't want to. I wanted to stay in this capsule of pure bliss. No worries, no thoughts, no pressure. Just this smart, beautiful, challenging woman in my arms and her warm mouth pressed to mine.

"Asher." Hannah's voice edged with nerves as she shoved at my shoulder.

"Dammit." No matter how I tried to ignore reality, it always came back and knocked me on my ass.

Or dug half-moons into my shoulder.

Reluctantly, I dropped Hannah back to her feet and forced myself to turn toward the source of our disruption. They better have a damn good explanation—

And found my grandmother hanging out of her driver's side window, positively cackling with glee.

"Too late, I saw you. I saw you! About time too." She whipped around my parked car and zoomed up the drive, nearly clipping the potted petunia I'd seen Hannah fussing with the other morning.

"I think I better move that planter. It's too close to the driveway for certain motorists."

"Asher," Hannah hissed. "She saw us. She knows."

"That I can't stay away from your mouth?" I shrugged and wiped my hand over my lips, already craving her cinnamon taste again.

My preoccupation could be why I wasn't flipping out my grandmother had witnessed a private moment I had not been ready for her to see.

Better answer was that I was fucking glad she'd seen it. That at least one of the things I was holding back was now out in the open.

No more pretending.

No more denying.

I glanced back at Hannah and noted that she was peering at me strangely again. "You swear you haven't been drinking?"

I moved closer to her and caressed her cheek with the tip of my finger. "Did you taste it on me?"

Hannah flushed to the roots of her hair.

I chuckled as I turned toward my grandmother as she hustled up the driveway with a large tote bag overflowing with packages. "Need some help?"

She waved me off before dropping the bag at my feet to wrap me in a giant hug. When I hugged her back, she whispered, "You did good, Snug."

I started to argue that I hadn't done anything—God knows Hannah and I were dancing around each other enough to wear out the carpet—but she'd already moved on to embrace Hannah. Hannah hugged her back and they spoke softly to each other for long enough that I frowned.

Were they talking about me?

I dipped my hands in my pockets and fisted them. Of course, they were.

"I have to say that I'm relieved." Gran stepped back and reached for her tote bag, frowning as I snatched it before she could.

I grimaced. Jesus, this thing was heavy.

"Glad to be home again?" Hannah asked. "How was your trip?"

"Oh, it was lovely. Met a fine young man. We're moving in together."

"Excuse me?" A sharp breeze moved through the trees and it suddenly occurred to me that we were having this discussion in the driveway. I motioned toward the house. "Can we take this inside?"

"Oh my God, my roast."

"And my granddaughter."

They both took off, chattering all the while. The door slapped shut behind them and I stopped on the porch, digging into the bag of presents.

"Snug, get in here with that bag," my grandmother called.

Busted again.

I followed them into the kitchen, depositing the bag in the foyer on the way. Hannah pulled out the roast pan from the oven, and the fragrant scent of the meat was nearly enough to make a man kneel down and beg. My grandmother had Lily on her hip, who was trying to pull off her dangling earring.

The quiet scene of domesticity nearly rocked me off my feet.

Hannah making dinner, my grandmother quietly chatting about her trip, my daughter bouncing and babbling to herself.

"So, I figured, why not move him in? I'm not getting any younger, you know. A woman has needs. I'd prefer not to place phone calls in the middle of the night when rolling over is just as easy."

I shut my eyes. Pretty domestic picture shattered.

With a mallet.

Hannah nodded and stuck her long-handled fork into the roast a little too vigorously.

"I imagine the same happened here. You put two attractive adults in the same space and boom, sparks." Gran shifted to use Lily's hand to smack against her stomach when she said "boom" and Lily giggled as if it was the funniest joke ever. Her cheeks were smeared with something orange. More Spaghetti-Os? I wasn't sure I wanted to know.

I moved to the sink and wet a paper towel before moving back to clean Lily's cheeks. She swatted at the paper towel, batting it away every time I tried to clean her up.

"Be still, Lily. I know you've been eating that pasta in a can crap again." I kept my voice even as I tidied her up, but from my grandmother's sigh, she didn't find me amusing.

Hannah didn't respond at all.

Then Lily fisted the towel and started chewing on it.

Well aware when I was outgunned, I stepped back. "Moving a man in you just met is rather sudden."

"Uh-huh. It is."

"Are you sure you shouldn't take some time?"

Gran pried the towel away from Lily and deftly wiped the baby's cheeks. "I'm not getting younger," she repeated. "I know what I want right now, so what, exactly, am I waiting for? Some prescribed time when proper society says it's okay for me to move forward? Screw that."

"Gran," I snapped. "Language."

My grandmother blew out a breath and passed the baby to Hannah, who had to drop her fork to take her. "I don't know how you deal with him. I love him like the dickens, but sometimes I don't like him very much."

She stormed out of the kitchen and I stared after her, stunned into silence. I was even more shocked when Hannah walked over and passed Lily to me. "You look like you need a hug," she said as Lily reached up with her chubby little arms.

Swallowing hard, I hugged her, holding on even as she started to fuss. She felt so good. Solid and warm and smelling of processed foods and powder and baby.

All the things that soothed me immeasurably right now.

"Should I be eating Spaghetti-Os too?" I wondered aloud.

Hannah snorted. "Let's not go that far. But I think your grandmother might like to see some of that Asher who was badly singing 'Lola' in the car. Really badly."

"I wasn't singing badly. Just not well." I wrinkled my nose at Lily. When she patted my cheeks and made the same face back at me, I would've sworn my heart squeezed. "Okay, badly. So, why would she want to hear it?"

"Because she'd know you weren't perfect. That you know you

aren't perfect. That you're human just like the rest of us and you're okay with it."

"But I'm not."

Hannah gifted me with one of her rare half smiles. "Not what? Not human? I've had cause to question that myself a time or seven."

"I'm not okay with being not perfect. Which is ridiculous. No one is. No one."

"He's learning." Hannah tugged on one of Lily's reddish-brown curls. "Slow but sure."

I gripped Hannah's hand and drew her down the hall as I shifted Lily to my other hip. My grandmother was peering into the unlit fire, her lovely face marred with worry lines I didn't like seeing. Ones I'd put on her face, not for the first time. Definitely not the last either.

When she looked over at us, I let it rip.

"Hannah's pregnant."

TWENTY-ONE

Asher

YET AGAIN, HANNAH STARED AT ME AS IF I WAS INSANE.

Perhaps I was.

My hold on her hand tightened as she tried to yank it free. "So, if you think I'm perfect, or trying to be, you're wrong. I mess up timing all the time. I mess up fucking everything."

Too late, I glanced at Lily. She was occupied with trying to dangle forward far enough to pull off her sock, so I probably hadn't scarred her too much with my language.

Hannah covered her face with her other hand. "Remind me not to try to give you advice again, okay? Like…ever."

Gran moved forward to pluck the baby from my hip and plunked her down in the playpen across the room. Then she turned back with narrowed eyes. "Okay, I'm no expert, but I do have a child of my own. I know it usually takes a period of time for such things to reveal themselves. I've been gone a week. Even if you pounced on Hannah the first day she came here for the interview—and thank you, Lord, because I had serious concerns about you, Asher—you must be like Superman."

"That's not exactly what happened," Hannah began.

"What concerns?" Although I knew otherwise, it didn't stop me from preening. I could use some Superman mojo right now.

"You live like a monk." My grandmother shook her head and glanced at Hannah. "He was practically born again."

"Christian?"

"Hardly," I snapped. "Just because I don't share information about my conquests with my grandmother doesn't mean I don't have them."

She rolled right over that as if I hadn't spoken. Probably everyone in the room knew that was bullshit. Even I did. Not that I told my grandmother about my love life, but I would've had to have one for that to be an issue.

Before Hannah, the most enduring affair I'd had in years was with my work.

"No, the other kind of born again. We both know when Billy died, part of you did too. You've been a corpse since, just walking around here hollow-eyed."

I dipped my hands in my pockets and moved to the window. What could I say? It was a truth bomb of the same kind Vincent had laid upon me last week. More and more kept coming at me, and a guy could only duck and weave so much.

"Bess, I got pregnant on New Year's Eve. Not this month."

"What?" My grandmother's voice lowered. "New Year's Eve. The night Asher didn't come home. The only night he'd been away from that baby since she was turned over to his care."

Lily let out a squeal and flung out a squishy block that hit Hannah in the leg. She retrieved it and brought it back to the baby, who flung it right back at her again. Hannah knelt with a smile and bounced the block into Lily's playpen. Lily plopped on her butt and brought the block to her mouth, gnawing on it with a contented gurgle.

I caught myself smiling and glanced at my grandmother to find she was smiling too, her eyes softer than I'd seen in a while.

"So, I'm going to have another grandbaby," she said quietly.

Hannah rose and brushed off her apron. "Yes, one is definitely cooking in there." She glanced down at herself. "It better only be one."

"Is there a chance there's more?"

"No," Hannah and I said in unison.

"One is perfect." My grandmother beamed, all earlier traces of concern gone from her expression.

Grandbabies trumped everything. Especially for my grandmother, who clearly had assumed I would never even date again, never mind have a kid.

I was still working my way around to grasping that concept myself.

Throat tight, I nodded. "Yeah, looks like the corpse can procreate. Quite a trick, huh?" At Hannah's pointed glance, I reached up to loosen my tie. "Hannah did some of the work too."

When my grandmother started to laugh and Hannah covered her face again, I rushed ahead. "I mean, her eggs. Jesus. Must you always live in the gutter?"

Smiling, my grandmother walked over to Hannah and cupped her cheeks. "You've accomplished an amazing feat, my girl. You've made him smile again. Whether or not he realizes it yet."

Before Hannah could deny that fact—something I knew she would do—I stepped up behind her and laid my hands on her shoulders. She braced, but she didn't move away. Little victories. "She also makes me sing off-key and eat ice cream in the middle of the night. Pretty sure canned pasta is our next frontier." I kissed the top of her head. "I'm going to talk to Gran for a few minutes if that's okay."

"Sure. Of course. Absolutely. I'll just wrap up the roast for later. Maybe we can do sandwiches. I made fresh bread..." She trailed off and fiddled with her updo. "C'mon, Lily, let's get lost."

"Hang on."

She glanced back at me and I framed her face in my hands, much as my grandmother just had. The difference was I covered her mouth with mine, kissing her gently. Her breath shuddered out. "Don't go too far," I murmured, squeezing her fingers.

"Right. Okay. Yes. What was I doing?"

Lily lifted her leg and tried to scale the playpen wall, propelling Hannah forward. "Oh, no, you don't. C'mere, Houdini." Deftly, she snagged Lily and turned her upside down, making her laugh so hard that her face turned red. Then she righted her and gave her a smacking kiss. "Let's go eat some mashed carrots so your daddy won't complain about you enjoying canned carbs."

With an arch look over her shoulder, Hannah flounced out of the room, baby in tow.

"I feel like I'm watching a soap opera, but somehow it's Friday and I'm just about to get to the cliffhanger without seeing all the days of lead up beforehand." My grandmother marched forward and poked me in the chest. "Do not cliffhanger that girl. Even more important? Don't tease her and kiss her and confuse her then go all Asher on her and freeze her out while you process your feelings."

I bristled. "I'm a man. We don't process our feelings, we ignore them."

"Maybe that's your problem then, you big adorable dummy." She grabbed my arm and tugged me toward the couch. "When are you going to get more furniture in this place?"

"I've been adding pieces as I go. When it was just me and an infant, I didn't have a need for—"

At her look, I locked my fingers behind my neck and leaned back. "It's not like that yet, Gran. We aren't playing house. She's Lily's nanny."

"And the mother of your child. Did you forget that part?"

"No." I slid a hand down the sleeve of my jacket before tugging it off altogether. Was the room heating up or was it just me?

Oh, right, it was the weight of my multiple...situations.

"It's just complicated," I added into the silence.

"You care about her. I see it all over your face. And her face too. From the first moment you two 'met,'" Gran pretended to cough, "you were sparking all over the place. At least now I understand why. She should have explained to me she knew you before I extended the job offer to her."

"Yeah, well, remember that the next time you call me Snug all over town. She didn't realize the position she was interviewing for was as my nanny."

"You didn't exchange contact information before you got biblical?"

"There was no praying involved, I assure you. But no, we didn't exchange anything. It was a hookup, Gran. You know, like the ones you have on vacation that lead to you moving the guy into your house."

"Hmm, seems like you did the exact same thing with yours."

I frowned. "This situation is entirely different."

"That's true. I didn't impregnate my young man." She patted my arm. "You win, Snug."

I couldn't help laughing. "You're incorrigible."

"What's your point?"

"Hell if I know. I don't know what the future is going to look like." I smoothed my jacket over my lap. "I'm trying to be okay with that when every part of me is used to controlling things down to the most minute detail. But lately, that's not an option."

"It's also not an option when you're dealing with a smart, capable young woman who has a pretty good head on her shoulders and isn't about to be herded."

"Tell me about it. But I love that about her. She stands up to me every time." Hearing myself, I frowned. "I like it. A lot."

"Mmm-hmm. So, you moved her in here solely to help with Lily, not because you can't keep your hands off her and want to see every moment of that baby's development."

"We aren't—it's not like that between us right now. Those kisses you saw are the bulk of what's happening."

"No, it isn't. Anyone with eyes could see plenty more is happening than that."

I rubbed my hands over my bleary eyes. "I don't know how to be a father to one baby, never mind two. But I've got to figure it out. Lily and Hannah deserve it."

"As does your new baby."

"Yeah."

"No one knows how to be a parent. Some people never learn, but that doesn't keep them from having kids. Sometimes a baker's dozen of them. They just don't put the mountains of pressure on themselves to do it all perfectly like you do." She scooped a hand through my hair.

"I still remember when you were a little boy, Snug. Your father was teaching you to ride a bicycle. Then he went in the house, but you wouldn't stop. You kept trying over and over again, that grim determination on your face."

"I finally learned."

"You did and got a boatload of scrapes and bruises for your trouble."

"I did. And I kept coming back for more."

"As you will with this. You'll probably have six kids by the time you're forty."

"Bite your tongue."

Shaking her head, she smiled. "Stop looking for the handbook on how to do it right and enjoy the little moments. And always, always do everything with love."

I swallowed deeply. She couldn't have given me a better segue if I'd asked for one. "Do you think that applies to work as well?"

"It applies to every-damn-thing, Snug. Are you going to tell your mother?"

"Well, I'll have to eventually, won't I?"

"Not necessarily. How many times has she stopped by to see Lily?"

I didn't reply, because I didn't want to think about anyone else who had let Lily down. My mother had never given two whits about parenting me, so why would she care about Lily?

"Christ, am I like her? Is that what this is?" I jerked to my feet and flung my jacket on the couch. It was a good thing I didn't have a much larger object to toss. I just might have. "I should warn Hannah not to expect anything more from me. I'm a decent provider, but anything else is off the table. Even the provider part is in question."

"Shut up and sit down." My grandmother patted the cushion beside her.

I sat. For once, I absolutely did not want to be right.

"You are the exact opposite of your mother and when you're lucid, you know that quite well. The reason you get so tied up about doing the right thing is because you don't want to let anyone down. Like she let you down, over and over again. Like your father did."

I said nothing.

"You can try to do well without driving yourself crazy that you make mistakes. No one gets it right the first time or even most times. Especially not when it comes to children and family. How many family events end up with someone in handcuffs?"

"Have you been watching those cop shows again?"

"You're scared witless to fail Lily. Instead of looking around and seeing that you're the one who stepped up for her. You have turned your whole life inside out to be that little girl's father. So what if you screwed up now and then? You didn't have any warning you were going to be a dad. One day you weren't, then the next you were."

That summed up what had happened in a nutshell, that was for sure.

"And in the meantime, you were also grieving your best friend. The only person who ever helped you to live for yourself and not just for your responsibilities." Her voice gentled. "Billy squeezed every drop out of every day. Maybe he knew something we didn't. He didn't have that long, so he was going to make the most of it."

My eyes prickled and I would've jerked to my feet again if her hand didn't come down on my upper arm to clamp me in place.

"You deserve to have love in your life. To love and be loved. To adore the hell out of that little girl and know that any screwups you make won't matter compared to how much love you have in your heart for her."

I knew she wasn't just talking about Lily. She was referring to Hannah and our baby too.

"We started everything backward."

"So, you begin where you are right now and take the steps you missed. Maybe find some creative new ones." She winked and I found myself laughing despite the constriction in my throat.

"I just don't want to let him down. To let down Grandad. Hannah. Lily. The baby. A thoughtless moment that became so much more."

"Was it really thoughtless? I doubt that. She wouldn't be looking at you the way she does if you two hadn't made some magic that night, even if you've tried to extinguish it since."

TARYN QUINN

"I don't want to extinguish it. I was singing tonight, Gran. Even in the midst of everything, with all that's so fucked up, I knew I was coming home to Hannah and Lily and it made the day bearable. So much more than bearable. Just thinking of them made me happy." I let out a long breath. "And I couldn't tell you the last time I truly was."

"You need to quit."

I blinked, sure I'd misheard her. "Excuse me?"

"You need to quit the business and figure out what makes your soul sing. You have one in there, I swear, under the Hugo Boss and wingtips."

I stared at her as if she was a stranger. "Have you turned into a mind-reader?"

"No." She smiled, and for a second, the lines on her face struck a punch right to my heart. She was still beautiful, but she wore the battle scars of a lifetime well lived on her face.

But that was the crux of it—she'd *lived*. And me? I'd done a whole lot of existing.

A whole lot of waiting for a tomorrow that was the same as all the days that had come before.

"Vincent has ideas. So many of them. They're good. Innovative. Ways to keep Wainwright from dying on the vine. Which is what it's doing with me at the helm."

She took my hand and squeezed. "You can't hang on and fight change forever, Snug. Life marches on. If you don't move with it, you'll get trampled."

"I want to try something different."

I told her the ideas I had for a news-focused podcast with a slant toward local trendsetters and movers and shakers. Not always the ones who got the press elsewhere, but the ones who were affecting change right at home.

No stagnation allowed.

"We have so many other holdings and things we're involved in, charities and foundations, that even if I step back, managing our portfolio will be an undertaking. But Vincent could handle more of the day to day, and I could function as a high-level consultant. I'm also

234

going to do this podcast." It was the first time I'd stated it as a *I'm going to* versus *I want to*—even in my own head. "I'm going to help Hannah with her meal delivery service too, if she wants the help." I took a deep breath. "And I'm going to raise my children."

"Aww, Snug." She let out a laugh, waving me off as she rubbed at her suddenly watery eyes. "You're such a beautifully direct arrow."

"Thanks?"

"It's a compliment. Your moral compass will never lead you astray." She cupped my cheek. "I'm so proud of you."

"Even if you don't always like me very much?"

"Spaghetti-Os are one of this life's most perfect foods, especially with a little grated cheese on top."

I grinned and drew her into my arms. "I don't know what I would do without you."

"Luckily, you'll never have to find out. My two grandbabies will keep me young forever." She gave me a misty smile. "Two," she whispered, and the backs of my eyes grew hot.

"Two," I echoed, letting the truth really sink into me for perhaps the first time.

I'd known it before, but I hadn't let myself truly believe it. Hannah still looked the same. Life hadn't changed yet.

But it would. Soon. And I wasn't going to run from those crazy, wonderful changes ever again.

I was going to face them.

Fucking finally.

Gran and I talked for a little longer, and I grilled her a bit about her new companion. She assured me he was a decent guy, and even suggested we go on a double date, which was a lot for me to consider even with my new progressive outlook. But I said I'd think about it.

I was probably going to say yes. Assuming Hannah was willing to give it a go.

Once Gran left, I went to look for Hannah and Lily. I found them curled up together on the bed in Hannah's room, sleeping peacefully. Hannah was curled around Lily and Lily gripped Hannah's shirt even in her sleep.

The sweetness of the scene before me made me grip the doorframe to stop myself from interrupting them.

Let them sleep. They both need their rest.

As if she could sense the weight of my thoughts, Hannah stirred and lifted her head. And without saying a word, she extended her arm to me as if it was the most natural thing in the world.

I joined her on the bed, wrapping myself around them both. I brushed a kiss over her temple, and Hannah fell back to sleep almost immediately.

I stretched my hand across Hannah's belly. For a moment, I could do nothing but trace the contours of her stomach, searching for any sign.

Soon.

So soon.

Then I reached for Lily too, curving my fingers around her hip.

Closing my eyes, I started to drift. No worries. No thoughts. I didn't nap as a rule, but I'd never had my family in bed with me.

I'd never had my own family before.

TWENTY-TWO

I'm taking my favorite girls on a picnic. I'll be home soon.

I swayed with Lily on my hip as we looked out the big picture in the living room. Sheets of rain were bashing the window and whipping the trees around. I was pretty sure Asher's big plans for a spring picnic were under around an inch of rain at the moment.

Possibly two.

I tucked my phone into my back pocket and set Lily down on her blanket with some Legos. Immediately a large red block went into her drooly mouth.

"Someday that tooth is going to come in, pumpkin pie."

Lily whipped the Lego at my head. Well-versed in dealing with her future pitcher arm, I ducked to the side and it sailed over my shoulder. She picked up a blue and yellow one and smashed them together with a giggle.

I went back to folding the endless piles of baby clothes that seemed to multiply overnight. Between the drool and learning how to eat with her own fingers, Lily was keeping me busy. Laundry was always on my to-do list.

Just as I was about to put on my favorite true crime podcast, the video screen for the home Alexa unit made its watery tones.

"Emma calling."

My chest tightened as it always did when one of them called me, but her smiling face filled the screen.

"Hey, Hannah Banana, how's it going in New York?"

"Spring in central New York, you know how it goes."

"Raining buckets?"

"You got it." I sat down on the hassock in front of the end table with the video-chat unit tucked in the corner. I pulled it forward so I could see my little sister better. "You are a sight for sore eyes. And God, you're so tan."

"Well, a week in Cancun will do that." Rachel, my other sister and Emma's twin, peeked from behind her. "Hey!"

My eyes welled up. "Oh, you're both calling me?"

"Yeah, we just wanted to call and tell you thanks for the extra money in our accounts. We can't believe you did that." Rachel tried to crane her neck. "What's up with this new job?"

"I'm a nanny for a very sweet girl." I twisted the video camera so they could see Lily. "The little girl's father is..." What was a good way to say loaded and not make it sound cold and calculating?

I never really thought about Asher's money in the day to day. This house was just his and Lily was more my...

Daughter.

Ugh, I couldn't look at it that way, but some days I forgot she wasn't mine. And I forgot all of this was a job, especially with the little bean growing inside of me.

Everything was so hard to define. The edges were growing hazier every day.

"Rich?" Emma moved her out of the way. "Dude, that place is swank."

I sat back down. "Asher comes from quite the line of wealth. He's a Wainwright—which might not mean much to you two. His family owns a lot of businesses, but the one you might know is the newspaper."

"Ohhh." They glanced at one another with wide eyes. "That's quite the job you landed."

"Don't get too excited. I'm not sure how permanent it is."

Emma rolled her eyes. "You always say that. How's the boxed dinners deal?"

We spent a few minutes catching up about their classes and my business. I carefully avoided the big subject that I really needed to discuss with them. I wasn't sure how to tell them. I mean, I could blurt it out like Asher had with his grandmother, but *eeep.*

"You seem like you're a million miles away."

"What? No. I'm right here."

Emma and Rachel were squeezed into the screen, both peering closely at me. "Something's different."

"No."

"There is." Emma tipped her head. "Did you get laid?"

"Oh my God. We are not discussing that."

"Is that scruff burn on your neck?"

"What?" My hand went right to where Asher had kissed me last night. He kept surprising me with sneak attacks.

"Ohhh." Both girls made huge eyes at me. "Who is it?"

"It's none of—"

"Hannah. Who ordered this monsoon? Didn't they realize we had plans?"

Emma's eyes, so much like mine, widened. "Plans?"

"Okay, gotta go."

"Oh, no, you don't." Emma's nose was practically in the lens.

"Of course, I didn't bring an umbrella." Asher bustled in, whipping his suit jacket off and dumping his laptop bag on the bench just inside the door. And he had to be wearing his glasses today. I was so weak against them. "Hannah?"

I tried to hit the end button, but suddenly forgot how to work anything, including my mouth to tell Alexa to end the call. Asher's white dress shirt was stuck to his body. Evidently, today he hadn't worn one of his white T-shirts under it either.

Dear God, he was positively soaked through.

"Oh, I'm sorry. I didn't realize you were on a vid call." He leaned down and kissed Lily on the head. "Can't pick you up, sweetheart. I need to change."

"Hello!" Emma, who had no chill, shouted.

Asher came up behind me. "Oh, hello." He leaned down and kissed me as well. Not on the lips, thank God, but he was behaving far too familiarly when my sisters were watching.

Boy, were they watching.

What the hell was up with him? First singing in the car, then singing in his office to a Matt Nathanson song last night. I hadn't even known Asher listened to music that wasn't classical.

I was so confused.

"I'm Asher. Can't wait for you guys to visit. We'd love for you to stay for part of the summer."

"We would?" I asked.

"Yeah, with the baby coming, I'm thinking you girls will want to enjoy the summer as much as you can."

"Baby!" My sisters shrieked in unison, and the video went black. "Sorry!" Emma righted her unit. "Baby? What baby?"

"Oh, shi—Skittles." Asher frowned and pushed his glasses up. "You didn't tell them?" he asked me out of the corner of his mouth.

"I was getting to it."

"Oh my God, what?" Emma looked downward, but of course, I was too close to the camera to see much.

I scooted back. "Not showing yet. I was going to tell you."

"Talk about burying the lead," Asher muttered.

"What? Now you start talking like a newspaper guy?"

He held up his hands. "I see you need to talk. I'm going to go change."

"Don't have to change on our account." Rachel smiled dreamily. "Nice job, sis. Rich and hot."

"Oh, God."

"I mean I'm assuming this is your boss. Man, I think I watched this on the Hallmark channel. Or was it read the book?" Rachel's eyes were dancing.

"Shut up." I was mortified. And I didn't want my sisters, or Asher for that matter, thinking that I was in this for the money.

"Actually, I knocked her up before she worked for me."

"You are not helping," I growled.

"Obviously not. And you definitely need to talk. I'll take Lily upstairs with me since she's face-planted into her Legos."

I twisted and sure enough, Lily was out for the count. It seemed as if she did her best sleeping in the middle of chaos. Which was a very good thing considering the insanity our lives had become.

"Bye, girls. And that invitation is open-ended." He gave me a long look, followed by a panty-incinerating smile. He stripped off his wet shirt without even looking at me.

My sisters were swooning behind me. Quickly, I moved the camera so he was out of view.

"Dammit, what's with denying me my Magic Mike moment, Hannah?"

I ignored Rachel, but I sneaked another peek or eleven of my own.

Damn, he was gorgeous.

He scooped up a sleeping Lily, then he looked over his shoulder with an arched brow. At this point, things were so far out of control that I went with impulse and gave him a wolf whistle.

The quick flash of his smile made my belly flip. I frowned a little when he went the long way around to go up the stairs. He probably wanted to take up his wet suit jacket too.

Or give us another chance at a peep show, the exhibitionist.

I turned back to my sisters.

"Now explain." Rachel pointed at me, so much like our mom used to do when she was looking for juicy gossip.

I sighed. "This is going to take a while."

"Let's start at the beginning." Rachel propped her chin on her hands. "Don't leave anything out."

Emma elbowed Rachel over. "I want to hear too."

"It all started on a snowy New Year's Eve."

Rachel gave an exaggerated sigh. "Yeah, this is going to be good."

I indulged my sisters for a little while. Knowing Asher would be taking care of Lily let me have some much-needed sister time. Even if a lot of the teasing was at my expense. I might have given a little more detail than I should have for impressionable nineteen-year olds, but I fell into telling them about Asher.

About Lily.

About the crazy life we were making by accident.

We discussed absurd baby names and that I might end up with an October baby depending on how the pregnancy went. How dates for actual pregnancy didn't make sense at all. Not to mention that the two of them needed to be way more careful about protection than I had been.

"You don't have to tell me, but just please be careful."

"Ugh, don't pull on your Aunt Hannah suit. Stay in the sister role, please." Rachel buried her face in her hands.

"I'll tell you one thing. Do not hook up with guys from Crescent Cove. There's now a bumper sticker circulating that there's something in the water here. Literally."

"Really?" Emma's eyes got huge.

"There's a ridiculous baby boom going on here. Each time I make a delivery for *Hannah's Helping Hands*, I hear another report of someone having a baby."

"So, the boom-chicka-wow-wow is going viral in Crescent Cove? This I gotta see."

I lifted the camera to my face. "No, you will not."

Emma's peal of laughter was so nice to hear. It had been a long time since we were able to talk. Some of it was my own fault. I didn't want to be a burdensome older sister when they were just finding themselves.

"We need weekly check-ins," I said impulsively.

"Now that you are growing a human, I think that's a certainty. But we really do miss you, Hannah Banana." Rachel smushed her cheek against her sister's and they both made guppy faces. "We miss you. And we're definitely coming to visit this summer. I did get an internship, so it won't be the whole summer."

"That's wonderful. I'm so happy for you."

"I'm actually going to work on a cruise ship for two months out of the three." Emma made a face. "I know it's probably going to be terrible, but I think it's the only way I'll get to see some of the world until school is over. I thought about taking a year off—"

At my stern expression, she laughed.

"But I don't want to lose a whole year. A few months of being locked in a sardine can should be enough."

I'd heard horror stories about cruise liners, but I knew that had to be more of an outlier kind of thing than the norm. I had to trust that Emma knew how to take care of herself.

"Look at you biting your tongue." Emma's laughter was addictive.

I couldn't help but smile back at her. "Just promise me you'll be careful, and that there's a way to get out of working there if it's awful. I don't care what it costs, I'll get you home if need be."

"That's because you're the best."

"All right. Let me go check on Asher and Lily. It's far too quiet up there."

"I'm really happy for you, Han. He seems pretty awesome. Even if you are sleeping with your boss. So scandalous."

"Thanks, Rachel." I shook my head. "I don't know what's going to happen with him. We're taking it a day at a time."

"Well, don't take too long. That man is super fine, and some other girl will be ready to swoop in. He's hot with all caps."

"Thanks, I think." I was still afraid to label anything about us. Even if I did find myself looking forward to his arrival each afternoon. Lately, he was often coming home with a smile and jumping in to help in the kitchen.

How many times had he shooed me out of the room to play with Lily, just so he could give me a break? He wasn't avoiding her anymore. Sometimes when I was trying to figure out a recipe, he'd even take Lily to his office for some time together. I'd found them curled in his reading chair on more than one evening after dinner.

So much was changing, most of it in good ways.

I swallowed hard and focused in on my sisters. "I love you."

Rachel's eyes misted. "We love you too."

Emma looped her arm around her sister's neck. "We miss you and expect reports in between calls. And we'll be sending you more names."

I laughed. "I can't wait."

They waved and then they were gone. I blinked away the wash of tears. I missed them so much, but I was so proud of the women they were becoming. Both of them overachievers. Emma was still waffling about what major she wanted to stick with, but Rachel had a plan in place. She was going to be an architect, creating sustainable energy housing.

Our parents would be so proud of them, especially our mother.

I dashed away the wetness and finished folding the baby clothes in peace and quiet. I'd have to figure out what we were going to eat now that a picnic was not part of the game plan. Maybe the three of us could go get a pizza in town. I was a little sick of my own cooking at the moment.

I tucked the basket of clothes under my arm and headed upstairs. A soft, pleasant male voice came in clearer the closer I got to the top of the stairs. It was a country singer, but I couldn't name which one. I was more of a rock and pop kind of girl.

Asher's office door was open. Lily's was closed. I quietly went to check on her. She was sleeping with her arms splayed over her head. Totally out for the count. That was her exhausted sleep stance. Considering she'd been fighting her morning naps lately, I wasn't unhappy to see it. That meant she'd be out for a little bit.

Maybe we could call Bess over for a date night. No picnic, but perhaps we could salvage the day.

I set the basket of clothes on her changing table and back out of the room, then followed the music. I found Asher setting grapes and brie on a plate. Sort of. The grapes kept rolling away, but I had to give him an A for effort. Especially since he had a bottle of sparkling grape juice in an ice bucket set up on a huge gingham blanket spread in the middle of his office floor.

He'd pushed his desk back and stacked the boxes of equipment that kept showing up every few days. Two pitchers were overflowing with spring flowers. Crayola-colored gerberas and daisies, even a handful of soft yellow and pink tulips. There was an honest to God picnic basket sitting at the edge of the blanket. White linen napkins and silverware were set next to the plates.

I even saw an apple juice box peeking out of the cooler he'd tucked behind the basket. He'd thought of everything.

"There you are." Asher stood with an easy smile. No pinched lips or frown lines now. Thank God. "How was your talk with your sisters?"

"Good."

I tried to reel in my reaction to all of his hard work. I didn't want to make him feel self-conscious about it, but at the same time, I was so afraid to make it too big of a deal. Instead, I went with my instincts and smiled back at him.

Pleasure unfurled in my belly, along with a warmth that I hadn't felt this deeply since that very first night.

That night had included the floor and a fireplace as well.

Instead of a suit, Asher wore a pair of jeans with a button-down white shirt. Not the kind he wore to the office every day, but one that looked like it had been with him for a long time if the frayed tails were anything to go by. The sleeves were rolled back on his forearms and he was barefoot. Such a domestic look, at least for his temperament.

Right then, I felt a little frumpy in my old college hoodie and yoga pants. I'd meant to change for our picnic, but with the rain—well, it just didn't seem important.

Now? I really wished I'd taken the extra steps.

He crossed to me and curled his arm around my waist. "Had a bit of a rain delay, but I thought we could maybe do a carpet picnic. Seemed stupid to waste all the food."

"As I was just thinking downstairs that we should go out for pizza."

His smile slipped a little.

I went up on my toes and kissed him. "This is so much better."

His hold tightened and the kiss lengthened, his ink and leather scent seeping into my bones with each sweep of his tongue. The muscles that flexed and rolled under my fingers urged me closer. Each little touch the last few weeks had been leaving me starving for more.

Maybe that had been his plan all along. Right now, I didn't care.

His fingers slid away from me, coming up to cup my face. The kiss was sweeter now. The undertow of emotion and raw passion that rose up between us was more like frothy lace. The kind that tickled and teased.

I felt his smile in the kiss before I opened my eyes.

"What?"

"I've missed touching you like this." His voice was thick and gentle. "Feeling like I should touch you like this."

"Things are complicated."

"They don't have to be."

I leaned my cheek into his touch. "Easy for you to say. You're not technically my employer and baby daddy."

He winced. "When you put it like that…"

"Yeah."

"But that's not what it is about for me." I tried to pull back, but he held me tighter. "It's more that I don't deserve you."

"Asher—" I twisted my fingers into his shirttails.

"No, it's true. You came into my life when I couldn't see my way clear to find any kind of happiness. I didn't even think I should be happy. Not after what had happened with Billy. He died, and here I was, living the life he hoped to have with his baby girl."

"You've done right by her. So right."

"Now I want to do right by you." His Adam's apple rose and fell. "I still can't believe you're here. That someone as strong and amazing as you would stick around and give me a second chance. Or hell, fifth chance by now." He lowered a hand to my middle. "And that there's a piece of us growing right here no matter how many times I fuck things up."

I opened my mouth to answer him, but he kissed me again.

All I could do was hold on. He was like a wild storm. He blew into my life with snow, and now with rain, he was asking for so much more. One season and we were speeding toward something bigger than both of us.

It wasn't just me I had to worry about.

Finally, I tore my mouth away from him. "Just be careful with me, Asher." I hated the weakness in my voice. Hated that I needed to voice it.

"Let me in. Give me a chance."

I looked down at his chest. The wide expanse of it urged me to lean in. To let him shoulder some of the weight. But what if I leaned? Wouldn't it be even harder to stand on my own if he got tired of the novelty of us?

He kissed my forehead. "You're thinking so hard. I know I have work to do, but I'm not afraid of us. Not anymore."

I lifted my gaze to his. I didn't have the words. But I could show him. I lifted onto my toes and slipped my fingers through his hair. He lowered his mouth to mine. We were a pressure cooker that finally let the release valve free.

I breathed him in as my shoulders relaxed. I could feel his heart beating against my chest, knew it was echoing in the wild beat in my ears. His warm fingers slipped under my hoodie to find my belly. He trailed his fingertips over my stomach and up to my bra.

He watched me as I attacked his buttons with shaking fingers.

I felt more reassured when his hand trembled lightly against my breast. This was just as big for him as it was for me. This man had been the only one to touch me like this. Part of me knew he'd be the last one to touch me too.

Even if we didn't work, I wasn't sure I'd be able to let anyone learn my body and get to know me as Asher had.

I pushed off his shirt and trailed the pads of my fingers over the swirling ink of his many tattoos. So traditional in so many ways, and wild in others.

I knew that firsthand. I was carrying the proof of it right now.

Even when we'd tried to be safe. When we'd tried to take a slice of a lonely night between us, we'd created a tether that would never be broken. As if the universe had ideas we couldn't fathom.

He lifted my sweatshirt off and then crouched in front of me to remove my yoga pants and simple cotton underwear. "You are so beautiful."

I looked down at him, sifting my fingers through his untamable hair. Here too, he couldn't quite stay in the aristocrat box he believed he belonged in. There was so much more to Asher Wainwright.

More than even I knew.

"Let me take you to bed, Hannah."

"No. Show me here on the blanket you set up for us for our springtime picnic." I smiled faintly. "Rain be damned."

He drew me down with him, stretching me out on the soft blanket. "You deserve more than this cotton quilt."

"Pretend it's just us and the sunshine. That we have that afternoon free to be just us. That we're two people who can take the day off just to have fun and get naked."

"Every time I've touched you, it's been more than just sex." He drew his fingers between my breasts up to my neck.

I stretched into his touch, my eyes fluttering shut as he lightly scored over the column of my neck and back down. "Yes."

His lips followed the same trail as he deftly curled me closer so he could unsnap my bra. He slid the lace down and drew a lazy trail over the tops of my breasts before finally taking a nipple into his mouth. He groaned around the tight tip and I arched to give him more access. I rolled him, so I could get my leg over his hip.

"Why are you still wearing your jeans?"

"Because if I take them off, I'll be more worried about getting into your sweet heat than what you need."

"What if that's exactly what I need?"

He rolled me onto my back, taking my nipple into his mouth again as he cupped and rubbed my other breast. "Let me worship you first."

"What if a certain little girl wakes up?"

He moved lower. "Guess I'll just have to make my way downtown a little faster." He inched farther down the blanket and hooked my knee over his shoulder. "I miss this, Hannah. I miss tasting you on my lips."

I hissed out a moan and arched as he nibbled his way over my belly to my inner thigh. "It feels like you haven't been there in so long."

"I haven't. And I'm going to rectify that mistreatment."

I laughed. I didn't realize I had laughter in me right now, but there it was. I tightened my knee against his head as he licked every inch of me then found some specialized map to all the places that made me wild.

I was a shuddering mess and he was just calmly working his way around me with a tongue that should be bronzed.

"Let go," he said against my thigh. He nipped me, then laved his tongue over the little hurt. "Don't fight this."

"I'm not."

He looked up from between my legs. "You are."

I twisted my fingers into his hair. This disheveled and purposeful version of Asher made me want him even more. "Maybe I want it to be us, not you giving all the time."

He crawled back up to meet me, his mouth harder and surer this time. The Asher I dreamed about and wished for when I couldn't push away the longing.

I scraped my foot down his jean-clad leg. "Off," I said against his mouth. "Inside me. Make me come again. Just us."

He groaned against my neck. "I was trying."

"And succeeding. But I just want you. If you want to spend the rest of the evening going for gold medals and lightning rounds, I'm good with that. But right now, lose the damn jeans. I need you."

The rasp of his zipper made me sigh in relief. I reached between us and fumbled with the boxer briefs keeping him from me.

"Hannah," he said in a strangled voice.

I didn't want to wait anymore. The hot length of him fit my hand perfectly. Then with his slow push into me, there was the fullness I could never seem to get enough of. I curled my legs around his hips and held him deep inside me. "There. God, yes there."

"Jesus." He raced kisses up my neck and found my mouth. He fisted my hair with one hand and braced himself over me with the other.

I didn't even care that his jeans were chafing against my thighs. I raked my nails down his back and into the back of his jeans to grip his ass. The flex of his muscles pushed me closer to the bliss I was chasing. The one I only seemed to find with him.

I wrapped myself around him and embraced the storm we were together. Even as I let it take me under, I trusted that he'd have me. That breaking under him wouldn't splinter me apart. That he'd put me back together when it passed.

He chanted my name against my mouth, my neck, even my shoulder as his teeth scraped over my flesh. I didn't think he could get any deeper inside of me, but I was so wrong. That he lost control with me and trusted I'd catch him too was so humbling.

And as powerful as anything I'd ever known.

I cried out his name, and his intense eyes snapped to mine as he slowed. There was nothing but him and me. The rough, almost frenetic pace slipped into the dreamy in-between. Where I didn't know where he ended and I began. The kisses slowed and the friction between our bodies started a slow burn.

I wasn't even aware the end was coming. I wanted to bask in the closeness we'd been too afraid to ask the other for. But he knew my body too well.

God, he fit me as if he was the missing puzzle piece the universe had created just for me.

"Hannah," he said against my neck.

I couldn't control the sob. The almost unbearable twisting release that was pleasure and pain and the sort of drowning that stole breath and sense. When I surfaced again, it was his hazel eyes searching mine.

His wet eyes mirroring every emotion I'd dared to wish for.

I cupped his face. I didn't have words for what we were yet, but I was so glad I wasn't alone anymore.

TWENTY-THREE

Asher

"You wanted to see me?" Vincent appeared in my doorway, appearing more disheveled than I'd ever seen him.

I leaned back in my chair and closed out of the spreadsheet I'd had open detailing the rest of the year's marketing plans. I had a feeling a lot of them would be changing at the very least, if not being cancelled altogether.

That bothered me less than I ever would've guessed.

"I did, but unfortunately, I have an appointment I can't miss."

That was an understatement. In a little while, I'd be picking up Hannah for our first real baby doctor's appointment. Well, other than the one where she'd originally gotten the news. She was three and a half months along now, and from my reading—I shifted to make sure my leg was firmly covering the pregnancy book I'd been perusing on breaks—she was behind on her required visits.

Not that I would tell her this, of course. I had no desire to be disinvited from my own child's doctor's visit.

We'd been doing well lately, but a smart man knew when not to push his luck. I was also enjoying the perk of regular sex. It had only been a week or so since our carpet picnic, so early days yet on that score, but I wasn't about to count how long it had been since I'd had even that much regularity in my life.

"Sorry. I know I was supposed to meet up with you earlier, but Connie had an issue with one of the photos in the weekly and all hell broke loose. One of the new guys thought it would be funny to sub a picture of the mayor for a dude dressed up as a hot dog and the caption called him head wiener." Vincent raked a hand through his unusually shaggy dark hair. He was usually clean-shaven with perfectly coiffed hair, but then again, I used to be that way too.

I rubbed the scruff I hadn't had time to deal with this morning, due to lingering over coffee with Hannah and Lily. And before that, lingering with Hannah in bed until the baby's cries had drawn us down the hall.

We had a lot more of that in our future. We were getting the hang of it—well, starting to anyway.

So much new. So many fresh starts.

And I wasn't responding to Vincent, although to be honest, I found the hot dog thing pretty fucking funny.

I cleared my throat. "That's unfortunate."

"It's ridiculous is what it is, and Connie is going to fire that idiot." Vincent tucked his hands under his arms. "I figured that's why you want to meet with me too. So, if you want to fire me, just tell me straight. I don't need you to soften the blow. What I did was insubordination, plain and simple."

"You didn't intend for Daly to run to me and squeal like a little piggy." At Vincent's shifty expression, I checked my watch. I had a feeling we would be cutting it close for the appointment. "Or did you?"

"Deep down, yeah, I probably hoped he would. If I thought you would listen to my ideas, I would have approached you. Hell, I should have anyway. It's none of Daly's business, and we're friends."

"Are we?"

"I thought so."

"So did I until Daly's call. While I understand your motivations, I really wish you'd chosen another route."

"In retrospect, so do I." He exhaled. "If you intend to let me go, let's do it and get it over with."

"Why, so you can run to the Rochester Daily and share your ideas with them instead?" I shook my head. "Sorry, can't let that happen. I want Wainwright to be a force into the next generation, and you're the man to take us there."

Vincent's brow furrowed. "I am?"

"You are. I want to discuss in depth exactly what that means, and how your role will be changing—and mine, for that matter—but the appointment I can't miss is my baby's first doctor's visit. Well, in utero."

"In—what?" Vincent looked over his shoulder as if he expected said baby to appear behind him. "Where did you get another baby?"

"It sure wasn't off eBay." I stood and grabbed my suit jacket off the back of my chair.

"Wait, now you're cracking jokes?" He rubbed the side of his face. "Was it really you singing 'The Gambler' in the john yesterday? I thought it was you, but then I decided it couldn't be. You don't sing."

"I do now." My voice was remarkably cheerful considering I was pretty sure my ears were fire-engine red. "I sing not particularly well, I make not funny jokes, and I step back in a company when someone else has all the drive and ambition that I no longer possess. But I have some interesting leads on new things to occupy myself with." I pulled on my jacket. "What do you know about podcasts?"

"A little bit. You're actually going to step back? You live and breathe this business, Asher." Before I could respond, he scraped a hand through his hair. "Look, what I said probably came from a little bitterness. Not your fault, and you've never done anything to deserve it. You've been the best fucking boss a guy could ask for." He cleared his throat. "Pardon my French."

I laughed and bent to pick up my briefcase. "To pay me back, tell me what you know about podcasts while you walk me out."

"Sure. And uh, Boss, you left that behind." He pointed at my chair.

"It'll give the cleaning staff a thrill." I rounded the desk. "They should especially enjoy the underlined parts."

Vincent glanced back as I tried to nudge him out the door. "What's underlined? Is that really a preggo handbook?"

"More of a primer, let's say. And don't even think about looking at it. You do realize where my new home is, don't you? Apparently, the whole town is under a baby spell." I shut my office door behind me.

"What the hell are you talking about?"

Vincent's reaction was similar to my own when I'd discovered Crescent Cove was well-known for something more than quaint lakeside views and charming shops. "If you're curious, stop into Brewed Awakening in the Cove. Ask for Macy, the owner. She'll give you an earful."

She'd surely given me one when I stopped in for a cup of java the other morning. I'd mentioned that Hannah was Vee's dog-walker for little Latte. Hannah had met Vee during her brief time working at the café—a job she'd quit shortly after she'd taken on the nanny job. Vee had a passel of children, thanks to an ad searching for a baby daddy in the Cove. And also, due to drinking too much of Crescent Cove's water.

The last part was just speculation.

Vincent yanked on his tie. "I'm not sure I'm man enough to."

"Me either, but I survived." We crossed the newsroom and passed the fleet of offices that surrounded the main hive to emerge in the hallway that led to the exit. "I'm pretty sure Hannah and I got caught up in forces bigger than ourselves. Sage may be a baby pusher too, for all I know."

"Who's Hannah?" Vincent cocked his head. "Oh, your baby mama?"

I frowned. "Don't call her that."

"What should I call her then?"

I didn't know. We didn't have any labels for each other. We were just existing in this free space where we made the rules and figured out the path forward. "The answer," I said softly before I caught Vincent's strange look and realized what I'd said.

But it felt true, so I didn't correct my statement. Just kind of...lived with it for a moment.

254

That she could be my answer when I hadn't even realized I was still full of questions seemed like an unspeakable miracle.

The topic shifted to Vincent's knowledge of podcasts, which I think he appreciated. I understood the desire to relegate the subject of settling down and babies to a box at the back of the closet. God knows I hadn't been looking to expand my family on New Year's Eve.

Luckily, some unseen hands had guided us together. Or…Sage.

I was still sure she had something to do with it. Or my grandmother. Maybe both of them. Every town had a matchmaker, didn't they?

Perhaps Crescent Cove had two in the making.

Vincent and I parted with an agreement to discuss the transition on Friday, including the specifics of what exactly that would mean. But I made sure he understood that while my overall role would be smaller, I would still be keeping my hand in. I would also be working some longer hours in the weeks leading up to officially handing him the reins, just to ensure the change would be a success.

We ended the conversation with a handshake—and a hug, which I appreciated much more now that I was becoming the sort of man who sang Kenny Rogers' songs in the men's room at nine am.

The old austere Asher probably would've sprayed his hand with sanitizer and forgotten the whole thing had ever occurred. Good thing I'd sent him packing.

He was sort of an asshole.

I texted Hannah on the way to let her know I was running late.

Oh, don't rush. I just went into labor.

Despite that impossibility, I nearly swerved off the road.

You nearly made me drive into a ditch.

You shouldn't be texting and driving anyway. What kind of example are you setting for the children?

The word *children* sent a chill through me as it always did. At least it wasn't nearly as paralyzing anymore.

The children can't see what I'm doing right now and I'm using text-to-speech anyway. Did you miss me?

Who is this again?

Laughter rolled through me, filling the car. That was me laughing like that. Not just a polite chuckle at parties, but actually fucking *laughing.*

I swallowed hard. Billy would be proud of me. And he'd tell me it was about time.

He was right. It was past time.

When I pulled up at home, I made sure the radio was cranked up and that I was singing John Mayer's "Your Body is a Wonderland" at top volume. Hannah came out laughing, carrying Lily in her little yellow rain slicker, and I forgot how to breathe.

"You didn't finish," Hannah said breathlessly as she bent down to lean in my window.

"Finish what?"

"The song?"

"What song?"

"Asher." Hannah grinned as she pushed her finger into my forehead. "What's your damage today?"

Lily babbled a word that sounded an awful lot like "Asher" and tilted precariously forward to grab for my face. Then she gave me a sloppy kiss that smelled of grape jelly.

"Daddy," I corrected her without thinking, my gaze connecting with Hannah's over Lily's reddish-brown hair.

Hannah's throat moved as we both waited for something that didn't come. But I couldn't claim to be disappointed, because I'd never come so close to wanting that before.

Had never figured it was in the cards for me.

Hannah came around the car and got Lily into her carseat before joining me in the front. I turned down the radio and backed out of the driveway, my thoughts so loud she probably was getting a headache.

"You can be her Daddy too, you know." She touched my thigh. "It's not an either/or situation. Her father will always be her father."

"Yeah." I tightened my hands around the wheel. "You're right."

"You've earned that name and then some, which is why she'll be calling you that sooner than you think. Right now, she's pretty obsessed with sounding out *jelly*, but I bet that will be the next word on her list."

Smiling, I slid her a sidelong glance. "Or maybe Mommy."

She held my gaze until I reached over to grip her hand. She tangled her fingers with mine and I pressed them to her belly, needing her to know I wasn't only talking about Lily. Our family of four was new and special and scary as hell, but I was all in.

Now I just had to convince Hannah.

We arrived at her doctor's office a short while later. I grabbed my glasses out of the visor on the way in, raising my eyebrows innocently as Hannah shot me a look.

"I'm sure we'll be looking at paperwork."

"Right. You're sure you want to make me all hot and bothered."

I tugged her against my side as we reached the door. "Side benefit. Right, Lily Patch?"

Lily screwed up her mouth. "Asher."

I sighed. "I'm going to be the only one at parent-teacher nights whose kid calls them by their first name, aren't I?"

Hannah's lips twitched. "No. Because she'll probably call me by mine too."

The acknowledgement that Hannah intended to stick around for the long haul made my grip around her shoulders tighten. I brushed a kiss over her hair and Lily leaned between us from her perch in Hannah's arms, offering her face up to me for a kiss.

Hannah chuckled. "See, she thinks you're handsome in your glasses too."

I kissed Lily's forehead and steered them to the desk in the waiting room. We filled out some paperwork, then took our seats.

257

I was only hyperventilating a little about the purpose of this visit. Baby steps sometimes felt fucking huge.

We weren't waiting long, shockingly enough, although it seemed as if half the people waiting were entranced by Lily. Lily, however, only cared about the big foam blocks on the floor.

When Dr. Ellis's nurse ushered us into her office, Lily was still clutching a block with the letter F that she refused to release. I'd tried to pry it away twice, only for her to howl as if I was trying to murder her.

Kids were cute. And terrifying.

"Hi, Hannah. Good to see you. And Asher Wainwright, it's a pleasure to finally formally meet you. I've heard so much about you." Dr. Ellis smiled as she and Hannah exchanged a look that I didn't understand.

"You have?" We shook hands and I glanced at Hannah. "What has she been saying about me?"

"Just that you double bagged the night you knocked me up."

"What? I did not." I frowned, thinking back. "No. I didn't. It had been a while, but not quite long enough for me to forget everything I know."

"If that was you after forgetting..." Hannah trailed off and set down Lily on the children's mat on the floor to play with her block.

Dr. Ellis laughed and leaned against her desk. "Happy accidents happen all the time in my line of work." She cocked her head at Hannah. "Your mood has changed since our last appointment."

Hannah rose from her crouch beside Lily. "I've had some time to sit with the idea."

"Yes, you have. And you seem to have a supportive partner. Am I correct, Asher?"

I didn't know if all doctors got this personal, but I had a feeling Hannah and Dr. Ellis had a different dynamic than the usual doctor/patient relationship.

"Yes. Since we've kicked things off with a bang already, I've brought some questions. I have a book, but I haven't covered everything yet." I pulled the folded piece of paper I'd ripped out of my

Day-Timer from my jacket pocket. "How long can we safely have intercourse?"

"You did not just ask that," Hannah muttered. "And I can answer that for her—that time has already passed. The door is locked on you now."

"I didn't mean how late, although that's a good question too. I meant actual duration."

Hannah shook her head and took the seat beside me. "If you weren't wearing those glasses, there's a good chance I might walk right out of this office."

Dr. Ellis laughed. "It's a good question to ask. As far as how late, some women find sexual intercourse to be helpful in stimulating a natural birth, especially if it ends in an orgasm. As long as the woman is comfortable and healthy in other ways, we don't really put a date on when to stop. As for the other," she winked and Hannah shut her eyes, "that's entirely up to personal preference."

Hannah didn't say a lot through the whole visit, although she did ask a few pertinent questions about what she should be eating and not eating and different milestones. But I was far more vocal, especially when I learned she'd actually lost three pounds since her last visit instead of gaining.

"We're getting a steak dinner after we leave here," I informed her. "One you didn't make, no matter how delicious your cooking is."

Hannah sighed and slipped her shoes back on. "I think stress burns calories, because I'm definitely eating plenty."

"Eating for two is a different animal, but some women don't gain much at all. I wouldn't worry. You're doing everything right." Dr. Ellis smiled at Hannah. "You're in great health, Hannah, and once we do the sonogram in about five weeks or so, you'll be able to see your baby."

"Including the gender?"

Hannah immediately shook her head. "I want to wait. It should be a surprise."

"For the whole nine months? That's a long time."

"You've already covered the first three," Dr. Ellis reminded me.

I released a slow breath. "Good point. That's still far too long."

"We'll discuss it." But Hannah sounded about as flexible as she did when I gave her business ideas. Although she was getting a bit more open-minded there.

As for the gender reveal timing, we'd just see about that. I had an ace up my sleeve.

On the way home, I made an unexpected detour. Lily was fussing in the back, so I decided to show my own flexibility by stopping at the McDonald's drive thru and getting a soft serve vanilla cone for Lily and a Big Mac for Hannah. She rolled her eyes, but she ate it, licking the special sauce off her fingers in a way that was far hotter than it should have been.

"Is this your first time through a drive-thru?" she asked.

"Why, just because I asked where the silverware was?"

"You have a burger and fries. You don't *get* silverware, Mr. Silver Spoon." She reached over to wipe salt off my chin. "I like when you don't shave," she added, licking the salt off her fingertip.

"Like glasses, check. Like scruff, check. Like to make me uncomfortable when there's a baby sitting nearby, check." I glanced over my shoulder at Lily, whose face was covered with vanilla ice cream. I couldn't keep from laughing. "You enjoying that cone, Lily Patch?"

Hannah looked back too and laughed with me. "Lily Patch is such a cute nickname for her."

"It was Billy's. He always joked he found her in the cabbage patch. She was the red-headed doll, although now she's getting more brown. Aren't you?"

Lily tossed the remnants of the cone on the floor.

Hannah sighed, unbuckling herself. "I'll just—"

"No, I've got her. Eat your lunch. The baby is hungry even if you aren't." I unclicked my seat belt, stopping when I realized Hannah was staring. "What?"

"You really want this baby." She cleared her throat. "Our baby."

I didn't have to think. "Yes, I do. And I really want you too." I gripped her hand. "Not as an incubator. Because you're Hannah

Jacobs, and I haven't been able to take my eyes off of you since I saw you scribbling secrets in a diary."

Her cheeks pinkened. "It's more of a business planner now."

"Did you tell it about us having sex?"

"It? You realized it's a bound book?

"Yes. Did you?"

She licked her lips, nice and slow. "Maybe. Maybe not."

I shook my head. "You have an evil side, and I'm not sure what it says about me that I find it sexy."

She gave me a rare full smile. "Me either."

We finished our lunches and got back on the road. I had a surprise destination, one I didn't clue Hannah in on.

"Where are we going?"

"You'll see." I tossed her a grin.

"Are you kidnapping me?"

"Maybe. I wouldn't mind tying you up and having my way with you. Probably not with the baby present though."

"Asher Wainwright, you're a kinky sort. I never would've guessed."

My grin widened. "Imagine that."

I pulled into the parking lot of Tattoo You and Hannah whipped her head toward me. "I'm not getting a tattoo. I don't like needles. Especially big needles. No, I hate them all."

"We aren't here for you."

"Then?" Her gaze dropped to my chest, although it obviously wasn't visible through my shirt. "You don't have that much real estate left to get inked, at least on your torso. Which still doesn't fit with any of the rest of you."

"See what happens when you have a crazy buddy who encourages you to do wild stuff?" I flicked my thumb along the corner of her mouth. "Or your crazy boyfriend?"

Saying it made my pulse pound in my ears so I quickly unbuckled and got out of the car. "You and Lily can stay here. I'm just going in for a quick consultation with my regular guy. He doesn't know if he can get the outline started today or not."

"Okay."

"Or you can come in if you want—"

She'd already pulled out her phone. "I'll be fine. I may come in if I need the ladies' room. Joy of pregnancy, peeing every five minutes."

On that note, I headed in.

Lance, my longtime tattoo artist, came out to greet me with a grin and a clap on the back. "I thought you were done with tats for a while." His expression clouded. "After Billy—"

"Yeah. This is for him though. And for my girl and my kids." More things that sounded weird on my tongue, but I forced them out because I couldn't wait around for the magical time when my life didn't scare the holy shit out of me.

Maybe being scared meant I was finally living again.

"Oh, yeah? You told me a little on the phone, but lay it on me. I'll do some sketches while we talk. If you like any of them, we can start laying down the outline today. Can do some more filling in in a couple weeks. We're jammed in here nowadays, man."

"That's great." I glanced out the big glass windows and noticed Hannah was now leaning into the backseat to fuss with Lily. "Let's work on those sketches and by then, Hannah should need the bathroom. I'll see if she can wait while we get it started."

Lance laughed. "Is that how it is?" He turned and craned his neck. "She's the pretty brunette in the front seat?"

"Yeah."

"You did good. She's gorgeous."

"She is."

"You said kids?" Lance waggled his brows as we moved toward his station in back. "It hasn't been that long since I've seen you. You've been busy."

"Well, Lily—"

"Yeah, Lily." Lance scraped a hand over the top of his head, skimming down over his stubby ponytail. The back of his neck was tattooed with intricate Chinese characters. "How is she?"

"Good. Growing like a weed. She's already at the top of her percentile." The pride in my voice made my steps falter.

Was it odd that I was proud of something I'd had no hand in?

No. I didn't have to take ownership in her accomplishments and milestones to appreciate them. And thank God for that.

"Not surprising. Billy was a damn string bean." Lance pulled out a chair for me and grabbed his sketch pad. "Okay, let's talk turkey."

I told him what I had in mind, giving him the freedom to sketch whatever he thought would work. As I talked, he nodded and sketched and erased and added more shading.

"I was thinking a vine."

"Where do you want it?"

I rolled up my right sleeve. "I was thinking my forearm. Not too far down, because of work—" Hearing myself, I shook my head. "Nah, I'm going to be working more out of my house for a while. I can have the fucking ink on my hand if I want it there."

Lance grinned. "You sure can. You can have it come right down like this." He sketched out his drawing with a fingertip on the back of my hand. He had the ink climbing toward my fingers, which was definitely more than I'd planned on. But I didn't want to hide the design. If anything, I wanted to be able to look down and see it anytime I needed the visual reaffirmation.

I had a family now, one that was anchored in the past and growing stronger by the day.

"Not a vine though. I'm seeing a tree. Lots of gnarled branches, thick roots. And the names can be woven in between the gaps." He turned his sketch pad toward me. "Like that."

"Oh, that's awesome. Can you start it today?" I rolled my shirt up even higher. "You can do it mostly black, with the names maybe in—"

"Colors like leaves I'm thinking?"

"Yes. That's good. Autumn." I looked up again just as the bell jingled over the door. Hannah walked inside, holding Lily on her hip, her sunglasses propping back her long fall of hair. "Hey, babe, come look at this."

I didn't know why I called her *babe*. I also didn't expect her eyes to widen at the sight of me as if she'd forgotten entirely who I was. Then she pressed her lips together and rushed off with Lily in the direction of the restrooms. Somehow she knew where to find them.

Women were geniuses.

"Yeah, she's smokin'. Got some curves on her too." At my narrow-eyed look, Lance cleared his throat. "Just saying. I could see tattooing her name on my branch too."

I choked out a laugh. "Jesus. But yeah, let's get it started today. If she won't look at the sketch, she can at least see the outline."

"She has a problem with ink?"

"Some needle phobia. Since she's pregnant, hope she gets over it."

"Oh." Lance nodded knowingly. "Kids, huh? Don't blame you. I'd want to get that one on lockdown too."

I frowned. "It wasn't like that. It was just a…" Dr. Ellis's phrase came back to mind. "Happy accident."

"Good for you, man. Let's get this ink started then before we get swamped."

I tried to shift to see Hannah and Lily emerge from the bathroom, but I was positioned wrong. In no time, Lance had a good bit of the main trunk done, with the climbing branches extending up my hand. Some of them were knottier, the ink dense and dark in spots. Other spots had room for the names. He put them down in thin black ink for now, with the idea to add highlights and color shading during the next visit.

Billy.

Gran.

Lily.

Hannah.

And the word Happy.

Just…happy.

"Oh my God. That's—" I turned my head and glimpsed Hannah standing a few feet away, her hands up to her mouth. "Holy shit, that's hot."

Lance looked up from his work with a smirk. "Somebody's getting lucky tonight."

With effort, I tried to keep my face sober as I spoke over the noise of the tattoo gun. "You like it? Come closer. There's—"

"I see." She pointed at the sketch book that had fallen off the table and landed face up on the floor. "You have all of our names. And…happy?"

"Yeah, since we don't know the gender yet, and we won't for a while, we can't pick a name. So, happy accident seems to fit, right?"

Hannah moved forward and cupped my cheek, leaning down to give me a hard kiss. "Yes, we can find out next month. No, you didn't outwit me. Yes, I know you're conning me. No, I don't care." She stepped back as my head revolved off my shoulders—not from the effect of the tattoo either—and smiled at the receptionist, currently carrying a giggling Lily. "Thanks for watching her for a minute."

"Oh, no problem. Your baby is an angel."

Hannah's gaze met mine as she answered softly, "Yes, she is."

TWENTY-FOUR

"I HATE WHEN HE'S RIGHT." I JUGGLED MY PHONE WITH MY IPAD AS I tried to keep my video call going with Gabby.

"No, you don't."

"I so do."

I brought the phone up to meet her gaze. "Especially when I wasn't prepared for the influx of orders."

I tucked my phone into the stand I'd found in the pantry. No idea why it was in there, but then again, I often found weird things in the house. It was as if Asher had bought the house as is and forgot to finish filling all the rooms.

But the last owner had to have been a cook because the stand was the best thing on the planet. I was forever snatching my phone out of some puddle of sauce or pile of flour. With this thing? Well, it was official, I might actually marry it.

I quickly checked my site on my iPad and found seven more orders for this afternoon. I sent them to my label printer and for the first time since I'd opened Hannah's Helping Hand Box, I had to turn off the delivery option.

"Don't worry, we'll get them all delivered."

Since things had been going so well between myself and Asher, he'd felt comfortable enough to tell me what I was doing wrong in my business.

Looking at his gorgeous new tattoo had helped soothe my annoyance at his suggestions, I had to admit.

It had taken a few trips to the tattoo parlor, but now it was all done. Perhaps I spent a little more time than necessary making sure it was properly moisturized. Mostly because it was ridiculously thoughtful and hot in some crazy way I didn't know how to explain. Ink had never been my thing, until my traditional, workaholic lover had gone ahead and done something so over the top and special.

Something for just us and our growing family.

That was Asher. He was so linear with certain things like business. Almost rigid enough to make me want to smack the crap out of him. Then he tossed me a sweet curve ball that left me confused and nursing a mushy heart that felt almost too full.

As my menu had been too full. I honestly hadn't believed cutting it in half would help. In fact, Asher had told me to cut it down to five items.

I did it, simply to prove him wrong. And now—chaos.

Damn him.

"Thanks for helping me deliver. It's going to be crazy, but I think if we both do it, we'll be fine."

The video shook a little and the sound of a slamming car door flooded me with relief. She was already on her way over, thank God. The vid righted itself. "I'll be there in ten."

"Bless you."

Gabby gave me a thumbs up. "We're good, mamacita." Then the video went off.

I scooped up Lily and deposited her in the pack and play. She screeched her displeasure, and I gave in and gave her the puffed treats she loved. As well as her new favorite toys, a plastic bake set.

I couldn't say I minded that she was taking after me in some regard, even if I wasn't her mom. Though I felt like she was mine more every day. Asher too.

At least until lately.

Of course, he wasn't around to help today. I probably should have called Bess, but if I was going to make this business a success, I needed to find my own balance. Then again if Asher had been around, I would have been happy to let him pitch in. I'd gotten way too used to him being home in the evenings, and that was on me. I only had myself to lean on—and Gabby. She never let me down.

Already, I was thinking about asking Gabby to become my partner, not just my helper with deliveries. That was if things kept on the same trajectory. I'd thought Asher might be interested in making my company a bit of a family business, but lately, he'd been distant again. Working late hours like he had when I first started taking care of Lily.

Only this time, he continued to crawl into bed with me at night. No matter how exhausted we both were, there was no true sleep until he was curled around behind me in the deepest part of the night. It was the only thing I could hang onto at the moment.

Luckily, I was usually too busy to think about it most of the time.

Lily was walking now—not well, but just enough to get into trouble all the time. Between chasing after her and my slowly increasing customer base, I was in bed at almost the same time as Lily. Even if I wanted to stay up to have some adult conversations—or playtime—it just wasn't happening.

"All right, baby girl. Let's get this party started." I flicked through the settings on my phone and found my packing playlist. It started with "Lay Your Hands on Me" by Bon Jovi and instantly clicked my brain into gear. By the time Gabby arrived, I'd packed up my beef stroganoff, spicy lemon shrimp, and half of the grilled veggie pasta.

She knocked on the back door to the mudroom and I let her in. "Hey."

She swooped in and hugged me. "I can't believe you ended up with that many orders in one day."

"I'm convinced the universe likes to mess with me. I only changed the menu to show Asher he didn't know what he was talking about."

"We'll give him the win since it tripled your sales."

I laughed. "He'll end up all strutting peacock with the knowledge."

"You know how to bring him back down to human male levels."

"All I have to do is read aloud from the baby book. Usually does the trick."

"Would work for me. Between Mami's labor stories and yours, I'm never having a kid."

"You say that, but then your whole world changes."

"If you say so." She followed me in and took an appreciative deep breath. "Girl, it smells amazing in here."

"Thank God, I'd made enough of the stroganoff that I could extend the recipe. Serves Asher right that he won't get to have any."

"You are a cruel woman."

"Damn straight."

As usual, we worked well together. Within thirty minutes, we had everything packed up, including Lily Patch, and we were both loading every soft-sided cooler I had into our cars. We double-checked the addresses and ensured that our GPS units could actually find them before splitting up.

"I have to head to my parents' house after deliveries."

"That's fine. Tell Bonnie I said hello and that I want a cooking lesson. I'd love to add some of her Spanish Italian fusion recipes to my repertoire."

"God, her head will be swollen, but I'll tell her." Gabby slammed the door and rolled down the window. "I'm so proud of you for making this happen, chica."

I grinned at her. "Thanks. Couldn't do it without you, babe." I waved as she headed down the drive then turned to my little charge. "You ready to go for a ride?"

Lily blew kisses, her new favorite trick. "I'll take that as a yes."

"Asher!"

I shook my head. "Nope, just Hannah Banana today, kiddo."

"Bnnaaa."

Delighted, I blew raspberries into her neck. "Close!"

When she was a giggling ball of happiness, I locked her into her crazy harness. The baby seats were no joke. I turned on some more Bon Jovi for her, since the rockers were her favorite band as of late. I was a little more partial to current music, but nineties' rock would do for this sunny afternoon.

The first six drop-offs were perfection. I even managed to get an applesauce squeeze pack into Lily without too much fanfare. Eating in the car was a trick sometimes. I ate one too for a little sugar boost.

I plugged the next three drop-offs into the GPS, and we sang our way through the *Have a Nice Day* album. At least we were finally heading into the 2000s with that album. We were clapping along to the songs so loud that I didn't hear the grinding noise at first.

When the song changed over to the slower "Bells of Freedom", I heard it.

It got even louder as I stepped on the brakes. I turned down the music and winced. It had been awhile since I had driven my car, but I'd definitely never heard that sound before. Suddenly, the grinding became a screech and Lily put her hands over her ears.

"Nahh."

"Yeah, I know, kiddo. Hang on." I pulled over to the side of the road. "Shit." We were just outside of town on a country road.

I grabbed my phone out of my bag and quickly went for my contacts. My thumb hovered over Asher's name. He was in meetings all day, according to our family Google calendar. This definitely wasn't an emergency.

I was an independent woman with a roadside assistance subscription. I glanced at the time with a wince. I still had a half dozen deliveries to do, and it was already after four in the afternoon. Checking the rearview mirror to make sure Lily was still happy, I dialed the tow company.

A pleasant woman picked up. I explained where I was and that my car wasn't drivable.

"Unfortunately, it's rush hour, and I can't get anyone out there for at least ninety minutes."

"Ninety? I have a child with me."

"Are you in immediate danger?" Her voice became clipped.

"No."

"Can you turn the car on to keep it heated?"

"Well, yes." Obviously, she had a checklist of some sort, and I had a feeling I was not getting any of the good checkmarks.

"Are you on the side of the road with high speed traffic?"

"Look, I get it. We're not a priority, but ninety minutes? That seems excessive."

"You are in a low tow area, ma'am."

I rolled my eyes. "I have food in the car that will spoil."

"I'm sorry. I'll have a tow truck there as soon as possible."

"Never mind."

"Are you sure?"

"I can't sit here for ninety minutes. I'll find an alternative."

The voice paused and the background noise went silent. Damn mute button. I hated when customer service people used that. Like we didn't know they were doing it. She came back on the line. "We'll leave the service call in. If you find an alternative, just try to call us back."

"Fine, fine."

I rummaged in my bag when Lily started to fuss. I took out one of her favorite teething rings and passed it back to her before I hung up.

Crap. Crap. Crap.

Again, my finger hovered over Asher's number and I thumbed down to Gabby's number instead. "Hey."

"What's up?" The air was whooshing in the background. Hands-free on a pretty spring day was no joke.

"How many deliveries do you have left?"

"I'm on the last one."

"Great. Where are you?"

Gabby rattled off a street that was at least fifteen minutes away. I sighed. "I ran into a little trouble."

Suddenly, the air noise lessened. "Are you okay?"

"Yeah, we're fine. Something sounded off with my brakes, so I pulled over."

"Oh my God. Where are you?"

"The old country road near the Leonard house."

"I'll be right there." Then the line went dead.

I sighed and bounced my head against my headrest. "Seriously, how is this my life?" I turned to check on Lily. She was gnawing on the ring, drool glistening from her chin and chubby hand. One tooth had finally come in, but she was already cutting another one. "You're going to have a full set of chompers before you turn one, kiddo."

She squeaked out a barrage of babble followed by a giggle. I couldn't help but smile back at her. Even at our worst moments, this kid had a smile at all times.

I did a search for tow companies in the area, then remembered Kramer & Burns from Main Street in Crescent Cove. They did more detailing and design work than mechanics, but maybe he'd take pity on me since we were officially town residents.

"Yo." Came a female voice. "Shit, I mean, Kramer and Burns Auto, how may I help you?"

"Hi, this is Hannah Jacobs. My car broke down, and I was wondering if you were available for a tow?"

"Call Triple A, sweetheart. We only do customs."

"Wait! I live in Crescent Cove. I've heard that Dare will help out people in town."

"You heard wrong."

"Dammit, Tish." I heard the muffled voice in the background, then the phone being fumbled. "This is Dare, how can I help you?"

Lily tossed the rings at me and suddenly started to wail. Perfect.

"Hi. This is Hannah Jacobs. I tried to call Triple A, but they can't get to me for ninety—"

"Don't give it a thought. We don't leave moms stranded. Even if you weren't a mom—besides, Kels would skin me. Sorry about Tish. God, I'm turning into my wife. Let's start this again. Where are you?"

I laughed and turned in my seat to give Lily another applesauce pouch. That might buy me five minutes. "Thank you. I'm so sorry to bother you."

"Not a bother. Just let's get you situated."

I sagged against my seat. "That would be wonderful. I'm on the old county road. Just not sure exactly where."

"Can you see a marker?" I looked out my front window and saw one. Thank God, something going my way. I rattled off the number.

"Perfect. I'll be there in less than twenty."

"Thank you."

I looked at my screen again. Maybe I should text Asher. But then I'd worry him for no reason. We'd be home and in bed before he got home anyway.

I huffed out a breath and plugged it into my car charger. At least I wouldn't have a dead phone on top of all of this. I slapped my hazards on and got out to sit in the back with a whimpering Lily. By the third round of "Born to Be My Baby", Gabby was pulling up behind me.

She got out. "Okay, let me get you and the baby into my car. We can get the baby seat going. Maybe we can even get it installed before dark."

"It's not going to be dark for at least an hour."

"Yeah, but it's you and me doing the car seat." Gabby blew a lock of dark hair out of her eyes.

I laughed because if I didn't, I'd cry. "That's true. Can you help me grab the food first?"

"Yup, got it."

I leaned into the front of the car and hit rewind on the song one more time then got out to help her. When we were loading the last of the coolers into her backseat, a monster tow truck pulled in front of my car.

A rangy, blond man hopped out in a chambray shirt with the sleeves rolled back over massive forearms. "Hannah?"

"Yes!" I peeked around from the trunk. I stopped and waved to Lily in the backseat, who was doing a good job of eating her hand. "Thank goodness. I have orders that need to be delivered."

Dare scratched the back of his neck. "Well, we'll get your car all hooked up and see what's what. Your friend have the deliveries?"

"Yes. They're loaded. Kinda took up the whole of her car."

"Well, I've got a baby seat in the truck. Always seems to come in handy since my son, Sean, is forever wanting to ride with me. Think we've got you covered if you want to send your friend off."

"Oh, thank God. That would be amazing."

"Go on and get your little one. We'll get you taken care of."

He ran back to his rig and backed it up to my car. I hurried over to the backseat and unbuckled Lily, then hooked the diaper bag over my arm as I slipped the baby out of her straps. Gabby came over and I handed Lily over. "Can you hold her for a sec?"

"Are we getting the baby seat?" Gabby's eyes widened as she awkwardly took Lily. "Hey, little girl."

Lily slapped a drooly hand against her cheek. "Asher!"

"Got that one down, kiddo," I muttered and opened the front door to get my purse. I unhooked my phone and swallowed down a string of curse words. My charger didn't work. Wonderful. My battery was at ten percent.

I turned it off to keep whatever I had left available and grabbed my purse.

"Dare has a carseat in his tow truck. I'm going to go into town with him."

"Are you sure?" Gabby's voice lowered. "I don't want to leave you alone with some dude."

"And I don't want my customers to not get their dinners. It's fine, truly."

Gabby bit her lower lip.

"Honestly. His wife is a first-grade teacher. Or she was. Might be on maternity leave like half the town if any of the stories are true. Whatever. He's a stand-up guy." I took back Lily and settled her on my hip with a smile then did the bounce-sway thing she liked. Her head thunked onto my shoulder.

"If you're sure. Keep your phone on you."

"It's dead. My car charger isn't working."

"Girl, I told you to get one of those extra battery things."

"I know, but I was rushing around and didn't take it off the charging station. Whatever, it's fine. I turned off my phone, but I have a little juice left. If I get into trouble, I'll call you."

"I'll be back to pick you up after I'm done."

"No, you said you had a thing at the house for your parents."

"It's fine. They'll understand."

"I'll call Asher if I have to. I just know he's wrapped up in meetings until later tonight."

"I'm coming to get you." Gabby's voice firmed. "Then I'll take you to the house."

"No, you're going to go home and take care of whatever it is you had plans to do."

She gave a dramatic sigh. "Gina has birthdays every year."

"Oh, geez. No. You will go to your sister's birthday dinner right after the last delivery." When she opened her mouth to argue, I pointed at her. "That's an order."

"You're the worst."

"No, I'm the best. And I want us to seriously talk about doing this thing together. For real."

"What?" Gabby's dark eyes went wide.

"We do all the things together, don't we? This should be included."

"I don't know what to say."

"Say you'll think about it. Then we'll crunch some numbers and see what we can come up with. Especially if we're going to keep getting orders like this."

"Yeah. I mean, I have a lot of ideas if you're really serious."

My throat closed up a little and I swallowed down the lump. "Yes. I should have asked you sooner." I patted my slight bump. "Things are going to get hairy soon."

"And not because you can't see your cooch to shave." She impulsively hugged me and even kissed Lily's forehead without being coaxed to do it.

"You're terrible." I laughed and patted her arm. "Okay. Go before the deliveries are even later."

"Going." She dabbed at her eyes. "Okay." She blew out a breath with a laugh. "I'll find you tomorrow. But text me to let me know you're home."

"I will."

She ran back to her car and took off with a wave.

I turned to find Dare already hooking my tires up to whatever winch thing he had going on. He gave Lily a half smile and she buried her face into my neck.

"Sorry. She definitely missed her nap."

"She's not screaming the world down. It works for me. Ready?"

I nodded and followed him to the truck. We got Lily in the seat and I sat in the back with her. It was cramped, but she was happy to have me sitting beside her. She wouldn't let go of my finger at first. Until she looked out the window and realized she had a very different vantage point than my little car.

I relaxed against the seat and dug into my purse. I hadn't checked in with him all day. And he usually texted me a few times to make sure there was nothing amiss.

Then Dare asked me a few questions about what I'd heard when I pulled over. When I made the sound, Lily laughed. Dare gave a small laugh and made a phone call to the shop. I was just about to ask Dare if he had a charger when we hit Main Street.

By then we were getting into the shop, and the noise was intense. Lily's eyes grew huge as she took in all the big machines.

"Tell you what. I'm pretty sure it's your rotors. You probably were driving on the last slivers of your brake pads. It's not a huge deal. Will probably take me about an hour to get them fixed. So, if you want to head over to the café we'll have you on your way."

"Are you serious? It sounded so much worse."

"Nothing quite like metal grinding on metal to scare the crap out of you. If it's worse than that, I'll come down and have a talk with you."

"Thank you so much."

"Happy to help."

I unbuckled Lily and let Dare help me get out of the huge truck. A stunning redhead came out with a welding mask in her hand.

"So, this is the mom you helped. I swear you people are so mush with the kids and moms."

"It's called being a human, Tish." Dare shook his head. "Don't mind her. She forgets how to talk to people. Why we usually keep a welding tool in her hand."

Tish shrugged and put the shield on. She threw up a peace sign and sauntered away.

I glanced around at the custom motorcycle getting worked on in the corner, and the very posh vintage Mustang on a lift. I really didn't want to think about how much this was going to cost me. This was no quickie mechanic place.

Luckily, I had quite a bit of money socked away these days.

"My phone is almost dead, so I'll just come back in an hour or so?"

Dare shook his head. "No. I'll come to you. Or I'll send Rylee a message to let you know to come down. I think she's working at the café today. She's my brother's wife."

"Oh, okay. Sounds good. I really can't thank you enough for helping me."

"Anything for a Cove resident. Even if you're pretty new."

"Good to know. We're not going anywhere." At least I was pretty sure we weren't. I stuffed my purse into the diaper bag and headed out into the near dark. The days were getting longer, but I'd definitely been pushing my luck with everything today.

Brewed Awakening was busy as usual, but not quite as bad as the lunch rush. I was running on empty on a number of levels, so I ordered a mom-to-be friendly cappuccino for me, juice box for Lily and decadent piece of chocolate cake for me.

I freaking deserved it.

I found a table by the window and set Lily in one of the high chairs. Lily shoved her fist into her eye and rubbed hard. "I know how you feel. Just a little bit longer."

At least I hoped so.

TWENTY-FIVE

Asher

THIS WAS IT. THE DAY I'D BEEN WORKING TOWARD FOR WEEKS. MONTHS really, even without fully knowing it. On a number of levels. And as a reward, we'd even finished our final meeting before the reveal a couple of hours early.

I shuffled files into my briefcase, already looking forward to ceremonially dumping the bulk of them into my filing cabinet once I was home. No longer would I be tethered to my office on the go. "Tomorrow's the big day. Are you ready?"

Vincent took a breath, flashing me a grin. "Yeah, Boss, I really think I am."

"You can stop calling me Boss anytime now. You'll officially be fulfilling that role yourself in," I glanced at my watch, "under six hours."

"God. Intense. But you'll still be the boss for all intents and purposes."

"Yes, just less seen and heard from unless you need me. Which you won't. I have every confidence in you."

Vincent got to his feet and gripped the back of the padded chair. "You're really sure you want to do this? I gotta say, I never saw you as the house husband type. Even when the thing happened with your friend, you continued on for the longest time as nothing had fazed you."

"When Billy died, you mean. Not a thing. And if I acted unfazed, it was because I was trying like fucking hell to keep everything together for a little girl who didn't deserve the hand she was dealt."

"Yeah." Vincent pinched the bridge of his nose. "My apologies. I don't mean to diminish it. I give you all the respect in the world for stepping in. I don't think I could've done that. I mean, kids? Yeah, no, not ready yet."

"I thought the same. But luckily, life wouldn't wait for my balls to drop so I had to figure it all out." I gripped the handle of my briefcase, imprinting the feel of it on my hand. Hopefully, I wouldn't be carrying it again anytime soon. "You'd be surprised what you can do when you have no choice."

"But to step back from a successful career—"

"I'm just changing my career. Going in a different direction. I'm hoping to launch the podcast by summertime, so don't think you've seen the last of me. The goal is to pair it with *In Focus* as a tool to go deeper on those news stories."

Vincent nodded. "It's a great angle. I'm looking forward to kicking everything off."

"Tomorrow we make the announcement and do the ribbon cutting for the inaugural issue of the magazine, and then we go from there." I moved around the table to clap him on the back. "Congrats, Boss."

Vincent laughed. "Not true, but it still sounds nice. Thank you for this opportunity. I won't let you down."

"No, and more importantly, you won't let yourself down. Every day is a chance to start the rest of your life. Make it a good one." I glanced at my watch again. "On that note, I'm going home to hopefully do the same."

"Oh, big plans tonight? I'll walk you out."

"Yes, need to pick up some sparkling grape juice and maybe some flowers." I smiled, remembering. "Tulips, I think."

"Romantic night on tap then?"

"Among other things. I've been keeping this all under wraps to surprise Hannah. Figured she might want to be at the big cover reveal tomorrow. Depends, of course, if she can take time off from her meal delivery service—"

"Oh, she does that? That's good to know. I've been looking into those delivery services myself. Good when there's not much time to cook." Vincent and I reached the exit and headed out into the parking lot. "Unless my ordering from your girlfriend's business would be weird."

"No. She doesn't do all the deliveries herself. Gabby does some, and I will be helping out too. So, just be prepared for me to deliver your pork loin some night."

"There's a trick. How exactly do you tip a millionaire?"

"Generously."

Vincent laughed. "Of course now I'm getting hungry. If I ever settle down—which is unlikely—I need to find myself a chef. You got lucky."

I grinned as we reached my car and I opened the door. "I sure am. Get a good night's sleep. I'll see you bright and early."

He blew out a breath. "Will do. You too. Enjoy your night. Thanks again."

"I will."

As was now my tradition, I sang all the way home. Tonight's song on repeat was "Natural" by Imagine Dragons. On the way, I stopped off at the grocery store for a few essentials. The aforementioned sparkling grape juice, a pint of vanilla ice cream, some fresh strawberries, and a rather ostentatious rainbow bouquet of tulips, although I probably lost points for where I was buying them. On impulse, I grabbed some of the bath bomb thingies I knew Hannah enjoyed. Maybe we could enjoy some hot tub time after Lily was asleep.

If Hannah wasn't too tired. And if hot tubs were okay for pregnant women. I'd have to look it up. Or she could take a regular bath, even without me. I wasn't fussy. I just wanted her to enjoy the celebration too.

I was becoming a house husband. Kind of. I mean, not really. I would be outfitting my office to do the podcast in a professional manner, and I intended to keep my hand in at work so I wasn't a stranger. Wainwright had a number of different interests, and just keeping up with them would occupy a chunk of my time.

Plus, there was Hannah's delivery service. I intended to help out there too in whatever way she needed me. Or if she didn't, I'd just keep myself busy elsewhere.

When I rolled into the driveway, I was singing a song from the Black Keys. Then I realized the house was dark.

There wasn't a single light burning anywhere. Even the porch light was off. I hadn't realized how I'd become so used to coming home to a well-lit house. Stepping inside to delicious scents with the music blaring and Lily's giggles while she whaled on whatever toy she was torturing that day. Some days there was an added bonus of Hannah's creative swearing under her breath at whatever she was cooking.

Noise and lights and life. A happy home.

Getting there anyway.

Seeing the place so dark and still made me swallow hard. It was like a flashback of my life pre-Hannah. No one to greet me, no waiting warmth. Just an empty shell of a space waiting in silence until even my footsteps sounded like echoes.

My eyes narrowed on the empty spot where Hannah usually parked. Her car was gone. Not a surprise, but still, the proof she wasn't home struck me low in the gut.

I turned off the radio and pulled out my phone to doublecheck she hadn't left me a message. Nothing. I checked the Google calendar we shared, just in case she'd added an appointment I'd forgotten, but that was blank too. The only thing there were my last few meetings with Vincent and some of our advertisers, advising them of the transition. That part was over now, but she didn't know that. I'd expected them to run later. Maybe that was why she hadn't contacted me to let me know she'd be late.

Maybe.

Quickly, I called her. My racing heart said it wasn't the time for a text. The call went straight to voicemail.

"She's probably just running errands," I said aloud. "No big deal."

I tried her phone again, knowing she wouldn't answer. Needing to do it anyway. I got her voicemail again and told her to call as soon as she got my message. Then I called Gran.

"Hannah isn't with you, is she?"

"No, why?"

"She's not home and I don't know where she is. Is Lily there?"

"No. Neither of them. I haven't talked to Hannah since yesterday."

"Let me know if you hear from her, okay?"

"Why would I hear from her? Snug, what's going on?"

I shut my eyes and leaned back in my seat. "Nothing. Nothing's going on, but tell that to my head. Tell me that this isn't like when no one heard from Billy, and he was lying dead behind a house for hours without anyone knowing. Tell me that. Please."

"Oh, Snug, it's not like that. She's a busy mother. You know she's probably out doing a million things. Maybe even delivering those meals of hers. She didn't answer when you called?"

"No."

"Why don't you come here and we'll go look for her? Just drive around and see if we can track her down. That's what family does."

I wanted to take her up on the offer. God knows I didn't want to be alone. As it was, my hand would've jangled if I hadn't gripped the phone with all my might. But I had to do this myself.

"Thank you. I'm going to do that, but if I need you—"

"If you need me, I'm there. In a heartbeat."

"Thank you," I repeated, voice thick. "I love you, Gran."

"Just as I love you, my Snug."

I didn't want to end the call, but I did. I backed out of the driveway and drove in circles around town, passing by all our usual haunts and Hannah's typical stops. The grocery store I'd just left, the tailor, the pizza shop we frequented on the few nights Hannah didn't feel like cooking, the post office—long since closed—and the playground where we took Lily to swing. Then I just cruised up and down the streets, aimlessly searching for her car. It was an older model. Not big enough, not safe enough. Why hadn't I replaced it? Even if she argued.

Even if she fought me. I didn't care. Her safety was the most important thing.

Her and the girls.

Twisting my hands around the wheel, I hit the gas when the stoplight on Main Street in town finally changed. I didn't know the baby's sex. We were waiting just as she wanted. But just like that, I knew she was having a girl. It was clearly meant to be so I'd be thoroughly outnumbered.

I couldn't wait.

My shoulders were so tense that pain radiated through my back the longer I sat behind the wheel. But I kept driving, hope against hope I'd see her familiar vehicle at one of our usual spots. I even checked home once more, just in case. Maybe I'd missed a note—

No, I had not. She'd left nothing for me on the refrigerator, or in the notebook we used to scribble notes about Lily, or anywhere else.

So, I dropped off the sodden container of ice cream along with the other groceries, keeping just the probably wilting tulips. But I needed to find her to give them to her as soon as possible.

This time, the flowers were meant for her and her alone.

On my next circuit through town, a suspiciously similar car to Hannah's rolled out of the bay of the custom car shop next to Macy's café. I brought my car to a stop at the curb with a squeal, blocking the exit. Grabbing the tulips, I climbed out of the car, only to see the person driving Hannah's car—or a damn near double for it, right down to her recent addition of fuzzy pink dice that doubled in a pinch as a toy for Lily—was *not* Hannah.

As the tall, scruffy dude unfolded himself from the front seat, I fisted my hands, probably crushing the damn flowers. "Where is my woman?"

The guy cocked an eyebrow. "This ain't the Desperate Singles app."

I stared at the guy, not amused. "You're driving Hannah Jacobs' vehicle. I demand to know her location."

"Depends." He scratched his cheek, looking me up and down. "Are you some kind of criminal element? You look pretty sketchy."

I looked down at myself. My suit was a little wrinkled, but it was a custom Hugo Boss, like many of my suits. Meanwhile, this individual had on a worn chambray shirt with a hole near the hem and jeans that looked like they'd been purchased in 1982. "I'm Asher Wainwright." I hated the cold note in my tone, but it couldn't be helped right now. "And you are?"

"Oh, fa-la-de-da. Should I genuflect now or later?"

I would've responded in kind except I'd happened to turn my head and glimpsed a honey-colored updo on a woman in the window of the café next door. I forgot all about pissing matches with grumpy mechanics—at least that was a reasonable guess, although serial killer was my second thought—and crossed the parking lot to the front door of the café at record speed.

"Hey, wait, Wainwright—"

The guy's voice disappeared with the thunk of the coffee shop's door behind me. Instantly, I heard the theme music of some horror movie, playing on a small screen in the reading nook. A bunch of people were clustered close, eating popcorn and squealing at the bloodthirsty maniac on screen.

Speaking of serial killers...

My gaze swung to Hannah and my fingers flexed around the already tortured stems of my flowers. I stalked toward Hannah's table just as the door opened behind me and mechanic-serial killer dude lurched forward to seize my arm.

"Hey, wait a second—"

At his voice, Hannah spun around in her chair, her blue eyes widening comically. "Asher? Dare?" Then she frowned. "Why are you accosting him?"

"Good question." I shook him off and straightened my tie. "He stole your car." I knew good and well he probably had not done any such thing, but consider me pissed off.

She let out a giggle. An actual honest-to-goodness giggle. I didn't think I'd ever heard her do that before. She still didn't even smile all that often, never mind have to wipe the mirth out of her eyes. "Dare didn't steal anything. He's the part owner of the shop next door. My car started acting up and—" She stopped and zeroed in on the mangled tulips. "What are those?"

"For you." I shoved them at her and took a quick glance at Lily in her high chair. She was sucking on a juice box and watching me owlishly, her mouth smeared with what looked like chocolate. "Asher," she said distinctly.

That was a fight for another day.

I glanced at Hannah. I had no idea if Dare and the rest of the patrons of Brewed Awakening were still watching us, but at that moment, I did not care. "You didn't leave me a note. You didn't call or text or hell, send up a goddamn smoke signal."

Sorry, Lily. Sometimes swearing was necessary.

"I know. I'm sorry. I think you need this. It works magically to make you feel better, I've heard." She passed me a wrapped candy, and I blinked, not understanding until I realized it was ginger.

Just like my grandfather's magical elixir.

I grinned. Everything really would be okay.

"I really am sorry. I thought you'd be working and that I'd be back before you were. Then the car was acting up and the stupid charger wasn't working and—" She broke off and finally took the flowers from me, sniffing them experimentally. "What's the occasion?"

"I'm turning over the day to day operation of the business to Vincent. Tomorrow we're revealing the news magazine he's launching and officially announcing his new role. And I'm going to work from home from now on."

"Oh, man," Dare muttered behind me, but I didn't stop to see the facial expression that went with it. I did shoot him a mental middle finger though.

How dare he intrude on my romantic fucking moment?

Hannah gave the flowers an experimental sniff as she watched me as warily as a ticking time bomb. "Are you sure that's what you want to do?"

"Yes, I'm sure. I've been sure since we talked that night over ice cream. Well, it set me down the path anyway, and speaking to Gran helped to get me the rest of the way there. Vincent is excited about the business. He wants to take over, and I'm going to let him."

Hannah gave me a tentative smile. "I'm happy for you. And what are you going to do?"

"I'm going to do what I'm excited about, including the news podcast and helping you with your business. We make a good team, don't you think?"

Hannah sat down with a heavy thud, still clutching her flowers.

"And don't ask me if I've been drinking—"

"Fine, I'll ask," Dare said from behind me, answering that question.

"No." I gritted my teeth. "I'm just resolute. I want the picture in my head. You and our girls and time spent building a life, not making money. I have enough of that. Hell, I don't even have to work again if I don't want to. Neither do you."

"Hey, Mister Moneybags, what about springing for our tab?"

I ignored the voice from the peanut gallery.

"Now I realize who you look like. Sure you aren't related to the Hamilton brothers? They like to brag about how they're made of coin too."

"Who?" I looked at Hannah, who shrugged.

"No clue. I'm still new in town myself."

"No," I said over my shoulder to Dare. "Also, go interrupt someone else's Hallmark moment."

Instead of listening, he planted his legs wide and crossed his arms.

Okay, then. Maybe he could get some tips.

He probably needed them.

I focused on Hannah. "You can still work if you want. As long as you want. I'm still going to as well. But the difference is that I'll be doing it for the right reasons, not just to fulfill a legacy that will do just fine with Vincent at the helm."

Her chin wobbled. "You said our girls. Did you somehow pay off some tech and find out what the baby is?"

"No, I just know. It came to me all of a sudden tonight when I was driving around looking for you, hoping like hell God or whomever is up there wasn't vengeful enough to take you and my girls from me just like Billy was taken." I fell to my knees in front of her and cupped her belly. "I can't lose you. Only forever will be long enough."

Hannah sniffled and scooped her hand through my hair. "I'm sorry. I was so thoughtless. It just all spiraled out of control. But I never imagined you'd think the worst." She leaned forward, laughing a little as her range of motion was a bit less than it had once been. Her belly was barely anything at this point, but it was enough to make her pause. And me pause as she gripped my jaw. "I want to share my business with you, but I already have a partner."

"Who?" Indignation filled my voice.

"Gabby. I just asked her tonight. She took over the rest of my deliveries when my car broke down." She covered my hands on her belly with her own. "But we have our own collaboration going right now."

I swallowed hard. "Yes, we do." I leaned up until our noses were an inch apart. "You're going to have to marry me. There's simply no other solution."

"What?"

"You heard me. I'm on my knees. I'm asking you to marry me. Be my wife. Commit to the lifetime of insanity that is guaranteed to be ours—"

Lily banged her juice box before pitching it right between us, managing to splash little purple droplets all over Hannah's white shirt. I don't know who laughed louder, the baby or me.

Or Hannah.

"You're not—" She pressed her lips together at my raised eyebrows. "I wasn't going to ask about alcohol, I swear. This time, I was saying you're not going to change your mind."

"Not a fucking chance. Sorry, Lily," I said without looking her way. "I love you. I love you so much."

Hannah's eyes went bright and she blinked over and over. It still didn't keep the tears from sneaking free. "I love you too. I think I always have from the first night. For sure from the time I came to your house for the nanny job and you acted like a jackass."

"Shocker."

Dare's reaction barely registered. Right now, I had more important considerations.

"Good thing you love assholes." I rubbed her cheek, blotting up her tears.

"You aren't an asshole underneath. But you do a very good impression of one. Just like I do a good impression of wanting to be alone. I thought I didn't want to have to take care of anyone, when I've never been happier than these days I've spent with you and Lily." She sniffled. "I just never wanted the ones I love to leave."

"I'm not going anywhere," I said roughly, catching her tears as fast as they fell. "This is all I want for the rest of my days." With my other hand, I reached for Lily. "No matter how many there are, there will never be enough."

Hannah's smile was like the sun emerging after the darkest of days. She shifted on her chair, clutching the juice box in one hand and the flowers in the other as she pressed her forehead to mine. "Let's get married, Asher Wainwright."

The café erupted in applause as we kissed. Even Dare joined in.

When I eased back, he clapped me on the back. "Congratulations." Then he tucked something in my pocket—Hannah's service bill.

I pried it out, expecting a reason to grouse. Hey, I was ridiculously happy right now, but I was still me.

Instead, a big fat zero with a smiley face had been written on the bill. "You're not charging?"

"Nope. On the house. Consider it a wedding present." Dare smiled at Hannah. "Congratulations."

"Thank you. Aww, that's so sweet of you."

"Welcome to the Cove. You too, Money Bags."

"Thanks."

"Dare is a sweetheart, isn't he?" Macy swept forward and planted a bill on Hannah's table. "But I'm not. Although if he messes up, call me, Hannah. I'll help you bury the body."

We all laughed. Even me.

Mostly.

EPILOGUE

September

THERE WAS A POINT OF WAITING TO THE VERY LAST MINUTE TO DO something, and I'd reached it.

I wasn't a procrastinator by nature. Until my life had become so full that even escaping for an hour to visit a jeweler—in secret—was a feat.

"You told your girl that you were going out drinking, but you're really getting her ring?" From the driver's seat of his truck, Austin shook his head. "You're supposed to lie about drinking, not use it as an excuse, dude."

"It's a thing with us," I muttered. "Can this thing go any faster?"

"Not unless you're going to pay my speeding ticket."

"No time for speeding tickets. Besides, don't you get special dispensation or something?"

"I work for the fire department, not the police. Who are also not above the law, thank you very much."

I rolled my eyes at Austin's indignation. "Fine, just step on it."

"I'm stepping. I thought you were already engaged. Why do you need another ring?"

"I never gave her one."

"Wow, lame." Austin coughed into his fist. "Oh, I see."

"It was a spur of the moment thing. I wasn't prepared."

"You didn't ask her parents first?"

"Her parents are dead, unfortunately."

"What about her priest?"

"I don't think she has a priest. Is that a thing?"

He jerked a shoulder. "Seems like a good idea to ask a man of the cloth. He'd probably give you some of that premarital counseling. I could too, but mine would be short." He flipped on his turn signal to veer down the street where the jeweler's was located. "Run. Fast."

"You're just jealous."

"Of regular sex? Yes. The rest?" He shuddered. "I might be ready for that when I'm like sixty-eight."

"Such a precise age."

"Well, I have the better part of a decade until my kid sister is old enough to move out, and I'm not going to confuse her with relationships that might not last."

"Marrying kind of ensures they'll last."

"Are you a hippie?"

"No?"

Austin shook his head. "Just saying, I don't want to mess with Joey's head. So, by then I'll be pressing forty, and I figure with Viagra, I'm probably good to go for another thirty years. By sixty-eight, I'll be ready for canasta tournaments and a pair of lounge chairs in Florida."

It was my turn to shudder as he stopped the car in front of Zagan's Jewelers. "Your idea of the future is horrifying."

"Least my expectations leave room for improvement." He shrugged and got out of the truck.We walked inside and I informed the woman behind the counter I was picking up a special order that I'd already paid for. She emerged a few moments later with a small green box. Without prompting, she popped open the lid.

Inside, nestled on fabric the same green, was Gran's vintage engagement solitaire ring with two important additions—a small canary yellow diamond on one side for Lily and a small green diamond on the other side for our daughter. Or son, if my spidey sense turned out to be wrong.

I smiled at the jeweler. "It's perfect, thank you—" I broke off as my phone buzzed in my pocket with Hannah's ring tone. And she was calling, not texting. "One moment, please."

I stepped away to take her call. "Hey, you. I'm almost done—"

"It's probably good you have a drink in you. I think this baby is impatient."

"What? What? What?"

At my clear distress, Austin came over to me. "You need oxygen again? I kept it in the truck from the last time you nearly fainted when we were together."

I had to assume he was kidding, but part of me hoped he wasn't.

"Just a few contractions is all," Hannah said soothingly. "I already called Gran to sit with Lily and I doublechecked my bag is ready to go."

"Go? Go where?"

"Asher, if the baby's coming, we have to go to the hospital. Remember? We practiced this."

"Yes, but you weren't actually in labor." I sucked in a breath. "Nothing we practiced included hyperventilating."

"Holy shitballs. She's squeezing it out now?" Austin winked at me. "Better hurry up and get that ring on her finger. If it'll fit."

"What ring?" Hannah asked.

I sighed and tipped back my head. Oh, look, I could see stars. That probably wasn't a good thing, considering I was inside on a cloudy day. "I'm not actually drinking. I went to pick up your engagement ring."

"My—oh my."

"You didn't freak at possibly being in labor, but now I hear you breathing fast because I got you a ring?"

"Yes. And I'm freaking a little at the labor thing too, because ow." She hissed out a breath. "Can you come home? Like…soon. So your buddy Austin doesn't have to deliver this baby in the driveway?"

Since Austin was right beside me and Hannah was speaking more loudly than usual due to impending birth, he heard every word. He backed up so fast he nearly stumbled and held up his hands. "I'll just get you home." He raced out the door like his…well, like his ass was on fire.

Appropriate.

Nodding to the jeweler, I grabbed the ring box and backed out of the door. "I'm on my way. Don't have the kid for about twenty minutes, all right? Promise me."

She wheezed out a laugh. "I'll do my best."

It took three hours and forty-eight minutes for me to officially become a father for the second time. Rose Elizabeth—for Bess—Wainwright was born in a hospital, not a driveway, thank God, but Austin had insisted on driving us in my car.

Even so, Austin had needed the oxygen this time, not me.

I was too busy cuddling my perfectly beautiful baby girl and holding my wife-to-be's hand, her triple diamond ring nestled between our fingers like a wish.

The best one we'd ever made.

Gran hadn't met our little girl yet, because she was watching Lily. But she'd bring her here soon to meet our little one. Gran had broken up with her live-in guy, but she wasn't upset. She knew love came along when you least expected it.

I smiled at Hannah. So did we.

EPILOGUE 2

I TIED THE BELT OF MY ROBE AND SHUFFLED DOWN THE HALLWAY. I WAS sure I'd get used to these 2 AM feedings someday. Probably just around the time our little girl didn't need them anymore.

But for now?

Yeah, the boobs didn't lie and our daughter would soon be looking for me. Instead of waiting for her to cry and wake up her sister—who refused to sleep in any other room—well, it was just easier if I reached her before she screamed.

I glanced at Asher's office door. The light was on and the door cracked open. He'd been up late doing an interview for his podcast with someone in Hawaii.

I sighed. Hawaii sounded really good right about now. Maybe for our honeymoon.

I got to the door and paused at the unfortunately flat singing voice of my fiancé. But what he didn't have in talent, Asher definitely made up for in sweetness. Each of our girls had a different song.

He said he wanted them to always think they were special.

Dammit, he was always stealing my breath by saying stuff like that when I least expected it.

I leaned on the doorjamb, unwilling to disturb them just yet.

Our new baby daughter, Rose, was nestled in the crook of his arm. The thimble-sized nursing bottle looked like a toy in his hand, but he was so gentle with her. There was no fear in how he handled a baby now. Only a huge love that seemed to only get bigger with each day we were together.

He turned as his whispery and rumbly voice hit a high note that sounded just about perfect. He spotted me and smiled.

I went over to meet him and kissed our daughter's cap of feathery dark hair.

"She's finally asleep," he whispered. "I wanted to let you get some rest. And I couldn't resist coming in here."

"And here I was trying to let you work," I said softly. A little discomfort on my end was totally worth the wonderment in his voice.

He pulled me in a little closer and we both swayed for a few minutes. The little baby squeaks and grunts were only here for a short time. I wanted to remember them all.

But we were asking for trouble if we didn't put her back in her crib. We had so few hours to sleep between feedings. He settled Rose back into her bassinet as I checked on Lily, whose crib was right next to hers.

Originally, I wanted Rose's crib in our room for the first few weeks, but her older sister was quite insistent on getting her way when it came to sleeping arrangements.

Asher's hand slipped up my back and tangled in my hair. I straightened up and cupped his face. In the dark, with our two girls sleeping, all my emotions bubbled up. "I love you."

He curled his arm around me gently. My body still felt like one huge swollen bruise from giving birth a little over ten days ago. "I love you too, Hannah. I love you and our family so much. I can't believe how lucky I am to have found you."

I rested my head on his chest and glanced down at the daughter of my heart with her arms up over her head. "We both lucked out that stormy night."

I was pretty sure I'd have this little snapshot in my memory banks forever. And that was a very nice word that I was more than happy to have in my vocabulary these days.

Especially when it came to my little family. Something I never thought I'd truly have—or want—again. Yet here I was with not one, but two little girls in my life again and a husband-to-be.

And I wanted the three of them with a ferociousness I never expected.

All because of a winter storm that had originally made me feel so alone and hopeless. Now I had Asher and our two daughters that filled my life with laughter and happiness again.

I'd even given up the last bit of my past by selling my old house to Gabby, who was thrilled to have a space of her own for the first time.

As for me? I had everything I ever wanted right here.

Thanks so much for reading CEO DADDY.

If you'd like to read more about our crazy town, Crescent Cove, please flip the page and find all the books in our series. It's ever evolving and we try really hard to make sure our readers can jump in and enjoy at any time.

But…if you love series books, you definitely get a lot of extra fun when you read the series in order.

We also have a fun newsletter & Facebook group where you can find more about us, our books, and fabulous giveaways.

GO HERE: bookl.ink/TarynQuinn

If you loved the book, please let your friends know. That's what this community is all about. If you're so inclined, we'd love a review on your favorite book site.

CRESCENT COVE CHARACTER CHART

BEWARE…SPOILERS APLENTY IN THIS CHARACTER CHART. READ AT YOUR OWN RISK!

Ally Lawrence:
Married to Seth Hamilton, mother to Alexander, stepmother to Laurie, best friends with Sage Evans

Andrea Maria Fortuna Dixon Newman:
Mother to Veronica 'Vee' Dixon

Asher Wainwright: CEO Wainwright Publishing
Involved with Hannah Jacobs, father to Lily and Rose

August Beck: Owns Beck Furniture
Brother to Caleb and Ivy, involved with Kinleigh Scott

Beckett Manning: Owns Happy Acres Orchard
Brother to Zoe, Hayes, and Justin

Bess Wainwright:
Grandmother to Asher Wainwright

Caleb Beck: Teaches second grade

Brother to August and Ivy

(Charles) Dare Kramer: Mechanic, owns J & T Body Shop
Married to Kelsey Ford, son Weston (mother is Katherine), son Sean, brother Gage

Christian Masterson: Sheriff's Deputy
Brother to Murphy, Travis, and Penn, sister Madison 'Maddie'

Cindy Ford:
Married to Doug Ford, mother of Kelsey and Rylee
Damien Ramos:
Sisters Erica, Francesca, Gabriela, Regina

Doug Ford:
Married to Cindy Ford, father of Kelsey and Rylee Ford

Gavin Forrester: Real estate owner

Gabriela 'Gabby' Ramos:
Brother Damien, sisters Erica, Francesca, Regina, best friend Hannah Jacobs

Greta: Manager of the Rusty Spoon

Hank Masterson:
Married to JoAnn Masterson, sons Murphy, Christian, Travis, Penn, and daughter Madison

Hannah Jacobs:
Involved with Asher Wainwright, mother to Lily and Rose, best friend Gabriela Ramos

Hayes Manning: Owns Happy Acres Orchard
Brother to Zoe, Beckett, and Justin

Ian Kagan: Solo artist
Brother to Simon, engaged to Zoe Manning, son Elvis, best friend Rory Ferguson, friends with Flynn Sheppard and Kellan McGuire

Ivy Beck: Waitress at the Rusty Spoon and owns Rolling Cones ice cream truck
Sister to Caleb and August, engaged to Rory Ferguson, best friend Kinleigh Scott, friends with Maggie Kelly and Zoe Manning

James Hamilton: Owns Hamilton Realty
Father to Seth and Oliver Hamilton

Jared Brooks: Sheriff
Brother to Mason Brooks, best friend Gina Ramos

Jessica Gideon: Famous actress
Ex-wife to John Gideon, mother to Dani

JoAnn Masterson:
Married to Hank Masterson, sons Murphy, Christian, Travis, Penn, and daughter Madison

John Gideon: Owns Gideon Gets it Done Handyman Service
Daughter Dani, ex-wife Jessica Gideon

Justin Manning: Owns Happy Acres Orchard
Brother to Zoe, Beckett, and Hayes

Kellan McGuire: Lead singer Wilder Mind, solo artist
Brother to Bethany, married to Maggie Kelly, son Wolf, friends with Rory Ferguson, Ian Kagan, and Myles Vaughn

Kelsey Ford: Elementary school teacher
Married to Dare Kramer, son Sean, stepson Weston, sister Rylee Ford

Kinleigh Scott: Owns Kinleigh's
Cousin Vincent Scott, best friend Ivy Beck, involved with August Beck

(Lucas) Gage Kramer: Owns J & T Body Shop, former race car driver
Married to Rylee Ford, daughter Hayley Kramer, brother Dare Kramer

Lucky Roberts: Works for Gideon Gets it Done Handyman Service

Macy Devereaux: Owns Brewed Awakening and The Haunt
Best friend Rylee Ford

Madison 'Maddie' Masterson:
Sister to Murphy, Christian, Travis, and Penn

Marjorie Hamilton:
Ex-wife of Seth Hamilton, birth mother of Laurie Hamilton

Mason Brooks: Owns Mason Jar restaurant
Brother Jared Brooks

Maggie Kelly:
Married to Kellan McGuire, son Wolf, best friend Kendra Russo, friends with Ivy Beck and Zoe Manning

Melissa Kramer: Owns Robbie's Pizza
Married to Robert Kramer, mother of Dare and Gage Kramer

Mike London: High school teacher

Mitch Cooper: Owns the Rusty Spoon

Murphy 'Moose' Masterson: Game Designer/Construction Contractor and Owns Baby Daddy Wanted
Married to Vee Dixon, son Brayden, brother to Christian, Travis, Penn, and Maddie

Oliver Hamilton: Owns Hamilton Realty and the Hummingbird's Nest
Married to Sage Evans, daughter Star, twin brother Seth Hamilton

Penn Masterson: Graphic novelist
Brother to Murphy, Travis, Christian, and Maddie

Regina 'Gina' Ramos: Waitress at the Rusty Spoon
Brother Damien, sisters Erica, Francesca, Gabriela, best friend Sheriff Brooks

Robert Kramer: Owns Robbie's Pizza
Married to Melissa Kramer, father of Dare and Gage Kramer

Rory Ferguson: Record Producer/Rhythm Guitarist
Brother to Thomas and Maureen, engaged to Ivy Beck, best friend Ian Kagan, friends with Flynn Sheppard and Kellan McGuire

Rylee Ford: Barista at Brewed Awakening
Married to Gage Kramer, daughter Hayley, sister Kelsey Ford Kramer, best friend Macy Devereaux

Sage Evans: Owns the Hummingbird's Nest
Married to Oliver Hamilton, daughter Star, best friend Ally Lawrence

Seth Hamilton: Owns Hamilton Realty
Married to Ally Lawrence, daughter Laurie, son Alexander, twin brother to Oliver Hamilton, ex-wife Marjorie

Tish Burns: Owns J & T Body Shop, custom fabricator
Friends with Gage Kramer

Travis Masterson:
Brothers Christian, Penn and Murphy, and Maddie, daughter Carrington

Veronica 'Vee' Dixon: Pastry Baker, owns Baby Daddy Wanted
Married to Murphy Masterson, son Brayden

Vincent Scott: partner in Wainwright Publishing Industries
Cousin Kinleigh Scott

Zoe Manning: Artist/photographer
*Sister to Beckett, Hayes, and Justin, engaged to Ian Kagan, son Elvis, cousin
Lila Ronson Shawcross Crandall, friends with Ivy Beck and Maggie Kelly*

GET HOOKED!

Have My Baby

Claim My Baby

Who's The Daddy

Pit Stop: Baby

Baby Daddy Wanted

Rockstar Baby

Daddy in Disguise

Crescent Cove Standalones

CEO Daddy

ALSO BY TARYN QUINN

AFTERNOON DELIGHT

Dirty Distractions

Drawn Deep

DEUCES WILD

Protecting His Rockstar

Guarding His Best Friend's Sister

Shielding His Baby

WILDER ROCK

Rockstar Daddy

HOLIDAY BOOKS

Unwrapped

Holiday Sparks

Filthy Scrooge

Jingle Ball

Bad Kitty

For more information about our books visit

www.tarynquinn.com

ABOUT TARYN QUINN

USA Today bestselling author, *TARYN QUINN,* is the redheaded stepchild of bestselling authors Taryn Elliott & Cari Quinn. We've been writing together for a lifetime—wait, no it's really been only a handful of years, but we have a lot of fun. Sometimes we write stories that don't quite fit into our regular catalog.

* Ultra sexy—check.
* Quirky characters—check.
* Sweet–usually mixed in with the sexy...so, yeah—check.
* RomCom—check.
* Dark and twisted—check.

A little something for everyone.

So, c'mon in. Light some candles, pour a glass of wine...maybe even put on some sexy music.

For more information about us...
tarynquinn.com
tq@tarynquinn.com

QUINN AND ELLIOTT

We also write more serious, longer, and sexier books as Cari Quinn & Taryn Elliott. Our topics include mostly rockstars, but mobsters, MMA, and a little suspense gets tossed in there too.

Rockers' Series Reading Order

Lost in Oblivion

Winchester Falls

Found in Oblivion

Hammered

Rock Revenge

Brooklyn Dawn

OTHER SERIES

The Boss

Tapped Out

Love Required

Boys of Fall

If you'd like more information about us please visit

www.quinnandelliott.com

Made in the USA
Middletown, DE
05 November 2019